EPICS OF MICHAEL

EPICS OF MICHAEL

THE WARRIOR WITHIN

B.J. NICHOLS

TATE PUBLISHING & *Enterprises*

Published by Tate Publishing & Enterprises, LLC
127 E. Trade Center Terrace | Mustang, Oklahoma 73064 USA
1.888.361.9473 | www.tatepublishing.com

Tate Publishing is committed to excellence in the publishing industry. The company reflects the philosophy established by the founders, based on Psalm 68:11,
"The Lord gave the word and great was the company of those who published it."

Book design copyright © 2008 by Tate Publishing, LLC. All rights reserved.
Cover design by Jonathan Lindsey
Interior design by Kellie Southerland

Published in the United States of America

ISBN: 978-1-60462-969-9
1. Fiction: Religious: Apocalyptical
2. Fiction: Action & Adventure
08.08.06

CONTENTS

PROLOGUE

IN THE BEGINNING

All glory and praise be to the Ancient One, the most holy and wise Eternal One. Here, in my trembling hands, is a priceless set of ancient scrolls. I discovered these only moments ago. These scrolls have recorded on them some of the most renowned stories of the Kingdom, never before heard by mankind. My name must remain anonymous and you may only know that I am a humble scribe in Heaven. The stories you are about to partake in are the accounts of Michael's battles and the highly dangerous missions for which God commissioned him. No human on earth has ever heard the extraordinary details of these monumental battles and perilous missions. For it was commanded: Their ears will be shut and their eyes will be closed until the Lord chooses to show them.

However, the time is at hand for the final battle is drawing nearer. I am thrilled that it is my duty and most gracious privilege to tell the children of God about the scrupulous and painstaking efforts to which the highest King has taken. These difficult and trying struggles were solely undertaken in order for the Lord to protect his children. To guard them from the forces of evil—the demons that lie in wait to devour the spirits of those who choose to follow the LORD with all of their minds, hearts, and souls.

I feel it is absolutely necessary that you have all the facts so you can be fully informed on the history of Heaven. I will begin by reading from the ancient scrolls that were recorded before mankind was in existence. These scrolls have been sealed and locked away in the innermost vaults located deep beneath the house of scrolls.

Securely guarded within the vaults are countless scrolls of various kinds, some of which contain words that have yet to be written by the prophets. There is a unique and old book in the center of the innermost vault. This is the *Book of the Seven Seals*, which holds the words to the prophecy that will one day determine the fate of all mankind. The words of this prophecy were written before the foundation of time.

The vaults also hold the original Ark of the Covenant. To answer the question you are now asking yourself: The Ark of the Covenant built by Moses was actually not the first Ark, but a contrived replica from a God-inspired vision. Truth be known, the vault is home to a vast collection of precious artifacts, the original blueprints for Noah's Ark in God's handwriting, the tablets that the Ten Commandments were written on, Elijah's robe that was filled with God's power, David's slingshot, which was used with pinpoint accuracy to kill Goliath. And among these, there are many more irreplaceable treasures that are still being inventoried by hundreds of angels directly under my supervision.

Until now, the ancient scrolls' seals have not been broken. The words have never been recited pending this very moment. You should feel honored and fortunate to be a part of this historic moment. After reading this, life for you may never be the same. You will become enlightened and given an insight into the spiritual warfare that has been, and still is, fought in the Heavenly realms. Feel free to tell whomever you may please, but listen to me when I say they probably won't believe the stories you are about to share in.

I will now read from the eldest of the ancient scrolls titled *The Warrior Within*.

In the beginning there once was neither earth nor vast universe, only complete darkness. But from the darkness a single light shone through. A light so pure, so innocent, and yet so mysterious and terrible that in its very form no eye could behold lest it go blind from the immense glory of its being. In the beginning, before there existed galaxies or planets that lie within the universe's seemingly endless boundaries, there was the light and the light was God. Truly I say to you, in the beginning was the word, the word was with God, and the word was God. When God spoke into the darkness, he created the light and a place more beautiful than any place throughout the universe—Heaven. Picture a place more glorious, breathtaking, and awe-inspiring, and you might get close to picturing Heaven. Yet you'd still be far from embracing its incredible potential. God fashioned it after his own glory and it was a place of inconceivable beauty and peace.

Then God created angels to dwell in it. These were creatures of immense splendor and brilliance. Fashioned in God's glory, they were created to worship him. God created one angel, in particular, different from the rest. This angel possessed strength greater than that of ten hundred men and with wisdom that exceeded even that of King Solomon (who was to reign on earth thousands of years later). He was favored over all the angels and God loved him deeply. He named him Michael, which means, "Who is like God."

Michael was both handsome and powerful. His face was remarkably masculine and yet refined. It possessed a soft and delicate feature that was distinguished and noble. What is more, he possessed features on his face that looked very much chiseled. He truly resembled the statue of David with cheekbones that were highly protruded and much defined, a broad kingly nose, and a royal set of lips. He had wavy bright blond hair, which shone vibrantly whenever light reflected on it just right. He had especially brilliant eyes that were a unique quality and their appearance mysteriously changed from blue to green with each glance he cast.

In addition to these dignified features, his physique was incredibly sculpted. Michael always remained humble, confirming the great wisdom God had instilled in his spirit. His gown consisted of a bright white tunic with gold threading that accentuated the borders of his sleeveless outfit. His shoulders were draped with a magnificent cloak. Fit for a king, the entire edge was richly bordered with purple and gold stitching. It was attached to his tunic by one large, solid gold emblem. One thing you should know is that his garments were truly unique—set apart and designed by God himself. Henceforth, no angel in all of Heaven was adorned so richly as Michael, nor has there been since.

From nearly the dawn of time, the battle between good and evil has been raging. Of all places, Heaven is where the first conflict commenced. It was one decision that set the war in motion and ever since the wheels haven't ceased turning. The choice that initiated the war of the ages was made first by only one angel, who happened to be the most beautiful of all the angels, Lucifer.

There once was a time when Lucifer loved to worship the LORD. His name actually denotes "light bearer." Lucifer was appointed to be the chief angel of the heavenly choir of seraphim. God dearly loved his songs and his voice could bring your soul to tears of joy and lift your spirits to new heights. His one true passion was writing songs for praise and worship. This gift he possessed was unrivaled by any and cherished by all.

Out of nowhere, it happened one day. A seed of evil sprouted in the heart of his innocence. The poisoning of his heart began subtly, as a small tug on his soul, but it gradually grew to the point where he questioned whether or not God was the one true Creator. Deep down in his spirit, feelings of hatred and resentment brewed and churned. They continued to swell and grow to the point where they ate away at the core of his being; steadily chipping away at the heart and soul of his beauty and character, until one day all purity vanished, along with his innocence. He became selfishly driven and without any regrets, he could now create his own path to life. He made a way for himself by first deciding that serving God wasn't an option he wanted to choose. Ultimately, he came to the false realization that he could never satisfy his power hungry ambitions until he alone had control.

From that point on, he fearlessly sought to challenge the very throne of God even if it meant spreading his poison or influence as he thought of it.

NOTE FROM THE SCRIBE...

Here are some things, to name a few, that you should know about this restless and rebellious spirit named Lucifer. He was tall and intimidating and menacing, yet incredibly beautiful. His long back hair flowed just past his shoulders adding a fine and striking essence. His deeply set blue eyes aired a quality about them that was both cunning and resolute. As astounding as his appearance was, it was his influence that attributed even more to his charismatic appeal.

Lucifer had managed to win over a significant force of angels. Even more ghastly, he persuaded these angels that he should rule over Heaven and even have sovereignty over God himself. As Lucifer continued to spread his wicked manipulation, he meticulously planned and waited for the right time to orchestrate his revolt. As the numbers grew, his time to rise drew nearer and nearer. Soon, he had amassed a great army, but the greatest of his followers was Beltezar who was closest of all to Lucifer.

Beltezar was a high-ranking angel. He possessed a strength that was brutally powerful, yet he maintained a facade that was quite refined. He possessed a charismatic quality that attracted masses of angels to his will. It was this characteristic that appealed to Lucifer most of all. He was the number one recruiter for Lucifer so, needless to say, he quickly climbed the ranks becoming the top general in Lucifer's increasingly large army. Elite, stonehearted, and feared by all rebel angels, he was truly a force to be reckoned with.

The Warrior Within ...

THE FIRST BATTLE

On a certain day, a seraph named Remiel was strolling in the Garden of Tranquility. The garden was remotely located about ten thousand paces outside the east gate of the Holy City. The centerpiece of the garden is the Fountain of Life, which flows continually from out of a large smooth stone. Remiel was among Michael's closest and most trusted friends. He was imposing in height and what he lacked in physical strength, his intellect made up for. He had an ability to vigorously absorb knowledge like pure light soaks up the darkness. Though what he took pleasure in mostly was gaining new wisdom from the time he spent with the LORD.

He was walking down one of his favorite paths with his brother Raguel. Raguel was similar to his brother in appearance and stature. Like Remiel, he too loved to learn new things. His personality was as different from his brother's as night is from day. Remiel has a cheerful, giving heart, is exceedingly organized, extremely disciplined, and quick to follow orders from any superior seraphim; Raguel, on the contrary, is clever beyond measure, and loves to debate any who are up to his level. To add to his buoyancy and confidence he can't help but boast, humbly of course, that he is brave to challenge orders. That is, if he believes they don't fit the big picture, being his description of God's plan and purpose.

Remiel loved to write music and Raguel could play the harp with impeccable talent. Praise songs were something they both shared a passion in, and they often spent hours on end discussing the topic. Remiel was in the middle of sharing a new song and Raguel was sorry to interrupt, but he recalled a meeting with a friend he was supposed to attend. He hugged his brother and took off with great speed for the town square in Jerusalem. *If your legs can run somewhere, why walk them*, Raguel always said.

Remiel did not let this unexpected change in plans keep him from enjoying his walk in the garden. He decided to head towards his favorite spot, a large smooth rock in the middle of the garden. He was leisurely walking down a familiar path when suddenly a noise pervaded his ears and interrupted the serenity of the garden. The sound was that of voices whispering and they seemed to be coming from behind a cluster of cedar trees.

Immediately, Remiel searched for cover and he positioned himself behind a small boulder. From the safety of his hiding place he could distinguish a couple of things, only two voices could be perceived and he could distinctly match them with a pair of faces. It dawned on him. He was witnessing a secret meeting between Lucifer and Beltezar. A strong gust of wind was blowing through the garden, so Remiel could only make out bits and pieces of the conversation. What he could understand greatly alarmed him. From Lucifer, he gathered they were making preparations for war. From Beltezar, he learned that millions upon millions of angels had already joined their forces. Together they were planning to overthrow the throne room within the hour. Remiel could draw only one conclusion—heresy.

"What diabolical scheming," he said, which was clear enough for them to hear.

"I must tell Michael," he asserted to himself. Without a second to spare and before his adversaries could react, Remiel ran like the wind.

"Don't trouble with the seraph. There's no time to waste. Gather our troops. You know what to do," Lucifer ordered his trusted general.

"It will be my pleasure to usher in the new age with the crowning of my lord, Lucifer," he boldly replied.

A few earth miles away Michael was sitting under a giant cedar tree situated in the great forest outside Jerusalem. He was meditating on a word from the LORD. He was breathing in the air slowly and taking in the beauty that surrounded him. A fresh breeze brushed gently across his face. Heaven's serenity was intoxicating to his senses. He couldn't help but drink in the air that was so refreshing to his soul and spirit.

Suddenly a rustling in the leaves produced an anxious Remiel. He saluted him and immediately Michael knew something was amiss. Before now, Remiel had never addressed him in such a way.

"Michael, my captain, I have grave news to deliver," he said with a serious, unwavering tone. Michael listened carefully as Remiel unraveled the diabolical scheme and before his very eyes, Remiel watched his friend transform into the leader he was made to be.

Upon hearing the report Michael saluted him.

"I must run to Mount Zion," Michael said with a resolute voice. "The LORD will know what to do. Go and summon the captains: Gabriel, Raphael, Uriel, Saraqael, and of course your brother, Raguel. They will assist you in gathering the faithful. Order all to rally at the throne room and there we will make our stand against Lucifer and his forces. Travel with great haste, Remiel."

Remiel nodded in agreement and turned darting away to summon the others. Michael ran with great haste straight to Mount Zion where the throne of God stood.

Michael climbed the steep mountain as quickly as his sturdy legs could possibly take him. He knew before the throne there would be an answer to this calamity. He only had to reach the summit, where the LORD's help awaited him. After reaching the top two huge seraphim's, Justice and Mercy, were all that stood in the way. Their sole purpose was to guard the entrance to the throne room. Justice stiffened his arm and held Michael to a halt.

"Justice, I have an urgent report for the LORD. I don't have time for this," Michael declared. He insisted still that Michael state his news, but Mercy insisted they let him pass.

Michael entered the throne room. The glory of God's presence could be felt straight away. The LORD dearly loved Michael and he was allowed to approach God's throne as close as the four cherubim. These were the angels created for the sole purpose of worshipping God. They surrounded his throne with praise continually on their lips. Their singing is famous throughout Heaven and from their mouth's come the most beautiful sounds you could truly hope to hear.

God was sitting on his throne, as he approached. Michael presented himself with a reverential and gracious bow.

"My Lord and King, I come with news that deeply disturbs me. Remiel has informed me that Lucifer has plans to overthrow you. More terrible yet, he and Beltezar are prepared to follow through with their plans within the hour. What must we—" before he could speak any further, God interceded in a commanding voice.

"Fear not Michael. Do not be anxious from what you've heard. Do you not realize that I already know of Lucifer's heresy? I am an all-knowing and all-seeing God. No thought of Lucifer's is beyond my wisdom. His mind, I realize, has grown wicked indeed and his heart is perverted beyond anything I have created."

The Lord raised his right hand forming a fist and his eyes gleamed with a ray of power.

"Let Lucifer come this hour. May Beltezar and their forces attack," God shouted with a voice that echoed like resounding thunder. "They will discover the power I alone possess and even in the tip of my smallest finger there is more strength than in his entire army."

The presence of the Lord was so powerful Michael could not stand, but only kneel before God's throne. The weight of his glory was nearly too much for his angelic being to bear. Michael looked up and the Lord was shining like the sun.

"I am at your will my King. You have but to give the command and I will give my life to your glory," Michael spoke with the zeal of a great general.

God rose from his throne and stood like a mighty pillar. He looked Michael in the eyes, searching his heart with his holy presence.

"Michael I am raising you up. No longer will you remain just a seraph, but you are now the commander of the Host of Heaven," declared the Lord.

Michael eyes lit up. He was speechless.

Suddenly an angel, whom Michael had never before seen, appeared from nowhere and approached the LORD. He handed God something quite large wrapped in a beautiful purple silk. God pulled the cloth away and revealed the most breathtaking sword Michael had ever seen.

"The Sword of the Spirit," said the LORD.

He descended the steps and handed the sword to Michael.

"This sword possesses the power to vanquish all evil and defend the kingdom of Heaven. Do you, Michael, accept your duty to Heaven," God boldly said.

"I do," shouted Michael with great fervor.

"Will you defend Heaven with all of your mind, heart, and soul," asked God, his eyes blazing with glory.

"With everything I am, yes," Michael answered. He felt a strength surge through his legs and he found himself standing before the LORD of Hosts.

"As you stand here, the faithful are being called," God proclaimed. "The time has come for the Host of Heaven to stand and defend the throne."

Michael's face was in awe and his heart felt an unspeakable peace. At that moment, Remiel entered the throne room. His face beamed with hope and his eyes spoke only determination. He bowed to the floor and addressed God.

"My LORD and King. I have gathered as many seraphim as I could. I was astonished to find most already knew of what was coming."

The LORD thanked Remiel for his brave service and he informed him that Michael was no longer a captain but the general.

"Commander of the Host of Heaven," Remiel rose to his feet and exclaimed with unrivaled joy.

The captains were soon together and were given magnificent horses to ride on, along with Michael. Within moments, God's noble army was assembled, the righteous angels that would lay down their lives for the LORD Almighty.

Ranks of 7,404,926 were formed with thorough efficiency. Thirty-six ranks were formed, so the total number of the Host of Heaven was 266,613,336. Either a lance or sword was dispensed to all the seraphim.

Twelve ranks, led by Jeremiah, were covertly sent outside the city through the south entrance. They silently hid in a giant forest of cedars outside Jerusalem. Twelve more ranks, led by Joshua, were sent secretly through the east gate and placed in the Garden of Tranquility. The other twelve ranks, led by Gideon, lay hidden behind Mount Zion. All ranks patiently and fervently awaited their orders from the Lord of Hosts. The captains who were to ride with Michael were Gabriel, Raphael, Uriel, Remiel, Raguel, and Saraqael. The plan was now executed and the maneuvers had been orchestrated with scrupulous proficiency. Now, it was up to Lucifer and his forces to set off the chain reaction.

It had not been long after the Host of Heaven was in their assigned places when the news reached the throne. The enemy forces were positioned just outside the Holy City in the Fields of Gladness. There were 666 legions formed with an estimated 200,160 angels in each legion. Each was led by a master sergeant. The enemy forces all together totaled 133,307,226.

Suddenly, Lucifer, accompanied by the captains of his army, entered the throne room. Lucifer proceeded towards the throne with an arrogance rivaled only by the evil in his heart. No sooner had he stepped within fifty paces of God than he set his mouth in motion and challenged the Most High.

"I, Lucifer declare war—" he said and froze when he witnessed a most impressive and frightening force. The throne room was shaking from the sheer magnitude.

God had opened his mouth and a blinding light had poured forth. His voice was like the sound of many waters and his face was terrible to behold.

"I am the Almighty, Creator of Heaven and the universe, the Beginning and the End. I am the great I Am," he thundered.

God raised his hands in a display of awesome might and power as a brilliant whirlwind of light encircled him on the throne.

"When I spoke into the darkness I created the light. I created you Lucifer. Now, you dare defy your creator," shouted God, his voice echoed throughout Heaven. "There is no peace left in you, only deceit, lies, and evil. From this point on your name will be

Satan, prince of darkness. You want so badly to have control. I will give you a kingdom to rule. Your dominion will certainly not exist in Heaven, but I banish you to the fiery pits of a realm I call Hell."

God then looked over the faces of the angels that were betraying him. The captains that stood with Lucifer could not bear to look their creator in the face.

God's eyes were full of sadness as he addressed them, "As for my angels who have rejected me, you have trusted in lies and found safety in deceit. You are no longer worthy of being called seraphim. Instead you are now demons, lower than vermin in my sight."

God then focused his gaze upon Satan once more and his face beamed with a dreadful light.

"Your kingdom will be one of fire and ash, one of pain and agony," declared the LORD, wielding his tongue with unrivaled authority. "You will roam the earth looking for souls to torment and spirits to imprison. Heed my words, Satan, your reign on earth shall not last for an eternity. When I come for you I will lock you in a chasm unfathomably deep and after a thousand ages have passed I promise you this—I will destroy you."

The entire vastness of Heaven literally trembled in the fury of his righteous anger. For when men shout in anger they are merely raising their voice, but with God, his wrath is true justice. All of Heaven could hear his voice. It echoed like booming thunder throughout the entire vastness of the universe. The light that radiated from his face was so intense no angel in Heaven, not even the cherubim, could gaze upon him. For the LORD appeared more magnificent now than ever before.

Terrible and pure was the fury of the LORD. Satan shuddered in terror of God's wrath. He had tried in vain to hide his fear, but failed miserably. He fled from the presence of God; his captains trailed him out of the throne room and quickly descended Mt. Zion. As Satan approached the foot of the mountain, he signaled his men to take up their weapons and retreat to the fields. Needless to say, the entire rebel force was panicking from fear.

Suddenly, Michael and the valiant Host of Heaven were

empowered by the Holy Spirit. With the extraordinary strength of a hundred men each, they were more than prepared to pursue the enemy. Ordinarily, angels have the strength of at least twenty men at all times, but on this day there was an extraordinary increase in their power. Michael and the captains led the Host of Heaven seated on brilliant white horses. These were most definitely the strongest and noblest steeds in all of Heaven.

As the enemy fled through the fields, Michael and his captains awaited God's command. The ranks of angelic warriors held their breath as they waited for the signal from the throne.

"This is the moment we make our mark in history," Michael proclaimed to the captains. "All of Heaven will speak of your virtues for a thousand generations. Mighty and steadfast are we—warriors of God."

"Fear not, Michael. Have faith and I will give you victory," the LORD silently spoke to his heart. Michael looked to the LORD and his eyes were ablaze with a mighty power. A surge of strength and confidence flowed in Michael's spirit. Without speaking aloud, God provided hope for Michael's heart.

"Fear not, seraphim. Be not dismayed, for my mighty right hand will deliver you. Faithful servants of the one true God, charge," God commanded with a thunderous shout.

The trumpets sounded from Zion. Michael and all of the angels felt a flash of light enter them like a lightening bolt.

"To the glory of God," Michael raised the Sword of the Spirit above his head and cried out.

The horses stampeded with a charge that sent tremors through the golden streets of Jerusalem. Without looking back, Satan and his captains fled the city. Their only hope was to reach the Crystal Mountains that lay within a few miles of the east gate. The demons panicked and were fleeing to the mountains in hoards, but Jeremiah and his force ambushed them cutting off their escape. Confusion instantly overtook the demons and the major sergeants frantically made every attempt they could to reset their ranks.

Michael and the courageous six on horseback charged down Mount Zion and through the Fields of Gladness. They had Satan and his captains in their sights and they were determined to keep anyone or anything from obstructing their path. In one accord, their mindset was resolute—overcome the enemy with the power of the Most High. Gideon and twelve million seraphim were on foot rushing like a landslide down the side of the mountain. From the highest point in Jerusalem, Mount Zion, the LORD watched and waited from his throne for the right moment. Victory could only happen in his timing.

Michael spearheaded the attack on the captain Magnimus' forces. His legion was saturated with huge, strong demons. Gabriel fought with the zeal of many warriors. Uriel slew demon after demon. Raphael was too powerful for any to dismount; even Magnimus failed to topple the giant seraph from his horse. Saraqael, Remiel, and Raguel fought side by side as they flanked the rear guard of the strong legion. The general and the seraphim were a mighty force of strength and might. They overpowered the legion, driving them back to retreat.

As they pursued Magnimus' legion, Michael took down a vast number of massive demons effortlessly and without being dismounted from his noble steed. His captains fought valiantly by his side, and despite the fact their swords could not even be compared in strength to Michael's Sword of the Spirit, they wielded their swords with power and precision. With perfect timing, Gideon and twelve million of the most zealous angels swept over the hillside like a fierce tidal wave. Each warrior had his lance in hand, ready to harpoon the enemy. Gideon ordered them to divide: one half joined with the warriors on horseback the other half flanked the legion forming a tight impenetrable circle.

Before long, the enemy's efforts quickly turned to desperation and retreat. Michael and the courageous six cut off their escape and Gideon and his forces speared thousands upon thousands of demons. Satan, accompanied by his captains, watched in horror from the side of the Crystal Mountains. They had managed to evade Jeremiah and his forces and retreat to the safety of the mountain or so they thought. Satan was enraged at what he was witnessing. He ordered all of his captains to rally the legions to launch one final assault. Only Beltezar remained by his side as he watched and hoped in vain that this last effort would turn the tide.

The captains took charge of the legions from the major sergeants. The momentum was beginning to sway in their favor. Gideon's forces were entrenched in a ravine fighting against millions of rebel angels. Jeremiah's army had their backs to the mountain, battling with six million demons they had trapped. In spite of being vastly outnumbered, the enemy was prevailing against the Host of Heaven. The tide had turned, yet hope still lingered in God's seraphim, but it was fading fast.

"Send your salvation my God," Michael looked to Mount Zion and cried out with all of his might.

"Michael, look. Help is coming," Uriel said, pointing towards the Garden of Tranquility. Then all of sudden, a cloud of dust stirred in the air and Michael could see the shadows of millions of seraphim rushing across the field to their aid.

"Joshua," Michael yelled at the top of his lungs.

"Salvation is here," Gabriel proclaimed.

The Host of Heaven was once again empowered to fight.

"To the glory of God," Gideon's forces raised their voices in unison.

"For the King," Jeremiah's army cheered.

Satan looked on as Joshua and the twelve million seraphim came down on his legions like a wall of might, crushing the demons' spirits and their bones. Michael and the valiant Host of Heaven took back the momentum by force.

"My liege, what can we do against his mighty will," Beltezar said, looking to his master for an answer.

"I must kill Michael. Then the enemy will flee before our wrath," Satan said, his eyes enflamed with hatred. His spirit was boiling over with anger.

"I will ride with you my lord and, with my sword, I will smite his captains," Beltezar declared. Together, they rode down the mountain screaming profanities at their enemies.

Michael looked to the mountainside. A landslide was coming down fast, right on Jeremiah's army. The rocks pummeled the angels. Amidst the cloud of dirt, Michael saw him.

"Satan," Michael uttered.

The captains looked towards the mountain and saw Beltezar riding by Satan's side. He and the captains took off in their direction. Michael spearheaded the charge with Gabriel on his right and Raphael on his left.

Their mighty steeds split the forces of darkness just as Moses parted the Red Sea. Michael had his eye set firmly on Satan. The captains fanned out taking down hundreds of the major sergeants as they rode forward.

"He's falling right into my plan," Satan said to Beltezar.

"Gabriel and Uriel will be the first to feel the edge of my blade," Beltezar said. "By my sword, may all the captains feel your justice, Lucifer my lord."

The legions scattered as Michael rode forward to meet Satan in battle. Beltezar engaged Gabriel and Uriel, knocking both of them off of their horses by a blow from his fist, but not without losing his balance and falling to the ground. Michael timed his jump perfectly and landed a blow to Satan, routing him from his steed. Angels and demons alike stood and watched as Michael dueled with the prince of darkness.

Satan had his weapon drawn and he waved it about with futility in a display of swordsmanship. Michael lunged at Satan, but he missed him and struck the ground with a thud. Satan somehow evaded every one of Michael's efforts to take him down. He retaliated with a jab, but missed piercing Michael by no more than an inch.

The duel continued for quite some time with neither of them touching one another. Each successfully blocked the other from being triumphant. Then something incredible happened that has been passed down, from seraphim to seraphim, through the ages. Suddenly, Michael's sword began to glow with an intense light. The blade illuminated the entire battlefield with an enchanting, yet terrible iridescence. Satan was nearly blinded by the pure light.

Michael raised the Sword of the Spirit and came down on Satan with every ounce of strength he possessed. Satan tried with all efforts to block his swing, but it was to no avail. The Sword of the Spirit struck with a flash of lightning that thundered and lit up all of Heaven. Satan's sword shattered to dust. When the dust cleared, Michael was standing with the Sword of the Spirit raised in victory. The pride of Satan was overcome. Satan's arrogant face vanished and in its stead the most horrified look appeared. The prince of darkness laid face down and helpless. Michael stood with his foot on Satan's back and gave glory to God for victory was now at hand.

"Raise your voice in triumph, all you angels of Heaven. For victory belongs to our God," Michael declared with a mighty shout.

Once Satan was disarmed, the legions threw down their weapons and accepted their defeat. God rose from his throne and shook Heaven with his voice.

"It is finished. Satan, you have been defeated. Remember this though; your time has not yet come to be destroyed. You are forevermore banished from Heaven, and Hell will be your domain as long as time remains on earth."

The ground then opened up beneath Satan and the demons' feet and a giant incinerating flame shot up. The flame swallowed the forces of evil, dragging their spirits to Hell. The ground closed shut and appeared as if it had never before opened. Bear in mind, God could have driven Satan and his demons out of Heaven with the power he possessed in the tip of his smallest finger. However, this battle was a test and a challenge; meant to strengthen Michael and the Host of Heaven for what God had in store for them.

All of Heaven was in awe of the glory of God. Never before had they seen such a display of mighty power.

"Victory is the LORDS.' Victory belongs to the one true God," Michael shouted.

The entire Host of Heaven joined in, until an ominous voice grew louder than their cheers. Right away, they focused their attention on Mount Zion. There stood God shining like a bright morning star, beaming in glory, and radiant as many gems. His voice was like a rushing wind.

"Michael, come near to me," he said. Michael obeyed at once and ascended Mt. Zion.

Michael mounted his horse and rode to Mt. Zion. There he climbed the mountain alone. As he came closer to the top, he could clearly see a kind and gentle smile on God's face.

"Come closer valiant one," God said to him. Michael approached the LORD and bowed low.

"Oh most high and mighty King of kings and LORD of lords, please forgive me for ever being anxious of Lucifer's betrayal. You are an all knowing, all seeing God and to you be the Glory forever and ever. For our victory belongs to you and you alone," Michael said.

"Fear not, my servant," God said, putting his hand on Michael's shoulder. "Today you have proven yourself and shown me that you are ready for what lays ahead of you. This is just the beginning of the mighty things you will accomplish in my name to my glory. Only I can see what is ultimately in store for you, but you must trust in me with all of your heart. And know that I am always with you no matter where you are. Remember that nothing is impossible with the power I bestow on you. For today you are deemed and most respectively given the title, Archangel Michael. Know that the angel you were before will never be the same. For I am doing a new thing. Kneel Archangel Michael, most highly honored angel among the Host of Heaven."

"From this day forward you will forever be known as an Archangel of the Most High. May the Sword of the Spirit be a light upon your path and may my Holy Spirit empower you and guide you," proclaimed the LORD. He took the Sword of the Spirit and touched each of Michael's shoulders.

The LORD then produced a beautiful emblem and before he fastened it to Michael's cloak, he spoke.

"Stand Archangel Michael. I now bestow you with a new badge to replace your former one. This Holy badge symbolizes the authority I have given you and it signifies, to all seraphim, your position as the commander of the Host of Heaven."

God fixed the emblem to Michael's cloak and an eruption of cheering spread like the wind through the crowded streets of Jerusalem.

The badge was exemplary in all respects. The emblem was made of pure gold and shaped like a shield. A dazzling red ruby was embedded in the center and the finest of diamonds in Heaven were encrusted all three of the edges. Consider this, the diamonds and precious jewels found in Heaven are far more beautiful, beyond comparison, than that of any found on earth. So, needless to say, this was an especially breathtaking gift from God.

Immediately following the ceremony, the LORD of Hosts descended Mount Zion with Michael on his left. He addressed the angels: "Today a great battle was waged and all seraphim fought zealously and valiantly." The LORD's eyes gleamed with light and his face appeared solemn as he continued.

"This is only the beginning of what is to come. There will be many battles before the war has finally ended. You have chosen wisely to stay and fight for the sake of my righteousness and, rest assured, I will win the war in the end."

God turned to Michael and clasped his hand in the Archangel's and raised his arm in the air.

"My servant is no longer to be addressed by Michael, but he is to be called Archangel Michael. If anyone does not honor this then you have not honored me. Know that I am your God and the Archangel Michael is now the commander of the Host of Heaven. It is he who will lead you into the battles to come. With the Sword of the Spirit he has my authority to command the armies of Heaven."

After God had spoken a great shout arose like a wave of thunder. Multitudes of angels burst into praise. They worshiped the LORD for who he is and what he has done singing:

> *"Lift your voices in triumph*
> *All ye Host of Heaven*
> *Give glory to God in the highest.*
> *For he has defeated the darkness.*
>
> *Lift your voices in triumph*
> *All ye Host of Heaven*
> *Our God is a great God.*
> *Worthy, worthy, is the King."*

The angels worshiped God for days without ceasing. And even though they were created for this purpose, they willingly delighted in it more than anything.

First Time on Earth

Note from the Scribe

Praise be to God. The righteous seraphim were victorious. The battle between the forces of light and the legions of darkness had raged fiercely for three incredible days. In order for you to understand the immense struggle of such a revolution, you should know that a day in Heaven is equal to a thousand years on earth. Knowing this, you can only imagine what toll it took on all the seraphim that fought courageously to protect Heaven. Before the battle no angel had experienced war, nor had any felt a sword in their hand our lance in their grasp. Until the war, no weapon had been forged. But of course, there was no need for swords or lances or armor, for peace had reigned since the dawn of time.

During those three atrocious days of fighting the Host of Heaven spared their enemy no mercy. They were unshakable in the midst of combat. The seraphim tossed all kinships aside, as brother fought against brother. They also were forced to put all sympathies aside; considering a war of this magnitude there was no room for compassion. After all, the throne of God was at stake, and peace as they knew it, was hanging in the balance. They willingly and zealously put their lives on the line to save God's throne from the evil clutches of Satan.

On both sides, hundreds of thousands were slain. The spirits of the mighty angels, who gave their lives for the LORD, became known as the Neshawmaw. They were to dwell peacefully in the House of the LORD. However, there will come a day when they will be given new bodies, but this will not come about until the final battle between Heaven and Hell. Then, and only then, will they once again wield a weapon of war to defend God's kingdom.

The rebel angels who perished in combat became demonic spirits and were banished to the lake of fire. These spirits search the earth in desperation for souls to steal. Although demonic spirits cannot take physical form, they can take possession of a human only if a door is opened for them. They eagerly exploit a man's flesh for their evil intentions. In fact, it is common knowledge that these spirits can avoid the pain and agony of the eternal fire only if they are dwelling in a man's body. Moreover, demonic spirits along with the demons, cannot escape the creator's judgment. For in the end of days they will meet their demise at the battle of Armageddon.

The fiery depths of Hell had claimed more than one third of all seraphim and with them—the dawning of a new age had arrived. The angels of faith that united with Heaven became a brotherhood, tightly knit together and bonded for eternity in God's good grace. The fall of the demons brought a new life to Heaven: the air was more invigorating, the light was extra brilliant, and every plant was greener and all colors came vibrantly to life. All the angels were stronger for their triumph over evil, and all dissension had vanished in the midst of God's holy congregation.

On the other hand, life was very different for the demons and their prince of darkness. The demons were doomed to perform Satan's bidding. Roaming the earth and never finding rest, they hunted for souls to purchase and drag down to Hell with them. Some remained beautiful on the outside, but were still wicked and perverted on the inside. Even worse, some began to change in appearance, becoming wretched and vile manifestations of evil. To see one of these demons would terrify anyone unless they had protection from the LORD.

Concerning the prince of darkness, he began to change in

appearance and character. One of his most malicious skills is the ability to transform his body into any form imaginable. For he can be beautiful and cunning or he can be ugly and frightening; always shifting form into whatever will give him the advantage. From the moment he fell from Heaven, a dark hatred clouded his spirit. He desired to turn everyone against their creator, God. This became his top priority and whatever means were necessary, he would take them. Through his perverted thinking, Satan had convinced himself that no risk was too great and no foe was too fierce to overcome, as long as he sat securely on his throne in Hades.

Satan was only given permission by God to descend from Hell once every thousand years. It was in these times that Michael would assemble a large force of the Heavenly Host to descend upon the earth and wage war against the evil one and his legion. It was in these battles, and there have been a number of them to speak of since the beginning of time, that God has made Michael famous amongst all the angels in Heaven.

Through Michael's eyes his life was now just beginning. Michael's character and knowledge developed beautifully; after all, God himself was his teacher. The LORD also instilled in him wisdom beyond that of any angel in Heaven. He fully matured in stature becoming the tallest and strongest angel among the Host of Heaven. God purposefully created the archangel this way to prepare him for the battles and missions to come. Although Michael didn't fully know it yet, God was molding him and shaping him for a destiny far greater than Michael could ever imagine.

The great battle for Heaven was actually a test for Michael. Could he lead the Host of Heaven? Could he be victorious? Could he rely on God and not himself? These were the questions that needed answering. One test in itself could satisfy all questions. Could he defeat Satan and his devices? After pummeling the conceited prince of darkness, the duel had been won. Michael had come out triumphant and not by his might, nor his power, but by God's spirit. Moreover, the defeat and exile of Satan brought about a new stage in Michael's life. This was the start of his extensive training.

Michael had never wielded a weapon until the first battle when God bestowed upon him the Sword of the Spirit. Simply put, Michael was utterly in awe of this kingly sword; it completely took his breath away. This was no ordinary sword, but it was empowered with the Holy Spirit. Forged from the most precious steel in all of Heaven and earth, the blade was inlaid with gold and silver that intertwined and blended perfectly together. The sword seemed to radiate a brilliant light whenever it was removed from its sheath.

The hilt was ornamented with the rarest jewels; the most beautiful, dazzling, and precious gems that Heaven could produce. To say the least, these polished stones were far more breathtaking than any on earth. The handle was adorned with shimmering diamonds, soft in appearance, yet extremely durable and harder than steel. In addition to these fine qualities the diamonds were chiseled with flawless precision to fit Michael's hands perfectly.

The sheath that held the Sword of the Spirit was created entirely out of gold (a fine gold, much tougher and lighter than that which exists on earth). Lining the center of the sheath were large, handsome, shiny red rubies, in which one could see their own reflection. The sword and sheath were without defect, perfectly and uniquely designed by God himself. Although the sword is beyond comparison in beauty and strength, its greatest significance lies not in what the eye can see, but in what flows through the veins of the blade.

The power of the Holy Spirit lives and moves in the sword, from the very tip of the blade all the way down to the base of the handle. The sword's power comes not from the one who wields it but, conversely, the power of the Sword of the Spirit flows *into* its wielder. This is anything but an ordinary weapon for it carries the authority of God almighty. Henceforth, not just any seraph can possess this holy weapon but only one who is God's most trusted.

Following his victory, Archangel Michael danced before the God's throne as the four cherubim sang:

> *Holy, Holy, Holy, is the*
> *LORD God, the Almighty,*

Who was and who is
And who is to come

Michael loves worshiping his God and he knew to give credit where credit was due. His victory came only by the power of the Most High. More than anything else, dancing before the throne lifted his spirit and carried him to new heights. The LORD took great delight in Michael's worshipful dancing. God also loved Michael's companionship. They spent countless moments together walking in the Garden of Tranquility and they held their deepest conversations while sitting by the Fountain of Life (this fountain was known for its rejuvenating effects and, on a breezy day, its refreshing mist could be felt throughout the garden).

Michael loved spending time with the LORD and he thrived on his presence. Their discussions were not always leisurely but quite often they were deep conversations of God's plan and purpose for his archangel. Michael consumed himself with the LORD's teaching. He couldn't get enough of the wisdom and knowledge of the LORD. Just when he thought he had learned it all, God would pull something new from his sleeve, as he was continually instructing Michael in his righteous way.

At this point in Michael's training, God desired to fill his mind and heart with the wisdom and knowledge that has existed since the beginning of time—when God spoke the words, *I Am*. God knows everything and is wise beyond anyone or anything ever created. After all, he is God and he created all that exists.

The LORD's presence filled Michael with the Holy Spirit so that his heart and mind absorbed, like a thirsty sponge, all of God's teachings (including the wisdom and knowledge of what is to come). God revealed to him much of the future, but he didn't divulge when these things would take place or what part Michael would be playing in this predestined scenario. God alone knew the full details. Even so, Michael knew more about the past, present, and future than any angel in Heaven.

The Warrior Within …

Soon the day had arrived. The day Michael had long prepared for. The time had come to utilize the wisdom and instruction that was instilled in him by the Lord Almighty. It was a brilliant day in Heaven, like every day in Heaven, when God called Michael to his throne room.

"Archangel Michael, as I have promised, you are called for a great and mighty purpose, destined for my glory and honor," God said; his face shined with kingliness. "Your time to rise is yet to come but I will make certain you are fully prepared. That is what brings you here today. I have summoned you to serve in spirit and in truth, for I am the great I Am. Michael—will you accept your duty?"

"With all that is in me, I accept," Michael answered, looking into God's eyes. The expression on Michael's face changed from one of fear and doubt to an expression of pure elation as his eyes pulsated with the light of the Holy Spirit.

"I anoint you with the power of my Holy Spirit. Behold, I go before you and prepare the way. Go and be blessed in my name," God said and grasped hold of Michael's hands. "Close your eyes and believe in me."

Michael did as He asked and he held his eyelids tightly closed as God spoke words in the ancient heavenly tongue. Peals of thunder bellowed throughout Heaven and cracks of lightning flashed. The ground beneath Michael's feet trembled in the quake of God's awesome power. After many moments, the Lord's voice faded and the thunder and lightning ceased, until complete and utter silence pervaded his ears. The quiet stillness was unnerving to him, but the wisp of a cool breeze brushed against his face and an incredible peace swept over his entire being.

Michael had to summon up all of his courage in order to open his eyes. He squinted at first and, letting a little light in, he found the brightness to be less intense than that of Heaven. Then all at once he let go and upon opening his eyes, he beheld the earth that God had created. He was in awe and his breath was taken away by what he was now seeing. His senses were grasping the elements and his mind was wrapping itself around this beautiful creation— earth. His entire being was taken back as he gazed upon a great mountain; higher than any in Heaven. It dwelled in the clouds, high in the stratosphere, and it nearly reached the heavens.

Michael searched his surroundings and found himself standing in a bountiful plain with waves of long, soft green grass that swayed like feathers in the gentle wind. Tall rich cedar trees were growing here and there. Bushes with beautiful purple flowers hugged the bases of their trunks. Michael couldn't help but stare up in wonder at the mammoth-sized mountain of earth and rock. It was cloaked with trees and a pure white snowcap crowned its peak like a majestic halo.

Even though there was no music to be heard, Michael composed a new song to the LORD. He danced and worshiped as if there were a great symphony assembled. He praised God for bringing him to such a splendid place. He fell to his knees and prayed in reverence to the LORD thanking him for creating such a wonderful place. As he was praying, he looked up and witnessed a brilliant light streaking across the blue sky. It traveled with incredible speed; zigzagging and shooting through the clouds. Before he could react, the light turned and came directly towards him.

Suddenly, a being of light appeared before him—a seraph. He was tall as well as slender. His cheerful looking face was slightly round with very high cheekbones. He had a head full of long straight blonde hair. He had piercing blue eyes, beautiful but serious all the same. As this seraph looked at him, Michael knew that he meant business. He was clothed in a bright white tunic with a hooded dark green cloak draped over his shoulders. Though, one feature in particular caught Michael's eye and set this angel apart from any he had met before. There appeared to be a glowing circle, possibly a crown of some sort, which was floating in midair, right above his head.

Michael made a slight bow, as angels do in Heaven to greet one another.

"Fear not Michael. My name is Elijah. I am a messenger sent by the LORD of Hosts. I bring a message from He who sits on the throne," he said with a bow and pulled out a piece of parchment and began to read from it.

"I desire for you to search the wilderness for a creature, a lamb," Elijah read. "This animal is very dear to me; make sure that no harm comes to my creature. You will find the lamb on the Mountain of God. You must carry the lamb to the summit, for there you will find salvation. The path will be difficult and the way treacherous; your task will be heavy and your burden light. If you put all of your trust in my name, I will set a hedge of thorns around you so no evil will befall you. All you must do is believe and I will make a way where there seems to be none. My strength will be your rod and your staff. Now go with my blessing."

"God be with you," rolled of Elijah's lips and in an instant, he transformed into light and launched himself back into the heavens.

"Good-bye, Elijah," Michael said, a little belated, while his mind attempted to absorb what had just happened. Even more, he was full of wonder and excitement, and more than eager to respond to the LORD's calling. He had no idea what challenges lay ahead of him or what dangers he will face but, one thing was for sure, the lamb needed rescuing and he was the angel God had chosen for the task.

NOTE FROM THE SCRIBE

The Mountain of God is known by more than one name. God's word (the Bible) tells that Mount Sinai, also called Mount Horeb, is the very mountain where the LORD met with Moses and entrusted him with the Ten Commandments. The mountain holds claim to a rich history full of encounters with the LORD Almighty, a history that spans the time from Michael's arrival to present day. Rumor has it that Noah's ark is buried deep beneath the snowcapped peak of Mount Sinai. The *Mountain of God* is another name by which it is called.

The Warrior Within ...

Michael stood gazing at the snowcapped summit. He was convinced that a great challenge lay before him.

"The lamb needs my help. Now, where should I begin?" he asked himself as the sun set before his eyes. A familiar voice spoke to his heart reassuring him that he is not alone.

NOTE FROM THE SCRIBE

You know that peace you sense deep down inside, comforting you when everything seems like it will never get any better? That is God's voice. When you feel as if you're all alone in the world and you'll never feel any better; then, you experience this warm, comforting sensation rising from deep down inside of you. That is God's voice speaking to you in terms that you can understand. If you listen closely you can hear God's still small voice speaking to you. However, and this is unfortunate, most people on earth never hear God's voice speaking to them. Most everyone is too wrapped up in their own world to listen to God.

The Warrior Within ...

"I shall camp here tonight," Michael decided, confidently.

He knew that with what was in store for him, he would need the light of day to explore. The sun set briskly and the evening brought a cold wind up the valley stirring the grass. The icy chill was just about unbearable for Michael. He remembered his time spent with the LORD and with all he learned it didn't begin to prepare him for what cold felt like. Quite frankly, it came as a shock to the Archangel.

Michael did know that, in order for him to warm his body, a fire would have to be prepared. All fire in Heaven originated from Mount Zion. In God's throne room, there burns a torch that has never been extinguished. It has a flame with no beginning and there is no end to its blazing presence. It is rightfully called the eternal fire of the Holy Spirit.

Michael gathered some fallen branches and dried grass. He bowed his head low in reverence and beseeched the LORD.

"Oh most gracious Father, LORD of Heaven and earth. Please bring your holy fire and give me comfort. I wait on you my God," he prayed.

The moment his lips closed the sky opened up. A brilliant flash pulsated and a pillar of fire appeared before him. The wood and the grass, he had gathered, ignited instantly. The pillar vanished, but it left a fire that burned generously. Michael found the warmth of the flame pleasant and soothing to his chilled body.

Next on the agenda was to find a place to rest his head. Michael looked about him and found grass that God had abundantly provided. It was the type of grass that was softer than any feathers and smoother than any silk. He gathered up a large amount and laid it out making a comfortable bed for himself. He laid himself down upon his bed and gazed into the evening sky. It was beauteous to behold; full of stars and with a moon that glowed pleasantly. He was awestruck at just the thought of this creation. God the creator, being the master artist, had painted the sky with bright shining stars. The stars went on endlessly much like the infinite wisdom of God. Making this scene even more wondrous, the moon was at its fullest. It seemed so large, so close to him, and it was unlike anything he had ever seen in Heaven. He was truly intrigued.

Michael was relaxing and enjoying every moment of the evening twilight when, suddenly, he was pulled from his gratifying state of mind. A noise, which came from close by, had startled him. He stood to his feet and placed a hand on his sword. The firelight revealed a creature crouching in the bush. As the wind blew the grass, he could distinguish its body. Four slender, lanky legs held the creature erect. Two piercing gray eyes stared at him down a long narrow snout: it was a wolf.

Michael steadied himself. The wolf stood at bay, not moving to left or the right, as it stared intently into the archangel's eyes. Its broad neck budged not an inch and its eyes glared at him like a stabbing knife. Michael felt unnerved, but remained calm and controlled. The silence was too much.

"Beast, I am a servant of the living God. Come near and reveal yourself a friend or flee before the power of the Sword of the Spirit," Michael boldly cried.

The wolf took two steps back, turned, and crept slowly away. A sigh of relief swept over Michael's spirit. He had stood up to the wolf and now his strength felt drained from the encounter.

Michael lay back down and kept his mind focused on the LORD. As his eyes grew heavy, he thought, *what a place this earth. Out of the entire universe, is there any place as unique as this creation of God's? It is a place to be admired and revered for its immensity and splendor.*

He didn't know what tomorrow would bring, but one thing was for sure—the heat of the fire calmed his troubled soul. He loved the crackling sounds and sparks the fire made just as much as its aroma. Fixing his eyes on the radiant evening sky, he drifted into a deep sleep that he had never experienced before. For in Heaven sleep does not exist. There has never been a need for it.

Michael awoke the next morning to the rising of a new sun. The bright morning sun, climbing the horizon and wrapping the meadow with its majesty, warmed Michael's damp cool skin. The archangel rose to his feet, faced the Mountain of God, and gave thanks to the LORD. His heart was enraptured with the beauty of this creation. It was awesome in splendor and breathtaking to behold. It rose into the clouds and welcomed the new light the sun brought.

There were many miles to cover before he would reach the mountain, so he dowsed the fire with dirt and set off. He noticed many paw prints in the meadow just outside of his camp, all of which probably belonged to the same wolf.

"You were watching me closely last night. Weren't you, wolf?" Michael said to himself as he scuffed up the paw prints with his sandal. Although, there was one question he pondered. Was this wolf a foe or just a member of God's creation?

Michael covered the distance between he and the base of the mountain before the sun was high overhead. He discovered, though, that he had difficultly drawing his breath. This feeling of fatigue was completely foreign to him. He knew that, in Heaven, he could run and never grow weary. The atmosphere on earth was not like the atmosphere in Heaven. *Earth held more than a few surprises,* he thought. He rested for a moment under the shade of a large olive tree. He was on the perimeter of the mountain and now only a thick forest of cedar trees lay in his path.

"Thank you, LORD." he said loudly, for he discovered a path, straight and narrow, leading through the trees.

Before he took one step further, an ominous sound struck his ears like a blaring alarm. An incredible scene unraveled before his eyes. The trees in the distant forest began to lean and bend toward the ground, and then, would rise up again. One by one the trees bowed over until a tree, only a stone's throw from Michael, bent over and remained down. Complete silence permeated the forest. The stillness, alone, was unnerving to Michael. His hand gripped tightly to his sword's hilt and he scanned the perimeter searching for what it was that could be there. His mind couldn't fathom what creature could do such destruction to the large sturdy cedar trees.

The silence was almost unbearable for Michael. He figured he had better say something but, then again, maybe keeping his mouth shut might be more effective. He decided in favor of speaking.

"I am a servant of light—the Archangel of God Almighty. Show yourself," Michael shouted. Then, the same loud frightening noise started up again. But this time, the sound began to fade away and the trees were bending in the *opposite* direction. "Praise be to God," he shouted.

All was becoming silent once again.

"I hope I haven't spoken too soon," Michael whispered to himself.

But, giving him cause for relief, the trees continued to bend and snap until, at last, the noise had fully faded into the distance.

"Praise be to God," Michael said once again.

Long last, Michael was able to commence traveling down the mysterious path. Perfectly situated between the undergrowth, the trail wound and twisted narrowly along the dark forest floor. The woods were saturated with shrubs and plants of all sorts: sweet smelling wild flowers, delicious fruit bearing bushes, painful thorny hedges, and many more which would be too numerous to describe.

Michael's body was tiring quickly, but his will remained strongly determined. He hiked the path cutting away any thorns that stood in his way. The sun was high overhead; the hottest time of the day, and an extreme thirst began to take hold of him. The archangel had never before experienced thirst; it was terribly unpleasant. In Heaven he did not need water. He had drunk from the fountain of life and he never thirsted again. He knew there must be water near, since a trickling could be heard, only farther than he would like to stray from the path.

Michael decided to abandon the pathway in search of this stream. He cut his way through the underbrush for what seemed like thousands of paces. Then, through the darkness of the forest, he could see a light, bright and beautiful, appearing ahead.

"Praise the LORD. There is light, after all, at the end of this forsaken tunnel," Michael shouted with excitement.

His voice was so loud that it triggered off a storm of feathers, as thousands of crows flew from their perch in the trees. Michael closed his eyes tightly for protection and covered his ears to muffle the piercing screeches of the crows. When he finally opened his eyes, he could see that their feathers had settled to the ground and that the leaves of many trees had been swept off their branches. The wind force, caused by the massive number of crows in flight, had literally stripped the trees of their foliage making way for the light of the sun.

With anticipation, Michael picked his legs up and ran to see what waited ahead. He broke forth from the forest and stood, breathless, staring at the serene beauty that enveloped him like a cloud. A pasture of vibrant wild flowers and long silky smooth green grass lay before him and, as far as he could see, there were rolling hills. He was standing in a valley beyond the outskirts of the forest. He felt as if he were standing in the midst of a sanctuary. As he looked beyond the valley, his eyes captured the fullness and magnificence of the Mountain of God. The snow-capped peaks were sharing space with the clouds and from where he stood the trees scaling the mountain looked as if they were merely twigs.

In the midst of the valley were a herd of deer and a flock of sheep feeding together. There were numerous varieties of animals abounding among the trees and the spacious fields. Life here seemed to stand still. Michael felt like he had entered a completely new world, set apart from the wild plains and rough woodlands he had come to know as earth. He was so infatuated with its serene and peaceful beauty that he had momentarily forgotten about his thirst. Licking his dried lips, he was again reminded of his thirst. Indeed, thirst was new to Michael and he sought, once again, to satisfy his need for water.

The stream must be near, he thought, as the sound of running water filled the air. With a listening ear, he continued to look over the surrounding forest and valley for the source of the sound.

Michael made his way to the outer perimeter of the valley. At the edge of the forest he spied a brook bubbling over with crystal-clear water. He ran with haste for the water's edge. He dipped his hands in and drank until he thirsted no more. By the brook he found a large, smooth rock ideal for sitting and resting. Michael picked some fruit from the nearby blueberry bushes.

"Delicious," he exclaimed and lifted his hands to Heaven. "Father, I give thanks to you for creating such a wonderful place and for providing me with all my needs. You truly are a great God."

After his prayer, Michael noticed there were hoof prints by the stream.

"Very tiny. These could belong to the lamb," he said, bending down and touching the muddy prints with his fingers. This motivated him, so he sprung to his feet and started following the tiny hoof prints. The prints traveled along the brook and into the forest, but the leaves were so dense that the trail seemed to vanish. Michael's instincts told him to pray. *My God show me the way.*

Just then a subtle whimpering sound tickled his ears. It was close. Michael looked up and down and here and there. Then he saw the lamb, helplessly trapped in a thicket of thorns, life being choked from its tiny and fragile body. Michael knew that the animal was frightened, so with gentle hands, he carefully loosened the thorns and freed the lamb. Michael lifted the lamb into his arms and held it close to his bosom. The small creature, being thankful for the rescue, licked his face affectionately.

"Little lamb, your salvation is here. Now to bring you home. The Father has need of you, little lamb," Michael declared with a smile and held the lamb high above him. "A boy, no doubt; from here on, I guess I should address you as little sir." Michael laughed out loud.

There in the woods, the giant archangel cradled the smallest of creatures safely within his strong arms. The hands that had wielded the Sword of the Spirit with an untamed rile against the enemy and the fingers that were once covered in blood from fierce battle, now tenderheartedly embraced the lamb. Michael felt compassion, toward the lamb, like none he had experienced before. There in the forest he silently took a solemn vow to protect the lamb with his life. He would defend the creature with the same zeal he swore to his God and the kingdom of Heaven.

The lamb began to wriggle in his arms, so Michael lowered him to the ground. He walked by the lamb's side and they made their way towards the brook. Without hesitation, the lamb went straight to the sparkling water.

"You're a thirsty little guy," Michael exclaimed. As the lamb was slurping the water up, all of the animals began to clear out of the valley. They didn't scurry one by one, but by herds. This especially alarmed Michael's spirit. The stampeding subsided and the wind carried the clouds of dust away. And now an eerie silence pervaded the atmosphere with a foreboding presence.

Michael felt a strange premonition in his spirit. The fleeing animals had also sensed something only moments ago as they hastily vacated the valley. Evil was near. Suddenly, across the valley a dozen or so trees bent and snapped one by one. A large pine tree on the border of the forest bowed over and as it sprung back, a gigantic object spilled over into the valley. The monstrous creature was miles away, yet Michael's keen eyesight could make out its horrid features. The beast was brown and hairy with paws the size of boulders, each sporting long claws resembling razor sharp daggers. Its snout was brood and in its mouth were a set of teeth that were very large, looking to be as sharp as a saw.

"A bear," Michael shouted in terror.

A grizzly bear, in fact, and that outburst was all it needed to spot Michael. The bear looked across the field and stood on its hind legs, letting out a ferocious roar that shook the ground beneath the archangel's feet.

The bear swiftly lowered himself down and the ground gave way with a thunderous boom. The beast began to run towards them. Michael grabbed the lamb and ran like the wind. He leapt over the brook with a single bound—what supernatural agility.

Michael kept the lamb tightly in his grasp. He flew through the woods, dodging trees and hurdling over fallen trees. He slowed down for a moment and listened. The bear had reached the forest's edge. *How did it cover that distance so quickly?* Michael had to ask himself.

"Never mind, though, time to go lamb," he said, and took off running, abandoning all fear and doubt with each step.

Michael thanked the LORD, in stride, for helping him evade the monster. Though, without warning, he tumbled down a small hill. He found himself rolling downhill into, yet, another valley. He was in a wide-open space that backed up into a mountain of rock.

"This is clearly a problem," Michael said as he looked at an unsurpassable barrier—a cliff. There was no way out, for he was standing on open ground with nowhere to hide. Out of nowhere, without a sound of approaching danger, the bear plunged through the trees sending splintered wood flying through the air. A piece of sharp timber stuck in the ground not even a half a pace from where Michael stood.

The grizzly bear locked eyes with the archangel. Knowing its prey had no way of escape, the bear paced back and forth proudly as it slowly approached Michael and the lamb. Drool poured from its jaws and its eyes were red; it was bloodthirsty. Despite the bear's intimidating showmanship, the commander of the Heavenly Host wasn't about to go down that easy. He scanned the valley for any sign of hope.

"Do not forsake me my God," he said as his eyes continued to search for way out. Then he spotted it—a small opening in the side of the cliff, just big enough for the lamb. Michael ran to it and tucked the lamb into the opening.

"You'll be safe here," uttered Michael, showing no fear. "I gave you my word and, if it be so, I will give my life to protect God's lamb."

The bear came near and like a pillar of evil it raised itself onto its hind legs. Michael was unwavering in the face of what could be certain death for him. He reached for the Sword of the Spirit, but it was not there.

"How could this be," he asked himself. His confidence began

to wane and panic, even doubt, made its way into his conscious mind. He felt like death was stalking him like prey.

Amazingly, Michael became overwhelmed with a feeling of peace. He was able to look fear in the face and stand up to this monster with an unswerving confidence. He was implored to look to Heaven and he saw something that reassured his faith. It was soaring high in the air but, suddenly it started to dive towards the earth flying at an incredible speed. The bear kept his eyes steadily on Michael, eyeing him as if he were contemplating a delicious meal. The bear stepped closer and closer, as Michael backed up against the rocky cliff. He had nowhere to go and the bear let a roar to signal its hunt had come to an end. The grizzly was so close to him that he could smell its rancid stench and his skin could feel the hot air from its nostrils. Michael dreaded the thought of being the next thing to smell on the bear's breath.

A gust of strong and powerful wind blew against Michael. The bear turned to see what was happening and his face was met with a blow from a bird's giant talon. It was not just simply a bird, but a majestic eagle, bigger than any other eagle on earth. The eagle let out a shrill earsplitting cry and swooped back down at the bear. The grizzly stood to its feet and swiped at the bird, but the bird easily evaded him. But the eagle, with great accuracy, had plucked the bear's eye from his monstrous head. The bear was infuriated and went into a rage. As the eagle circled above the bear preparing for its next assault, the grizzly stood back up on its hind legs. It let out a roar so enormously loud that rocks began to fall from the cliff. Michael grabbed the lamb and hurried out from under the avalanche.

The eagle dodged a rock with brilliant maneuvering and pierced the bear's face with a deep cut. The beast lost its balance and toppled over. In spite of being knocked over and nearly defeated, the bear scurried to its feet. Suddenly a loose rock from the cliff struck the monster on the head. The bear, after recovering from the blow, fled the valley in defeat. The eagle had been triumphant in waging his assault.

Michael and the lamb watched, unscathed, at the edge of the valley as the eagle glided over to them. The majestic bird gracefully touched down on the grassy field. The eagle was truly unique, different from any creature Michael had ever encountered. The larger-than-life bird was nearly the size of a horse and its beak was about the length of a sword. The bird gazed intently into the archangel's eyes. Michael felt as if the bird was searching his soul and penetrating his spirit with its regal eyes. Somehow he knew, in his spirit, that meeting this bird was more than chance; it was a privilege and he was definitely certain of that.

As Michael stared into its eyes, he failed to notice the lamb had left his side. What he witnessed next overtook him with amazement. The lamb ran to the eagle's side and the bird leaned over and nudged the lamb onto its back using its long neck. The tiny lamb immediately made itself at home with the eagle. Michael now stood by himself, but his spirit was urging him to draw nearer to the eagle. He took two steps forward and the eagle took two giant steps forward. The eagle bowed low and with its eyes, was telling the archangel to climb on to his back. As soon as he came to rest atop the eagle, it started running and its huge outstretched wings began to flap. The air stirred rapidly, the wind roared, and off they went into the sky.

In a mere moment, they had climbed high above the ground and the valley started to fade away. Michael could still see the massive grizzly running in the woods. He gasped as he witnessed the bear vanishing into thin air. His mind tried to wrap itself around what he saw, but he was too busy concentrating on keeping his hold atop the eagle. As they flew higher up the mountain, his eye caught a pack of wolves running with swift strides in pursuit of a herd of dears. He saw a black bear climbing a tree in search of some honey. Then he had to draw close to the eagle's neck as a flock of birds was flying, what seemed to be, much too closely. The eagle flew above the noisy flock and the wind was rushing through his hair as they traveled at a speed that seemed faster than any bird could possibly fly. The deep blue sky was above him and everything below him was breathtaking. The countless trees from such heights appeared like splinters in the earth. The many crystal-clear lakes shimmered and sparkled in the sun's rays. A thousand streams flowed down the mountainside and fed the green flourishing valleys. His spirit drank all of it in and the invigorating cool mountain air refreshed his soul.

"Such splendor and majesty, the Father God created all of this for his glory. God, my LORD, my King, I adore thee." Michael shouted with a joyful noise and the eagle responded with a shrill but joyful screech.

Without any forewarning, the eagle swooped down closer to the mountain. They landed smoothly on the mountainside in a small precipice with a large opening in the cliff–a cave. As much as Michael had loved the ride, he realized it had to come to an end. Nonetheless, he was grateful beyond expression for the bird's timely assistance. He took the lamb in his arms as he dismounted. He put his hand on the bird's neck.

"I do not know if you understand me. I just want to say, thank you. Thank you, for coming to my rescue. You should know that your help was my salvation."

The eagle bowed low and took two paces back. The archangel and the eagle locked eyes and, there and then, Michael knew this was definitely an extraordinary bird. *This eagle is the noblest of creatures*, he thought.

"I shall call you king of the birds," he said. He took a bow, saluted the bird.

The eagle's eyes shined and reflected the sunset in an array of colors, unusual and mysterious filled with warmth and compassion. Then, in the blink of an eye, the eagle flew off into the sky with its feathers glowing in the deep orange and red sunset.

"Good bye. One day, we will meet again king of the birds," Michael said, and he picked the lamb up and held it close to his side.

The lamb was looking up into his eyes and he noticed its eyes were different from any other animal he had ever seen.

Why didn't I notice this before, he pondered.

"Well, they're special that's for certain," he said to the lamb. "It's getting cold little lamb. I don't know how you like it, but as for me, the cold isn't nearly as pleasant as the warmth of Heaven's air. If you could experience Heaven, you would never want to leave it, my tiny friend."

Michael carried the lamb to the cave.

An icy breeze came down the mountain, as they huddled together inside the cave. Michael was totally amazed and awestruck at the incredible display of artistry the LORD had created in only a day. The most gifted and talented artist on earth couldn't paint such beauty, not even in a lifetime of work. Michael then did what he loved best. He worshiped the LORD with all of his strength and might and created a new song:

LORD, Creator of all things,
You paint the sky
With the splendor of your majesty,
You rescue the righteous,

LORD, Creator of all things,
You have delivered your
Servant from danger,

LORD, Creator of all things,
I need you.
My soul longs for you,
For I belong to you, oh LORD.

In spite of not having a comfortable bed of soft grass, a place to rest his head, or a fire to warm his hands and feet, the archangel rested well that night. The lamb snuggled up to his chest and the warmth from the animal made the chilly night endurable. The sun peeking into the cave woke him from his deep slumber. He rubbed his eyes and looked around the cave. The first thing that drew his attention was the lamb was gone. Michael jumped to his feet and rushed outside to search for the missing lamb. There was no lamb. There was a rising cloud of smoke behind a massive bush, but where was the lamb? *Was the bush on fire,* he thought to himself. He hurried over to it and discovered someone crouching over an invitingly warm fire.

"I was wondering when you were going to wake up," spoke a kind voice. "Archangel, come have a seat and eat some food. You're going to need it, Michael."

"Elijah? Is it you," Michael uttered as he walked over.

"It is I. Happy to see me," answered Elijah, chief seraph of messengers, and took a bite of some meat.

"Of course I am. I have desperately missed the company of angels," Michael said. His eyes lit up briefly with excitement. Then he saw the meat on the stick over the fire.

"Stop! What are you eating? Not the lamb," Michael uttered.

"Of course not, what do you take me for? It was a ram, too fat and slow for its own good, if you ask me," Elijah replied with a look of sheer astonishment. Much needed relief came over the Archangel, but then he remembered the lamb.

"One thing though, is troubling me. I'm afraid I have failed my mission. The lamb is missing and I fear the worst has happened to the helpless little creature," Michael said. His voice was solemn and his eyes appeared heavy with despair.

The chief messenger looked at Michael with a big smile.

"Why are you smiling Elijah?" Michael asked. The seraph walked over and sat down next to him.

"Why I am smiling, you ask. Well, here's the situation—"

"You took him from me," Michael said, interrupting him. "I have failed."

Michael's eyes were full of worry.

"No, no, my friend. I did not take him from you and you have not failed your mission," Elijah said, patting him on the back. "Not yet, that is."

Michael stared at him completely flabbergasted.

"Archangel, why do you look so bewildered? You should know that I am struck with a sense of humor every now and then. I will continue telling you and I'll be serious. Michael, it was the lamb that called you and the lamb who led you this far. The lamb is safe now so no longer do you have to bother yourself worrying about him."

"What about the eagle? Do you know anything of this creature," Michael interjected, for he very much wanted to know.

"Eagle?" Elijah said, eyes widening. "The Father God will have to tell you of this eagle. I cannot help you. As for your mission, there is yet more to be accomplished for the LORD."

Elijah pointed to the snowcapped peak.

"Michael, you must reach the top before sunrise in three

earth-days from now. You must pass this test and then you will return to your home in Heaven."

"What if I fail," asked Michael, looking at the ground.

"There is no condemnation for those who are in God," Elijah answered firmly, but with a gentle smile. "Besides this, why ask such a question? All things have been made possible through our Father in Heaven."

Michael looked up to speak, but Elijah had disappeared.

"Wow, I'll have to learn that trick when I get back," Michael said.

A sudden pain came over him, a churning in his stomach. His instinct took over and he grabbed a hunk of meat off of the fire.

"Quite tasty and not bad compared to our feasts," he said. He ate to his fill and stood to his feet; before him laid a formidable challenge of jagged rocks, ice, and wind. The peak was in the clouds, so only a portion could be seen, but he wouldn't let that discourage his spirit.

"My strength is in the LORD," he said, lifting his hands to Heaven. "Lead me in your ways everlasting. Chase all my fears away. Let not danger overtake me, nor allow your enemies to destroy your servant. My hope is in you, my God."

He set off with his feet walking briskly. His body felt strengthened by the LORD and his spirit was encouraged by his holy presence.

"All glory belongs to You, LORD. For my help comes from you, maker of Heaven and earth," Michael said as he reached the side of the cliff.

He grabbed hold of the cliff and began to scale the mountain-side. He climbed steadily for many earth hours. Whenever he felt his strength wavering, he would call to the LORD for help. Each time, without failure, a jolt of power would enter his head and travel down to his feet. Dusk was settling in, yet he still climbed.

Finally, he reached a crevice in the rock. A deep opening was carved into the cliff. He took shelter from the freezing wind. At this incredible height, the stars were shining vividly. They appeared bigger now than ever; they dwarfed their appearance from the first night. The moon was young and Michael knew he had to keep moving if he was to conquer the summit before the sun rose on the third day. He climbed outside and just as he did, a fresh snow began to fall. The frigid wind blew fiercely and the snow pounded against his face. His sight was clouded and his body was nearly frozen, yet he kept climbing.

The ground far below was nowhere to be seen and he was in the midst of a thick cloud. Through the night and into the dawn he climbed. As the sun rose, the light gave way to a terrace above him. Michael latched onto the edge of the sharp rock and pulled himself up. The height that he had reached was far higher than any human in the history of mankind has climbed. At this elevation any human would cease to live and even Michael's spacious lungs were struggling to take in the thin air. He had no choice but to rest on the ledge for a while. The wind came rushing down the mountain at a terribly brutal velocity and like a force bent on destroying the archangel, it began to slowly drag his weary body towards the edge.

Michael lacked the energy to reach for something to grab onto; all his strength had drained from his body. As the wicked powers behind the unnatural wind pushed him closer to certain death, his life flashed before his eyes.

"Save me! Do not forsake me, my God," he cried out.

Suddenly, he caught hold of a rock just as he was about to fall, but it broke. He fell and his heart sank into oblivion as he plummeted faster and faster.

"No…Father…help me," Michael shouted with all the breath he had in him; but it was too little, too late, for he lost all consciousness.

Out of nowhere, help literally grabbed him by the waist and snatched him safely from his deadly fall. It was the eagle. In his most desperate hour salvation had come to the Archangel. The commander of the Host of Heaven was saved, spared from the clutches of doom. The enemy's plan did not prevail and now Michael was flying, unaware, through the clouds to the summit of the Mountain of God.

Michael heard a voice speaking to his heart.

"Awake, my servant. Your God is calling you," said the voice.

The archangel opened his eyes slowly. He was cold, in fact, he felt like he was freezing. *Is this how death feels*, he thought to himself. He was still dazed and definitely confused, all the while taking in his surroundings.

"You are not dead. You live because of me," shouted the voice, sounding like it had traveled in the wind.

Then it dawned on Michael, he was still on earth. He stood up and witnessed the clouds beneath the slope he was on. He was on the Mountain of God; more specifically, he was standing on the summit. Michael raised his hands to Heaven.

"My God, you are faithful. You are true to keep your promises," he cried, gazing at the sky.

Absolute excitement overtook him and so did the frigid weather. Then a faint sound took him by surprise, a low gentle neighing sounded as if it was coming from behind him. He turned sharply and he couldn't believe what he saw—the lamb.

He picked up the tiny creature and held him to his bosom. A tear began to drop from the archangel's eye as he spoke softly to him.

"You're safe little lamb. I am here."

Although, Michael didn't see himself as the lamb's comforter for long, since it was the lamb that saved him from the freezing temperatures of the summit's atmosphere.

Michael closed his eyes and prayed for strength for the lamb and himself. After he had prayed, Michael was no longer freezing and his body was without any pain. He found that he was still holding the lamb. He suddenly realized he was no longer on earth; he was standing in the throne room on Mount Zion.

"You're home my child," called a familiar voice.

He turned around and there was God walking down to him. The lamb vanished into thin air, but Michael took no notice as he ran to the LORD. He disregarded any reverent bow, yet not in disrespect, but in the pure joy of the moment. God embraced him like a father to a child and held him close to his chest. Michael was crying in joy and God had tears flowing from his eyes. As each of God's tears dropped onto Michael one more of his wounds was healed.

NOTE FROM THE SCRIBE...

Who says there is no crying in Heaven, for on that day there were many tears. Tears of celebration. For Michael had completed his mission and had returned home, safe and sound.

LOGOS

NOTE FROM THE SCRIBE...

It is known that the earth and Heaven are two different worlds; even so, they're intertwined—woven together in the fabric of supernatural power. God fashioned it that way, so he can watch over the creation he loves so dearly. Well, not even an angel can begin to comprehend the LORD's ways, so I can imagine how difficult it is for a human mind to grasp the many different complexities of God's kingdom. Enough then about the things that man can't begin to understand; instead, I will continue with...

The Warrior Within...

All of Heaven rejoiced at Michael's homecoming. He had been on earth for only days, yet this time passed as mere seconds in Heaven. A huge celebration was thrown in the honor of the archangel's return. The party went on for an entire day in Heaven, which would be equivalent to 365,000 days on earth. It was one incredible party with singing and dancing, not to mention the food. God provided a feast unrivaled by any that have been held by the kings of the earth. The entire Host of Heaven was in attendance, not even one angel stayed at home.

The Father God's table was full to the brim with every kind of scrumptious and savory food that one could imagine. Although angels don't require food for survival, they still take great pleasure in enjoying some on special occasions. The Father's table is beyond comparison—a supernatural wonder. For it is no ordinary table. It is made from a wood in Heaven that can grow with a touch of God's mighty hand. The table expands to meet the demands of growth, so the Father's table always has room for more and is never full. God's desire is to someday fill the table with his people.

The celebration was exhilarating, fantastic, and fun of course. The day finally drew to an end and all the angels retired to their homes, and God returned to his throne on Mount Zion.

Before the LORD left, he addressed Michael in private.

"Go talk with your friends and, in a short while, I will call you to Mount Zion."

God hugged him and Michael was off to be with his friends. Now the archangel has many friends, but these particular ones are considered to be his closest companions: Gabriel, Raphael, the two brothers Uriel and Saraqael, and the twin brothers Remiel and Raguel, who are identical in every physical aspect.

Michael was the sole angel, out of the seven warriors to God, to travel to earth. Elijah was the only other angel that had traveled to earth, but as the chief seraph of the messengers, he was sworn to secrecy. As for Michael, he was given permission to share his experiences on earth with his six companions. The seven were a band of brothers, completely devoted to one another in spirit and in truth. They had fought side by side in the great battle and it was their swords that slew many of the sergeants of the armies of Satan. Thus they earned their titles and were respectively called the seven warriors of God.

At the moment, angels had officially settled down in their homes to rest for a while. The golden streets of Jerusalem were bare and empty. Not even a single voice carried through the alleyways or from the seraphim's homes. Only the distant singing of the cherubim on Mount Zion could be heard, since worship is continually in their mouths. The seven walked quietly through the peaceful streets of the holy city. They headed for Michael's home on Bethlehem Street. All seven had homes on this street. The archangel's house was situated on a hill overlooking the great walls, so every one of his companions agreed Michael's home had the best view of the Gardens of Tranquility. Therefore, his house is where they usually gathered for fellowship.

NOTE FROM THE SCRIBE...

Of the six companions, Michael was closest to Gabriel. They were closer than brothers, bonded for an eternity. *Gabe* is what Michael called him, along with the band of warriors, but all other seraphim called him by his full name. Gabe is known as the *valiant warrior of God*. During battle, he never leaves Michael's side. He pledged allegiance to God that no harm would befall the archangel during Lucifer's rebellion. He cut down many demons during the great battle, of which some were assigned as assassins solely to kill Michael. He valiantly and fearlessly subdued countless demons. Many of those demons came close to destroying Michael and if it wasn't for Gabriel, they might have succeeded. That is how much Gabe loved his God and his best friend. He was devoted to the point that he would lay down his life, without having to think twice about it.

Michael is a great swordsman, due to the gifts and skills God bestowed upon him and the Sword of the Spirit he carries. Gabriel, though, was made to be an incredible warrior, unmatched in all of Heaven and only Michael is his equal among the angels. His raw skills and talents for battle are the best among the seven warriors of God. All seraphim respected and loved him for his great feats in defending Heaven and earth against the forces of darkness. Therefore, God appointed him as Michael's training partner. The two huge warriors prepared for their missions spending an infinite number of hours sparring against each other. No angel in Heaven has the strength, power, or skill to overcome Gabriel in a duel, be it with a weapon or without. Michael is the only exception, but even then he would need an impeccable performance to overcome Gabe in hand-to-hand combat.

Gabriel was nearly ten feet in height and his broad shoulders gave the illusion that he was even taller. His frame was unquestionably built for battle, a muscular physique that boasted strength, surpassing even that of Sampson or Hercules. His endurance in battle never wavered no matter the circumstances. Gabriel had dark curly hair, nearly black, that flowed just past his shoulders. His face was ruggedly masculine and very handsome, indeed. His large, round, dark eyes were warm and generous; yet dangerous if one was to look into them in the heat of battle.

Gabriel wore a bright white tunic. A royal blue cloak was attached to his shoulders by two gold and silver emblems (one on each shoulder) shaped like small shields. Embedded in the center of each emblem was a single large blue sapphire and brilliant green sapphires lined the perimeter of the blue sapphire. These badges signified that he was the second highest-ranking angel in all of Heaven. Moreover, he carried a magnificent sword, a weapon even more intimidating than his monstrous physique. The sword's name is Logos, meaning "the word of God." The LORD bestowed it upon him before the great battle commenced. The sword is endowed with the authority of the Most High God and only Gabriel can master this weapon.

Logos was of superb craftsmanship, second only in beauty and strength to the Sword of the Spirit. The sword was exceptionally long and extremely sharp, which gave Gabriel a big advantage over his enemies in battle. It was crafted out of very unique steel. Unknown to any man, this steel was derived from the deepest mines below the highest mountains of Heaven. What's more, this steel can withstand a blow of any magnitude and absorb any shock. Gabriel, if he liked, could use it to slice completely through a cedar tree or more impressively, solid rock. The sword was not only powerful, but truly stunning to look at as well. The blade was smooth and cool to the touch. It had a reflection like that of a pool of water. Sometimes it took on a translucent appearance as if it vanished into thin air. This made Gabriel especially dangerous to the Satan's forces, since they couldn't see Logos coming. The hilt was bejeweled with the finest green emeralds with the purest diamonds encircling each one and the handle was adorned with the brightest blue sapphires that were shaped and polished smoothly to flawlessly fit Gabriel's hand.

The Warrior Within …

They arrived at Michael's house and, in no time, they had made themselves comfortable. They reclined in the soft lush couches in Michael's fellowship room. They were exchanging stories with one another, but soon they all agreed it was time to hear about Michael's journey.

"Tell us, Archangel," Uriel gleefully shouted.

"Yes, it's about time you spilled the news, brother," Gabriel added. The big warriors pulled their couches closer in to listen closely.

"Ok brothers, but you better pay careful attention to every detail, because I don't want to have to tell it twice," Michael said, leaning in with a smile. Then he let out with a belly full of laughter and they immediately joined in.

After they all calmed their laughter, the archangel commenced to tell them everything he had experienced on earth. They were in wonder when they heard about the scenery. Smiles flashed across their faces when the lamb came into the story. They gasped when Michael told them about the encounter with the monstrous grizzly. Breath taken is how they looked, when he told them about the eagle and his near death experience on the Mountain of God. Michael spared no detail; he made sure they knew everything about what happened to him on earth.

When he finished, the six companions sat back in silence. They were completely amazed with the archangel's testimony. Then Gabriel leaned in. He felt someone had to break the silence.

"Everything sounds so incredible," Gabe said with a straight face. "But you know I could have climbed that mountain in three days. And I'll add, without the help of a huge eagle to fly me to the summit."

The other five looked speechless. They were shocked at Gabe's boasting. Michael's face looked very stern and offended. Suddenly, his expression went from serious to a huge smile and he started laughing. Gabriel laughed next and the whole lot of them burst into laughter.

"Hey Gabe—why bother climbing the mountain when you could jump over it. It would make for a faster route," Uriel added, beaming with sarcasm.

Gabriel started slapping his leg in laughter and everyone joined in. The amusing ruckus soon died down.

"That bear you ran from, it was a cub? Isn't that what you said," Gabriel said, raising an inquisitive eyebrow as he playfully put his arm around Michael's neck.

"If that bear was a cub, I would hate to see the mother bear," Michael said, grinning as he tossed his friend's arm off of him. All of them couldn't help but laugh at him.

"You're in fine form brother," Raphael remarked and burst out laughing.

"Keep it up and everyone will be asking for a joke instead of a story," Remiel said and Raguel agreed.

"Gabe, I think you could have killed the bear, with your terrible humor that is," Uriel said, controlling his laughter.

"Right back at you big fellow," Gabriel shouted back in good spirit.

Uriel and Gabe relentlessly teased each other, in good fun of course.

"Gabe if you had been there with me I think the bear would have been too scared to face a mighty pair of angels, like ourselves," Michael said, patting Gabe on the back. "The grizzly would have tucked tail and ran away, most certainly. Everyone had a good chuckle as the joking and laughter went on for quite a while."

Eventually the laughter died down and the seven friends began to share stories from the great battle. Michael loved this time he had with his friends and it was more valuable to him than almost anything. However, there was one thing he cherished above all else: time spent in the presence of God. In spite of the countless memories he had in common with his companions, it was the moments spent with the Father that dominated his thoughts and recollections.

The stories escalated as each told their side of the story. It was funny how each version differed from the others. According to Uriel, Beltezar had scorpions for hair. Even more incredibly, Raphael rendered that Satan's face could change into that of a wolf's appearance. They laughed some more as they went back and forth friendly debating the facts of the great battle. Remiel and Raguel swore they saw demons transform into giant vipers.

Saraqael, at first, didn't join in until there was a brief moment of modest laughter.

"Foolishness brothers. You know all that you say is rubbish. I tell you the truth…," Saraqael said. His face had turned red, because he was trying his hardest to look serious. He quickly composed himself.

"I saw two demons change into giant spiders," Saraqael claimed with two big eyes full of vigor. "There was a poof of smoke and there they were, two huge spiders with venom dripping from their fangs. Well, you know what I did? Did I run, or cry for help? No—on the contrary, I squashed them both with my foot. It was no sweat, no problem at all."

Saraqael boasted with a straight face, but his brother, Uriel, knew better.

"Honestly, brother, where did you come up with that one," Uriel said. "You were cooking it up while the entire time we believed you to be bored out of your mind." Uriel grabbed his brother around the neck and playfully rubbed his head.

Saraqael turned bright red in the face. He was embarrassed, but everyone joined in and patted him on the back for such a great story. They thought what Saraqael said was especially funny, since no one knew him to have a good sense of humor. In truth, Uriel would incessantly tease his brother about being a prude stiff-backed angel.

"I don't think I can top that one," said Gabriel as his eyebrow rose in intrigue. "But I can try. I didn't battle two huge spiders or a head full of scorpions or a brood of vipers, but I did destroy thousands of demons with my trusty sword, Logos. I promised myself I would always remain humble of this, so I felt I shouldn't speak up. I know pride is not a desirable attribute. But then I thought, well it's not much compared to all of your feats, my friends. So why not."

Gabriel's friends couldn't tell if he was joking or serious, because not one of them would deny his claim. In reality, they each said they saw him slay hundreds of demons. So it made sense to believe his story, after they totaled the numbers.

Michael, being Gabriel's best friend, always knew just how

to put him in his place. He put his hand on top of the big warrior's head.

"Gabe's head might get too big to fit through the front door. If that's the case, he'll have to live here permanently. Don't worry friend, I'll just stay at your house and we'll call it even," he said with a big smile.

"Very funny, Michael. You're a funny guy. Did anyone ever tell you that," Gabe mused.

Everyone was having an amusing time until suddenly when their fellowship was interrupted by a blast from the trumpet.

"That sounds like it's coming from atop of Mount Zion," Uriel observed.

"It is, and that is my call to come to the throne room," said Michael, his eyes were very serious.

Then another blast from a trumpet bellowed through the streets of Jerusalem and this time it sounded very different from the first.

"And that is my call, brothers," Gabriel said. His eyes lit up with excitement.

Could this be my call to duty, he thought to himself, *oh please let it be.*

"We must be off, friends. Stay as long as you like. My house is your house," Michael said to his friends.

"Gabe, will you walk with me," Michael said, looking at him as he stood up.

"Yes, of course." Gabriel's face beamed with zeal.

The two gallant angels, closer than brothers, walked out the door and headed briskly down the golden streets. The throne room awaited them and their excitement was truly hard for them to contain.

On top of Mount Zion, a heavy cloud had settled—the powerful presence of God rested on the mountaintop. Justice and Mercy were expecting them. They saluted Archangel and Gabriel and stood aside to let them pass. The cherubim were singing beautifully when they entered. The two seraphs, under the power of God, fell to the floor upon entering the throne room.

"Be strengthened, my faithful servants," announced the LORD.

They stood up and proceeded to the throne of God. Trumpets

blasted and lightning flashed, peals of thunder shook the ground beneath them. There was the LORD standing before his throne like a bright morning star.

"Fear not," spoke the creator with much authority. "Come, walk with me."

They followed him down a stairway that led down a secret entrance to the east gate of the city. Michael realized they were going to the Garden of Tranquility. This pleased him greatly.

"Follow me, I have something to show you," God said.

Once in the garden, they headed down a path that was all too familiar to the archangel.

"The Fountain of Life," Michael whispered.

Gabriel had been to the fountain before, but not by this path. In fact, he had never been this direction. The truth of the matter was that this pathway was for God's personal use and no angel, save Michael and now Gabriel, has experienced this privilege. It was truly an honor and Michael knew that, but Gabriel was just figuring that out.

They reached a vast opening with a majestic fountain positioned in the center. The trees were perfectly trimmed, the bushes were meticulously pruned in different shapes, and the grass was neatly maintained. It was a serene place, full of beauty, full of wonder, full of awe, full of a purity, and peace. The garden of The Fountain of Life was a place unique, unrivaled by any place in Heaven, except for the throne room. The air around it was pure—full of energy and full of healing powers.

"Sit with me a while," said the LORD.

They sat down next to the fountain on a large smooth rock.

"I created the two of you to compliment each other well. I did not create you as brothers, but you have grown to be closer than brothers."

The LORD looked at Gabriel.

"The commander of the Host of Heaven needs a general to help assist him in battle. You, Gabriel, have proven yourself worthy of such a calling. I hereby appoint you lieutenant general of the Host of Heaven."

God then gave him a signet ring to represent the authority given to him by God the Father. The ring was gorgeous in every respect. A giant blue sapphire was set in the center and count-less tiny diamonds surrounded the sapphire. It sparkled like a blinding light.

God then looked at Michael

"Your mission was a success. I also know that you endured much struggling on behalf of all the Host of Heaven and me. You risked everything, including your own life, to save the lamb. Because of your dedication, I have shown you favor above all other angels in Heaven. You are my devoted servant and I have mighty plans in store for you."

The Lord turned once again to Gabriel.

"And I have mighty plans in store for you, Gabriel, my mighty warrior, lieutenant general of the Host of Heaven," God said with a kind smile.

God then addressed them both.

"The time has come, the moment is here; for you, Michael and you, Gabriel, to join each other on earth. Together, you will do mighty things in my name and together you must accom-plish the mission. Michael, without Gabriel your mission will fail and, Gabriel, without Michael all will be lost. The challenge that lies ahead of you will require all the skills and wisdom I have instilled in you both. Are you prepared to sacrifice everything for my kingdom? Will you go in my name for my glory?"

"Yes Lord, we will go." They answered and saluted the Lord.

"Gabriel, go and prepare your heart for my service. I will call you when it is time to leave," The Lord said and stood to his feet.

The Father embraced him like a child and he was off. Michael remained with God. The Lord sat back down.

"Michael, stay with me a while. I have some matters to share with you: some that are dear to me and others that are for your ears alone."

Michael subtly nodded, but his mind was racing with intrigue.

"Don't bother your mind, for I haven't revealed anything to you yet," the Lord softly spoke.

Michael had to remind himself that all his thoughts are laid bare before the Lord of Hosts—nothing is beyond his knowl-edge. Something more passed through his mind, the very first lesson he had with the Lord. The words sounded in his head as vividly as the first time he heard them. *The fear of the* Lord *is the beginning of wisdom and the knowledge of the Holy One is understanding.* He didn't know why those words were fixed in his mind at this moment, but it must be important.

"That's right, Michael. The foundations of your wisdom and knowledge are fear and understanding," asserted the Lord with a gracious voice.

Michael's eyes lit up, because the Lord had done it again. God's face was full of glory, and as he stood up he appeared like a majestic beacon of virtue.

"Those were not your thoughts, but they were mine. Walk with me a while and I will explain all that you need to know," spoke the Father. A holy passion lingered from his voice; a gleaming radiance twinkled in his eyes.

Michael felt he was ready for that next step, so he fervently agreed and walked with the Father. He wouldn't dare turn away a chance to be in the presence of the Most High.

"Michael, my spirit is moving in you. My Holy Spirit is changing you and transforming you into a new creature. This is a process that won't happen instantly, but it will take perseverance on your behalf and unwavering, unconditional commitment to my kingdom. If you are ready, I am prepared to give you the keys to the Kingdom, the knowledge and understanding of what was, what is, and what is to come."

"Yes, I am prepared to give my all, even if it means dying for the cause of your kingdom," Michael said, his face shining in the light of God's glory.

He looked into the Father's face. God's glory faded and Michael beheld his beauty. The Father smiled and it was more brilliant than a thousand sunrises.

"Then I will share with you the secrets of the kingdom of Heaven. All that is on my heart will become treasure for your spirit," spoke the Father with a zealous voice.

Note from the Scribe...

The Lord shared with him many deep matters of Heaven and the coming kingdom, of which some have been recorded. As for the other matters, they were far too secret to divulge. God told him about the monster he faced on the mountain. In reality, it was not an ordinary grizzly bear, but a demon named Magnimus, a major sergeant, in Satan's forces. Magnimus quickly climbed the ranks and he had been given a position of lieutenant general. Satan trained him personally; much like Michael was guided by God's wisdom and knowledge. Magnimus had been convinced by Satan to try one of his experimental potions. The malicious concoction transformed him into a hideous creature that not even Satan could deal with. The prince of darkness made another potion to turn him back, but it backfired and turned him into a monstrous form. A vague resemblance to a grizzly bear: hairy, vicious claws, and a snout full of bloodthirsty teeth. Magnimus was told that he could only regain his former shape if he did one thing for Satan—kill the Archangel Michael. Thus he was sent as an assassin, misguided, and misused, but still evil to the bone and full of hatred for the Archangel Michael.

Father God also shared with Michael the mystery behind the eagle. As Michael had expected, this was no ordinary bird. Actually it was no bird at all, but Michael couldn't have ever been prepared for what he heard next. The eagle, in truth, was God's only son. The eagle was a majestic form he took, an illusion to fool the enemy. I will return to the story with the Father's explanation.

The Warrior Within ...

"My Son took this form to save you from certain death. However, his time is yet to come. The enemy need not know of his coming or going until he is sent to save mankind and free them from death. I tell you the truth, none in Heaven is greater than the Son and none of Hell can withstand his might and power. Truly, I say to you, if you know me than you know the Son," God boldly said.

Michael was speechless. He didn't know how to absorb such incredible news. This was huge. Before he could respond the LORD spoke again.

"Satan has asked my permission to sift you like wheat. He

desires your death and he will stop at nothing. Satan's spirit is saturated with hatred and bitterness. He sits on his throne in Hades and meditates on evil and his soul never finds rest. Perpetually making plans for revenge, all of his anger and strife are focused on settling the score. He wants to destroy everything you stand for, Michael, and he seeks to bring down the kingdom of Heaven. If he had it his way, his armies would topple Heaven and you would be crushed beneath his boot. One thing, though, stands in his way... me." A somber tone was in his voice.

"Father, I stand amazed in your presence; I am truly humbled by your magnificence. I will not allow Satan to defeat me. Through your infinite wisdom, Almighty God, I have been equipped with the supernatural abilities needed to defeat the enemy. I know that I can't defeat Satan by my strength alone, but only by your spirit will I persevere," Michael said in admiration. His mind was soaking it all in like a thirsty sponge desperate for water.

"Your last mission was just a sample of what kind of devices the enemy uses," God said. "This time on earth will be unlike your last mission. Where I send you will be very different indeed. All that is in you will be required to complete this mission. Everything that your spirit has absorbed from my teachings will be needed in order to overcome the plans of the enemy. Now go, prepare your heart. When the time has come to leave, I will call you by name and not by trumpet." The Father said and embraced him like he was his own child.

Before departing the Father embraced him like he was his own child. Then the Father continued on his walk through the garden, and Michael strolled along with a light heart, but a heavy burden.

"Father, guide me in your wisdom and understanding. I walk in your truth, my God," he prayed.

The archangel was still absorbing all the Father had shared with him. He thought about the demon, Magnimus, who was cursed to walk the earth as a wretched monster until he had the Archangel Michael's blood and with it, his life. This was troubling, to say the least, although his mind always wandered back to God's Son. Just the thought of him brought peace to Michael's spirit.

"What is he like? I want to know him," Michael thought out loud.

"If you know me than you know the Son," he recalled what the LORD had said.

Back in Jerusalem, Gabriel was making preparations. He sharpened Logos and his trusty dagger. Gabriel carried a knife in his boot that was perfect for throwing. No angel could match him in a contest. Once he hit an apple atop Michael's head from fifty paces away. No enemy would want to startle him, lest he fire his dagger into their chest. His pack was almost ready.

"Aha, I knew I was forgetting something. Rope," he said as he rolled up about a hundred paces worth and tucked it away.

"Know what else you're forgetting," spoke a friendly voice.

Gabriel stopped what he was doing and froze.

"Perhaps, I should ask again," said the friendly voice.

Gabriel turned around and there was Michael standing in the entryway.

"I thought I'd stop by on the way to my house."

"Michael, come in brother." Gabriel said and took a bow, as angels do when welcoming a guest into their home.

"Gabe, I see your head hasn't gotten too big to fit through the front door." Michael looked at the door and back at Gabriel while he spoke. Gabriel laughed.

"Good one, brother. I'll get you next time. Now, don't you have some preparations to make?" he asked the archangel. Michael nodded.

"You're right. I'll be off, but before I go I just wanted to say one thing. It's good to know you'll be coming with me, Gabe."

"I wouldn't want it any other way. You know that, Michael." Gabriel said and grinned, nodding his head in agreement.

Michael took a bow and disappeared through the door; Gabriel went right back to what he was doing.

Across the roadway, Michael sat down in his room and began meditating on the word of the LORD. He was able to recollect all that the LORD had taught him. All the wisdom and the knowledge that was instilled in him began to rise from his memory. It slowly flowed from his mind into his spirit and throughout his entire being. Only moments seemed to have passed, when he sensed God calling him to the throne room.

"I will call you by name and not by trumpet," Michael recalled what the Lord had said.

He laced his sandals, girded his belt, put the Sword of the Spirit in its sheath and stepped out the front door to answer the call.

"You heard him too?" Gabriel shouted from across the roadway.

Michael ran across the street, with a nod answering *yes*

"Just now, I heard his voice calling me to come," Gabe said.

"Then we must answer. Come with me," Michael declared and looked towards Mount Zion.

NOTE FROM THE SCRIBE...

TWO best friends walked down the golden streets. They knew not what lay ahead of them but one thing was for certain, the Lord had called them by name.

LUMINAROUS

Lightning flashed on Mount Zion and thunder boomed on the closing horizon. Tremors shuddered through the golden streets, momentarily transforming the paved roads into shiny rolling hills. Michael and Gabriel trembled with fear in the quake of God's power. Their anticipation increasingly grew as they steadily drew closer to Mount Zion. The thunder and lightning withdrew their fearsome rumbling and a single blow of the trumpet chimed throughout Heaven announcing, yet, another force of God's power. A mighty rushing wind blew through the streets and riding in the wind was the chief of the messenger seraphim. Elijah now hovered before the angels; his halo glowed brighter than ever. Michael and Gabriel were breath-taken.

He had a trumpet in one hand and a scroll in the other. He blew the trumpet and its ring spread like a mighty tidal wave. Within mere seconds, millions of doors flung open and innumerable seraphim poured out of their homes. He unrolled the parchment.

"Host of Heaven, hail each angel from their mansion," Elijah announced. "Declare one to another the glory of the LORD and spread the news. For this very hour the servants of our King, Creator of Heaven and earth, have been summoned to Mount Zion. Attention all and pay heed for the Archangel Michael, commander of the Host of Heaven and Gabriel, lieutenant general of the Host of Heaven, have answered the call of the LORD–their duty to defend the kingdom of righteousness against the forces of darkness. Take a hold, each of your musical instruments and make a joyful noise, because today is the day the LORD has made."

A supernatural presence permeated the air. The rushing wind had ushered it in and everyone could sense it, especially Michael and Gabriel. The streets of Jerusalem were alive with singing and dancing.

"Let's hear it for Michael and Gabriel, mighty warriors of God," yelled the angel named Jeremiah as he stood on the front stoop of his house.

An eruption of cheering followed them down the streets. Remiel grabbed his tambourine and with everything he had he was beating it with rhythm. Uriel and Saraqael ran into the street and gave a brotherly hug to Michael and Gabriel. Raphael and Raguel danced in the streets and shouted praises to God. Songs of joy filled the holy streets of Jerusalem. Not a single angel remained in his house this hour. The streets truly overflowed with seraphim baring their spirits and souls before the LORD of lords. There were angels, beyond number, dancing and praising God with their entire being.

Michael and Gabriel felt as if they were walking through an ocean of worshiping seraphim and the sea parted for them as they passed by. Smiles beamed on their faces and, with hearts full of joy, their spirits reveled in the presence of the LORD. So many angels blessed them as they passed that Michael lost count. Gabriel hugged numerous seraphim, some he didn't even know personally, but each hug invigorated him all the same. The streets never seemed as large before as they did that day. Shoulder to shoulder, the Host of Heaven eventually melted their voices into a single song. Worshiping in one accord, they sang:

Worthy, worthy is the LORD
Who deserves blessing and honor?
And glory forever and ever

Blessed are the servants
Of the Living God

May the Lord cause His light
To shine upon them

In the name of the One True God
Blessed be their path
Glory and honor be to the Lord
Forever and ever

Words are too few to describe the scene that day. Know this though, in that hour each angel was connected in the holy and omniscient anointing of the Holy Spirit. The eternal bonds of angelic brotherhood grew even deeper, creating ties that the enemy could never sever.

This is it, Michael thought, *the time to answer the call, gather my courage, and follow my destiny in God. How many times did I ask myself, what would I do if he called me to a purpose greater than myself? Countless times I'm sure of it, but then it happened. The rebellion of Lucifer transpired and with it the great battle and my call to duty; a beckoning to rise above the circumstances, stand in the presence of the Lord as a commander and archangel, and leave behind my ordinary life as a seraph. The wisdom and knowledge of the Lord empowered my spirit and soul with the ability to do extraordinary things: To conquer my enemies, to deliver the kingdom of Heaven, to climb to new heights, and mature in God's holy grace. God's power alone transformed me into the archangel I am today; the archangel that is making his way to the throne room to answer the call of the Lord.*

They had reached the foot of Mount Zion, and Gabriel's mind was racing. *Everything was happening so fast,* he thought. His promotion to lieutenant general was humbling in itself and then the call to duty arose in the midst of it. This was all too much, but his spirit and soul were able to cope with the weight he bore on his back. For he knew it wasn't he that bore the weight of the responsibility, but the Father that carried it for him. That thought alone was reassuring enough to inspire him to new levels in his relationship with God. Heaven and earth were counting on him now and he was at peace knowing he was not alone in the fight. The call of the LORD had tugged at his heart and he answered with a great big, "Yes, I will go."

The steps never looked so numerous and the climb never seemed as long as it did this day when Michael and Gabriel ascended Mount Zion. Mercy and Justice were singing, along with the entire congregation, when the two huge seraphs landed on the threshold. Mercy and Justice were more than happy to let them pass.

"Archangel Michael and Gabriel, servants of the highest God, have come to answer the call," Mercy shouted.

"The King of Kings awaits you," Justice announced.

The pearly gates opened and the glory of the LORD poured forth in a dense mist. The Host of Heaven waited in the streets and looked on while Mount Zion became immersed in a white cloud.

"I can only wonder what's in store for them," Uriel remarked.

Raphael and Saraqael were wondering the same and at the same time, Remiel and Raguel approached. They were standing on Bethlehem Street and watching the lightning flash on Mount Zion. Peals of thunder bellowed from the steep rolling clouds that formed atop the mountain.

"One thing is for sure, God has made his power known this hour," Raphael said and placed his hand on his brow to protect his eyes.

A terrible light had burst in the sky above; truly, a display of power infinite times more powerful than any firework produced by the hand of mankind.

"He sits on his throne and all stand in awe at the mighty work of his hands," uttered Remiel, speaking from the heart of his wisdom.

"Who is like God," Saraqael shouted.

Uriel seconded that with another cheer and then the others joined in. Raguel began singing a new song. His voice is known throughout Heaven for being more beautiful than a nightingale's. The brotherhood of warriors caught on quickly and jumped right in. The song spread like the wind, end to end, through the golden streets of Jerusalem and soon the entire Host of Heaven raised their voices in praise. In accord they serenaded the LORD, who sits on the throne in Zion.

The mist was so dense that Michael could see nothing but flashes of light that danced in the cloud. He and Gabriel both could hear the seraphim singing praises in the streets; they delighted in the sound of the music. More beautiful than any song he had heard, thought Michael.

Gabriel took a step forward.

"Wait. Stay with me until you hear his voice," Michael whispered loudly.

As soon as the words had rolled off of his tongue he heard the voice of God speaking audibly to his heart.

"Come Michael. It is time," said the LORD.

Michael looked at Gabriel, who was smiling, and motioned him to follow.

"You heard him too?" Michael asked.

"Yes, of course," Gabriel replied with a grin.

Michael needed no words since his face beamed with a thousand of them and, yet, that wouldn't do justice in describing the joy he now felt. The mist parted, gracefully rolling back like cloths of the finest silk; the harpist started to play the most harmonious and charming music that flowed throughout the throne room. The music filled the air and, in a fleeting moment, the cherubim's voices joined in with the harp and sang:

Holy, Holy, Holy
Is the LORD God Almighty
Who was, who is, and who is to come

Michael and Gabriel were completely mesmerized by the flowing chant of the song to the LORD. They walked up to the throne, each of them feeling as if they were suspended in admiration. They approached the foot of God's throne and falling to their knees, they worshiped the King. The only desire in their hearts was to please the LORD of Heaven and earth. Their spirits longed to have a heart like his: a heart full of love and tenderness; a heart slow to anger and quick to forgive; a heart passionate for justice and abundant with mercy. Their souls couldn't get enough of his glorious presence. If they had their way, they would worship at the LORD's feet for all the ages to come. Even until the end of time.

The Father sensed their hearts, for they were laid bare before his throne as Michael and Gabriel worshiped. Their hearts told him everything he needed to know. His decision may have been made before the dawn of time, but it took the willingness of these two special seraphim, more importantly their readiness at this very instant, to initiate the mission at hand. The Father fully knew all of the preparation that was needed to arrive at this moment in time: all the training, the instructing, the mission before hand, and not to forget the first test—the great battle. These stages were all necessary for Michael and Gabriel to mature in the LORD and ultimately arrive at their destiny. The LORD Almighty arose from his throne. He laid his right hand on Michael, his left hand on Gabriel, and with the speech of the ancient tongue he blessed the angels.

Streaks of radiant light emanated from his hands and his fingers. Power he alone possesses flowed unto their heads and through their bodies. The two angels instantaneously transformed into pure light and they passed through the ceiling like threads of lightning. They traveled to another realm and another time. Michael drifted from Gabriel in the vast space know as the *heavens* which are farther beyond the one true Heaven. They traveled a speed unheard of by mankind.

Michael remained a streak of light and yet he was mindful of all that went on around him. As he traveled, he could see a round object that grew increasingly larger with each second that passed. More and more definition sprouted forth from the circular object. Each second that passed revealed more of the orb—blue masses, green masses, white masses, and dark huge creases jutted out here and there. It became clear to him that this was a planet like Father God spoke of in his teachings. He realized he was now viewing it from many thousand earth-miles outside of its atmosphere. A burning sensation moved over his body and he was forced to close his eyes. His body had begun to penetrate the stratosphere. Before he made it safely through, he had lost all consciousness and he fell, like a millstone into the earth's atmosphere.

Gabriel couldn't believe what he was seeing: the countless stars, the numerous planets, and the entire vastness of the universe. He felt as if he was still floating, but he knew he was still moving as the planet earth continued to appear closer and closer. The stars flew past him in each and every direction, but they missed hitting him. He realized he was encased in a glowing ball of light. Then suddenly, a comet whistled right past him and shook the air around him. As its brilliantly colored tail moved into sight, the colors jumped out at him. The air around him illuminated so intensely he had no choice but to close his eyes.

He noticed that the whistling had stopped and he felt something solid beneath him. He found himself sitting on the ground; more specifically, a dense covering of leaves.

"Earth," Gabriel cried out.

His hands were touching every inch of his surroundings. He grabbed a fistful of dark dirt then he put it back, carefully patting it down.

"I won't take anything I can't bring back home," he said.

He looked around, beholding the dense forest of trees and colorful plants that encircled him. The thought of being on earth truly fascinated him. At the same time, though, he was completely perplexed at what he saw before him.

Gabriel was in the midst of a dark jungle and animal noises echoed all around him. God had sent him into the inner sanctions of a mysterious jungle. It was nearly dark enough to be night and the only light visible was coming through a tiny opening between the trees about a hundred paces from where he sat. This was his very first time to experience darkness; an extremely strange feeling came over him, an unpleasant feeling of sorts. What kind of danger lurks in the darkness? He couldn't help but wonder what evil might be hiding in the darkness, waiting to devour him in his moment of vulnerability.

NOTE FROM THE SCRIBE...

I will tell you something that is worth taking note of. There is no darkness in Heaven, only light. The glory of God provides all the light that is needed in Heaven and, along with the eternal fire of the Holy Spirit, there can be no darkness. Even in the mines deep beneath Mount Olive where Prioust Ohly (the strongest metal in all of Heaven and earth) is mined, there is light. Again I will say that not an ounce of darkness, not a smidgen, not even an infinitesimal amount of darkness can be found in the entire realm of Heaven. Now with all this being considered, imagine what Gabriel must have felt. If you had lived your entire existence surrounded by only the purest of light, well then, darkness would utterly frighten you.

Therefore, if you take into consideration what you have just learned, Gabriel was being quite brave up until that point. Put yourself in his place and try to imagine what you would do in that situation. Surrounded by darkness and shadows, in a dense forest, with only an ounce of light to guide your way, what would you do? Now that you have placed yourself there, I will return to the...

EPICS OF MICHAEL...

The shadows on the forest floor appeared as if they were alive and with a will of their own, they were closing in on the angel. An unexpected feeling of horror came over Gabriel. He was losing his breath and suffocating out of fear.

"What's happening to me," he asked himself.

The trees around him came to life. A few paces from him were strangely deformed trees with hideous branches that stretched out like arms driven by an evil unnatural force. His surroundings became unpredictable, taking on bizarre forms that he had never before seen in his entire life. Vines were moving, apparently, on their own; he couldn't believe what he was seeing but his warrior-like instinct rose to the occasion.

"Come and get me if you dare, I'll slice you in half. Just try it," he drew Logos and cried out.

A thick vine, seeming to appear from nowhere, wrapped itself around his ankle; with a flash of his sword he severed the vine and it fell limply to the ground. A heavy branch pierced through his shoulder—he turned and pulled it out. Another scraped his leg, drawing blood, and another knocked him to the ground.

The vines began to wrap themselves around his throat, clinching tighter and tighter. Despite the giant angel's efforts, he could feel the life being choked out of him. Gabriel looked deep within him and found the power of the Holy Spirit waiting to come forth. He had to speak the words and the enemy would flee; he tried with all of his might to shout the words, but only a mere whisper escaped his lips.

"Not by my might, nor my power, but by your spirit LORD," he boldly uttered.

Suddenly, the vines receded into the trees. He could breathe now. He was free. He blocked out the pain and taunted the malicious force.

"By the power of the Holy Spirit you can't take down a servant of the one true Creator. Go ahead and make your move if you dare," he shouted, defiantly.

The trees returned to a stand still and the undergrowth swayed in the breeze.

"They're only trees now. There's nothing to fear with God by my side," he remarked as he rubbed the painful cut on his shoulder.

He decided that now was as good a time as any to pray to the Father. As he thanked the LORD for his saving grace, a holy energy entered his body and filled him with new life. He felt renewed and refreshed. Before he finished praying a bright light, pure and white, like a ray of Heaven, shone through the trees. He covered his face with both of his hands. The illumination was too bright for his eyes to adjust. Then something both astonishing and comforting happened. A pillar of light hovered before him and it hatched like an egg shedding its outer walls. He could now see that a being stood before him.

"Gabriel, I am Elijah, chief of the messenger seraphim."

Before he could say anything else Gabriel interrupted him (Gabriel has a tendency to do this sort of thing).

"I know who you are. And am I glad to see you, anybody from home for that matter," he said, his face revealed a smile.

Elijah raised an eyebrow, indicating a decline in his patience.

"Gabriel, I come bearing news from the LORD. If you are ready to hear it, I will continue," he said, suggesting the eagerness Gabriel was feeling with a hint of sarcasm. From time to time, Elijah can have a sense of humor.

"I'm all ears," he nodded *yes* and said.

The messenger continued with his address.

"You are on earth. However, you are in another dominion separate from what would be considered the ordinary realm of earth; separated by the authority of the LORD almighty. The world in which you now stand is a place on earth where time has no master. You are on an island called Luminarous, surrounded by an ocean of water. The dense forest you find yourself in the midst of is actually the heart of Luminarous' jungle."

Elijah then unrolled a small parchment and commenced to read from it.

"God the Father sends word that you were brought here for an extremely important reason, to serve a mighty purpose for the kingdom of Heaven. Your first task, although it may sound simple, will prove to be more challenging than you realize. Find your friend who is closer than a brother, the Archangel Michael. Until you complete this important task no further assistance will be granted."

Gabriel shook his head in approval, but he couldn't help but wince.

"I will do as the LORD asks of me but where should I begin? Where do I go from here," he asked, shrugging his shoulders.

The messenger's face looked bewildered for a moment.

"The LORD sends his command: Whenever you feel lost and afraid, search your heart, and you will find his Holy Spirit. God also says that he will never abandon your side. At present, that is all I may dispose to you. I pray Heaven's blessing over you. Until we meet again, God be with you Gabriel," Elijah said sharply.

Elijah's body then transformed into a beam of light and blazed through the jungle with a tail of fire.

"Behold, the messenger left a path," Gabriel thought out loud, noticing the trail of singed underbrush.

With Elijah gone he was once more alone and a hundred fears invaded his mind. Like a thief, they found the easiest way in and the unlocked door, known as *loneliness*, or the broken window, known as *doubt*. He began to second-guess himself and he found it easier to relax into a seat of despair then trust in hope. Then, with a commanding force, the last words of the messenger popped into his mind. He looked to his heart and there he found the comforting presence of the Holy Spirit. The anxiety that preyed on his spirit and wanted so desperately for him to join it fled faster than a thief caught in the act of stealing.

Gabriel finally figured out that he was supposed to start on the path Elijah had left. Before he began his journey, he put his trust in the God who is bigger than circumstance.

"Almighty Creator of Heaven and earth, I beseech Thee," he prayed with open hands and outstretched arms. "You are the Holy One, creator of all living things, and I adore thee oh Lord. I'm here to do your will. I need you, Lord of hosts, to show me the way. You are my strong tower; lead me in your way everlasting."

His feet now urged him to move forward. Comfort and peace came over him as his spirit was soothed by the power of the Holy Spirit. He heard God's still small voice.

"I will never leave your side nor forsake you," God spoke to his heart.

With God's presence to guide him and Logos by his side, he made his way down the pathway of burnt brush and broken branches. The way had been prepared and the path was paved before him.

He stared this way and that as he walked along. He was breath taken with the life around him. The under-story was full of a variety of plant life. Huge shrubs full of blue and purple buds gathered beneath the towering trees. He noted the different types of trees: giant palms with coconuts, banana trees, fig trees, and kapok trees with thick buttresses that stretch out more than a dozen paces over the jungle floor. These trees he knew, but still there were some that he had never seen in his entire life. One, in particular, had bark that was bright red with orange hues that accented the lines and creases in its ageless hide. He was so curious about this tree that he stopped, for a moment, and peered up its lengthy trunk. Gabriel took note that its top could not be seen, for it stretched its mighty trunk through the jungle canopy and brushed the sky.

He patted the tree as if it were a pet and left it there to mind its business of growing as slowly as time itself. The trail didn't take long to reveal even more beauty beyond Gabriel's wonder and expectations. Trees everywhere were covered in mosses of different colors: blue mosses, deep and bold in textures, yellow mosses, almost glowing, red and orange mosses, vibrantly shaded. They all appeared like a brush had painted them. There were also masses of flowers. Gorgeous bromeliads were in bloom. Stunning orchids opened after a beam of light pierced through the jungle canopy and awakened the flowers from their slumber in the shade.

The forest was alive with brilliant colors. Camouflaged in the intense tones and hues of the living colors, were animals. In fact, the whole place was crawling with creatures. Snakes with red and yellow stripes slithered through the leaves, hissing as they licked the air with their forked tongue. Gabriel never liked snakes. Lizards lounged in the branches above him and cracked their tails like whips made of leather as he passed beneath them.

The angel put his hands out, palms facing upwards, to show the creatures that he was not a threat. He continued on, walking softly, making as little as noise as possible in effort to put the creatures around him at ease. He suddenly felt an urge to stop, dead in his tracks. Something like a black blur was moving fast through the forest. It was happening very fast and his eyes couldn't adjust to the movement of the object, which happened to be about a hundred paces off the path to the angel's left.

All of a sudden the black blur came to a stop and it appeared to be moving slowly in his direction. Whatever it was, it was jet black in color and it was steadily closing in on Gabriel. He pulled Logos from his sheath slowly so that he would startle the strange creature, which was now only a couple of dozen paces away. He could make out two things. It had four lanky but sturdy legs with sharp white claws that stood out like night against day on the dark leafy floor of the jungle and the creature had two yellow eyes that were slanted, enormous, and piercing.

The creature was, in fact, a black panther that appeared to be about six to seven earth-feet in length. It paced back and forth, keeping its eyes fixed on the angel. Gabriel couldn't decide if this animal was a threat or was friendly, but one thing was for sure, it couldn't be harmless with claws sharper than knives. After many moments, perhaps ten earth-minutes, the creature became scarce and disappeared into the dark forest.

Gabriel hesitated for a second and then he returned Logos to its holster. He looked around for any signs of the creature's presence and he took a sigh of relief since he had found none. He continued footing through the underbrush, but he stepped even more silently this time—like a prowling animal stalking its prey. What Gabriel didn't know was that there were bigger creatures lurking in the forest. Enormous beasts that were menacing and ferocious and thirsty for the blood of angels.

A bright intense light stimulated his eyelids and awakened the archangel. Michael felt a little groggy. He didn't know how long he had been unconscious. He realized he was lying down on a bed of coarse, yet delicate, substance.

What was he on or, more importantly, where was he, he wondered, as he lay motionless on a strange surface in a foreign land. He slowly raised himself to a sitting position. He forced his hands down to prop himself up, when he felt his fingers grip hold of a handful of grainy matter. It was like dirt, yet it was totally different from any dirt he had touched before. The dirt ran through his fingers easily. Its touch felt very light and porous on his skin. He eventually gathered his strength and courage and lifted himself up to a sitting position.

Immediately, many things flooded his mind and invaded his senses. A warm breeze washed over his face. A smell, unlike any he has ever known, caused the hairs in his nose to come alive. He found the aroma to be invigorating. The field of glass before him swayed as it moved up and down like rolling hills. It seemed to be both transparent and changeless all in the same manner. It had an appearance like that of deep blue crystal adorned with countless diamonds, all sparkling with each reflection of light it cast. It then came to mind what the Father had told him about his creation, earth. The deep blue crystal, he suddenly realized, was no glass field at all.

"An ocean," he exclaimed with pure joy.

And the dirt was not dirt at all, but it was sand and it was pearl white. Smooth as silk the sand was and it spread its blanket as far as the eye could see in one direction and the other. The energizing scent he was breathing in was the ocean. He suddenly felt courage inside of himself and it was powerful enough to motivate him to stand to his feet.

Michael gazed out at the ocean. The sun seemed to transform the water into a dazzling display of infinite colors. Shades of blue, turquoise, and even pink danced interchangeably with one another creating a spectacle that entertained the eyes. Quite frankly, the whole scene mesmerized Michael. He couldn't help but stare at this vivid show of God's masterful creation. As he looked out over the sea of endless shimmering crystal waves, he took a deep breath drawing in the refreshing aroma. As he inhaled its scent, he felt the Holy Spirit rising up from deep down inside of him. He felt a calling to a greater purpose than himself, a beckoning to endure the destiny that is and was his before the dawn of time—inevitably reserved for him alone by the God who created all things. The mission was set in stone and the hands of destiny had been set in motion. Now all that he needed was to know what fate lies ahead of him. Nevertheless, he fully discerned the Father would reveal his future course soon enough.

He turned and beheld the jungle. Up until now, he had no idea that a vast forest existed in this new realm. The dense landscape bordered the beach as far as he could see in each direction.

"Wow. What is this place," was all the archangel could muster up.

Michael wanted so much to stay on the beach. He was taken aback by this new world. It was fantastic in every aspect, he thought. The ocean was beautiful, the air was invigorating, and the sand was so soft that he wanted to linger along the shore, but his heart was telling him otherwise. He was to travel into the jungle. He paced back and forth for a moment, not wasting time, as he was deciphering the course he should take.

NOTE FROM THE SCRIBE...

Michael had to make a decision at this point in the mission and he fully comprehended what a big one it was. He found the choice of where to start to be simply mind-boggling. He needed to make his calculations based, not on his feelings, but on what survival knowledge he had gained from the LORD. Try putting yourself in his sandals. You have just arrived in a new undiscovered world. Yes, it could prove to be a place where life may welcome you or on the other hand, it could be a realm full of new and unknown dangers. What a weight to carry on your shoulders. Such pressures might amount to too much for human hearts to bear. The burden of being alone could be enough to drive a human mad.

Most people have short-circuited their connection with God, but angels have a supernatural tie to the Most High as certain as night will follow the day. Michael's heart and spirit were in agreement with the Holy Spirit, so he was not marooned on a desert island. Since he could never be separated from the presence of God, being alone was a falsehood. A fabrication of the enemy.

The Warrior Within ...

Michael was delving into his memory. He was deep in thought, concentrating on what possible repercussions might result from the route he decides on. If he ultimately comes to one, that is. Something had come to his mind. The life preserving knowledge he acquired from his time with the LORD would prove to be very useful. The fact that he needed fresh water to survive finally was enough to get him moving in the sand. He listened intently for the sound of running water, but the roar of the breaking waves drowned out most every noise. Although he liked the feel of the sand, he found walking in it to be quite cumbersome.

"This is going to take some getting used to," the archangel said with a sigh before he untied his sandals and freed his feet.

"Ah, that's better," he declared with a smile, as he felt the relaxing warmth of the sand on the soles of his feet. *What a wonderful sensation*, he thought to himself.

While he trod through the sand, an inspiration came to mind. He remembered that Elijah had visited him within moments of his arrival on his last journey to earth.

"Elijah, where are you," he pondered.

"You must journey in to the jungle. Take a leap of faith Michael and enter the unknown. Do not forget, I will be with you," God spoke to his heart.

Just as God's audible voice disappeared into the forefront of his conscience, a path opened before Michael. He had not traveled more than a quarter of an earth-mile when he came upon a breach in the thick outer layer of the jungle. It was scarcely a dozen paces across and a large, smooth stone marked the entrance. Michael took a seat on the rock and laced up his sandals. He wrapped them around his legs tightly and, as he did so, feelings of exhilaration flowed through his blood. Pure excitement was in his eyes when he peered into the dense inner recesses of the jungle. He took in a deep breath and placed his right foot in front of him. He had made the first step and his destiny drew even closer now. He could feel his calling to follow the LORD, no matter what. And, like magnets to metal, his feet were drawn toward the jungle.

He left the vast openness of the beach in exchange for the tight quarters of the jungle's underbrush. He had only traveled a dozen paces when the lower half of his garments tore away. The portion of his robe that had covered him from the knees down now clung to the branches of a prickly thorn bush. He secured his belt and he pulled the Sword of the Spirit from its sheath. He eagerly cut away at the underbrush that hindered his path. He was convinced that nothing would get in the way of his calling. Palm trees were thick as grass in these inner parts of the forest. Gum trees, fruit trees, and a variety of trees grew among the palms. Still, he noted that the palms dominated the undergrowth with their wide fanning leaves. Thus, light was sparse and shade was plentiful. However, Michael found it to be more like darkness rather than shade and, this of course, was not new to him. He yearned for the light of Heaven all the more.

"This is not going to be easy," he said out loud.

He caught himself missing home already and, if his calculations were correct, he had not been on earth more than three or four earth-hours. He found strength within himself, for the Holy Spirit encouraged him and gave him hope.

In the midst of his hike, there was something that he could not ignore. Something was troubling his ear. A series of faint sounds echoed from within the under-story of the forest. A noisy rustling in the leaves startled him, but when he heard a stirring in the bushes a dozen paces back he became very nervous. He glanced over his shoulder, but he could see nothing behind him. Not even a single animal.

What could cause such a racket, he thought to himself. Then he quickly turned around, but his hopes of catching the prowler off guard were only met with an eerie silence. He felt like something, or possibly worse, someone, was following him. He thought for a moment that the forest was conspiring against him. The jungle was set on trapping him the first chance it had. The undergrowth seemed like it grew thicker with each step.

Michael choked from the suffocating feeling. Michael knew exactly how to combat his horrible feeling. Pray. He stopped in his tracks and looked towards the heavens. Instead of a beautiful span of blue sky, he stared into a dense jungle canopy, which was too thick for all but a shred of light to filter through. He immediately felt his faith comforted by the Holy Spirit. Michael gathered himself and continued on the trail as courage flowed through him with a new strength. As long as the LORD was by his side, nothing could keep him down.

He hiked in the direction that he heard running water coming from. He was now far enough from the ocean's crashing tide to distinguish the sound of fresh running water. He recalled the taste of water he had experienced his last trip to earth and he grew feverish from just the thought of its taste. At home he had no need for water, for the Fountain of Life requires only a sip to satisfy your thirst for an eternity in Heaven. On earth, though, he was left with the experience of a thirsty palate and even though it was quenchable, it felt to him like a need that was insatiable. All the same, he pined for a good drink of clean clear water.

The sound suddenly faded to a slight trickle of water. Was he getting further from it or, perhaps, closer to another source? The question soon answered itself though, as he came upon a pile of smooth opaque rocks that piled upon one another. And from the center was the source of the trickling. Clean crisp water bubbled up from the top most stone and flowed gently down a slope that appeared to have been carved out of solid rock. Michael noted that this water had to have been bubbling over since the beginning of creation to carve such a smooth indentation. He drank freely from the water that trickled over the edge.

He wiped his mouth and took time to rest. Fatigue was beginning to set in after hiking for many earth hours. This was no surprise to him. He had experienced the same weariness on the Mountain of God. On the other hand, he was finding it very difficult to get used to the temperature. The sweltering heat was more than unpleasant; he was literally dripping in sweat from the extreme humidity. He continued to drink from the fountain God had provided. He discovered that each drink was less refreshing than the last. He was figuring out what it's like to be full or more like quenching his thirst. This was unusual, although it wasn't new to him, but he looked at it as fantastic nonetheless. While he finished drinking his fill, he noticed a certain noise in the surrounding forest. Michael was gifted with the uncanny ability to hear something many earth miles away; sounds that were much further and even fainter than any human ear could perceive. The sound seemed to be of a natural origin and it was strangely menacing. It began as a low rumble that reverberated through the jungle, but soon he felt a vibration under his feet. His ears couldn't pinpoint the sound, but if his calculations were correct, the rumbling sensation was coming from the eastern direction. The rumble grew to a loud and booming disturbance.

The hairs on his arms stood on end and he just stared at them. However, it immediately dawned on him this was some mechanism in his body warning him of some foreboding danger. Suddenly, an earsplitting crash sounded. He was almost certain that the origin of the sound was a tree falling but what toppled it? That was the question at hand; then there was another menacing boom, so close that it hurt his ears. His instincts were telling him to run, but he couldn't get his feet to move. Birds flew overhead and creatures, some small and some sizable, were running through the forest to escape whatever terrible thing this might be. They paid no attention to the angel as they shot past him. Then the strength of the Holy Spirit pulsated through his muscles and he too was off running away from whatever force could cause such chaos. He ran as fast as his legs would take him. Swift and driven with adrenaline, the archangel flew over rocks and leapt over dead trees like it was a minuscule stride for him. He dodged prickly thorn bushes and darted past huge tree trunks as he maneuvered his way down the spontaneous escape route. One thing was on his mind and that was to get as far away as possible.

Michael continued running until his legs collapsed. He fell and tumbled into a giant wall of shrubbery. A hedge that almost seemed like it had been deliberately placed there. He fainted and when he awoke he discovered he was in a dark place. He was, in fact, on the inside of the hedge wall. Subtle rays of light punctured the underbrush, giving way to an incredible sight. Michael looked down one side and then the other and sure enough, a wall of hedges stretched in a straight line as far as he could see the rays of light that were scattered throughout the undergrowth. The branches that intertwined with one another were thick and full of finger-size thorns, which looked very unforgiving.

The archangel crawled until he found a substantial opening, big enough for his broad shoulders to poke through. He pushed his hands down on the soft earth and stood up. He found himself standing in a lagoon, so to speak, with silky neatly trimmed grass. About a thousand paces in front of him, due west, he beheld an incredible sight. A majestic cliff climbed nearly a few thousand earth-feet into the sky. A sparkling waterfall poured, with a thunderous sound, into a most beautiful refreshing pool. A large stream flowed through the middle of the secluded meadow and under the hedges. He licked his lips as, fortunate for him, he was terribly thirsty. He walked over to the water and dipped his hands into the glimmering pool. As the sunlight shined down on it, he noticed that the water changed colors. He looked up and took in the sight before him. The cliff walls were embellished with thousands of orchids, in a variety of brilliant colors. This is what caused the illusion the pool of water formed.

It was at this moment that his nose picked up the sweetest aroma. The scent hovered over the water and he saw it must be from the honeysuckle that clung to the many kapok trees submerged in the water's edge. There were many plants that he had not yet seen. Shrubbery with leaves that iridescently gleamed in the sunlight edged the pool like a flock of sheep drinking at the water's edge. Flowers that were nearly his size floated freely in the lagoon water. Still there were more trees with fruits he had yet to taste. An intense hunger churned in his belly, so he took a smooth rock and threw it at one of the fruit bearing trees. The first rock just missed one of the giant greenish gold fruits, but the second won the prize and then some. A cluster of fruits fell, but that wasn't all that moved. A spider monkey was startled from his safe perch. The agile creature swung from tree to tree to get to its friends, a large family of monkeys that were grouped in a large tree. The distraction lasted briefly and the angel got back to eating his fruit, which his fingers felt over for a weakness in the thick impenetrable outer shell. There was none and since he didn't want to soil his sword, he found a sharp pointed rock and cracked his prize meal open. He tasted the soft interior and found it to be quite delicious.

Michael took this time to refresh himself. He bathed his face in the water after eating his fill of the mysterious fruit. He gazed at the paradise around him. It was like a world separated from the rest of the earthly realm.

"Like a little piece of Heaven," he remarked.

There were birds of countless species flying here and there. Parrots, parakeets, lorikeets, and toucans were among the innumerous birds that were perched in the tree branches that hung low over the lagoon. Michael noted their gorgeous bright feathers. Then something happened. He thought his eyes were deceiving him, but his ears also heard what he was seeing. The soft sound of flapping wings made of silk. The wings belonged to butterfly's and humming birds. The birds and insects darted about the lagoon from flower to flower. The hummingbirds moved in unison with the butterflies, their colors seemed more vibrant and glowing with each pulsating beat of their wings. A few even landed on his shoulders and arms bringing an expression of pure joy to his face.

"Thanks be to you, God, for bringing me into your sanctuary," Michael declared. "Praise is to you for all that you have created. All of nature belongs to you and the rocks and the trees shall cry out if I won't."

Michael continued in praise to God until an extremely disturbing noise awoke him from his praying. There was a thunderous boom. Tremors suffused the top of the water. The ripples became more like waves as another boom echoed through the forest. The monkeys shrieked loudly and leapt and jumped swiftly from tree to tree until they were out of sight. The birds vanished into the forest over the waterfall and the butterflies climbed to the top of the jungle canopy. Words are slow, for this transpired much quicker than its description. Unnerving calm settled in the jungle and only Michael along with a lethargic tree sloth too slow for his own good, were left behind. Another rumble, only louder now, and the ground shook as more ripples broke the surface of the water. At that point Michael felt it would be better to be the sluggish sloth two hundred feet high in a tree, than a mighty archangel on the ground. He truly felt vulnerable to whatever unnatural force could make the earth quake. His mind was telling him his worst fear. This creature, whatever it may be, is the same creature he ran from only hours before. He awakened from his thoughts when a roar bellowed from within the forest, just beyond the wall of hedges.

Somehow, I think those bushes aren't going to keep a monster out, Michael thought as he looked for an escape route. His back was to the wall. The only way out was to go through the barricade of bushes. He tried to process the situation with his mind, but confusion and panic disrupted his thinking. There was another roar and, this time, it was definitely close.

"Help me my God. Do not forsake your servant," he prayed.

It was then that Michael sensed that he should draw the Sword of the Spirit, so he did. Then it happened, the time to face his fear had arrived. A huge section of the shrub wall collapsed with a splintering crash and there it stood with its eyes searching for its prey and then it spotted the angel. The monster stood nearly forty paces in height. To add to the horror, the mammoth creature looked hungry and it was glaring right at the archangel. It stood still as a statue. An armor of thick greenish-gray scales covered the beast from head to tail. The giant lizard had deadly claws shaped like scimitars. Its mouth was long, narrow, and full of grotesquely large razor-like teeth, which had drool dripping from them. The most intimidating factor was not its enormous size, dangerously sharp claws, or even its meat-shredding teeth, but it was the steam coming from its slimy nostrils.

Suddenly it moved one of its enormous legs forward and then it's other, proceeding in a full out gallop towards Michael.

"Not good," Michael yelped and turned to run for the safety of the cliff.

He didn't know if the monster could swim or not and he didn't care to find out. He thought that the most dimwitted thing he could do would be getting in the water with a beast twenty times his size. He ran toward the cliff, hope still remained for there was an opening large enough for the huge angel to squeeze under. He looked over his shoulder and the beast was gaining on him. From about a hundred paces away, it began to raise something on its back. Giant leathery wings unwrapped themselves and spread out twenty paces in each direction. Michael was almost there. Only fifty paces divided him from the security of the cliff side but with a thunderous landing, the beast came down in front of him. It brought in its leathery apparatuses used for flying. It curled its body as to make a semicircle to entrap Michael. The beast whipped its tail at him, but he jumped over it and ducked as it came flying back. The monster now appeared furious. It stretched its neck out and let out a roar from deep within its belly.

Michael grasped securely to the Sword of the Spirit. He held it out as the beast tried, yet again, to topple the mighty servant of God. Its tail was met with a slicing cut from the sword and the beast shrieked in pain. Now it was definitely angry. It showed its teeth and began to salivate like a lion would before its dinner.

"What do I do, LORD," Michael said with a grimace. "Deliver me from this foul beast, lest I become his food."

The beast then bowed its neck back and steam poured from its slimy disgusting snout. Michael ducked just in time, evading a blazing ball of fire. The monstrous beast stretched out its neck until its face was only inches from Michael's body. Michael stood as still as a statue as he could feel the dreadfully hot steam pouring from the beast's nostrils. For a brief instant, Michael thought in vain that it might just leave him alone. The monster, though, opened its mouth and roared. Rocks tumbled from the cliff above. This could not be a good thing. Michael could smell its last meal on the lizard's breath. There were bones and other disgusting things stuck between its teeth, which were covered in plaque and emitted a nauseating stench. Then the beast stood up as straight as it could, towering above Michael, and it stomped one foot on the ground, as if ferociously claiming its territory. Then it bent over and opened its mouth only inches from Michael's face, roaring with such fury and power that it blew the hair on Michael's head straight back. Michael stood dead still.

Then, out of the blue, something incredible happened. A blurry object flew through the air, appearing to be large and powerful, and it landed with a thud on the lizard's scaly back. This was no blurry object at all, but it was the one and only Gabriel, lieutenant general of Heaven's armies. Before the beast had realized it, the brave angel took Logos and drove it through the monster's scaly back delivering a hefty wound. The monster let out a roar of pain and went into a mad frenzy. Gabriel hung on for dear life and in the face of death, he inflicted yet another wound. He struck a vulnerable spot on its back, making the monster hiss and shriek. Within seconds, Gabriel was thrown about forty paces high into the air. He landed with a big splash in the lagoon.

The monster spread its leathery wings and flew over the jungle canopy. Gabriel had disappeared beneath the water so Michael dived in to save him. After a few suspenseful moments, the archangel emerged with Gabriel tucked under his right arm. He pulled his best friend onto the land and laid him in the grass. Gabriel's eyes suddenly opened and he coughed up a mouthful of water.

"That'll teach him not to clash with a servant of the Lord. Come back and get some more," Gabriel said after he had caught his breath.

He sprung to his feet and shook his fist into the air. The reality was that he didn't particularly care for the beast to come back. Gabriel's nature is to taunt evil whenever a situation presented itself.

"I'm certain I wounded the monster. I felt Logos plunge deep into its hideous hide. Yeah, I don't think he'll be back here anytime soon," the brave angel asserted.

After listening to his best friend carry on, it was easy for

Michael to see that no harm had befallen him. He was his usual courageous, outspoken, and confident self.

"Thanks be to God for sending you here, the timing couldn't have been more perfect. Nevertheless, we should leave this place and seek shelter for the night. We can't be sure the beast won't return. One thing is for sure, we need not camp on open ground."

Gabriel concurred and Michael glanced at the crevice in the cliff he had tried to get to, with no avail, just moments ago.

"That definitely won't do," the archangel uttered.

"One might say a cave large enough for two might do," Gabriel said.

He knew his friend well enough to realize that he knew what he was talking about. Michael looked bewildered and Gabriel simply laughed.

"Well, don't keep it to yourself Gabe," Michael started in. "Where can we find these gracious accommodations that you speak of?"

Gabe smiled and chuckled.

"You're going to love this. It's up there," Gabriel said as he pointed towards the cliff.

"I guess we'd better get moving, Gabe. It won't be long until nightfall sets in," Michael noted, patting Gabe on the back.

Gabriel had not experienced night yet. The darkness of the inner depths of the jungle only provided a mere simulation of the blackness of the nighttime and it was nowhere near the blackness of a moonless night.

"Before we go, I think I owe you a thank you," Gabriel said, sincerely.

Michael looked at him as if he were thinking, *what are you talking about?*

"You would do the same for me," he said, smiling all the while. "Even if you wouldn't reciprocate, I would've still done it."

Gabriel noticed the smile on his friend's face. He knew the Archangel all too well, and laughed out loud at his dry sense of humor.

"It's good to laugh," Michael remarked and gave Gabriel a pat on the back.

"Laughter is a good thing, but you know you'll be tired of me before the day is over. In fact, I'll be so bold as to say, by morning you'll probably want to hand me over to the monster for a good meal," Gabriel said. The word *morning* sounded strange to Gabriel, since he had never before experienced a morning, in the earthly sense.

"Nonsense brother," Michael retorted with a chuckle.

The two angels' reflections in the lagoon water looked like giant towers. They started their walk towards the cliff wall.

"I think this is as good a time as any to let you know that there is no way around this monstrosity of a cliff. There is only one way and that is up," Gabriel said.

Michael agreed, though he didn't exactly like the sound of that, taking in to consideration what he had been through on earth before. His mind began replaying that image of falling from the mountain. Over and over he prayed silently and as a cool, calm peaceful feeling swept over his body. There was a nice breeze blowing off of the water that carried, with it, a refreshing mist. However, he sensed that the peace inside wasn't from the natural refreshment of the elements, but from the supernatural power of the Holy Spirit.

The cliff rose upward like an unconquerable pillar of rock. The rugged face of the rock wall was dominated with jagged sharp rocks and perforated edges, like blades that could cut a man. Both traits are seemingly unforgiving but, that was the least of their worries. The cliff was thousands of paces high and the sun was already beginning its decent in the sky. Daylight was running out for them and a climb such as this would normally require many earth hours. And even though there were still many words to be said between the two seraphim, they didn't have the advantage of time on their side. However, they did have the power of the LORD on their side. With a short prayer for strength and protection, they proceeded to conquer the unconquerable.

THE FALLEN STAR

NOTE FROM THE SCRIBE...

What a momentous event. Was it by chance that Gabriel had found Michael in his greatest time of need? There are no coincidences and it was no fluke that they came across each other at this particular point in their mission. Truthfully, it was predestined by the Almighty himself and decided long before Heaven and earth existed. Gabriel's extraordinary rescue was planned and set in stone by the Father. And who or what can bend what the Creator has straightened. The Holy Spirit was sent just at the right instant, with precise timing, to overthrow the enemy in his tracks. It was not by might, nor by power, but by God's spirit that Gabriel and Michael were delivered from beast—the monster that rules the dominion of Luminarous. Needless to say, this was no ordinary creature and Gabriel's strength to defeat it was no ordinary force.

History was truly made that day as Michael and Gabriel made their marks on the timeline of Heaven's rich history. Had the enemy won that day, Satan and his demons would have been rejoicing. Moreover, there is no doubt they would have launched a full assault on earth and all of its inhabitants. Give thanks to God and praise his name, for any force of the enemy cannot bend the plans of the LORD. Know for future reference that this event marked the turning of the tide. Remember that the LORD is in control and no matter how scary the story gets, no matter how ugly the enemy is, always trust in him.

Tens of millions of angels were praying for Michael and Gabriel, fervently interceding for the brave warriors at this precise point in their epic journey.

The Warrior Within ...

Gabriel was the first to grab on to the rock wall. He took hold and started climbing.

"Follow me. I can see a way up," he shouted, looking down from a dozen paces high.

Michael had a somber look on his face. He was dwelling on his memory of passing out and falling down the Mountain of God. The image replayed itself over and over again. The enemy forces were already at work, but the interceding seraphim were praying with power to break the spell.

"Are you coming or not," Gabriel shouted down. "I can't climb for you and you're much too big to ride on my back." Gabriel laughed to himself.

"What's that you say?" Michael came out of his trance and said.

"Just get moving Michael. We haven't much light left," Gabriel replied, a bit befuddled at his friend's response.

Sure enough the sun was setting and before long darkness would be upon them. Michael knew this better than his friend. The diminishing light, however, was enough for Gabriel's common sense to comprehend the situation and he had gone through training to prepare him for the earth's natural elements. Michael said a quick prayer to himself and he instantly felt a surge of supernatural strength enter his mind and body. The malicious spirit had to flee at the name of the LORD. The archangel fixed his right palm firmly on a ledge and he began his ascent. Gabriel was already a hundred paces ahead of Michael, when he glanced over his shoulder and spotted his friend climbing swiftly and effortlessly.

"That's it brother. Keep it up and you'll pass me," he said to encourage the archangel.

He wasn't joking; Michael was almost running up the rock. He pulled and swung from ledge to ledge, climbing higher and higher with each passing moment.

"Watch out, Gabe, here I come," Michael shouted back.

The rocky path steered Gabriel dangerously close to the thundering waterfall. On a good note, the giant angel found the mist from the waterfall to be refreshing to his exhausted body.

The sun dropped behind the cliff and the light became instantly scarce. The two angels were past the half way mark and closing in on the level ground that awaited them at the top. Michael had caught Gabriel.

"Michael? Wow. And I thought I was a fast climber," Gabriel uttered from astonishment.

"Well, what are you waiting for? You know I can't carry you on my back," Michael pointed to the top and said.

"Up above, I spotted a cave earlier. I think it's even big enough for the two of us," Gabriel shouted and like a dart, he shot past Michael.

"Sure you say the cave looks big enough. But will your head fit through the door? That is the true question." Michael yelled as he climbed after him.

Gabriel laughed as he pulled himself onto the top of the cliff. He turned and lent a helping hand to Michael, and both of them collapsed from fatigue.

Michael helped him to his feet. The two had been laying down on the soft mossy rock. They were utterly exhausted. This feeling was nothing new to Michael, but he didn't pleasantly welcome it either. In spite of this, he was fully aware that it was a sacrifice he had to make in order to follow the calling. Gabriel, on the other hand, was foreign to the idea of fatigue. What were these strange sensations? The feeling of being out of breath was not something he delighted in. While dealing with this complication, his legs felt like they were turning to jelly. He encountered a world of trouble when he finally stood to his feet. Gabriel's knees were wobbling and his legs were unstable like they were on a seafaring boat. Laughter felt natural for the both of them. After a passing moment of amusement, Gabriel steadied himself and searched for the cave. The sky was overcast but there was a strong wind overhead. The clouds were pushed along at a rapid pace with the wind. The two angels were amazed at how stealthily the clouds floated by without making a sound. These were among many aspects of earth that would take some getting used to.

Suddenly, the moonlight presented itself, but it was fading quickly behind a cluster of clouds. All vision would soon be obscured. Then Gabriel spotted it. The cave's opening was about seven hundred paces away and across the river. Their journey across would have to wait since the angels, along with the land-scape, at once became enveloped in pitch-blackness.

"You picked a fine spot for shelter," Michael exclaimed. The grin on his face was veiled, but he couldn't hide the sarcasm in his voice.

Gabriel offered no reply. Within a few seconds the moon was on display and he moved like the wind. Michael said nothing, but he followed as quickly as his feet would take him. Gabriel and Michael made their way across the water by jumping from one slippery rock to another. They kept their balance perfectly until Gabriel began to teeter on a large pointed rock when he was about halfway across the river. The moonlight vanished behind a veil of clouds and Gabriel was slipping. He fell and with a splash he hit the water and the current swept him down the river.

The waterfall was just a few hundred paces away. In a matter of moments, Michael's best friend would be lost in the deadly rapids of the mammoth waterfall. Michael chased after him dart-ing from rock to rock. He had no light, so only the judgment of his ears could guide him. The sound from the water, as it rolled over the stones and pounded against the rocks, was his only tool to measure his jumps.

"Send your salvation, my God," he prayed fervently, shouting over the resounding current.

"Michael, Michael, save me," Gabriel yelled, struggling to stay afloat. The powerful undercurrent was too strong for his tired body.

The waterfall was a mere dozen paces away. Gabriel tried one final attempt to save himself. He desperately reached out for a rock, but his fingers slid off of each one.

"Grab hold of my hand," Michael shouted at him.

The archangel had gotten to him just as he was about to be taken by the rapids of the waterfall. Gabriel stretched out his arm and Michael took hold of his hand. The grip could not hold against the torrential current. Their fingers let go and the water pulled Gabriel over the edge, and he plummeted down the waterfall.

"No, no," Michael yelled.

For Gabriel, his life was flashing before his very eyes. Michael was standing on a rock above. He could only watch and pray, in a mere moment it would be over.

"No, no. Father God, save him," Michael shouted.

The following happened too fast to describe. Words are too slow. The archangel had to jump to the bank of the water for something incredible was happening. The water reversed its flow. The waterfall began to flow upward. The water felt like a net to Gabriel. Whatever he was feeling it was too late, because he was about to crash into the pool below. He covered his face with his arms and then he felt a sensation that was unlike anything he had ever experienced. He found himself caught up in the waterfall like he was stuck in a web. He opened his eyes and the jagged rocks below went from being deathly close to a safe distance below him.

"How could this be," Gabriel exclaimed. "Thanks be to God."

Above, Michael witnessed the entire event unfold before his eyes. He couldn't believe what he was seeing but he could trust that the LORD had worked a miracle.

"Praise you LORD. My protector, deliverer and my salvation, all glory and honor belongs to you." The archangel prayed with his hands raised to the sky.

Michael ran onto a rock and with one swift strong movement, he pulled his friend out of the water. Gabriel looked stunned, a bit shaken, and entirely relieved. They reached the cave safely, and he took a seat near the water but not too close.

"That was a close one," Gabriel said, solemnly.

"What he did out there, I will never forget," Michael uttered.

"The LORD meant it when he told us he would never leave us nor forsake us," Gabe said, gazing up at the stars.

"He is the LORD Almighty and he is true to his word," declared Michael as he put his hand on his friend's shoulder. "He is who he says he is, Gabriel. Not a single hair on our heads has been left uncounted. Far be it from his will that your calling be left unfulfilled. That is not the nature of the LORD's promises, nor will it ever be. For, although the universe is ever changing around us, God never changes. He is the same today, as yesterday, and he will be the same tomorrow. My soul takes comfort in knowing that."

Gabriel stood to his feet and his eyes peered intently into the night sky. The stars seemed to come to life, dancing and playing as if the universe was their playground. Gabriel's eyes reflected the light of the moon as he peered into the heavens.

"His ways are higher than ours," proclaimed Gabriel. "This night, my first on earth, I have learned to put my trust wholly in the LORD. To literally put my life in his hands and I have discovered that nothing is impossible for him. In Heaven I thought I had already learned this. In fact, you know as well as I, that it is common knowledge that all angels trust entirely in the LORD. However, I somehow feel different now. Like a new window has been open. One that lets all the light of his glory in and I now find myself complete in his presence. I am, and always have been, utterly obedient to his will. And I revel in the knowledge that I serve a mighty King."

"Well put, my friend. I couldn't have said it any better myself," Michael said, wrapping an arm around him like a brother.

They were each more than ready to get some well-needed rest. The two angels were about to enter the cave and explore their accommodations when suddenly a bright flash of light streaked across the starry sky. To get a better look they ran to the bank of the river. The light was shinning brighter than anything in the sky.

"Is it a shooting star?" Gabriel pondered.

"I'm not sure, but whatever it is, it is coming closer," Michael noticed. The light then began to slow down and, at the same time, the light grew more intense.

"I think it's coming towards us," said Gabe.

"I think you're right. It's coming fast," Michael said, intrigued.

"Should we take cover inside?" Gabriel pointed to the cave and asked.

Michael shook his head no, which truly baffled Gabriel. If the light turned out to be what the archangel was thinking, they would be safe. However, if it didn't, they'd be in trouble. Nevertheless, their anticipation grew steadily with each fleeting moment. The light moved in rapidly and set itself above the water. A gleaming ball of light now hovered, unmoving, over the water. The orb was a mere dozen paces from the two angels. The light seemed to change its colors from within. How many times, they couldn't tell. The shining ball passed over the water and settled on the land in front of them.

The orb transformed into an odd shape. It was elongated and wider at the top than the bottom. Then almost instantly, the orb's illumination dimmed and changed from a pulsating intense light into a single ring of radiant light. At that moment it became obvious what the gleaming ball of light really was, Elijah, the chief of messengers. Michael's hopes were elated. Gabe, on the other hand, was prepared for something that was of an evil nature. His hand had held tightly to Logos' hilt, but when he saw Elijah, he released his grip with a sigh of relief. Gabriel would never back down from a fight and he took pleasure in beating down the enemy. However, this night had provided all the action and thrills that he could take for his first day on earth.

Elijah bowed in respectful manner.

"Dear seraphim, greetings in the LORD," he addressed them. "I come bearing news of grave importance. I carry tidings from the LORD of Hosts. He sends his blessings and his presence travels with you by day and by night."

"Shalom brother," they both greeted him.

"I knew it," Michael said with a smile on his face. "I could feel his presence with me. He was silently and subconsciously steering me and guiding my way."

"Am I glad to see you, Elijah," Gabriel said, abruptly changing the mood of the conversation. "For a moment there I was thinking you were something else, perhaps more dangerous or evil is more like it. Truly, we've had quite enough excitement for one day."

"Please, Gabriel, enlighten me if you will," Elijah looked fascinated as he spoke.

"We will share our adventures with you, Elijah, but first let us go somewhere safer," Michael interjected and motioned for them to follow him into the cave.

"It will do," Elijah said, glancing curiously at the humble accommodations.

At the entrance, they could see no further into the cave than the light of the moon allowed. Maybe a few paces but beyond that there was only pitch darkness. From nowhere, Elijah produced a staff; a wooden staff the likes of which neither Michael nor Gabriel had ever seen. It was long, narrow, twisted, strangely shaped, and out of the ordinary for certain.

"*Helliffi olhi lighlli,*" Elijah said, speaking in the ancient tongue.

The tip of the staff ignited and it emitted a golden flame. The handle glowed red like hot lava. At first, Michael took little notice of the supernatural light. Instead, he was astonished that Elijah knew the ancient speech of creation. He had learned what he knew of the secret tongue from the Father and he knew the Father and he spoke this tongue. He was absorbed in thought. He recalled the words Elijah spoke were the very same words spoken by the Father at the dawn of creation. God had repeated these words to him many times for the purpose of teaching him the miracle of his creation. In the human tongue, their meaning translates: Let there be light.

"Where did that come from? How did you—? Oh, never mind. Anyhow, you're going to have to show me that trick some time," Gabe blurted aloud, startling Michael from his thoughts.

Elijah smiled and laughed from his belly.

"I knew you would appreciate it," he exclaimed. "Indeed, supernatural power flows in the wood of the staff I hold in my hand. Though, you know well that it is not I that possess such power but the one who sent me." Elijah rested on a large smooth stone.

Gabriel starred intently at the staff.

"Gabe, maybe one day the Father will give you a staff like his," Michael put a hand on his brother's shoulder and said. He then reached for Gabriel's sword and unsheathed it. The blade shimmered fiercely in the light from the staff.

Gabriel grabbed at the sword, but the archangel held it firmly in his hand.

"Here, take it, Gabe," Michael said and handed him the sword. "I just wanted to prove a point—Logos is a gift, an indescribable one at that. Gabe, to each is his own and to each be his own," Michael said.

"Far be it from me to think of it as anything other than the perfect gift," Gabriel put Logos back in its sheath and said.

Elijah sat motionless, silently observing with the utmost patience.

"If you two are finished—" he uttered and cleared his throat. "—and prepared to listen to what I have journeyed an unfathomable distance to say, then I will begin. Otherwise, continue as you were."

Michael immediately looked at Elijah and noticed something different about him. His face appeared older, or perhaps wiser. His deep blue eyes were flooded with a holy knowledge. Michael pondered rather or not those eyes had seen things unknown to all seraphim, including him. Did his mind hold secret wisdom of the past? How did he come to know the ancient tongue? Did the Father teach him or did he learn from hearing it? *There is more to this chief of messengers than meets the eye*, Michael thought quietly. Elijah's eyes started to glow in a very unusual blue. They looked like two sparkling gems set in ivory.

The messenger turned and gazed directly at Michael.

"To begin, I must have a private audience with the archangel," Elijah said. "You must excuse yourself for a few moments, Gabriel."

Gabriel had just sat down on a smooth ledge that projected from the wall of the cave. It looked more like a chair than a rock. He hesitantly raised himself from his seat.

"So be it. I'll be outside if you need me," Gabe said. "If you hear me yell or cry in pain, there is no need to worry."

"An abominable monster will have eaten me....," his voice faded out as he departed from the cave.

Elijah was quite baffled, but Michael gestured with his hand, assuring him that everything is okay.

Gabriel was now out of earshot of the cave. Michael suddenly noticed the walls of the cave. They were strangely colored. The rock gave off a reddish-orange iridescent shine. The ceiling was about a dozen or so feet high. The light from the staff presented enough light to see dozens of paces further into the cave and the depths of the cave descended far beyond the light into hidden darkness. The halo, hovering freely above Elijah's head, cast strange shadows on the ceiling including ones that danced and seemed to move on their own accord. Michael was curious what the message would be and Elijah was preparing to read it to him. He revealed a small piece of parchment he had concealed in his robe. He unrolled it, rolled it up again, and put it back.

"This isn't it," he said to himself and pulled another out. "That's not it."

"Just curious, how many can your robe hold?" Michael inquired.

Elijah shrugged his shoulders and chuckled. Finally, the third piece he found was the one he was looking for. And he regained his composure.

"The word of the LORD says," he spoke softly but assertively. "You're here for more than just a test, but an intervention of the supernatural kind. My rod will test you. And, this may come as grave news, but you will also be tested by the prince of darkness and his evil minions. Satan has asked my permission to test you and prove me wrong. I have granted him permission to do so. I believe in you and love you, Michael. No test that the enemy puts before you will be beyond your ability. I will fill you with supernatural strength when you need it most."

Elijah paused for a brief moment to clear his throat. Meanwhile, outside the cave, a much different event was unfolding. Gabriel had sat down on the bank of the river. He sat with his arms wrapped snugly around his tree trunk-like legs. He was staring, in a dreamy gaze, at the stars. He noted that they were beyond counting and extraordinarily beautiful. Each was created unique and given ordinances to follow. Some were clustered together to form incredible shapes and others seemed to move freely across the sky like shooting beams of light. He was praying to the LORD.

"Father, I wouldn't be here if it wasn't for your saving grace.

Your salvation is all I need. Help me to grow in understanding so I may answer my calling."

"You have answered your call, Gabriel," a voice, deep and resounding spoke to his heart. "You chose to trust in me with all of your being. Now you stand in the wide-open spaces of my love and grace. My presence will never leave you nor forsake you."

He instantly recognized the voice to be God's and he was comforted.

Peering at him, from its hiding place, were two slanted eyes. They were watching him closely, studying his every move, and analyzing him like a skeptical peer. Unknown to the angel, the eyes began to move slowly through the jungle backdrop. They settled behind a bush that happened to be a mere dozen paces to the right of the cave. They watched and waited. The creature behind the eyes was planning its moves carefully, choosing the perfect time to make its presence known. The timing was of utter importance for the creature. It had to be just right or else the plan would be foiled.

Inside the cave, Elijah continued his message.

"The enemy desires to destroy you and he seeks revenge at all costs. The LORD says that there will be no test that you cannot overcome and, when all seems hopeless, he will be with you. Remember that he will give you strength to conquer the enemy. It is all in his timing."

Michael absorbed, with a receptive heart, all that Elijah had spoken.

"I have delivered God's message to you. Discuss this with no one, not even Gabriel; especially not Gabriel," he said, his brow was furrowed with concern.

"Now the time has come that I must speak to Gabriel alone," Elijah said and stood to his feet.

"What tests am I to face? Has the LORD told you? Do you know?" Michael had a notion what his answers would be, but he asked nonetheless.

"I know not of the tests or trials you will face. Only God knows the answers," Elijah quietly replied, almost in a whisper as if he knew the enemy might be listening.

"If you will please excuse me, Michael, I must talk with

Gabriel," Elijah said cheerfully, as if Michael hadn't just received exceptionally serious instructions.

Gabriel was skipping stones across the water when Elijah approached. Gabriel's face appeared curious. He was wondering what message he was about to receive, and what news Michael had just heard. Michael switched places with him and waited by the river.

Once inside the cave, Gabriel thought he should speak up first. He enjoys to converse but he loves to get the first word in. For an unknown reason, which he hasn't shared, he values the first words over having the last.

"Ok, what's going on? Why do I feel I'm being left out? It seems there are now things beyond my knowledge, beyond my knowing, and I'll be honest—it troubles me terribly to think this," Gabriel said, initiating the conversation.

"Gabriel, I was told you like to get the first word in," Elijah replied solemnly. "There will always be things beyond your knowing. There is an infinite wealth of wisdom and knowledge way beyond your scope and mine as well, but you need not let it worry you. Instead, you must learn to trust in the LORD. Have you not been through this before?"

Gabriel was reclining in the stone chair and he laughed to himself.

"Trust I have learned. Dealing with your lectures, I have not," Gabriel said under his breath.

Elijah was sitting on a large smooth stone. He leaned in and his staff ignited twice as brightly; his face gleamed with the anointing of the Holy Spirit.

"Gabriel, I have not come to patronize you. I was sent to help you," he said and his breath was felt by Gabriel.

"How'd you do that? The first time your staff came alive with fire, you spoke the sacred tongue of creation—" Gabriel said with a perceived attitude. "Maybe you have power of your own? Perchance you used sorcery to light your staff."

In an instant Gabriel's voice had changed like someone or something was speaking through him. The enemy was already beginning to work their diabolical tricks, starting with Gabriel. Fortunately, at that moment, Elijah had been filled with the Holy Spirit.

"My spirit spoke the words silently. The LORD needs no audible voice to be heard," He said, taking on a commanding tone. "Or don't you already know that, spirit!"

He then raised his voice, as one who speaks with authority.

"I rebuke you in the name of the LORD God Almighty," Elijah shouted. "You tool of Satan heed my command for I am a bondservant of the one true God. I cast you back to the fiery depths. Be gone demon, before I speak a curse over you—rot of hell."

Elijah stretched out his hand and spoke in the sacred tongue. Michael heard the commotion and came to the aid. He broke through the threshold of the cave just in time to see a shadow, blacker than night, stretch itself over the ceiling of the cave. Michael felt an icy wind pass through him as the shadow fled past him screaming profanities as it disappeared under the moonless night. Gabriel had the impression that an immense tension had been released from him. He felt like an ox that had its yoke removed from his shoulders.

"What just happened," Michael asked. He discovered his hand was firmly gripped to the hilt of the Sword of the Spirit. Silence settled heavy in the air.

"What was that Elijah?" Michael demanded to know.

The chief of messengers sat back down. He was exhausted.

"An agent of evil," Elijah gravely said. "Deep in the flaming bowels of Hell, Satan has been secretly crafting a breed of malicious spirits. He has no power to create, however, he does exercise his power to pervert and mutate, and he does so by extracting the spirits from demons that once disobeyed him or crossed him. Any that question his authority end up as one of these dark apparitions and they succumb completely to their master's will; being bound for an eternity to do his bidding."

"What you witnessed tonight was nothing more than a dark spirit, once a demon, but now a mutation of the enemy, better known as Ruah," Elijah continued, speaking quietly, in almost a whisper. "And these Ruah are only one of the many treacherous weapons Satan has at his disposal. Our sources tell us the demonic spirits cannot take physical form, but they may possess other demons, if they can overpower them. What you observed tonight was their ability to demonize. It is now confirmed fact that they can harass and manipulate both demons and angels alike. There is the threat, more so a possibility at this time, that they can even possess an angel."

Elijah got up and walked to the entrance to the cave.

"Moreover," uttered Elijah as he stood at the threshold. "There is one thing you should know about the Ruah, something that separates them from all other demons. No natural weapon can work against them, so your swords will be made useless when facing one. However, there is hope for you still. Although any natural weapon cannot defeat their malicious breed, there is a certain power that can break their stronghold. Prayer is this power and, when the time comes, you must focus on the Holy Spirit and he will shatter the Ruah into a thousand pieces like the breaking of glass."

"For the time being the Ruah is gone," Elijah said with a sigh. "Though, it will certainly bring word to its master. When that happens these parts will be crawling with their dark presence and fowl stench. Be on guard brothers and don't ever fool yourselves for they require only a moment, a concise second of weakness and you could be overtaken by their poison and influence, finding yourself on the threshold of madness. To be demonized is one step closer to possession. If Satan can't destroy you then he'll make every attempt to force you to join his evil masquerade, particularly, by exploiting his Ruah as weapons against you. Pray for discernment and protection from the enemy."

Michael's jaw dropped. This report was completely new to him, so needless to say, he was taken entirely by surprise. He felt helplessly unprepared. In all of his lessons with the LORD and with all of the secret knowledge he obtained, he wasn't prepared to deal with this supernatural evil. He recalled, one by one, the countless moments he spent basking in the wisdom of the Father. Even so, he wasn't prepared for the Ruah. He remembered all the training and instructing he had received thus far and he wondered why he had not been made aware of the Ruah. His thoughts were telling him he had been left out, nothing more and nothing less. Like being kept in the dark, he felt blind and useless. His spirit discerned otherwise. The Holy Spirit reminded him he was yet the leader God made him to be and he was still being groomed for his ultimate fate. Even now, as he stood in the cave, the wheels of destiny were in motion continuously turning while the enemy waited for him to stumble and fall.

Michael had not noticed until now that Elijah was peering deeply into his eyes from across the cave. The archangel came near to the messenger and raised an inquisitive eyebrow.

"Why was I not informed of the Ruah," Michael asked sharply. "Elijah, I was not prepared to battle a force of evil such as this. If there had been more, what would have become of us?"

Elijah's face turned very stern, more like a big brother than a peer.

"Well, take a seat, both of you. And listen closely, lest I repeat myself and I would strongly dislike having to do that," requested Elijah, with all the authority he holds as chief of the messenger seraphim.

When Elijah spoke, he commanded the attention of any angel. Michael and Gabriel nodded *yes* and took their place by the angel. They both sat unmoving, anxious to hear what he had to say. Elijah sat down and took a piece of parchment from his robe and proceeded to unroll it. To Michael and Gabriel's astonishment the scroll was unbelievably lengthy. The print was also much too small for their eyes to read.

"Are you going to read from the entire parchment," Gabriel inquired. "Wait, that is beside the point … how can you even read the tiny print?"

"Each letter, which I can't even distinguish, is smaller than a grain of sand," Michael added. Elijah had his face buried in the scroll and they didn't know if he had even heard them.

"With all do respect, Archangel Michael and lieutenant general Gabriel, I am trying to concentrate," Elijah said and set the parchment down on his lap.

"If you both can hold in your hands deadly weapons such as those," remarked Elijah, pointing to the swords by their hips. "Then surely you can wield an ounce of patience. Let me do my job and you shall hear the report from the LORD."

Michael and Gabriel said nothing. Elijah returned to his business and the two giant angels looked at each other like they were thinking, *what's gotten under his skin?*

Michael and Gabriel were extremely exhausted from the day's events. They were starting to wonder rather or not this was going to take the entire evening. Elijah glimpsed over parchment after parchment.

"Now to find that special inscription. I know it's here somewhere," Elijah said to himself.

Where he kept all the scrolls was baffling the two seraphim. Like a magician at a child's modern-day party, he pulled out one after another. He quickly formed a partially neat pile of scrolls. Elijah wasn't typically unorganized, but he was working on many assignments at the time. He prided himself in being good at multitasking. Finally, after what seemed like hours to the two angels, but was actually only mere minutes, Elijah found what he was searching for.

"By God's good grace, I do declare I've found it," the chief messenger cried out.

Elijah composed himself, lowered his tone, and urged them to come closer. They came near and sat before him. He looked at the entrance of the cave as if he was checking for any unwanted visitors. He scanned the back of the cave, looking suspicious at every turn, as he peered back and forth.

"You never know who or what may be listening. While you are in this realm, you will learn that you can never be too careful," he whispered. Elijah then unrolled the parchment and began to read in a sharp but low tone.

"I will begin by telling you the history of a certain star. This star was created for a very special duty. He was given the name Luminarous, by the creator, Father God. His name denotes bright and beautiful one. The Almighty set his course in the universe many ages ago. He was to provide light for many millenniums to the countless planets and galaxies in the universe. The sun was the only equal light in the universe. God personally showed him the path he was to travel in. His course was unique among the infinite number of stars. His path would essentially bring him to earth, but not until the fulfillment of the prophecy, which is written in the Book of the Seven Seals. He was created to play a major role in the end times."

Elijah held his tongue and peered towards the cave-opening. He thought he heard something moving outside the cave. Michael and Gabriel each put their hand to the hilt of their sword. It turned out to be nothing more than a deer, which darted off as soon as it noticed the angels.

"However—" Elijah said, and cleared his throat. "— Luminarous' own selfish ambitions filled him with arrogance and his light became poisoned. He chose to disobey the will of God and break the only commandment he was given—*trust and obey. Follow the path and your destiny shall be fulfilled.* His pride ultimately drove him to abandon the assigned course and choose his own path. He drifted in the heavens and before long he paid the price for his conceit. His light was extinguished and into the darkness Luminarous fell."

Elijah opened a new scroll to continue reading.

"Well, don't take all evening. I need to know what happens next," Gabriel blurted. Michael nodded with anticipation.

Elijah ignored Gabriel's antics, found his place on the new scroll, and commenced with his report.

"He was drifting in the heavens when he was sucked into a dark abyss (worm hole) which took him directly to the throne room to meet with the King. God decided against destroying him at that precise moment. Instead, he banished Luminarous to a realm within the earth. A secret island, where time has no control over its inhabitants; a place where there is no way out. The waters surrounding this island may appear beautiful but they are far too dangerous for any living thing to enter or escape.

Luminarous was sentenced to a timeless imprisonment on the island, that is to say, until the end times when the Book of the Seven Seals will be opened. Then and only then will his final judgment take place.

Moreover in the center of the island, a mountainous volcano towers high above all the inhabitants. Its job is to keep evil accountable. At the command of the LORD, the volcano will erupt pouring forth magma and ash that will vanquish the island of all inhabitants. Thus far, the volcano has remained dormant, but the time for action is drawing near. That is what brings you here Archangel Michael and lieutenant general Gabriel. You were brought here on a covert mission to capture the fallen star, Luminarous."

"But what about his sentence of imprisonment," Gabriel said and received a stern look from Elijah for his interruption.

"I will enlighten you on the matter if only you will let me finish," Elijah replied.

"We'll listen. Won't we, Gabriel," Michael quickly said.

"Please, as you were," Gabriel said.

Elijah found his place on the parchment.

"You both are here for a very important reason," he said, using a more serious tone than before. "Satan became aware of Luminarous' fall from grace. He was also mindful of the power the star possesses. His demons in charge of secret intelligence informed him that even though Luminarous' light had been extinguished; the star had still retained much of its power. Satan conceived, in his wickedness, that the power of Luminarous could somehow be harnessed and utilized. He commissioned his Ruah to search out the earth for this secret realm. Eventually, the news came back to him that the secret realm had been breached. A great number of Ruah were ordered to remain on the island as scouts. Satan commissioned an entire legion of demons to hunt down Luminarous and bring the fallen star unspoiled, to Hell. There, Satan devises to further pervert the star by breaking its will and commanding its power for his evil desires. This brings me to why you two are here to intervene. The plans of the enemy must be stopped.

Now, the enemy has hundreds of followers on the island. Included among them are many wild beasts turned against the Creator, dozens of Ruah that roam the island constantly in search of a soul to possess and finally, but certainly not the least, thousands of demons that are stationed in an undisclosed location somewhere on the island. Even so, in the midst of the evil that darkens the land, there yet remain allies of the LORD. They are few in number, but they are a faithful brotherhood of animals that are firmly committed to the Creator. Pray that when you need them most that the LORD will send them."

"Hold up for a moment," Gabriel interrupted yet again. "The island we are on is basically a death trap crawling with Ruah, demons, and wild beasts bent on killing angels. Where do we—"

That's all he could say before Elijah stopped him right there.

"Shish," Elijah put a finger to his own mouth and said. "I was getting to the point, Gabriel. Can you please hold your tongue? I'll tell you once more and I certainly mean it, not a word until I've finished. Now where was I? Oh yes, there are still many allies of the Holy One, but you must beware of the trickery of the enemy. Look into their eyes to perceive their heart. The eyes are a window to the soul, you know. Remember the discernment of the Holy Spirit, for no lie can stand in his presence. Your purpose here, Michael and Gabriel, is to find Luminarous. You must capture him so he can be relocated to a new realm, a place that is free from the clutches of the enemy. Once your quest has been completed, the LORD will cleanse the island from the wicked inhabitants."

Elijah stopped to pull out another piece of parchment. He unrolled it.

"Take a look with me," he said in a hushed tone. "This particular parchment contains a detailed map of the island. Ah ha, we are here right and your destination is on the other side of the island, about one hundred and thirty thousand paces away. Our most recent report said that the enemy has caught Luminarous and they have taken him deep into the earth. The only entrance is through a cave, which has an unfathomable depth. You will be amazed to find out this report came from Joshua himself. He was sent here secretly to scout the island ahead of you and Gabriel. Although his mission went terribly wrong. He was captured and taken, blindfolded, to the enemy's camp. His prayers and courage exceeded the enemy's expectations. For a fortnight ago he escaped and made it to the surface. He risked his life to deliver this report. He was accompanied by three other seraphim: Caleb, Sethur, and Ahab. What became of the other angels is terrible indeed. Joshua could not find them. He searched through the cave's corridors and the angels were nowhere to be found. He fears that they will be executed or, worse, tortured until they give in to the enemy's will.

That is why it is extremely important that you take great haste and leave this evening in search of the enemy's lair. The island is scattered abroad with wickedness, so be extremely cautious and journey with light steps to go undetected in the jungle. Moreover, the evil one never sleeps and his slaves are ever watchful of the cave."

He looked at them both with caring eyes and sincerely said, "This is my prayer for you both. May the Holy Spirit go with you and prepare the way and may the favor of the LORD rest upon you."

Elijah then glanced right at the archangel.

"Archangel Michael, please allow me and Gabriel a few moments alone," Elijah said. "I have a message from the LORD to share with him."

Michael agreed and stepped outside the cave and there he stood guard. Elijah now focused his gaze on the lieutenant general. His eyes were full of the glory of the LORD and Gabriel's face was stricken with anticipation.

"The LORD says," Elijah began with a zealous tone. "I have made you a captain over many angels and I have given you much authority in Heaven and on earth. I have promoted you to a prestigious appointment as the lieutenant general. Your deeds in the great battle were masterful and heroic. I have created you for Michael and the archangel for you. You were destined to be like brothers from the moment I spoke you into existence. Michael cannot fulfill his ultimate destiny without your aid and neither will you complete your calling if you lack help from the archangel. That is why I have assigned you to this quest and, at this moment, your main concern is guarding Michael from the evil attacks of the enemy. You are to watch over him always and he is not to leave your sight. You must not fail. Gabriel much is riding on your shoulders and your burden will be heavy, but remember you are not alone. I am always by your side in spirit and in truth."

Gabriel was very impressed and he was humbled as well. He had always looked up to Michael as a big brother and the LORD confirmed their friendship to be pre-ordained. Gabriel could tell by the expression on Elijah's face that he was waiting for a response.

"I consider it my greatest honor to be the guardian of God's most favored angel," Gabriel said with the fervor of a great general. "The LORD can trust me wholly in this. I will not let the LORD or Michael down. What about Michael? Does he know of this?"

"He is not to know, just as you are not to know of his instructions," Elijah said, sternly. "Gabriel, you must be steadfast, strong, and trust in the LORD always. You must excuse me. It is now my time to return."

Elijah rose to his feet and walked outside the cave. Gabriel quickly followed him and Michael was standing outside when they both passed by him. Michael and Gabriel followed him and spoke not a word. The chief messenger transformed once again into pure light. He hovered above the water for a moment and, without making a noise, he flew like a shooting star into the wide starry sky. Michael and Gabriel were left standing there at the bank of the river. Each of them was completely awestricken. Their minds were going over what each of them had been made privy to. They silently retreated to the safety and security of the cave's solid walls. Although some of the report had been disconcerting, much more of it was encouraging and inspiring. Michael knew wholeheartedly that there was a special reason God had ordained them for this arduous quest. Gabriel immediately took up pacing back and forth, as he pondered over the instructions he had just received. Michael remained seated with his hand resting under his chin, looking quite studious in his current posture; he appeared to be in deep thought.

"What are we waiting for," uttered Gabriel, breaking the silence. "Elijah told us to make haste. So, what are we doing in here wasting precious moments? We should be out there in search of the enemy's lair."

"Right you are Gabe," Michael stood to his feet and declared. "The time has come for us to employ the skills and knowledge that the LORD gave so generously to us."

"Yes! And not to mention the wisdom instilled in us by the Almighty himself," Gabriel said with courageous eyes.

"Join me Gabe in a prayer for LORD's protection," Michael said and pulled the Sword of the Spirit from its sheath. Gabriel in a second's time had Logos raised in the air. The two prayed fervently to the LORD asking him for guidance, protection, and the discernment of the Holy Spirit.

"Now, Gabe we must make haste. Let's pursue the enemy and with the LORD's help, may we not grow weary. Fly with me," Michael said in a whisper that steadily grew to a shout.

A grin came over Gabriel's face. Then the two each took up his sword and stepped out of the cave into the invigorating night air. They ran with great speed leaping from rock to rock to get across the waterfall. In a mere matter of seconds they had crossed the river and were descending the path alongside the waterfall.

The moon was full, which provided more than sufficient light for their path. Even so, there was the looming danger of the ever-watchful eyes of the enemy. Thus, the angels decided to travel under the disguise of the dark dense jungle that lay beyond the pasture. In the gloomy forest, they thought, not even their shadows could follow them. It was a perfect guard from Satan's prying spies, or so the angels assumed.

Though the light was barely discernable, Michael ran with the swiftness of an agile gazelle. Gabriel could hardly keep pace, which was extraordinary in itself, since Gabriel was used to out-pacing Michael during their foot races. How they hadn't smacked into a tree was a miracle, Gabriel knew; it seemed to him that Michael was being guided by something other than his eyes. *It must be the power of the Most High*, Gabriel thought, for his help alone could lead us through pitch-black darkness.

The angels had been traveling for a few hours when they came to a clearing in the jungle—a place where the forest canopy opened up to a clear view of the vast starry sky.

"This looks like a nice place as any to rest," Michael said, nearly out of breath. "Will you join me, brother, and give praise to the LORD."

"I couldn't agree with you more," Gabriel grinned happily and said.

They raised their voices to Heaven to give praise to the LORD Almighty. Although they were greatly fatigued, they still sounded more beautiful than the most harmonious bird in song. They praised God until sunrise, singing:

> *"Holy, Holy, Holy is the LORD God Almighty*
> *You are worthy of all Praise*
> *You command the moon to shine*
> *And the sun to rise*
> *We adore you oh LORD*

Holy, Holy, Holy is the LORD of Heaven
You are worthy of all adoration
You guide our path
And guard us from harm
We are in awe of you oh LORD"

NOTE FROM THE SCRIBE...

The enemy was working, nonstop, to find a means of attack against the angels. The Ruah of pride and destruction was unsuccessful with its first assault. Michael and Gabriel knew full well that it wouldn't be their last encounter with the dark apparitions of the enemy. Their worship provided a cover of protection against the enemy's dark will. Angels aren't totally immune to the spiritual attacks from Satan's demons, just as humans are not. A human, though, is more susceptible to the assaults of demons, without God in his life. Angels, on the other hand, worship the LORD in spirit and in truth, always, for that is the purpose they were created for. And a seraph's will power is beyond comparison to that of any earthly human.

However, the presence of evil was strong on the island of Luminarous and dozens of Ruah were on the loose roaming the island looking for bodies to possess. At this point in the quest, things were only going to get tougher for the two brave seraphim. Now that a Ruah had actually beheld them in person, the alarm would surely be activated; silently and desperately, Satan's dark minions would prompt the search for the servants of the LORD and the Ruah's focus would be honed in on the spirits of Michael and Gabriel. The enemy was prepared to stop at nothing to separate the seraphim, Michael more than Gabriel, from the presence of God. Fortunately, for the angels there were over a million other angels in Heaven assigned to continually intercede for Michael and Gabriel. The prayers of the seraphim provided a solid covering against the forces of the evil one.

BABYLON

While in worship the seraphim were completely unaware that an enemy scout was secretly spying on them. The scout was a jet-black wolf. The creature made no sound as it crept along. The wolf kept to the shadows and stealthily dodged the moonlight to remain undetected. The wolf was an animal long turned against its creator by the enemy. He was the first in what would be a long breed of hellhounds. He was trained to hunt the friends of God. He saw them strictly as adversaries of his master and like a good meal; he took great pleasure in devouring the flesh of his enemies.

The wolf didn't come any closer than a long stone's throw. His will was strong, for his flesh very much desired to eat them and he could barely tolerate the singing. Above all else, he couldn't stand the name of the LORD being praised. He silently observed them for a few moments. He tried his best not to pant in disgust at their worship. He noticed their large stature, especially that of the huge one. He had never seen an angel quite as strong nor as tall as the huge one. He made the mental notes he had been sent to take and without breaking a branch or a twig, he eluded their attention as he vanished like a ghost. Once out of earshot, he sped off swiftly to alert his master of the seraphim's whereabouts.

A twig snapped breaking the dead silence and the watchful demon had his axe in hand, ready to dismember any approaching threat. A low growl pervaded his hearing and he lowered his guard. The wolf approached the demon. Its broad shoulders and long powerful torso sat atop four lanky legs with claws sharper than steel beneath them.

"My dear Baal. Do you bring news of the enemy," asked Saul, a middle-ranking demon more mischievous than wicked, but nevertheless dangerous.

The wolf, with swift agility, steadied itself on its hind legs and placed its forepaws on the demon's shoulders. He whispered into the demon's ear in the tongue of beasts.

"Master Saul, I bring news of the enemy's presence. I have located two angels about two thousand paces from here," the wolf said in a loathing growl. "They are praising, worshiping the Creator, God."

"Watch your tongue Baal. Lucifer alone is our lord and master," Saul shrieked out of anger and struck the wolf in the snout. Baal scowled and snarled ferociously.

"Aha, if we can capture the angels we will definitely receive a reward for our efforts," Saul said in a soothing tone. What he actually meant was that he would take all the credit and leave Baal completely out of the prize. After all, Saul is a selfish demon that seeks only what can fulfill his own desires.

"But master, these angels are well armed," Baal barked. "They carry powerful weapons of the likes I have never before seen; swords that could cut anything. Even your iron axe wouldn't stand a chance."

"Fool. I am skilled with the axe," Saul snapped with pride. "And have you forgotten that you have a mouthful of tiny swords, teeth that can rip through any flesh. You will follow your master wherever he goes. Now, enough with your foolish fear, let's go."

Baal strongly disagreed with his master. He knew in his soul that a wolf and his master couldn't overcome the angels. However, he also knew better than to voice his opinion, since he would receive harsh and painful discipline for his actions. Thus, as usual, he kept it to himself. With the shake of a chain, Baal began creeping along. He definitely didn't want to wear his leash, so he led the way. Soon they were running as fast as they possibly could without making a noise. Saul's plans were to ambush their enemies. Baal may have feared what the powerful ambassadors of God could do to him, yet he was repulsed by them and wanted to make them suffer more than mind his instincts.

They had only been stalking their prey when they came upon the spot the seraphim had been in only moments ago. Baal discovered, through sniffing the place Michael and Gabriel had been worshiping, that their foes had not been gone for long.

"I can almost hear their voices singing still. It sends shivers down my spine just thinking about it. Come, I've picked up their scent. Follow me," growled Baal.

The master and his wolf crept swiftly along in hot pursuit and soon they were running in a full gallop. Baal had picked up their scent and, this time, it was extremely potent.

"We are getting closer master," hissed the wolf.

"Well then, go faster you fool. We mustn't lose their trail," Saul replied quietly, yet sternly. "Can't you taste their blood now, Baal? Their flesh will make a nice reward for your generous appetite, my pet."

"The best there is," he thought out loud as he leapt over rocks and crevices. Baal's legs sped up and his mouth salivated at just the notion of a well-deserved meal of angel flesh

In the meantime, Michael and Gabriel were running like the wind, leaping in great bounds over nooks, crannies, rocks, and the fallen remains of once-mighty trees. The landscape was thick with bushes and dominated by thorny vines that tore at their flesh as they ran. Finally the seraphim began to fatigue, so they did what came naturally. They slowed their pace to a leisurely walk. At this precise moment the angels were far ahead of the demon and his wolf. Of course, they were completely oblivious to the fact that they were being stalked and with each passing moment the looming threat of danger was closing in on them.

"Michael, how far do you think we've come?" Gabriel inquired.

"Most likely five thousand or so paces, give or take a few thousand," he replied.

"We should stop for a break. Don't you feel fatigue plaguing your legs and feet," Gabriel said.

"We will rest here, but not for long," Michael came to a stop and said. "As we speak, Gabe, as we sit here—the enemy is searching Luminarous for their prey. We are that prey, so we must keep moving towards the destination." The entire time the archangel spoke, he looked like he was listening or searching for a particular sound.

Gabriel nodded in agreement, although he was a bit curious at Michael's peculiar behavior. Even so, he spent the remainder of their rest in complete silence.

Morning had come and gone and it was nearly noon by now; they had been traveling for over twelve earth-hours. The air was peaceful and the jungle noises were relaxing to them. Birds of a certain species, and very colorful, were chirping in the trees around them. They were a bright red with black streaks and a yellow head that gave the illusion that the birds wore masks. Their music was so soothing that Gabriel began to sway back and forth. Soon enough, he had fallen into a deep sleep.

He had never experienced sleep before, but it seemed wonderful to his consciousness. His mind drifted into a dreamlike state. At first, he had visions of home. The streets of Heaven were full of singing and dancing; much like the day he remembered leaving for earth. He found himself walking down Main Street in Jerusalem. Everything was so real: the sights, the sounds, and the familiar angels that were close friends. Every one of his closest friends lined the street. He saw Raphael and Saraqael, Remiel and Raguel, and one of his closest friends, next to Michael, Uriel the Daring. They were waving at him at him, but not one of them had a smile on their face. Their expression was difficult to interpret. Their faces looked blank, if any description was to be used.

Then it dawned on him that everyone was there except for his best friend, the Archangel Michael. He thought, *maybe he's at his house or might he be in the throne room with God?* As he walked, he searched the streets for just a glimpse of the archangel's face. He wanted so much to run through the streets to find his best friend, but his legs wouldn't stray from their path. He had no control over them and, on and on; they took him through the street that seemed endless now. Main Street was never this long, he recalled, still he couldn't get his legs to move off the one way track they were on. As he moved on, he suddenly noticed that Raphael and the rest of the angels had their feet bound in shackles. As he moved on, the faces changed. Now he didn't recognize them as seraphim, but as demons and they were grinning with a devilish smirk. Then he felt a strange sensation against his back. He turned to find a blade held firmly against him.

"Move on, move on," said a voice. "It's time to receive your punishment, Gabriel, friend of God."

"What is the meaning of this," Gabriel shouted. "Where is Michael? Where are the seraphim? When I get a hold of you, demon, my God's wrath will come upon you." Gabriel tried to retaliate but, he couldn't reach around. He felt helpless at the will of the demon.

"God?" The demon heckled." Haven't you heard that your God was overthrown? Lucifer, may he live forever, is lord now."

"Nonsense, there is none more powerful than the LORD of Hosts. The Heavens and earth tremble at his feet, and so will you, vermin," Gabriel snapped back, he couldn't believe his ears.

"Your God's time is over," the demon struck him in the side and spoke arrogantly. "And Michael you speak of. He was captured and killed on Luminarous when an assault was launched against LORD Lucifer's army. As you can see, the forces of Hell were victorious. We raided Heaven and took the throne for Lucifer. With your God locked away in the pit of despair you no longer have any power. That is why you cannot move your legs in any direction other than the one lord Lucifer assigned."

Gabriel was dumbfounded and his lips were speechless.

Was this true, he thought. He soon caught sight of Mount Zion. The throne room was toppled. In its place was a giant heap of rubble and ash and as he got closer, he could make out more and more. First, he noticed a red throne, bright as the color of blood and in it sat a being clothed with a robe of the exact same color. Soon he found his feet ascending the once holy mountain.

Where was God's presence? Gabriel had never felt more alone in his life than now. All was lost. As they reached the pinnacle, he saw more than he wanted to see. He beheld a red dragon, gigantic and hideous, with seven heads and ten horns and each of the horns had a pair of eyes that peered down on Gabriel. Every one of the dragon's heads spoke blasphemes against God and Gabriel noticed a mark at the center of each of its heads. The mark was in fact a number, 666. The red dragon was adorned in chain mail of the finest gold and precious jewels that shimmered and sparkled with each movement or shudder. The huge robust dragon sat before the throne with its leathery wings folded behind its back.

All of this was coming at him so fast. Next he witnessed four abominable beings in place of the four cherubim that once praised God continually with their lips. These beings, although Gabriel had yet to learn about gender, were female and they were scantily clothed, dressed from head to toe with gold and silver bands with red jewels encrusted in them. They danced provocatively for the pleasure of the one who sat on the throne. Finally, Gabriel glared with intensity at the one who now sat on the throne. He was no other than Satan, the prince of darkness.

Suddenly, Gabriel felt a thud against his back.

"Kneel before Lucifer, lord of hosts. Bow infidel," screeched the demon.

Gabriel wanted nothing more than to take Logos and avenge his God, but no sword was at his side and his limbs were useless against the dark power of Satan. The next thing he realized was that he was kneeling before the throne and with his face prostrate to the ground, he could feel the dragon's breath against the back of his neck.

"Hail, hail, the lord of hosts, Lucifer, ruler of Heaven and earth. All must kneel before his might and power," the dragon said and hissed at him.

The feminine creatures that had been dancing around the throne began to move towards him. They surrounded him on all sides and ran their fingers across his shoulders and body. He couldn't move, even though he tried with everything he had. With each disgusting touch from the creatures, he felt more dis-honored and humiliated. He searched deep within himself to find the power to move his limbs for just an ounce of strength to retaliate, but none could be sought out.

The beings whispered profanities in his ear and repulsive sug-gestions. As he remained continuously silent and still, the beings cursed him and the Creator. Tears began to flow from his eyes. From deep inside, an epiphany of defeat consumed his spirit.

"Look at me Gabriel. Look into my eyes and face your sentence," shouted Satan from his throne.

The angel ignored his wretched voice and wept. Lucifer stood and descended the throne. The dragon bowed its head to the floor, making way for Lucifer's last step. Gabriel felt a strong hand grab him by the back of the neck and lift him to his feet. Lucifer's hair was no longer black, but it was now a fiery red; his eyes were lifeless and black. The beauty that was once in him had vanished.

"Would you rather I look different," Satan smirked and transformed.

Now the Archangel Michael stood before Gabriel; his eyes lit up with hope for just a minuscule moment and then his hope vanished. Satan laughed at him, all the while appearing like Michael.

"I think I shall keep this likeness. It fits me well. Don't you agree, Gabriel?"

Gabriel was filled with anger and he spit at the feet of Satan. He couldn't move his arms to attack, so what else was there to do than to spit in disgust. Satan laughed and the beastly dragon did as well. The dragon's laugh sounded nothing like a natural creation of God. The noise it made was mechanical and hideously repulsive to Gabriel.

"Gabriel, that's no way to win my favor," Satan heckled. "If you want to live I suggest you start behaving like one of my slaves, submissive and reverent. At least be civil and grovel at my feet. Beg for your life swine."

Gabriel ignored his haughty words; he was meditating on the Holy Spirit.

"Please be there. Help me my God, do not forsake me," he prayed to himself.

A demon approached the throne. He was tall and menacing with green eyes that were as cold as ice. He had a scroll in his hand.

"Beltezar, I see that you have the seraph's sentence in hand. Give it to the dragon," Satan said.

Beltezar bowed low and like a good puppet, he did as he was

told. The dragon held on to it with his right claw and, before reading from it, he reveled in self-righteousness.

"I Babylon, bringer of pestilence and destruction, maker of miracles, instigator of the mark of the beast, and supreme dragon of Hell, declare the LORD Lucifer's sound wisdom. Let the nations kneel at the king of king's feet, Lucifer, ruler of the heavens and the planets. His power and might have spread on to the four corners of the earth. All men have heard the rumors of his coming and, when he does arrive, every man, woman, and child will receive the mark of the beast. This will be the sign of the New Age, the dawning of Lucifer's reign."

Babylon then unrolled the scroll with his two careless claws and began to read.

"Attention all servants of the true god, Lucifer, lord of hosts, who's dominion shall last for an eternity," the dragon shouted with a thunderous resonance.

"All have heard of the tyranny and treachery of the former lieutenant general of the Host of Heaven, Gabriel. Listen up. The seraph Gabriel's soul has been weighed, his spirit has been measured, and the scales of justice have found him wanting. Therefore, Lucifer, through his sound wisdom and knowledge of evil and good, has come to a decision of judgment."

The beast then gazed at Gabriel, whose head was now down in humility.

"Gabriel, your fate has been decided. Your sentence will be served for a timeless age. You will be imprisoned in a chasm of fire where you will be tortured by the venomous serpents of Hell. Your sentence may be reduced to a mere hundred ages. You only need to kneel before his majesty, Lucifer, king of kings and lord of lords, and declare that he alone is god. What say you Gabriel?"

Gabriel had been focusing in on the Holy Spirit and he heard a still small voice speak to his heart. At first notice, it was too inaudible to perceive, but it began to rise steadily from within his spirit.

"What will it be, Gabriel," shouted the dragon; his voice shook the ground Gabriel stood on.

"Speak the name that is above all names," said a voice inside of the angel.

"What do I speak, LORD? Just tell me and I will shout it with all my might," Gabriel concentrated and whispered. Gabriel's words were loud enough for Lucifer to hear. Lucifer found the look in Gabriel's eyes to be intriguing. He stood from his throne, desiring to have a closer look at Gabriel.

"If you have no answer, I will make you bow. Kneel fool, and receive your punishment," the dragon roared with a booming voice, trying as hard as it could to intimidate the angel.

"Gabriel, speak his name and the enemy will flee," the Holy Spirit shouted within Gabriel. "The name above all names, my son, Jesus." The Son of God's name echoed like resounding thunder.

Courage and hope swept over Gabriel's face. The name was beautiful and majestic. He had heard this name before, but where from? His mind explored the possibilities and it all came back—déjà vu. Maybe he had heard this name in another time and another place? His mind was racing through the possibilities, and he concluded that he must obey the Holy Spirit.

"Speak his name Gabriel," commanded God's voice with great authority.

Gabriel focused his gaze upon Lucifer and all fear vanished from the angel. Lucifer perceived the strength and confidence that was in Gabriel's eyes. Great tension crept over him like a mad disease. Panic began to crawl beneath his skin and he failed to overcome the feeling. The power he thought he possessed dwindled in the shadow of his fear. He could no longer look the angel in the eyes, so he stared at the beast instead and barked orders at him.

"Babylon, kill him now. Kill Gabriel before—"

Gabriel turned his gaze at the dragon. It was too late for Babylon to do anything for Gabriel had opened his mouth.

"Jesus, Son on of the Living God, Deliver me," Gabriel shouted to the rooftops of Heaven.

The beast cringed in pain and Lucifer covered his ears.

"Jesus, come now—rescue me," Gabriel shouted again with all his might.

Lucifer bent over in agony, Babylon collapsed on the ground and, like a corpse, lay deathly still. A single horn fell from his head, shriveled up, and crumbled into dust. The four abominable beings stood by the throne, cowering and covering their ears with their hands. Suddenly, a gigantic angel appeared out of thin air. He was three times larger than the Archangel Michael. He did not stand on the ground with his two feet; he appeared to hover or float. His long black robe moved like it was flowing in a breeze, or as if a continuous wind were passing through it. His entire body glowed in a strange dark light and a name was written on his chest. The name, Thantos, according to the Holy Spirit's interpretation, means Angel of Death. The four abominable beings crowded around Lucifer for protection. Thantos raised his arm, pointed it at Lucifer and spoke aloud. His lips moved not, but the voice that came forth was piercing and terrible.

"Your days are numbered Satan," the angel of death said. "Your life span is ever decreasing. On your judgment day, the one true God will call for me. And when he does, I will take great delight in coming for you. By the authority of the LORD of Hosts, I do declare, how dare you attack his servant, Gabriel, with blasphemous malice. Your evil trickery has been struck down. By the power of the Almighty, your authority has been kept in check and it has been thrown down."

Thantos had a staff in his hand with a large, sharp, curved sickle on the end. He raised it above his head and the four abominable creatures fled from Satan's side. With one quick swoop of his sickle, the angel of death assailed the wretched spirits and they burst into fire and ash. Before the blade could strike Lucifer, he vanished out of sight.

"It is finished," Thantos said with a fierce shout.

The angel of death then looked at Gabriel.

"Waken Gabriel, waken. It is time to wake—time to go," he said soothingly.

"Wake up, Gabriel," Michael urged him and shook him. Finally, he came around.

"How long was I out," Gabriel asked. He looked somewhat incoherent.

"What do you mean in saying, how long," Michael said, looking at him incredulously. "Your eyes have been closed for no less than a few moments. I woke you because I heard a disturbing noise in the jungle and I thought you should know about it. I think I saw the origin of the sound, at least I think so. I noticed a black blur flying across the jungle floor. It made little noise and when it completely stopped, for only a split-second, I saw that it was a long black creature on four legs, but that is about all I could distinguish."

Two things were going through Gabriel's mind. One was the dream or vision he experienced, but the details were fading fast and soon enough he would lose memory of what had happened in his dream. The other thought started to move to the forefront of his mind. Could the creature Michael saw be the same one he encountered only a day ago?

"Did you notice anything else about the creature," Gabriel said. "Two large yellow eyes by chance."

"Why yes, it was only for a split-second, but its eyes were yellow. That I am sure of," Michael recalled, staring intently at him.

"Then it is as I thought," Gabriel said.

"What do you mean, Gabe," Michael asked with a very curious expression.

"It may well be—" Gabriel uttered. "—the same creature that stared me down, only yesterday."

"Tell me more," Michael said with intrigue. He was eager to find out.

"I believe the creature was a panther. He came awfully close to me—too close for comfort," Gabriel remarked.

"Now that I think about it, it could very well have been a panther," Michael said with some certainty.

"If it is the same panther, we should have nothing to fear," Gabriel asserted.

"What makes you say that," Michael asked. His eyes beamed with fascination.

"The panther could have attacked me if it wanted to," Gabriel said. "In fact, I was prepared for a fierce fight. I had one hand on Logos and the other ready to slug the beast, should it have come too near. Instead, the creature stared at me with huge yellow eyes; it was showing me it meant no harm. Truly, the animal was smarter than I thought. Perhaps it would have even let me pet its head if I desired to. Though, it was clever enough to notice my defensive stance and, not to mention, Logos by my side."

"Nevertheless, we should keep a lookout for this panther," Michael suggested. "You look different to me, Gabe. You look worn out, like you've been in a battle."

"That is something else I must share with you. Where do I begin ... " Gabe said before his face turned into a blank stare.

"What's wrong Gabe," Michael said with concern.

"Why can't I remember," Gabe uttered. "It's like my mind is on the very brink of remembering, yet I can't recall a single thing." His thoughts or lack thereof were deeply troubling him.

"What do you mean?" Michael was flabbergasted. "Gabe, you're making no sense. No sense at all."

"I know, I know, but if I could only remember," Gabriel said, while both of his hands pinched his temples. He was in deep concentration.

"Then stop for a moment," Michael suggested. "Don't trouble yourself to such extents. Did you ever think that maybe you're not supposed to remember?"

"Well no. Maybe I didn't have a vision after all," Gabriel pondered.

"Or, maybe you did," Michael said. "Don't question his ways, for they are higher than ours."

"Right you are and, not to mention, they're mysterious," Gabriel said. His voice resonated joy and confidence instead of doubt.

"He is all-powerful and all-knowing. And I feel him telling us to get moving," Michael said with a smile. Gabriel smiled.

"Then by all means—let's go," Gabe said.

The angels continued on their quest for the enemy's lair.

Saul and Baal were hot on their trail. They were still a few earth-miles behind, but they were aggressively in pursuit. The demon and his wolf had just passed through a small pasture and Baal came to a sudden halt at the edge of a strange forest. Here the undergrowth progressively thickened with palms and shrubs that grew snuggly close to one another. Saul could easily make out the path the seraphim had taken. Michael and Gabriel had cut down many branches and vines as they had hiked through many moments ago.

The wolf sniffed the air, snarled in a low menacing growl and didn't move. Baal's ears drew back and the hairs on his back stood on end.

"What is it now Baal," Saul grumbled. "We mustn't stop for anything. We're getting closer. I can feel it."

The wolf acted as if the demon wasn't there. He was in his natural element and his instinct took over; he had ignored Saul's every word.

"Even an elephant could travel the path these angels have left," Saul said, exaggerating of course, as he peered down the path.

"What fools," added Saul with a sinister laugh. "It's almost as if they wish to be your dinner Baal."

The wolf paid no attention to the demon. Saul turned red with anger.

"Well, I've tried the nice way," Saul said and kicked Baal in the side. "Get moving, you filthy mutt."

Baal snarled and snapped at his hand, a fair warning not to try that again and he was serious. Saul pulled his hand away and, at the same moment, he took notice of something moving fast through the jungle. It was long, with broad shoulders, and jet black in color. Baal took two steps forward, barked, and then growled. The creature was standing about two-dozen paces away. Saul could make out two huge yellow eyes peering at them.

"Now Baal, there's no need to get in a tussle here. Stay your ground and the panther will leave," Saul said nervously.

Baal dug its feet in and howled. The panther moved closer and made a low rumbling noise. The sound was like a growl, but even more intimidating. The panther turned itself around and disappeared into the thick undergrowth. Baal's ears popped back up and the hair on his back turned down.

"He delivers a message," the wolf whispered. "He says, stop now and turn back. Danger follows the angels and if we pursue them, death will surely befall us."

Saul remained silent for a moment.

"I have thought it over. Let's keep moving forward," said the demon.

The wolf didn't budge from where he stood.

"But master, we shouldn't go any further unless you desire death," Baal pleaded.

Saul kicked him before he could speak any further. The wolf howled.

"Stupid mutt, you're a wretched and useless thing. You will keep moving. This whole island belongs to lord Lucifer and all obey his command. That includes you, Baal," Saul yelled, and kicked Baal in the side and for his efforts received a nasty bite in the leg from the untamed wolf.

"Ouch," screeched Saul.

Baal took off and fled out of sight into the forest across the pasture.

"Who needs you anyway, Baal you stupid fool," Saul shouted, he was furious. "I can track the angels without help from your worthless hide."

What Saul was forgetting, though, was Baal's ability to see in the pitch-black night and without the aid of the wolf's night vision, he would be as blind as a bat. The demon's anger became his source for energy that drove him down the path; his evil longing for promotion fueled his pursuit of the seraphim. The inevitable soon came to pass. The sunset and it grew dark beneath the jungle canopy. Under such unfavorable lighting conditions, he virtually couldn't see his own hand in front of him. A seed of fear sprouted in his mind and it increased and expanded until it had permeated his entire being, terror walked freely in the passages of his mind and the corridors of his thoughts. He couldn't escape the feeling of helplessness and panic had overtaken him. Then out of the corner of his ear, he heard a rustling in the leaves.

"Baal, are you out there," he whispered for the wolf. "Baal is that you?"

A moment went by with no answer.

"Is that you Baal," Saul cried into the dark.

No answer. There was plenty of silence. Too much for a usual night in the jungle on Luminarous. Out of desperation he crouched in a fetal position. The trees near him cracked and bowed and the ground beneath him trembled.

"No," Saul screeched in horror.

Meanwhile, the seraphim were creeping along in the darkness at a stagnant pace. The undergrowth was extremely overcrowded with thorny vines and prickly bushes. The air was humid. Strange noises intermittingly startled them. From time to time, they could hear a roar or two in the distance. At one point, a low growl sounded within a few paces of them and to their backs. Whatever made the noise seemed as if it was taunting them. Michael was in the front and Gabriel had his back to him as they moved pace by pace and as quietly as they could. Nothing could be distinguished in the dark, yet with Logos drawn, Gabriel was prepared to slash at any attacker.

Michael led the way and his Sword of the Spirit was in hand. Anything that approached from the front would meet his sword before him and the same could go for any threat to the rear post Gabriel provided. Each time they heard the growl it was somewhere new and different, so needless to say they could never make out the origin of the noise nor did they stop to investigate. Instead they prayed silently, each to oneself, for protection and guidance in the dark. Soon the growling ceased and to their relief, the noise of insects chirping was all that could be heard. *The enemy will flee at the name of the LORD*, Gabriel thought.

Their strenuously sluggish hike was becoming too taxing on their bodies. They had traveled for what seemed like another thousand paces when Michael felt a giant palm leaf strike his face. When he lowered the palm branch, he discovered a vast opening in the jungle. What relief he felt. When he let go of the leaf it nearly smacked Gabriel in the face. Michael walked forward and nearly stumbled over a fallen tree. The moonlight illuminated everything so intensely that they were able to behold the entire opening in a single glance. The clearing was quite large and Gabriel estimated it to be about five hundred paces across. A giant redwood tree laid fallen right in the middle and its unfortunate demise also brought about the destruction of dozens of other trees.

"Here is a good place to rest," Michael said, taking a seat on top of the fallen redwood. Gabriel rested next to him and felt instant relief. He dangled his feet in the air. The cool night air felt wonderful on his aching toes. Michael did the same.

"How do you think this tree came to fall on the jungle floor?" Gabriel asked.

"I'm not sure. Do you notice all the others? Look over there," Michael replied and pointed in the direction of dozens of toppled trees all in a row.

"All the trees are leaning in the same direction. It appears that something's knocked them over," he added.

"Well, the trees didn't fall on their own, that's something we can be sure of," Gabriel remarked. "It's very unusual. The trees are cut in a straight line with a very specific pattern."

Michael's eyes were very tired at this point. He caught himself dozing off.

"Sorry Gabe ... I just can't seem to keep my eyes open. They're getting heavy."

"You rest. I'll keep watch," Gabriel insisted.

"No, no, that wouldn't be fair of me. You need sleep just as badly," Michael said. Though with his last word, his eyes closed and he reclined against a large branch.

"That's it. Get some rest. I'll keep guard," Gabriel said.

The archangel was fast asleep. Gabriel rose from his seat and walked around the opening. He wanted to explore the territory, but he also wanted to keep himself awake. He knew if he sat still long enough, sleep would inevitably set in. The dream he had before was nearly wiped from his memory, but the fear it had caused was fresh on his mind. Although he couldn't recall the details, he remembered the vision was disturbing.

"Maybe the LORD wiped it from my mind," he thought out loud. "But why would he do so?"

"Don't worry about what you have no control over," God spoke to his heart. "Do not be anxious about the past, Gabriel, but look to the present. My presence will heal you. Draw near to me and I will draw near to you."

Gabriel gazed into the night sky. The stars were twinkling. Each of them was shining with all they had for the glory of their

Creator. Gabriel fell to his knees and worshiped Father God. As Gabriel worshiped, he did not take notice that a few creatures emerged from the surrounding jungle. The animals were curious to see an angel. An antelope came forth, along with a gazelle and her two fawns. A small boar came out of the woods, followed by its father boar, a giant boar with huge tusks. There was a lioness, and her cub close by her side. Gabriel didn't notice any of them until he returned his gaze to the ground, just in time to witness a large black panther staring him in the eyes from only a few paces away. The creature was sitting erect and its eyes were staring straight through him. He reached for Logos; the panther gave a low growl and vanished like a ghost. The other creatures didn't move at all. Gabriel looked upon every one of the animals. He was astonished at their gestures. They all approached him one by one as if to greet him. The angel welcomed them.

"You must be friends of God," he exclaimed as he gently patted the lioness on the back. Her cub purred and rubbed against his leg and he laughed.

"Michael must see this. Come and greet my friend," he said to the animals.

He figured they might understand. They started to follow him, until a low rumble vibrated the ground beneath their feet. Gabriel looked at the antelope as its eyes grew huge, and then it darted swiftly into the forest. One by one each of the animals ran off.

The rumbling had ceased and silence was all around him. No rustling of the leaves could be heard, not a single disturbance. The noise of insects calling to one another ceased. Then there was another rumble, followed by a bigger vibration in the ground. Then a foreboding silence settled on the jungle once again.

Gabriel ran to the archangel's side.

"Wakeup. Wakeup, Michael," Gabriel whispered and nudged him.

"What is it?" Michael said, rubbing his eyes. "How long have I been asleep?"

"Maybe an earth-hour, maybe more or maybe less. I don't know," Gabriel said nervously.

"What did you wake me for," said Michael, impatiently.

"I heard something," Gabriel snapped back.

"What did you hear," Michael inquired, still groggy.

Gabriel looked busy searching the jungle perimeter.

"Well, what is it? What'd you hear?" Michael looked fully awake.

"I heard something, a rum—" spoke Gabriel until he was interrupted by another small earthquake.

"There's no time to run," Michael said, now fully awake. "We must take cover."

Another fierce tremble shook the ground.

The two seraphim jumped behind the tree and hid in between two huge tree branches. The earth shook again and again and then again.

"The beast is getting closer," Gabriel stated. A nervous tension was in his tone.

"Fear not Gabe. Prepare your heart for battle, prepare your spirit for victory," whispered Michael, with zeal.

A blanket of clouds smothered the moon and gave the angels cover.

"He sends his protection," Michael looked up and observed.

"I see," Gabriel said. A mighty confidence flowed in his words.

Everything around them grew invisible; the darkness was thick and blinding. The rumbling sound intensified and it became more and more apparent that the monster was drawing closer and closer. Then they finally heard it. The sound of the ground splitting open echoed through the air and pierced both of their ears making them ring annoyingly. The monster manifested itself with a fiery blaze. A ball of fire shot over their heads and incinerated a tree behind them. Then they both heard something that sounded like someone screaming and yelling. It dawned on them that the ball of fire wasn't intended for them; instead it was aimed at someone else, perhaps an angel or even a demon.

They sat motionless in the pitch-blackness awaiting the monster's next move and listening for any more spine-chilling screams. Michael had his hand on the hilt of his sword. Gabriel held Logos tightly with both hands. Sweat rolled down Michael's cheeks. Gabriel's heart was pounding with the anticipation of a fight. Someone was definitely running. They could hear footsteps scurrying through the leaves. There was a sound of pursuit and the thunderous sound of the monster's feet pounding against the soft ground. Then a shriek rang out, followed by a blood-curdling scream. The monster had caught its prey. Gabriel crouched low under the tree to look. A blaze of fire flashed and, for a mere moment, he saw what looked like two feet dangling in the air and two huge armored feet dug securely into the ground.

"We must do something," Gabriel whispered, wincing at the sight.

"We must and we will," Michael answered. "Wait for the perfect moment."

"We can't wait much longer," Gabriel whispered out of frustration. "Soon Michael, we must act fast."

Michael nodded as another ball of fire shot over their heads. Surprisingly the monster's prey wasn't dead, they could hear the sound of feet stumbling across the forest floor.

"Help me. God save me," cried a voice.

"Now, Gabriel. Create a diversion. Run across—" and that is all Michael could say before Gabriel took off like a cheetah. He ran out into the open and immediately he had to hit the ground on all fours. A flaming ball of fire grazed his back.

The following transpired rapidly. Words are slow and I warn you, it is unpleasant to bear and certainly not meant for the faint of heart.

Gabriel stood to his feet and saw the monster holding, in its grasp, the shriveled form of an angel. Its green eyes locked Gabriel in its sight and it tossed its prey aside. The angel lay lifeless on the ground.

"Come and get me you foul beast, if you dare," Gabriel yelled and ran in front of the fallen redwood. "You will taste Logos and die."

The monster chased after him.

"Take courage Michael. Move now and I will deliver you," Michael heard the LORD speak to his heart.

"To the glory of the Most High," the archangel shouted with all his might.

The giant beast jumped in the air and spread its wings. It had locked on its target and it was about to pounce on Gabriel. Michael was running with full speed along the length of the fallen red wood. He leaped into the air and landed on the monster. With the Sword of the Spirit he cut through one of its wings as if it was sheer cloth. The beast lost its balance in midair and toppled to the forest floor. Gabriel rolled on the ground beneath the redwood. The monster let a ferocious roar and Michael dismembered its other wing.

"You can't get away now you filthy creature," Gabriel said.

He jumped out from under the tree just as Michael plunged his sword deep into its scaly hide. Gabriel took Logos and, with one swift swing, the monster's head dropped to the ground. Within mere moments of its death, the monster spontaneously burst into flames and disintegrated into a smoldering heap of ashes.

"Wow, that's something you don't see everyday," Gabriel exclaimed.

"You're telling me, Gabe," Michael said, out of breath. "By the grace and mercy of God we're still alive."

Gabriel searched for the injured angel. He was lying deathly still in the same spot as before. They quickly walked over to him. When they got there, they could see he was breathing.

"He's alive." exclaimed Gabriel.

"We must pray for him. That is his only hope," Michael said. His eyes filled with compassion.

Suddenly, the moonlight shone down. The clouds moved and they could see the angel's face. It was black and bruised, indistinguishable and beyond recognition. He tried to open his eyes, but he barely managed to crack open one eyelid.

"Michael…Gabriel is that you?" he said in a low, solemn voice.

"Yes," they both replied and looked at each other, wondering who this was.

"Who might you be—most unfortunate one?" Michael asked. He leaned over and grabbed the angel's hand.

"My name is Saul," he said, coughing to clear his throat. "I am grateful to you both for rescuing me from that dreadful monster."

"Saul, what business did you have with the beast?" Michael asked.

"The monster was neither an ally nor a foe. He was much too wild for me to control…" Saul said, pausing to cough. "You did a great justice. For the monster has killed many allies of God and it's fed on the flesh of my brothers ever since we've been in this forsaken realm."

"He's a demon—a traitor. Give me the word and I'll finish him off," Gabriel snapped in anger.

"Calm down brother. At least, let's hear what Saul has to say," Michael said sternly. His eyes gleamed with a serious light under the moon.

The demon wanted to speak, but it was a struggle just to open his mouth.

"Thanks to you, Michael and Gabriel, now the feared beast's dominion has ended. Please—" Saul uttered and coughed up some blood. "Trust me ... I don't want to be the enemy."

"Sure, he says that now. When his spirit is fading," Gabriel blurted out.

"Let him speak Gabriel. Show some courtesy. A little respect wouldn't hurt you," Michael said.

"Courtesy? Respect?" Gabriel said in a skeptical tone. "Those words are of no value to demons," he added under his breath.

"Please hear me out," Saul looked at them both and said. "I fear I made the wrong decision by turning from the LORD. I am a traitor and I deserved what the beast did to me. I am but a mere shadow of what I once was in Heaven. The awful thing is that I vaguely remember what my life was like in Heaven. My mind is poisoned with the thoughts of my miserable existence as a demon. I've felt nothing. Torment and hatred has consumed my spirit every second of every day since my fall from grace, from Heaven."

Dawn crept over the trees and a faint amount of light swept across the forest floor. Saul's face now glowed in a vibrantly deep orange color as did the vast opening they were in. Michael and Gabriel were astonished at what Saul had said and at how his appearance was beginning to change.

"It is neither I nor Gabriel that can offer you forgiveness, nor can we judge you. These things are completely in God's hands," Michael softly said with compassion in his voice.

"I have despised my life as a demon," Saul sincerely said. "I have lived my life for a wicked master and given my spirit over to the evil one. I want peace in my spirit. I need the LORD."

With his face turned upward to Heaven and tears flowing profusely from his eyes, he summoned all the breath he had left in him.

"Please forgive me, LORD. I want to serve the one and only true God, the LORD Almighty. I need you, Father," Saul uttered, spending all of his strength.

They couldn't believe their ears at what they were hearing. Though, both of them felt pure joy and vitality from just being a witness to this incredible conversion. What happened next was both bizarre and beautiful to watch. Saul's expression completely changed. The darkness of evil lifted from his face and a new light replaced the darkness. His appearance was no longer characteristically wicked and demented, but his face now had a handsome and serene quality. Michael and Gabriel were overwhelmed at this transformation from evil to righteousness and it seemed to transpire in a brief instant. The aging effects of hatred and malice that had wrinkled his face were suddenly removed. He looked younger, even under his broken and bruised face.

Saul with his eyes gazed toward the heavens, smiled a brilliantly sweet smile and breathed his last breath. A moment passed brief enough for a single heartbeat and then a small sphere of light came forth out of Saul's mouth. The sphere of light was his spirit and it hovered over his body.

"Thank you. Thank you, Michael and Gabriel," a voice said from within the sphere. It was Saul.

Then the sphere shot into the sky, blending perfectly with the stars, and it sailed across the galaxy until it was completely out of sight.

"What will happen to him," Gabriel asked, still staring at the twinkling stars.

"Only the Father knows. He will do what is right in his infinite wisdom," replied Michael.

"Wisdom—yes of course; but I feel that it is the LORD's compassion and grace that can save Saul."

"Saul's going to need all that he can get," Michael said and patted Gabriel on the shoulder.

"I can't help but feel that we haven't seen the last of Saul,"

Gabriel's words rolled off his tongue with awe and wonder. It was hope, though, that produced those words.

"It's interesting you should say that, Gabe, because I was just thinking the same thing," Michael remarked.

"Must I remind you, we are closer than brothers," Gabriel said with a hint of humor. "By now, you should've figured out that we're prone to saying what the other is thinking."

"Yes, maybe I should, but why waste my time trying. How can I forget when you're always reminding me?" Michael said and smiled.

Gabriel grinned and laughed a little, so did Michael.

Their laughter was soon silenced from something totally unanticipated. A bright light flashed across the night sky. It shone more intensely than Saul's light that had just ascended moments ago and Michael knew that it was not his spirit returning. Gabriel had other suspicions and his right hand clung securely to Logos' hilt. The light descended rapidly and it was upon them. The light hovered right above the ground, only feet from the two seraphim that stood speechless in its presence. The light took form, and Michael's hopes were fulfilled.

"Elijah," Michael exclaimed.

"Welcome chief of messengers," Gabriel added.

The chief messenger greeted them with a bow. His halo emanated an immensely bright glow and its luminosity created an illusion of dancing shadows—the result of the trees that projected shadows on the forest floor as they swayed to and fro in the wind. Words cannot begin to describe the entire beauty of the scene. Michael and Gabriel awaited patiently the message from Elijah. He was in the midst of finding the correct parchment with the report from Heaven. He didn't take very long this time. Elijah unrolled the scroll.

"Praise be to God for Babylon, the dragon has been slain," Elijah read with a bold clear voice. "The Most High sends word that he watched and waited for the exact moment. In his precise timing you, Archangel Michael and you Gabriel, were filled with his supernatural strength to defeat the wicked Babylon. By his power you were victorious. He has delivered you from the hand of evil."

Elijah then pulled a scroll from his robe and handed it to the archangel. Michael eagerly received it.

"My instructions were to give you this message, and yes, I was supposed to tell you one other thing..." Elijah's voice trailed off. He had lost his memory for a moment, an uncharacteristic lapse in the chief messenger's usual sharp wittedness.

"Ah yes, I remember now. Do not open it yet," Elijah said and right before Michael was about to unravel the parchment.

"That's it. Roll it back up, nice and neat," Elijah said. "Use the discernment of the Holy Spirit. He will reveal to you the time and the place to open it. It is for your own good, Archangel Michael."

"Hey—over here Elijah; any messages for me," Gabriel cleared his throat and said.

"None other than the one you have already received," the chief messenger replied.

"Ok, now that we've cleared that up," Gabriel nodded and said. "Will you at least do me and Michael the liberty of informing us where we are on this deathly island?"

"I was not instructed to give you that information," Elijah smiled nicely and said.

"Elijah, anything will suffice," Gabriel grinned and entreated him. "Even just a hint will do, please."

"You never know when the enemy is watching," Elijah came near and whispered. "I do not know your exact location. However, during my descent I did notice a large mass of demons gathered many thousands of paces in that direction," he said and pointed due northwest.

"How many," Michael asked.

"Hard to tell from such a great distance. They appeared as ants on the ground," Elijah said and shook his head *no*. "I've already said too much. I'm not supposed to be telling you any of this. I was only meant to deliver God's message of victory and that was it. Now I'm getting in over my head."

"God is merciful and our quest is difficult," Michael urged him. "Gabriel and I could use all the help we can get."

"Judging by the height from which I viewed the legion it was hard to tell how many," he whispered. "If you truly need my help, then I won't abandon my fellow angels. After all, there is the code we are to abide by."

Gabriel and Michael nodded in agreement.

"I estimate their numbers to be in the thousands. Maybe two thousand, maybe three, or possibly more," Elijah continued. "As I said, the distance was great between me and the enemy and to add to it, I was traveling at an immeasurable speed."

"Thank you for telling us—I think," said Gabriel

"Yes, you were brave to share that with us. We sincerely thank you. The demons might be too many for us, but what are their numbers compared to the power of the Most High," Michael said gratefully and Gabriel agreed.

"True, but I feel that information was too much to share. That is why I received no instructions from Heaven to do so. I must ask your forgiveness for honoring the code above the command of the LORD. I will leave now and ask for mercy from the LORD."

"Wait, Elijah. I take full responsibility," Michael said sincerely.

"Not if I take it from you, brother. I will carry the burden," Gabriel insisted.

"That is kind of you both, but it was my choice," Elijah bowed and said. "Please stay the course and do not stray from the path. May the LORD protect you and his Holy Spirit guide you. Go in strength and go in peace brothers."

He transformed back into a pillar of light and ascended into the morning sky.

"Oh King of Kings and LORD of LORDS, take care of them. May it be your will, my LORD that I return to them once more as your messenger," Elijah prayed as he traveled through the galaxy.

THE POOL

NOTE FROM THE SCRIBE...

I would ask you to stop reading right now and pray for them, but of what use would that be? What you have read took place countless ages ago. However, their quest can serve as a reminder to you that you should pray for the Archangel and Gabriel. In fact, pray for all of the seraphim of Heaven. For as you are reading these words, they are somewhere on earth (or in the heavens), defending the universe against the forces of the evil one. And they will be fighting the good fight until the race is finished, until the prophecies of the Book of the Seven Seals are fulfilled and finished. Then and only then will they rest and receive their reward.

Once again, I tell you the enemy has many tricks up their sleeves and they plan on using as many of them as it will take to destroy Michael and Gabriel. God is not blind to the actions of the enemy, nor does he turn the other cheek.

The Warrior Within...

The dawn had ushered in the light of God's holy presence with Elijah's visit, but the messenger had long since left, and with him, the peaceful presence of God. They hadn't spoken to one another since Elijah's departure. At this point, many things were going through Michael's head. He was contemplating their course, but his mind began to wonder to other thoughts—dangerous thoughts—thoughts that could even lead to questioning God's authority. That indeed is hallowed ground and only God can go there. For his ways are higher than ours and never to be questioned. Not seraphim, not man, and the Archangel Michael are definitely no exception. He realized this and managed to maintain his spiritual composure through nothing other than prayer.

Gabriel was preparing himself for a fight and a big one at that. The number of legions that Elijah had reported observing burdened his mind with constant worry.

How can I protect Michael from legions upon legions of demons? Gabriel wondered. *How can I save Michael from certain death? I am only one seraph; how can I preserve the mission without Michael,* his mind pondered. *What would become of Heaven and earth if I failed the LORD,* he thought. Gabriel was tormented with fear and doubt. Only yesterday his life had been saved from the clutches of death and, now he was on the verge of doubting the power of God.

"Gabe, do not fear the unknown, but have faith in what we do know," Michael said reassuringly. "He will never leave us or forsake us." It was easy for him to see that something had been troubling Gabe.

"I appreciate your words, but I'm feeling much better now," Gabriel's voice showed courage as he said. "God spoke to my heart. He said to take courage and that he is with us always and forever."

"Elijah's report could be disheartening if we took it the wrong way," Gabriel added. "That is, if we were to face a legion of demons alone on Luminarous, but you know as well as I that isn't the case. Not only is God fighting alongside us, but also there are allies here to help us. I've seen them Michael."

"Allies? Tell me more." Michael looked thrilled.

"While you were sleeping, there were about a dozen that came to visit: a boar the size of a tiger, a gazelle, and an antelope. There was also a lioness and her cub. Then there was this particular animal. I've seen him before—the panther."

"Really," Michael queried. "Do you think it could be the same panther I saw in the forest?"

"I don't know," Gabe said. "But I do know there was something unusual about this one. I was praying when I noticed the panther standing a few paces in front of me. Its huge yellow eyes peered straight into my soul and its face appeared to be wiser than the common animal. It was quite amazing. Well, up until the point I reached for Logos."

"Why did you do that?" Michael looked baffled.

"If you had seen its giant claws shining like ivory knifes in the moonlight, you would have done the same thing. I was only being cautious. Anyway, the movement I made startled him and the panther vanished into the jungle. Somehow, I feel it meant no harm."

"Did the other animals seem to notice him," Michael asked.

"I don't know. At least, I don't think so. It happened all too fast. Why do you ask?"

"Just thought it was interesting, that's all," answered Michael.

"Wait, now that I think of it," Gabriel pondered for a moment and added, "I do recall that the other animals formed a circle around me, but not until the panther had gone. Maybe it's a coincidence."

"I don't think so," Michael shook his head and said. "Gabe it was no coincidence. I think he has been following us. Without making it obvious, glance behind me to the left of the red palm tree."

"What is it? I don't see anything," Gabriel whispered as he bobbed his head side to side, trying to get a good look.

"I said, take a glance. I didn't say study the tree," Michael said with a stern tone; he creased his brow.

"Sorry. I guess I haven't mastered the art of glancing," Gabriel whispered back, patronizing him.

"Never mind," Michael said, irritated with him at this point.

"Wait just a moment…I think I see him. Yes. I do," Gabriel exclaimed in astonishment.

"Hush. Don't startle the creature. I think he means no harm. But it wouldn't hurt to find out what he's up to," Michael said. He was becoming more curious about the creature.

"How do you suggest we do that," Gabriel said. "It seems like a precarious task, if you ask me."

"Walk with me, Gabe, and I will tell you," Michael whispered. "Slowly follow me and make no sudden movements."

"Act natural, Gabe. Don't look behind you," Michael persisted, since Gabriel had glanced over his shoulder.

The seraphim moved forward slowly and nonchalantly. Michael kept the animal in his peripheral vision and it was clear that the panther was sitting motionless. Then, without hesitating, the panther flew into the jungle. The mysterious creature leaped into the air and onto a tree limb. The panther instantly camouflaged into the background.

"He's out of sight," Michael supposed.

"Then why are we whispering," Gabriel remarked.

"Quiet. Keep moving. Trust me," Michael shoved his hand over his friend's mouth and whispered.

"Do you think this is the work of the dragon, Babylon," Gabriel asked. They were now traveling straight down the path that had been formed by the toppled trees.

"It's conceivable," Michael replied. "But why go to such great efforts?"

Gabriel grinned and laughed to himself.

"What do you find so humorous," Michael asked with a serious tone to his voice.

"You said great efforts," Gabriel said, looking at him with disbelief. "By chance, did you catch the size of that monster? Cutting down a tree might take some effort for you or me, but for that mammoth dragon, I think not. Truly, its tail alone could have cut the trees down."

"I witnessed the dragon nearly slice you in half with its tail," he added, pointing to some fallen trees. "Yes, you dodged it perfectly, but if there had been just a slight hesitation in your timing, you could have been good as dead."

"The dragon didn't whip its tail at me. Yes, our fight might have been traumatizing, but I think I would have remembered that." Michael pointed out and added with a sarcastic tone, "Maybe you hallucinated."

"Actually, what I saw didn't happen in this last fight. It happened—" Gabriel said before Michael interrupted.

"You mean to say that you were standing idly by while

Babylon nearly made a meal out of me," Michael remarked contentiously. "How long were you standing by before you decided to jump in and help?"

"It's not exactly as you say," Gabriel responded. "You see, when I heard the dragon's roar that got my attention, but when I heard you yell that really got my attention. I thought I've already explained this."

"No, a matter of fact you didn't but continue. As you were," Michael said with a clever grin.

"Alright then, where was I? Yes, I was telling you that I heard a cry for help. I knew that had to be you. I ran as fast as my legs would take me. I think I covered two thousand paces in a mere matter of earth-seconds," he exaggerated. "When I arrived I scurried down the path by the waterfall. The path led to a ledge and that is where I saw the dragon swinging its tail right for your head."

"Okay, I know how you got there," Michael interrupted. "But how long did you stand there?"

"Maybe an earth minute, maybe two. I don't know," Gabriel said, irritably. "As I was saying, I timed my jump with precise accuracy. It was my efforts that saved your life."

"Who was it that almost drowned," uttered Michael, now agitated.

"Wasn't it you that nearly got eaten," Gabriel said, raising his voice. "Yes, I think it was. If I hadn't intervened you could have been done for."

"Oh, I think I could have handled the situation myself," Michael retorted, now visibly angry. "As for you, if I hadn't jumped in the water and pulled your drowning body to the surface in time, you could have been done for."

"You are impossible. I was your saving grace and you know it," Gabriel shouted.

"You were my saving grace," Michael quickly countered. "On the contrary, I believe I was your saving grace."

"This quest seems to be far too big for the two of us. Maybe I should take my own path, because danger seems to be drawn to you like bees to honey," Gabriel remarked with a spiteful expression written across his face.

"Not me, but you," Michael insisted. "For danger needs no

bidding to run to you. As for the quest, you are right about that. The way isn't big enough for the two of us. And I'll tell you why. Your ego-inflated head has simply grown too big. Your head alone takes up enough room to cover the entire path. There's clearly no room for me on your path—quite literally."

Michael's harsh words struck Gabriel like a knife.

"I guess I'll be taking my own path. In fact, I think that's the best idea I've had since I've been on this God-forsaken island. No, I know it's the best idea," Gabriel struck back and, like in a dual, the archangel knew he had to pack a bigger punch.

"Go your own way, choose your own path, but before you go I think you should hear the truth," Michael snapped back. "It's not the island that's forsaken, but it's you, Gabriel."

Gabriel ran ahead of him in a heated frenzy.

"Run Gabriel. Run away," shouted Dissension.

"Forget him Michael. He only drags you down," Resentment came near to Michael and whispered cold words into his ear. "You don't need him. In fact, you never did. He's been a stumbling block to you all along, keeping you from fulfilling your destiny. He always held you back."

Resentment and Dissension were satisfied with their work so far.

"I feel much better now. I should have taken care of him from the start," Michael said to himself. The Ruah's persuasive speech worked its way into Michael's ego first and, like poison flowing in his veins, the words slowly made their way into his heart.

Resentment flew after Gabriel and Dissension stayed close by the archangel's side.

"It feels good to be free of such a burden. The Father will be pleased with you, very pleased," the Ruah whispered, soothingly, into Michael's ear.

Resentment soon caught up to Gabriel and fed him vicious thoughts of hatred.

"You can find Luminarous without him," Resentment spoke manipulatively, using a pleasing tone. "You never needed him. He only used you, Gabriel. He wants nothing more than to take all the credit for a job that, you know well you did on your own. He was always a thorn in your side and to think you called him your best friend. He never was anything of the sort. You know what he truly is; you see past his superficial façade. A scoundrel is what he truly is. He's self-absorbed, pompous, egotistical, spiteful, and the list goes on and on. Don't waste your time thinking about him. Instead, dwell on how God will praise you when you return with Luminarous. He'll promote you to commander of the Host of Heaven. And if Michael is lucky enough to make it off this island alive, then he'll be your servant, as low in rank as a dog."

The Ruah's words were like fuel for Gabriel's anger. He became driven to run harder. He turned and ran off the beaten path. He hadn't gone far when, out of nowhere, the panther appeared standing on a large rock. Gabriel tried to stop his feet and lost his balance. He fell helplessly onto his rear end. The jet-black animal stared down the angel. It stood its ground and growled with a low menacing growl.

"My work here is done," Resentment hissed as it spoke.

The Ruah fled the scene and called out to its partner Dissension to come along. The panther looked menacing as it glared at Gabriel, as if it was ready to tear him to shreds.

"I guess I was wrong about you, creature. Your heart is black," said Gabriel, petrified with fear and the panther could sense it.

"Michael. Save me," Gabriel shouted out of desperation.

Michael was hundreds of paces off, but still near enough to hear his cry for help. He sprung into action. His feet ran swiftly through the jungle.

"Michael, help!" Gabriel cried.

The panther was reared back on its hind legs, preparing to attack with its posterior arched up in the air; it was in perfect position for the kill. Without flinching or even hesitating, the beast suddenly gave in to its primal instinct and pounced. The panther flew through the air, it led with its claws and its long strong torso was stretched out to balance its weight. Gabriel rolled over just in time. The creature missed him and landed nimbly on its paws. Gabriel jumped to his feet and drew Logos from its sheath. The blade shined magnificently in the sun's rays. The panther stole a glance and then darted into the jungle.

"Run all you want. I'm coming for you panther," Gabriel

exclaimed, and took off in pursuit of the beast. Surprisingly enough, he found his legs keeping pace with the animal's strides.

"It's your turn to be the prey," he said as he ran.

Michael heard his voice and sprinted in his direction.

The panther dodged tree after tree, as agile as a gazelle in stride. Gabriel was gaining on it. Then the animal turned suddenly and sprung a dozen paces into the air, landing gracefully onto a large clearing. Gabriel's pursuit had been delayed, since he had tripped over a tree root. Fortunately, for him and not so much for the panther, the ground was soft from an earlier shower. And as Gabriel lay prone on the ground, he could clearly see the panther's paw prints in the earth. He regained his footing and tracked down the panther.

Michael caught up to him and was running by his side.

"What are we chasing," Michael asked in the midst of running.

"The panther," Gabriel strained to shout from being winded.

They ran side by side, with equal strides. A small ravine was just ahead of them; they gathered their strength and hurdled over it. They hadn't seen it before they jumped, but a downward slope was waiting for them on the other side. They hit the ground rolling, and found themselves lying flat on their backs.

Blue sky was overhead, for they were in a clearing quite spacious, in fact, and with a very bizarre centerpiece that immediately grabbed their attention. In the middle of the small meadow, stood a twisted pile of tree trunks, tree limbs, dried grass and other natural rubble.

"A nest," Michael guessed.

"Forget the nest. Look what's standing on it," Gabriel pointed and said.

On the rim of the nest and sitting upright, straight as a board, was the panther. The panther didn't blink, even once, as it stared at both of the angels and it looked as if it was grinning. The panther had a kindly sort of grin from ear to ear, nothing of the cynical kind.

"We've got him now," Gabriel whispered loudly.

The moment was brief, although to Gabriel it felt like a day. Before they had the opportunity to make a single movement, the panther hopped off the nest. The creature then walked leisurely into the far jungle on the opposite side, away from the angels, and disappeared.

Gabriel immediately took to pursuit, but before he could get two paces, Michael reached out and grabbed hold of his arm.

"Stop, Gabe," he asserted. "I think he means no harm."

Gabriel tried to break free of his grasp.

"I think not. That panther nearly made minced meat of me. Its claws came this close to shredding me in half," replied Gabriel, gesturing with a pinch of his fingers to express the literal meaning of his words.

"I'm sorry, Gabe. I didn't know that," spoke Michael with all sincerity.

"No need to apologize. Maybe he did want me to chase him after all," Gabriel said as he looked towards the nest.

"You make a good point. It is true, we wouldn't have found this if you had not chased him," Michael remarked and briskly strode over to investigate.

"Wait for me," Gabriel shouted and ran ahead of him.

The nest was deep and wide across. They knew it was constructed of everything from trees to shrubbery, but what they discovered on the inside proved to be grotesque. There were dozens of skeletons from all sorts of creatures, and they had been woven right into the frame of the nest.

"It's huge. Thirty paces across, maybe more," Gabriel exclaimed.

"Yes it is," Michael said, closely examining the nest. "Actually, it's big enough for a dragon; only a beast like that would use the bones of its prey to build its nest."

"Hey, take a look over here," Gabriel said with excitement. "What do you make of this mess, Michael?" A giant egg lay cracked open.

"I don't think it hatched, if that's what you want to know," Michael said.

The archangel got down on his knees to take a closer look. He saw a yoke, green in color, and white mucus that was still wet and slimy. Besides that, the stench permeating from the egg was rancid, to say the least.

"Okay then, but what or who would do this," wondered Gabriel.

"Perhaps, wild beasts, or maybe—" answered Michael, pondering the possibilities.

"—demons," Gabriel finished his answer for him.

"Exactly," Michael said with a keen look in his eyes. "Look over here, Gabe."

Michael ran over to a mound of black ashes that were still burning.

"This looks awful familiar. Doesn't it," spoke Michael.

"You mean this pile of burnt dust was once a dragon," Gabriel said.

"That's right, Gabe. Most likely Babylon's mate."

"If demons are responsible for this—" Gabriel pointed out and scanned their surroundings. "—then they couldn't be far from here."

"We better take guard and we should pray for God's covering," Gabriel added as he put Logos back in its sheath; though, his fingers stroked the hilt and stayed near. He was prepared to fight if action need be taken.

"Yes, of course," agreed Michael. He, too, kept his hand close to the Sword of the Spirit.

"Before we go any further, I need to say something," Michael said, kindly.

"Stop there, brother. It is I who should say something," uttered Gabriel.

"Wait, let me speak first," Michael insisted.

"You know as well as I that I must have the first word. You know you'll be counted as being much braver for taking the last," Gabriel said, his tone was serious and lacking any sarcasm.

"As you wish, Gabe," said Michael, motioning for him to proceed.

"I don't know what came over me back there," Gabe said. "That wasn't me. I don't behave like that. Sure, I can be a bit obstinate from time to time. And occasionally I can be a little difficult to deal with."

"A little," Michael interjected with a sly grin.

"Okay, a lot, but only sometimes and you know that's the truth," Gabriel said. "I'll admit I started the argument. I don't know what took control of me?"

"Gabe, before you say anything else. I want to say I too am deeply sorry for my spiteful remarks. I believe it was the enemy. In fact, it wouldn't surprise me one bit if the Ruah were behind this."

"Do you really think so," said Gabriel who shuddered at the thought.

"I do. Whatever they meant for harm God used for good. Look around you, Gabe. If it wasn't for our argument you wouldn't have run off ahead—"

"Yeah, sorry about that," Gabriel spoke up. "I shouldn't have been so hasty."

"It's forgiven and it's already forgotten," Michael shrugged his shoulders and continued. "As I was saying, if you hadn't run off, you would not have encountered the panther and you wouldn't have chased after him. You wouldn't have run down the unbeaten path and, ultimately, we would not have come to make this incredible finding."

"I'm still sorry about what caused it all," Gabriel added, sincerely.

"And you're still forgiven, but I need your forgiveness as well, Gabe."

"Of course, don't mention it," Gabe exclaimed.

"It's in the past now and we shouldn't bother ourselves with it," Michael looked him straight in the eyes and said. "Besides, the mistakes made in the past serve only to prepare us for what's to come. Instead of dwelling on what we have no control over, we need to look to the present."

Gabriel smiled, that wasn't the first time he had heard that message.

They established it was a deliberation of the enemy. The seraphim knew what action needed to be taken next–pray. They joined hands and prayed for guidance and, most of all, protection from the enemy; especially the LORD's covering from any attacks of the Ruah. By the time they finished praying, the sun was high overhead.

"The sun's been shining for nearly six earth-hours, I estimate," Michael said.

"So, how much daylight do you suppose we have left," Gabriel inquired.

"Perhaps six or seven more hours, so we better get moving," Michael estimated.

"I agree. Which way do you think is west," Gabriel asked.

"This way," Michael looked in each direction before he pointed and said. "Let's be as swift as gazelles. Run with me, Gabe."

Their path was hard and thick overgrown shrubs with sharp-edged leaves blocked the way. They had to hike roughly three thousand paces through the harsh shrubbery. After what seemed like a few earth-hours, they had finally passed through the dense shrubbery and into a forest of palm trees. They traveled another thousand or so paces without saying a single word. They were exhausted and thirsty. To add to it, their stomachs began to growl from hunger. The air was extremely humid. Michael pined for the fresh mountain air he had experienced on the Mountain of God. Gabriel longed to be home again. As he trudged through the mud and in between palm trees, he envisioned the Garden of Tranquility. He could almost feel the mist on his face from the Fountain of Life. He had closed his eyes for a brief second, but the sharp edge of a palm leaf reminded him where he was.

"Can you see anything ahead of you, Michael," Gabriel shouted from about two-dozen paces back.

"I'm up here. Come and see this," Michael answered with excitement.

His voice sounded like it was a great distance ahead of him so Gabriel, feeling a burst of energy, picked up his feet and ran in Michael's direction.

"Where are you," Gabriel yelled after he had covered many dozens of paces.

"I'm over here," Michael said.

Gabriel tripped over a tree root and rolled through a bush and into a huge clearing, landing on soft bed of grass. The ground was as pleasant as a cushion and it felt wonderful on Gabriel's back.

"I was wondering when you were going to get here. I was beginning to think you had gotten lost," Michael said. He reached down and lent a helping hand.

"Well, I'm here now. What is this place," Gabriel wondered,

as he looked across the meadow, which stretched out for thousands and thousands of paces.

"Let's find out," Michael said.

The archangel led the way as the two explored the meadow.

They found a large smooth stone sitting at the top of the highest point in the meadow. The seraphim sat down and rested on the rock. A fresh cool breeze swept across their faces; it was quite a relief from the dreadfully stale and stuffy air of the densest parts of the jungle. The clearing, by far, was the biggest they had encountered on Luminarous. The meadow rolled and sloped downwards into a vast opening that appeared to be a valley. The smooth grassy pastures stretched out as far as their eyes could see; even as far as the volcano, which was a days walk due west. As they sat contentedly on the large smooth stone, they found themselves surrounded by vibrant blooms growing in the soft green grass. Another gentle wind blew across their faces and brushed through their hair. The invigorating breeze was beyond relaxing, creating the sensation that hundreds of tiny fingers were running across their heads and massaging their scalps. They were more at peace now then they had ever been on Luminarous.

"I'm reminded of the Fields of Gladness. For a mere moment, I felt as if I was home," Gabriel remarked. He observed the flowers swaying to and fro, and moving in harmony with the wind.

"This meadow is nearly comparable to what we have back home," Michael smiled and said. "The flowers truly remind me of a rainbow fallen straight out of the blue sky. This meadow, although it can't compare to the Fields of Gladness, does remind me of them. I do miss Heaven, Gabe. I long to be strolling in The Garden of Tranquility and to sit by the Fountain of Life and feel the mist against my skin—I can almost feel it. It's moments like these that make my aches and pains seem to vanish."

"I can picture the golden streets of Jerusalem," Gabriel uttered. "I can see the mansions that line Bethlehem Street. Although now, it seems like a distant memory and I am but a part of the scenery, fading into the background, destined to be forgotten," his voice faded with a hint of underlying anguish.

"Never, Gabe," Michael declared. "You are a part of the big picture—a major part. You were never meant to be in the background. Truly, as long as the LORD sits on his throne, your destiny will not allow you to fade into the background like some rebellious angel that's been banished to Hell, to be forgotten until judgment day. In God's eyes you're a hero, Gabe, and in my eyes you're a brother and a hero. You were called by the LORD Almighty to share in this quest. Your destiny will never be a part of the background—a mere ingredient in the grand scheme of things. God has called you to do mighty things in his name and to his glory. That is your calling—what you were meant for. Decided even from the dawn of time when God spoke into the darkness and created the light. If you will try to remember, it will come to mind that you kneeled before God in the Holy of Holies and accepted his calling. God's hand is directly involved in your presence on Luminarous."

"Michael, I'm sorry for despairing; there is no excuse. Thank you, what you said is exactly what I needed to hear," said Gabriel whose voice sounded joyful.

"You will walk the streets of gold once again and you will be received with singing and dancing. On Mount Zion, the LORD will embrace you as a Father to a son," Michael patted him on the shoulder and keenly said.

"You truly believe that is our destiny," Gabriel said. "There is not a single chance, not even a rumor of a chance that we could perish on Luminarous?"

"No," Michael shook his head and said.

"You're telling me that your mind has not concealed a infinitesimal notion, deep down in the recesses of your consciousness, that we are meant to sacrifice our lives to capture the fallen star," uttered Gabriel, his eyes were wide open.

"No, not one hair on my head, not one bone in my flesh, not one thought in my mind, not my soul and certainly not my spirit," Michael shook his head emphatically and insisted.

"To put your troubled mind at ease," the archangel said. "I will say that if that were our destiny, we should accept it. There is no greater thing you could do than to give your life for the LORD. At the great battle, thousands of demons were slain by your sword, Gabriel, but what can that compare to the ultimate sacrifice of giving your life for his glory. By God's favor, I am now commander of the Host of Heaven, but if I give my life for the LORD, I say count it not. Would I want to be remembered as the Archangel Michael or Michael the angel who gave his life for the LORD and all of Heaven? Yes, I say that, because he would do the same for me, the same for you, the same for all of his faithful servants. That is why I say if I perish for the sake of my God, then so be it, for there is no greater thing than an angel should lay down his life for the Father."

"Forgive me brother for ever thinking such a thing," Gabriel cried with tears flowing down his face.

"My life is in his hands, not my own, lest I run it into the ground by my own faults," Gabriel said as he wiped his tears from his eyes.

"Look around us," to further inspire him, Michael said. "Watch as the deer and the sheep graze on the plentiful grass. Notice the birds adorned richly with colorful painted feathers and observe their intricate dance. They fly about searching for food so their young can live and grow. Watch as the bees and the butterfly's dart about the meadow in search of pollen, the flowers cannot flourish without their aid. I could go on, but you know much of what I speak of for the Father has shared this with us. God created all of this and it works together, perfectly balanced, just as the hands that created it meant it to work. If God provides for even the smallest of his creatures, then of what greater value are his angels?"

"He knows the number of the hairs on our heads, so why should I worry about what tomorrow brings," Gabriel added, from his memory of God's teaching.

The day was perfect: the weather, the meadow, the sky above, and the animals around them were all perfect. It was a moment made for worshiping God, so they took their sandals off and stood among the animals in the soft lush grass of the pasture. The seraphim gave praise to the LORD for all of his wonderful works. The sun shined down brilliantly on them and warmed their faces. Their eyes beamed with hope with each new word that arose from the depths of their spirits. Their hearts were alive with love for God and their lips gave way to the joy that was overflowing in their souls. After they finished their song they noticed a well—a small pool of fresh spring water. It was just beyond the large smooth rock and it was quite sizable at more than three-dozen paces from edge to edge. They were baffled.

"Where did that come from," Gabriel wondered.

"I don't know, but I can say with certainty that it wasn't there when we got here."

"It's a miracle," Gabriel declared.

"Thanks be to God," Michael said.

"Thanks, praises, and everything I am. I'm thirsty if you can tell," Gabriel said with a big smile.

They knelt down by the pool and drank to their heart's content. The water tasted sweet and its moist touch was cool to their lips. It was, quite possibly, the most refreshing water they had ever drank. As they sipped at the pool's edge, they both noticed that a few feet below its surface, there was long grass, accompanied by colorful flowers, moving with the current. This served as further proof that a miracle truly had transpired, but there was no need for such evidence for in their spirit they had already settled it as fact. Michael stood looking at the water and pondering what they should name it.

"The Pool of Bethesda," Michael uttered.

"It has a nice sound to it. What does it mean," Gabriel said.

"The word just came to me," Michael concentrated for a moment and said. "I saw a vision of God's throne room and the words *house of mercy* spoke to my heart; then parts of the word came into my mind, first *beth* and then *esda*. Put them together and you have Bethesda. The Holy Spirit spoke this to my heart. I'm sure of it."

"Bethesda. It must be from the LORD—" Gabriel gazed into the sparkling clear pool and said. "—because a name as beautiful as that couldn't have come from your mind alone."

Michael gave him as straightforward and serious stare as he could manage. Then Gabriel started laughing and it must have been contagious, because Michael broke out with laughter too. Their hearts were merry and for the moment, their minds were free of all worry. An attack from the enemy was the furthest thing from their thoughts. They sat down and dipped their aching feet in the cool water. They felt completely relaxed and in a blissful state of mind.

"The Pool of Bethesda was truly a God-send," Gabriel remarked.

"I couldn't agree more, Gabe," Michael smiled and said.

FOLLOW THE LEADER

"Look at them just sitting there," growled Baal. "Please let me eat them. They look so delicious sitting there by the water. I can make it quick and painless for them."

"Silence you imbecile. Do you want them to hear you," a voice, stern and imposing, said.

Hiding in the bordering jungle was Baal and a certain individual. His name at this point was unknown and his face was hidden behind the veil of a palm branch. Only his voice could be heard. They were positioned in the jungle at the border of the pasture. Baal was studying the seraphim's every move with his keen eyesight.

"I haven't come this far to let my plans go to rubbish," said the voice in a condescending tone. "Baal, master of wolves, you should learn to master your tongue. Should I remind you that you left your master alone to face the monster and, because of your cowardly actions, he probably met his demise. I'll dare say if it were up to me, I would hand you over to that beast to be torn to shreds. As far as I'm concerned you're walking on hot coals right now, so hold your tongue or reap the pleasantries of a beating."

Baal let out a low menacing growl.

"Besides, Baal, we must work together if there's any chance of making my plan work," he patted Baal on the back as he spoke, softly and cunningly. "Heed my commands and Judas will honor you. And do you know what that could mean for you? A promotion, Baal, a place of honor among the legions. This prize could be yours."

He paused for a moment and put his hand on the wolf's head.

"You're my friend Baal," utilizing his skills in manipulation, he said. "You know that, don't you?"

The wolf gave a subtle nod.

"We don't want Judas discovering through some random news that you've abandoned your master Saul. Do we," said the voice.

"No," the wolf nodded and growled,

"Since you are my friend, Baal, I am willing to look past your faults, your disloyalty to your former master. Today, you have been given the chance to prove your worth, Baal, master of wolves," the voice said.

Baal, with some hesitation, nodded in agreement.

"We must be loyal to one another. We must stick together my comrade," he said, his tone was very pleasing to Baal.

This calmed Baal a little, at least enough to control his urges to eat his enemies right then and there. More significantly, he knew now that Baal recognized him as his new master.

Note from the Scribe...

Before you read further, I think it is necessary that you are made aware of some important details. I will enlighten you of the moments leading up to the miracle of the Pool of Bethesda. Read carefully and take notes. I am about to disclose some information that will prove to be of great value to you.

What you have read, thus far, has enlightened you to the fact that Michael and Gabriel were not alone on Luminarous. However, it may come as a surprise to you that Saul and Baal were not the first to track down the angels. There were others, bigger stronger demons, with a higher ranking in the legions, were assigned to search for the seraphim. In fact, Michael and Gabriel had been under surveillance from the moment they arrived on the doomed island of Luminarous. I'll take you back to the place and time; it was a few earth-days before the seraphim arrived.

At this time, rumors were spreading and causing quite a stir at the enemy base. At the center of the enemy's base was a cave. Not just any ordinary cave, but one with powers of dark sorcery. A dark veil of evil lay over the cave at all times. This evil magic holds the power to make the cave completely invisible. The cave's opening is cut out of the earth's surface and it is nearly a thousand paces across, from east to west and north to south. The depth is yet to be measured, but it's suspected to be unfathomably deep. I despise sharing this particular information, but you should know that many creatures have stumbled, unaware, into the caves opening and fallen to their deaths. It's hard to say how many animals in all, but approximately forty friends of God had fallen to their deaths. Each one of them sacrificed their lives in the service of their Creator.

It is also believed that the wicked presence that lives in the cave feeds on the souls of the fallen creatures. This evil needs no sleep and is always watching for an opportunity to steal another soul from a helpless victim. The demons, however, thrive on this sinister presence and they dare to call it their ally. I say, whatever it is, it cannot be trusted. Nothing that malicious is worthy of the title of ally. I would rather say that the sinister spirit is not their ally. It is not even their slave, as they would like to think it answers to them. Instead, it is their master that they blindly serve and believe in as a friend and ally. Nonsense, I say.

I tell you, if you were empowered with supernatural discernment given by the Holy Spirit, you could easily see the trap set by the enemy. You would see the cave in its entirety. And, if that was so, you could see the steps carved out of the rock. These stairs spiral downwards, descending thousands of paces into the dark cave. The hands of hundreds upon hundreds of demons constructed them. The depth and darkness of the cave was only surpassed by the eerie and evil foreboding presence it manifests. Imagine if you will, standing at the edge staring into the deep dark cave. You feel a cold whistling wind blow from the belly of the abyss and sweep across your face. This is followed by a heavy sensation that slowly and methodically comes over your entire body. Then you would feel a pair of huge invisible claws pull violently at your skin until your body can no longer endure the agony and as it gives in to the pain, you plummet over the edge, never to return again. At the mere notion of such an experience the hair on your arms should stand on end.

As for the rumors that were spreading throughout the enemy camp, the cause of the commotion was a report of great importance. The report allegedly had come from the supreme general of the legions of Hell. His name is Beltezar the Terrible. This fact would turn any news instantly into extremely important news. The rumors themselves varied from one legion to the next throughout the enemy base. Some rumors were saying Beltezar was preparing an all out assault on the island. An attack that would rout out all of the friends of God and wipe them from existence. Another rumor that was making its way through the legions stated that Judas was to be made a prince of Hell and if that was so then everyone under his immediate command could stand to benefit from his promotion. This would be a good rumor, but most every demon had come to the conclusion that Judas was far too selfish to share his spoils. Still, other rumors spoke of vengeance. Saying that the report was actually a decree signed by Lucifer himself to go to war. That was the most popular, seeing many of the demons would grasp any chance to retaliate against Heaven. Many started saying that a massive battle was being planned—a battle with numbers so huge that Heaven wouldn't stand a chance. This rumor eventually dominated and smothered the flames of the other rumors.

I will now take you to the enemy base where two demons are discussing the rumors of war.

The Warrior Within…

"A war I tell you, I can feel it in my spirit," Sihon said.

"I believe it too. The rumor of a coming battle is becoming real to my thoughts," Haman uttered. "A golden opportunity to prove my self worthy of promotion."

Sihon was a sergeant over one hundred demons and his friend, Haman, was of a lower class. Although he was only a corporal, he had reached the rank very quickly, surpassing many other hopefuls with recommendations from demons of upper class. Haman had high hopes of becoming a major someday and lead one of Hell's more elite legions. In order to fulfill this dream of his, he had strategically surrounded himself with demons of prestigious ranks. Sihon on the other hand wasn't quite as ambitious as his friend, nor was he as smug, but it was Haman's passion for succeeding that drew him to the corporal. Sihon, though, was greatly respected by all his soldiers. His demons served him with their lives and would proudly give them, if he asked. The two demons became friends the day that Haman was put under his command. That was many earth years ago.

"My boy, if you stick with me, you'll be getting that promotion," Sihon boasted. "I have come to know Judas quite well now and a good word from me could go a long way for you."

"Now, don't make any promises to me that you can't keep, sergeant," Haman said.

"It's not a promise, Haman. It's the truth."

"Sergeant, permission to say so—prove your truth," Haman remarked.

"My boy," Sihon asserted. "I am a sergeant over many and I need not prove anything. My word is my word. Wait and see, wait and see."

Their talk was suddenly put to an end by a loud resounding blow from a horn. They rose to their feet to answer the signal. They had been taking their leisure time, but both of them were eager to put an end to the rumors and hopefully the call of the horn meant their questions would be resolved. Hundreds of fellow demons passed by in lines and droves and Haman stepped in a line and followed.

"I must issue a call to my men," Sihon grabbed hold of his arm and said. "Look for me soon. Take charge in my leave and locate the others."

Sihon then hurried off. A large portion of Sihon's men were on reconnaissance. Many of them were experts in stealth.

Haman and the legions of demons came together at the designated meeting place. Near the center of their base, just outside the cave, was a large mound that was the only suitable spot for their commander to address them properly. Haman had already gathered about two-dozen of Sihon's men to his side. He sent four tall demons to search the crowd and find the others. A putrid stench filled the air, coming from the hoards of demons that were crammed together shoulder to shoulder. The meeting area was really only suitable for maybe a few hundred demons; however, the numbers gathered were in the low thousands.

A small majority had been on the island for many earth years. Nearly every demon had allowed their appearances to waste away and to imply the best they were a sore sight for decent eyes. The legions consisted of a wide variety of demons. Some were huge almost witless brutes, the biggest by far, was Goliath. There were also smaller demons, crafty and scheming in nature; the majority happened to be sergeants and majors, the most devious was Haman. And there were the demons that fell in between; these were the followers and not the leaders. They were the mindless soldiers that blindly followed any and all orders. These demons, not by chance but by plan, were the greatest in number on Luminarous. Satan knew fully well what he was doing. His tactics revolved around the fact that many of these, so called, brutes would jump at the chance for a suicide mission. In spite of these demons' lack of intelligence and efficiency, they had proven themselves to be incredibly dangerous and effective. Satan saw to it that their bitterness and resentment would never let them rest until they saw all seraphim dead by their doing.

"Silence. Order. I said, order," yelled Zoar, who was a stealth specialist and brother of Zoan, the captain of Beltezar's elite guard.

"All hail Judas, governor of the island and commander of Lord Lucifer's legions on Luminarous," Zoar announced and descended the mound.

The tall, slender demon climbed up the mound of earth. Judas stood erect on top of the hill, his long blond hair whipping back in the wind. His cold blue eyes were cruel and menacing, sending icy chills into the hearts of the demons. His nose was elongated and it resembled one a fictional witch is portrayed as having. He was fine groomed, not surprisingly, seeing that he was deeply vain and absurdly superficial. He practically maintained a spotless appearance at all times: no dirt on the face, no facial hair of any sort, and his tunic and robe were kept tidy as well. His shoulders were narrow and he lacked muscles thus his physical strength was diminutive, at best. His strength was of a different kind. He possessed skills of a cunning and manipulative nature. Although he worked hard to maintain a facade like that of freshly fallen snow, his character was corrupt and his heart filthy. Needless to say, he was an especially wicked demon of Hell.

The crowd had begun to stir and talk among themselves, so Zoar was called on to quiet the crowd once again.

"Silence. Come to order, in the name of Lucifer," He placed his hands to the sides of his mouth and shouted. The masses of demons fell into silence allowing Judas to properly address them.

"I need your absolute attention," Judas raised his voice as loud as he could. "I have ordered this assembly to deliver some serious news. The report I hold in my hand was delivered by a messenger from Beltezar the terrible, supreme general of the legions of Hell—"

Mumbling swept through the crowd.

"—the report is an exact dictation from a private council between the supreme general and the Lord Lucifer, may he live forever. And it states that two seraphim are coming to our island. They are dear to the God of Heaven and are of prestigious ranks. Our intelligence report states that they will be arriving within only a matter of days. "

The legion of demons burst into an unruly uproar. The demons shouted and cursed the Host of Heaven. To show their contempt, some were throwing handfuls of dirt into the air.

"Quiet—quiet. Be silent, brothers," Judas raised his voice to a commanding shout. "Listen here! There is yet more for you to learn. One of the angels is believed to be the lieutenant general of Heaven's armies. You know his name, Gabriel. He is large and powerful and more dangerous than you could imagine. He killed many of your brothers at the great battle. Our sources tell us he has become even more proficient in hand-to-hand combat. In fact, his sword fighting is said to be unrivaled in all of Heaven."

"We'll show him who has the deadlier sword," a demon in the crowd yelled.

The legions cheered and shouted curses, demonstrating their agreement. Judas regained order once more.

"The other seraph is even greater than Gabriel," Judas said. "Truly, he is God's most favored angel. He holds the most prestigious rank among all the Host of Heaven. He is the one who defied our master in battle. Through treacherous sorcery, he was able to disarm Lord Lucifer at the great battle. All of Hell agrees that this angel claimed victory through nothing short of the devious devices of his God. All who are faithful to our Lord Lucifer should know of the one whom I speak of."

The demons whispered his name to one another.

"The Archangel Michael," shouted Judas, confirming their suspicions to be true.

The demons spit and angrily cursed Michael and all of Heaven. Judas, once again, calmed down the rowdy legions. A riot was barely subdued, he thought to himself.

"We are most fortunate of all the demons of Hell," Judas said with a zealous tone. "Lord Lucifer is relying on us to capture the seraphim. Our commands, although they may sound simple enough, will require the cooperation on behalf of all demons on Luminarous. If we do not work together, we will not be able to successfully execute our orders."

"Brothers, are you with me," he shouted and rubbed his hands together.

"Once they are in our hands we will make them pay," he addressed them with a look of pure evil. "We will brutalize them. We will beat and torture them until they submit to Lucifer."

When the demons heard this they barked obscenities at Heaven. The entire legions raised their fists in the air and cursed the servants of God. Judas calmed his eager soldiers.

"The ambassadors of the God of Heaven are coming here to retrieve the fallen star Luminarous. If they get to him before we do, then all will be ruined. A party has been selected to hunt down the fallen star. The brothers that have been chosen will be notified this evening."

"We must not let this happen," Judas ruthlessly yelled. "We must capture Luminarous. We must conquer our enemies. We will not be defeated, we will win. Do you understand me?"

"Victory is ours. Victory belongs to Lucifer," The entire legion broke out into an uproar and chanted in unison.

Judas descended the hilltop and called for Nimrim, his personal servant.

"Here is the list." He handed him a small scroll and ordered him, "Gather these demons together and bring them to my quarters. I desire to meet with them."

Nimrim unrolled the scroll and glanced very briefly at it; he nodded his head and off he went. The masses quickly split up as soon as they had adjourned. Nimrim must have recognized the names on the list, because it didn't take him that long to find each demon. He led the private party below the earth into the recesses of the mysterious cave.

Judas was alone in his quarters. He was anxious to capture the fallen star. His mind wouldn't rest until Luminarous was in custody and securely trapped within the cage made specially to contain his unique powers. He sat at his table preparing a message to send to Beltezar. The scroll read this:

> Most revered Beltezar,
> supreme general of the forces of Hell,
> Your orders have been sent out. I have executed your plan with superlative efficiency. It is only a matter of a very short while until the star, Luminarous, is in our custody. In addition, I have taken it upon myself to ensure that the Archangel and Gabriel are given a proper welcome. The moment they are under our capture I will send prompt word.
> I am also positive that you will approve of the progress I have made here on the island. The legions, generously placed under my authority, have greatly improved their skills under my leadership and training. The construction of the base has come to a completion. The cage meant to hold the fallen star has been finished. However, its ability to hold him cannot be proven until Luminarous is securely inside. I assure

you, though, that an ample number of soldiers will be on hand, and I am taking every precaution feasible.

Signed in blood,
Major Judas
Governor of Luminarous

Judas pricked his finger and smeared it across the bottom of the page and then stamped it with the seal of snakes, his mark as the major. He had just finished sealing the letter when a heavy knock sounded at the door.

"Come in," he said.

Nimrim appeared in the doorway holding a flaming torch. Shadows danced on the ceiling as four demons came through the door and lined up.

"Thank you my dear Nimrim. You have served your purpose well. You may leave us now," Judas said to him.

Nimrim gave a subtle bow and retreated into the dark corridor.

"Stand up straight and let me get a good look at you," Judas ordered and grabbed a torch and proceeded to examine their faces and their arms.

"Excuse me major, what is the call for this," one of the demons spoke up.

Judas backed up and stared the demon in the face. This particular demon wasn't as tall as the other three and he looked as if he lacked the same strength.

"You are Rehoboam? I thought so. What is the meaning of this—for you dare ask your major such a question," Judas asserted himself. "You along with the others have been selected for an extremely important mission."

Judas' speech was suddenly interrupted by another demon.

"Major, we serve you and Hell proudly," he zealously said.

"You are Korah, am I right," Judas said and looked him over and nodded his head. The demon nodded *yes* in response. He was the largest of the four. His broad shoulders were nearly too big to fit through the door.

"I selected you, Korah, as well as your brothers, Dathan and Abiram, for your strength and power." Judas said and glanced back at Rehoboam and added, "I chose you for your leadership abilities. Your sergeant Sihon recommended you above all of his soldiers for this mission."

Rehoboam gulped with anguish, for he knew the extent of what was being asked of him. He believed it to be a suicide mission, since the last party to be commissioned had but one survivor out of a dozen demons.

"Major, I respect and appreciate your appointment," Rehoboam said. "Sir, if you will allow me to ask—why only four? Twelve were sent out before and only one returned."

Judas raised his arm. He was about to discipline Rehoboam for his contempt, but he lowered his fist and laughed mockingly.

"I will finish saying what I started." Judas, visibly ignoring Rehoboam, addressed the others. "You were not only chosen for your strength and power, but you were found to have the ability of stealth and speed. It was these qualities, foremost, that decided your appointments. In this case, we have gone with quality before quantity. For why should we send out another dozen or better yet one thousand that Luminarous should be alerted from his perch and smote them? I won't lie to you; this is a mission that could possibly bring about your demise. On the other hand, your success could mean an even grander appointment."

"Major Judas. Could I make sergeant, sir," Dathan spoke up.

Judas didn't reprimand him for his sudden outburst; on the contrary, he grinned.

"Why yes Dathan," he replied. "And the same goes for you, Korah—you too, Abiram, and even Rehoboam."

Judas gave their leader a sharp glare.

"The four of you are to tell no one of your departure. You will leave at nightfall, within the hour. And when you return, you are to report directly to me," Judas ordered with a smirk on his face.

"Last of all, Luminarous is incredibly dangerous," the major added. "Take extreme caution when dealing with the star. He is cunning and cannot be trusted. Also, the extent of his powers is unknown. Your swords and your fists will be useless against him. You will need only this."

Judas handed Rehoboam a net woven from an unknown material.

"This was made in the bowels of Hell and a spell has been

cast on it by LORD Lucifer himself and the fallen star will be helpless in its web."

"What if it doesn't hold him," Rehoboam queried; his eyes revealed skepticism.

"Blood and spit, you'll be finished. Dead," Judas slapped him across the face and cursed him. "Never question the sorcery of the lord of Hell and earth. Never, I tell you. Now go before I change my mind and turn you over to the bloody serpents to eat the flesh off your bones."

They saluted him and they filed towards the door.

"Oh, and if you choose to abandon your mission or fail—," before they could reach the latch, Judas added. "—you will be destroyed. Do I make myself clear?"

They nodded and proceeded quickly through the doorway. Only a moment had passed, and someone pounded on his door.

"What is it," Judas demanded. "Did you miss something?" Judas swung the door open. He found Nimrim standing in the light of his torch. Another figure stood out of sight, just outside of the light.

"Oh, it's only you, Nimrim. Can't I catch a moment's peace? Who's that with you?"

"Major, please forgive me for the intrusion. Sergeant Sihon has accompanied me. He wishes to have an audience with you," Nimrim bowed and said.

The tall handsome demon stepped into the dimly lit quarters.

"Leave us, Nimrim," Judas commanded.

"As you wish," he bowed and solemnly said.

"Now, what brings you here my friend, Sergeant Sihon, "Judas said with a crooked smile, and sat at his chair in a reclined position and rested his feet comfortably on the table.

"Major Judas, I came because I was just informed of the report you gave."

"You mean to say you did not attend the meeting," Judas asked, his smile disappeared and he sat up.

"It's not as it looks," Sihon quickly replied.

"It's not as it looks," Judas was angry as he continued, "Don't you realize what happens if you fail to make a meeting?"

"Yes, but let me explain—" Sihon answered him.

166

"—grounds for immediate dismissal and your return to Hell to be judged by the supreme authority," Judas said, cutting Sihon short.

"I will explain, if you will allow me," Sihon blurted, in haste.

"I was about to say before you interrupted me," Judas spoke up. "You are my friend Sihon and since I am so generous and wise, I will give you the benefit of the doubt. You may speak freely."

Judas returned to his reclined position.

"My soldiers were away on reconnaissance and since I fully realize the consequences of missing an official gathering called by the major, I left in haste to retrieve them."

"Why didn't you send someone in your stead," Judas inquired.

"At that moment, I had no soldiers at my disposal and I thought my men would gain respect for me if I personally called on them. I did send my trusted friend, Haman, to the meeting. We were in conversation when the horn blew. I sent him ahead to seek out my men at the meeting. I also asked him to tell me all of what took place, if I shouldn't return in time. It happened that I returned with my men only moments ago. I just heard the full report from Haman. He was kind enough to fill me in and he also made sure my men were gathered together for your address."

"Haman—" Judas said and sat pondering what he heard for a brief instant. "—tell me more about this Haman."

"He is a corporal and he's skilled and reliable. He does hope to become a major someday," Sihon replied, he caught himself saying too much.

"I shall like to meet this Haman. Summon him to me immediately."

"Yes major, right away," Sihon said. He found himself addressing Judas more like a superior than a friend and this troubled him dearly.

"Alright, as for your testimony, I will consider all of this at your hearing."

"What, a hearing," Sihon looked shock as he remarked. "I thought you understood. I meant no harm by what I did."

He felt like he was suffocating. The room suddenly looked much smaller, as if the walls were closing in on him.

"I know I am your friend, but you should also recognize that

I am your superior. And with this position comes great responsibility," Judas said, his face was indifferent.

"I am expected to follow protocol. It is simply duty to Hell above my friendships."

Sihon rose from his feet and sulked out of the room. Since he felt used, he reluctantly went about his errand for Judas. Within his heart, resentment was beginning to brew. His legs carried him angrily to the surface where the sun was setting.

"Sihon, friend, how did it go for you," a voice called out to him.

He turned and there was Haman sitting on a rock on the outskirts of the cave.

"Haman my friend—," Sihon swallowed his pride and said. "—you're just who I was looking for."

Haman was eating an apple. He threw it to the ground.

"Really? Whatever for," Haman asked and yet his voice hinted that he already knew the answer.

"Major Judas has requested a private council with you."

Haman's eyes lit up, but the dark shadows hid it very well.

"Sergeant Sihon, lead the way," Haman exclaimed; *promotion*, he thought to himself.

Sihon recognized that same cordiality in his voice that spoke of protocol. His friendships were dying. Soon it would be him alone against all. *I still have my men*, he thought and led the way for Haman. He grabbed a torch from Moab, the demon on guard, and they began the long descent into the mysterious cave. Haman claimed to Sihon that he had never been in the cave before, but to Sihon he bled lies and more lies. Suspicion no longer cowered in Sihon's mind, but his soul was poisoned with hatred for Haman.

He deceives me. Surely, they are conspiring together. They want to destroy me, Sihon thought.

"Nimrim," Judas called impatiently. "Nimrim."

The door flung open and the demon nearly tripped over his feet.

"You took long enough," Judas scorned him.

"I am deeply sorry sir. I was tending to my work," Nimrim shyly spoke.

"Don't bother with your blubbering excuses. I do have an

errand for you to run, important indeed. A secret errand, you understand," Judas said harshly.

Nimrim nodded and came closer.

"I want you to deliver this to Prince Baasha," Judas handed him a parchment, rolled and sealed, and ordered. "You know how to get there. Now go, by way of darkness. Be swift and be quiet. Go."

Nimrim put his black cloak on over his head and scurried out of there.

"We are nearly there. A few more stairs and we should be at the threshold of the passageway," Sihon whispered.

"I see another light coming up the path towards us," Haman whispered, his words echoed somewhat.

The light was suddenly extinguished.

"Where'd it go," Haman wondered.

"Hush, we must be quiet," Sihon replied in a hushed tone.

Suddenly they felt a breeze and then someone bumped in to them, nearly knocking them off their feet.

Whoever that was, was in a hurry, thought Sihon.

"Who would be such an idiot," Haman said.

"Hush, I don't know, but keep following me. We're nearly there," Sihon insisted.

The demons soon came to a corridor, dimly lit with torches. Two strong-armed demons were on guard.

"Halt," spoke one of them.

"What business have you," the larger of the two asked.

Sihon handed him a small scroll. The large burly demon unrolled it. He studied it for sometime, repeatedly looking up at Sihon, Haman, and then at the other guard.

"You may pass," he finally said.

Sihon ripped the scroll out of his hand, as the two went down the corridor. The cave was like a maze and Sihon had traveled it before, but he hadn't memorized the way yet. The paths twisted and split off to more paths. It was very complex and quite confusing. He waved the torch onto the wall and found an inscription of two snakes.

"This is the way," Sihon declared.

He found the door and raised his hand to knock, but the door opened slowly, on its own, it seemed. Judas was standing near the door.

"I've been waiting for you. Haman, is it," Judas said and extended his hand to lock arms with the demon.

"Go on your way Sihon, but don't go far," Judas sternly said. "You will be needed to give your testimony once more."

That's right. Don't go far, Judas thought. *When Beltezar comes you'll be good as dead. I have to prove that my authority is confirmed. You're the perfect candidate, Sihon.*

"Go rest sergeant Sihon, my friend," Judas said and hiding his smirk in the shadows, he extended his hand and locked arms with the demon.

After Sihon's footsteps had faded, Judas motioned with his hand for Haman to sit down at the table. Judas took a seat and rested his feet on the table.

"Thank you for coming. And, I appreciate your haste as well."

"I came as soon as I heard. Thank you for inviting me Major Judas."

"Sergeant Sihon has had many good things to say about you."

"He is a good friend, almost like a brother," Haman said; there was some disdain in his tone.

"Is he really a good friend," Judas asked as he sat up and leaned in.

"Yes—yes he is," Haman answered, hesitating somewhat. He began to wonder if this was some kind of test.

"I ask only because you seem like a respectable soldier," Judas said. "The kind that would sacrifice everything for the better cause of the kingdom. I know little about you, but I surely get that impression and that is the kind of soldier LORD Lucifer needs."

"Thank you sir," Haman exclaimed. *A promotion is coming I know*, he thought.

"You're a corporal, are you not," Judas asked.

"Yes, sir," he answered confidently.

"You climbed the ranks quickly, didn't you," Judas said, his tone showed interest.

"I've worked hard and benefited from it. I mean to say, I am ambitious and hard working, sir," Haman answered; he was beginning to feel like this was an interview for a more prestigious appointment. *Possibly major or even sergeant*, he thought to himself, trying to contain his bliss.

"Or do you mean to say you knew the right comrades," Judas probed. "Because you know as well as I that hard work is pleasing to your superior, but it is who you know that really matters."

"I don't think I fully understand what you mean, sir," Haman said.

"Let's dispense with the small talk and get down to business, the things that really matter. Sihon informed me that you desire to be a major. Is this true," Judas inquired and put a fist under his chin, resting his arm squarely on the table.

"I spoke of being major with Sihon in confidence, purely as a friend," he responded with carefully chosen words. The last thing he wanted was for Judas to think he wanted his position.

"As friends," Judas exclaimed, bursting forth with laughter.

"Maybe it was as friends, but it doesn't change what you said," he regained control of himself and said. "As for being friends, no longer think of Sihon in that way. Especially if you desire to be more than just a corporal."

"Why do you say that," Haman shyly asked, but he was thinking, *I know that, Judas, you lame impression of a major*.

"Haman, I say that because there are no friends. We are brothers, yes. We're in this together, yes. However, it takes more than friendships to make a name for yourself in LORD Lucifer's army. Unless, that is, you desire to be a whipping boy for the infirmaries in Hell? Because if that's the case then our conversation here is over and as far as I'm concerned, you never were under my authority on Luminarous."

Judas, you fool of a major, Haman thought to himself.

"With all due respect, that's the farthest thing from my mind. I want to serve in LORD Lucifer's army, but I do want to be major, maybe even a prince one day," Haman said with a haughty stare.

"Good then," Judas said, jeeringly. "And you think you have what it takes to sit in my seat? Even more, you desire to be a prince in the LORD Lucifer's prestigious royal court. This is truly too much."

Haman stood to his feet and to stand in the presence of a superior, unless told to do so, is considered a high crime of treason.

"If you have asked me here to mock me, then you can consider me no longer under your authority," Haman declared.

Judas jumped to his feet.

"Lower your tone, sir," Judas, in a menacing voice, said. "Sit down or you will be executed for treasonous crimes. You would be wise to heed my words."

Haman, for the first time, felt like he was truly under his authority. He had never seen this side of Judas. The major's eyes were glaring with a commanding presence.

"Haman, I did not call you here to make a mockery out of you. I requested a private council with you in order to consider you further for a prestigious appointment."

Judas walked around the table then paced back and forth. Haman's back was to him and he feared penalty of death should he turn and face the major. He now realized the authority Judas could exercise; if he wishes death he could have it in an instant. Judas was brushing his fingers across a pair of swords hanging on the wall.

"However, I am beginning to have second thoughts," Judas rubbed some dust between his fingers and said. "I am starting to see that you may not possess the abilities I am looking for. You see it takes certain attributes, nobility being one; highly regarded but seldom found in a corporal. And you are a corporal aren't you?"

"Yes you are—" Judas answered for him. "—and that's all you might ever turn out to be."

Haman was beginning to doubt his own abilities, even his keen sense of manipulation, which was the talent to credit for his numerous promotions. He could feel Judas' presence standing right behind him and could feel him breathing down his neck. *I'm a blubbering idiot*, Haman thought to himself. *What have I done? How can I recover?*

"Of course there is a way to prove your quality," The major said, speaking in a sympathetic tone.

Those words were exactly what Haman was hoping to hear at the very moment and he took the bait. His eyes widened as Judas walked around the chair and sat at the table's edge and stared at Haman like a falcon would a field mouse.

"Do you have what I'm looking for? Do you have the qualities that are required for what I am asking of you," Judas demanded.

"Major Judas, I do have what it takes," he stared Judas in the eyes and declared.

"I possess the qualities and the skills that are hard to come by," Haman continued. "Furthermore, I am a soldier that will sacrifice anything to get the job done. I will stop at nothing to advance LORD Lucifer's kingdom." Haman didn't know yet what task he was being asked to undertake nor did he think twice about it. He sat high in his chair, as tall and as straight as he could.

Judas grinned and let out a small chuckle. Haman didn't appreciate Judas' expressions of amusement, but said nothing.

"I like your enthusiasm Haman. You have passed my test, sergeant," Judas said without laughing. Haman's eyes lit up. He couldn't believe his ears.

"Did I say sergeant," Judas commented. "Why yes, I did. Sergeant Haman has a nice ring to it. That is what you will become if you pass my next test."

Haman didn't care what it was. It didn't matter, because promotion is all he thought of.

"You will accompany me on a journey, a reconnaissance mission to be exact. And an important one at that. I will relinquish no further information until you complete something first. You must locate a certain soldier for me. I think you might know of him; he is a brute and possibly the strongest soldier under my authority. His name is Goliath."

"Do I know of him," Haman nodded his head and said. "Of course, he's a friend of mine and I know exactly where to find him."

"Great," Judas clapped his hands together and exclaimed. "We will leave tonight. In the secret of darkness, we will make our way to the beach. The report from headquarters states that the Archangel Michael will supposedly land somewhere on the beach southeast from here. Go summon Goliath and bring him without haste to the spring well outside camp. I will be waiting where the rubber trees weave together."

"Major, I am your willing servant. I am at your disposal," Haman, after listening carefully, declared.

"And I appreciate that, Haman. I request of you nothing less than your total allegiance to this mission," Judas, with a soft but cunning tone said. "Also, Haman, make sure you tell no one of this conversation. Especially Sihon. Actually I would rather you have no contact with him at all, you know, until he's had his hearing. It would be a conflict of interest and the supreme council would frown on a witness mingling with the would-be guilty. Besides that, I wouldn't want anything regrettable to come to pass if the others should find out. They might get jealous and lose their tempers. You know how ill-tempered many of the soldiers are and a good excuse to fight is always welcomed by many."

"Yes, Major. Your bidding is my pleasure," Haman bowed his head and said. He then rose to his feet and saluted Judas.

"On your way out, tell one of the guards—choose whichever one you like, that I need something delivered."

Haman nodded and exited his quarters. Judas took out his pen and paper and began writing a message. The letter read:

Elymas the Sorcerer,
Your skills in the mysterious arts are respected and admired in all of Hell. Your expertise in sorcery is much needed on Luminarous. Truly the advancement of the kingdom is relying on your agreement to come to my aid. I bid you ascend to earth immediately and leave any task you are currently engaged in to someone competent under your authority. Moreover, should the Lord Lucifer himself deal out discipline due to your personal presence on Luminarous, rest assured the guilt will be on my head and my hands.
I am writing you to make a special request. There is a certain angel that is coming to my island. He is the lieutenant general of the host of heaven. You know him as Gabriel. I would place soldiers under your command: Sergeant Sihon and Sergeant Og. Your mission would be to spy on the angel. I respect your skills in sorcery and they would be very useful in driving the angel out of his senses: mad, insane, or whatever else you can accomplish with him. You have the freedom to use any

spell. And you may exploit the soldiers to whatever discretion you see fit. Though, I say this in confidence, Sergeant Sihon is disposable. However, please ensure that no harm befalls sergeant Og.

Please come quickly. I will be gone on a secret mission of my own, but Sergeant Zoar will be in charge. This is a top-secret quest. Please tell no one of this and destroy this scroll promptly.

Signed in blood,
Major Judas
Governor of Luminarous

Note from the Scribe...

The scroll was sent in secret to the great sorcerer and in secret, Elymas answered. He arrived at the island within a matter of earth-hours after receiving the call, and Zoar placed the sergeants Sihon and Og under his authority just as Judas had commanded. Like pawns in a chess game they were strategically placed against the seraphim of Heaven. Under the cover of night, they set off to cover many earth-miles to search out Gabriel. Elymas had prepared a set of incantations specially designed for Gabriel. He also prepared a spell for Sergeant Sihon, should the moment come to dispose of him.

The scouting party led by Judas had already rendezvoused upon Elymas' coming. Goliath was a nice addition, Judas had thought. This particular demon was nearly as tall as Michael and as strong as Gabriel. He was a quite the brute; in fact, he possessed a very unique physique. He was more muscular than two strong demons combined. However, he wasn't particularly sharp and he lacked common sense. I'll characterize him as a dimwit and an absentminded, oversized bully. He didn't think of himself this way, since there wasn't a demon on Luminarous that would dare tell him this to his face. They feared a nasty punch in the gut or even worse a stab from his sword. His look was very intimidating, a face that was darkened from the sun and a black disheveled beard that flowed nearly to his waist. His personal hygiene was repulsive. He had an overwhelming body odor that preceded him for several paces. His down wind had a dreadful stench; Haman made certain that, whichever direction the wind was blowing, he was on the opposite side of Goliath.

Haman had acquainted himself with Goliath from the moment he arrived. Haman realized that if he were going to advance himself on the island of Luminarous, he would need to have the biggest and strongest demon on his side. He promised Goliath a respectful position as head of security for him if he should be promoted to major. The main reason for his friendship with Goliath could be attributed to his smaller stature. Haman was not particularly small, but neither was he large by any means.

Since Haman had come to the island, he developed an appetite for the local food. He quite often overindulged in the variety of fruits that grew there. In spite of Haman's active eating schedule, or lack there of, his appearance was always up to code. He paid meticulous attention to his uniform and it was spotless. He kept his face clean and wiped free of any food remnants. From his meager start as a foot soldier, he had realized the relevance of his appearance and what it meant to be up to code.

After Judas gave a brief intelligence report, Goliath was up to date on the situation, or at least Judas thought he was. Goliath, in spite of his massive size, never asked a superior officer to repeat themselves. The covert operation to seek out the archangel had begun. They hiked through the jungle, under the cover of night, and they left no tracks for the first thousand paces by wading through the stream that led towards the beach. Judas did not want anyone following them, for he did not want his plans foiled. Nor did he want any other demons stealing his glory from him. If Haman only knew how petty and insecure Judas really was, he could easily execute a revolt against the major without much resistance.

Losing his position as major and governor was Judas' biggest fear, so he practiced keeping any over-ambitious demons close to him. By promising promotions to these demons, he kept his would-be-rivals at bay. He provided them with a believable, but false, sense of security by parading them around on the base as equals and confidants for all to see. He never rests in conspiring against any demon that gains respect and admiration from his soldiers. Judas sees this kind as more than just a potential threat, he sees them as enemies worthy of death, and he stops at nothing to make it happen. However, he does take great caution in making their deaths appear as nothing more than an accident.

That is why Judas called for the assistance of the sorcerer. Elymas owed him a favor since Judas had saved his life at the great battle. When the sorcerer had his back turned to an attacking angel of God, Judas intervened by killing the angel with his sword. Sihon was gaining in both favor and reputation and Judas wouldn't have any of it; thus, he kept an eye open for an opportune time to plan his assassination. He started planning Sihon's death from the moment the sergeant missed the assembly. Sending him on a reconnaissance mission was too easy. Everything was falling into place and, for the time being he only needed to worry about Haman.

The Warrior Within ...

Judas led the two demons stealthily through the jungle and in three earth-days time they had reached the beach. In the morning, Haman took eye of the Archangel Michael.

"Yet another reason for promotion," Haman said to himself. Goliath beseeched Judas to let him attack and Judas reprimanded both of them.

"Lower your voice, Haman; Goliath, control yourself. Heed my commands," Judas whispered.

"What shall you have us do," Haman spoke up.

"Quiet, I said keep your voices down," Judas sternly whispered. "We wait and watch. That is what Beltezar wants and that is what we shall do. Be patient, the both of you."

They spied on him from their hiding place on the border of the beach. They followed Michael, carefully keeping their distance and trying not to be detected. Their first challenge arose when the archangel decided to venture inside the jungle. Judas stopped them from pursuing him right away.

"This will be hard," Judas addressed them. "We can't make a single noise and no matter what, we must not be seen. To be seen by him or any of the enemy would mean certain death for all of us. Beltezar would have our heads if we fail this mission. We must track him like a hawk. There will come a point when I will send you, Haman, to gather more forces. Until that time comes, we must be patient and be watchful of the enemy. Do the both of you understand?"

Haman and Goliath nodded and they proceeded to creep along, staying out of view, as they made their way through the dense underbrush.

THE DAY THE
RAIN CAME

"Gabriel is close at hand," Elymas whispered. "I can sense his spirit. It's strong, but not strong enough to withstand my power."

"The undergrowth is dense here, sir. Should we go around," Og suggested and pointed to a narrow pathway. "Look there. I've discovered an easier route."

"That way does look like a better choice," Sihon agreed.

Elymas forced his hands over their mouths.

"Silence—" The sorcerer removed his hands and said, "—we'll go the way you've suggested, but from this point on there will be no more talking. We must use a series of signals to communicate; we have to use stealth to our advantage. The seraph we're dealing with is the lieutenant general of the Host of Heaven. There is no telling what he's learned or how his skills have advanced since the great battle. We are not to attack. I will use my gift of sorcery as a weapon against his will. The plan, that we must execute, is already laid out in my mind and it is completely flawless."

"Sihon, Og—you both are a vital part of my strategy," Elymas continued. "We'll work together to disrupt Gabriel's line of communication with his master. Sergeant Sihon, when the time comes, I will give you the signal to get quietly into position and from there you will wait for my next signal. You will hear a crow squawk twice, then you are to pour this onto the base of the closest tree."

Elymas then handed Sihon a potion in a ceramic vial.

"Handle this *very* gently, it is extremely powerful," Elymas ordered.

"What does it do," Sihon asked and held the vial up, examining it closely.

"Never mind what it does, Sihon. Your puny little mind could never comprehend the sorcery I wield." Elymas' eyes ignited in anger as he snapped at him.

Sihon looked shocked by the harsh reprimand he received. He hadn't seen this side of the sorcerer before. On the other hand, he really didn't know much about Elymas, other than the fact that he is a superb sorcerer, respected by many and held in high esteem in LORD Lucifer's royal court.

"You will see what the potion will do and your question will be answered," Elymas said, in a slightly kinder tone.

"What would you have me do," Og spoke up, his voice was very bold and this surprised Elymas, although he did not scorn him for asking.

"Sergeant Og, I will position you across from Sihon," Elymas uttered. "Your signal will be that of two crows from a rooster. Here is a second vial; dispense it onto the base of the tree nearest you."

Og complied with a nod.

"Let's move out," Elymas addressed them both. "Be as quiet as possible, move as if you didn't exist. When we come upon the angel, remember that timing is crucial; you must be vigilant in following my instructions without making a single mistake. If either of you make one single error, Beltezar will have your necks wrung. Do I make myself perfectly clear? "

They nodded a *yes* and followed Elymas. The sorcerer led the way down the narrow pathway. Og and Sihon were both amazed at how Elymas made no sound whatsoever as he crept along. His sandals left no impression in the soil and it was like he was invisible.

Once upon a time, Elymas was known as Hagnos' in Heaven. The name means pure. He had earned his new title from his skill in sorcery. Now, he is a far cry from the innocent nature he once possessed, he is immensely cynical and highly irreverent toward the LORD God. His stature is quite tall and he is very slim, with a long narrow face and sunken cheeks. His eyes are narrow with a lifeless green-blue hue to them, but when practicing sorcery his eyes take on an eerie glow. He is truly tainted with malevolence, morally depraved, and sickened with resentment.

Sihon and Og were actually brothers, nearly identical in physical stature and appearance. Both of them were huge, barrel-chested, and were somewhat handsome. They both had shoulder length, chestnut-brown hair with a receding widow's peak, and protruding eyes with an unusual bluish-yellow hue. Og was the more dominant of the two and whenever he felt it necessary, he had no problem asserting his seniority.

"Do you hear that," Sihon whispered.

"Hush, fool," Elymas commanded.

They were within a stone's throw from the angel now and their mumbling might have revealed their presence to the angel. They continued to creep slowly along. Fortunately, a large wall of shrubs gave them cover from their enemy. Elymas peered through the bushes and spied him. Gabriel was standing in the middle of a small opening, praying to the LORD. Elymas gave them their signals and the demons crept as quiet as spiders into their positions. The sorcerer rested on his knees behind a thick hedge and from there he could keep a watchful eye on his enemy. He waited patiently for Sihon and Og to reach their posts. The sorcerer was reveling in this moment. Elymas excelled in times like these. It was this reason that his reputation precedes him.

He studied the trees surrounding the angel and thought, *these will do nicely. Gabriel won't know what hit him and when he comes to his senses, it will be too late. Everything is falling neatly into place.*

Gabriel appeared to be finished praying and was looking about the jungle. Elymas, being a master of imitating animal sounds, gave his signal to Sihon and the demon emptied his potion onto a palm tree. The sorcerer then gave the signal for Og, and the proud sergeant poured the contents of the second vial onto a rubber tree. *Perfect,* thought Elymas, as he began his formidable incantations. He stretched out his hands and spoke in the forbidden tongue as he exercised his talents in the dark arts. He could see the spells were working.

Yes, yes, you're like putty in my hands, seraph of God, thought Elymas. Branches moved and twisted; roots came up from the ground and wrapped themselves around the angel's feet. A branch stabbed Gabriel and the strong angel toppled to the ground like a rotten tree from its stump.

"You're mine now, Gabriel. One more spell ought to do and you will be my slave to do my bidding," Elymas whispered, knowingly breaking the code of silence he had ordered his soldiers to follow.

The sorcerer began his final incantation—the spell that would put the angel under his control. Waves of light emanated from his fingertips and the light transformed into snakes. Slithering along the ground, they came upon the helpless angel that lay on the jungle floor. Suddenly, the angel sprung to his feet and a light appeared in the forest. A beam of pure illumination shone like the dawning sun. The snakes were driven back from the light.

"No, no, this can't be happening," Elymas whispered to himself.

The light transformed into another angel.

"Elijah," he whispered bitterly. "I will settle my score with you later and you have yours coming too, Gabriel, soldier of light."

The sorcerer lay prone on the ground. He had spoken an incantation of invisibility. He hoped that it wouldn't be broken by the power of God's presence. He could sense the Holy presence of the Most High and it repulsed him. Then it happened. The power of the Holy Spirit's presence had rendered him totally immobile and he was the one that lay helpless on the ground.

Elymas thought, *even though I can't move, I can still take note of what the angels are speaking about. What's that sound they're making? I can't understand a word they say.*

The power of the Holy Spirit was present and came the ability to confuse the enemy's tactics, which was very useful in moments that spy's might be eavesdropping. After Elijah left, blazing a trail through the jungle, Elymas regained his footing and attempted to cast another spell. He discovered that his words trailed off his tongue like drops of dew covering the grass lightly and barely there. He stuttered and tripped over the words of his spells. He found himself reversing the order of his words, which was something that should never be done by a sorcerer, even if desperate measures were called for. The spell could result in an implosion, destroying everyone around the sorcerer, but it could also kill the one who cast the spell—the sorcerer. It was the ultimate sacrifice and Elymas was willing to make it. As he spoke the spell into existence, he could see that Gabriel was moving down the path Elijah had left. He was getting some distance away. His spell could not reach that far and no matter how hard he tried to stop speaking he just couldn't do it. It was as if a power greater than what lived in his spirit had taken hold of him and wouldn't let go.

Finally, the last word of the spell rolled off of his tongue and to his relief, he felt certain that nothing had happened to him. He brushed his hand across his forehead and let out a sigh, but then something strange began to occur. He felt a tingling sensation inside his stomach and at first it was nothing much.

Maybe it was something I ate, he thought. Sihon and Og had made their way through the underbrush and were now by the sorcerer's side.

"What's wrong? You look a bit weary," Og said.

"Sir, you don't look too good," Sihon added.

Elymas couldn't say anything; it was as if he had forgotten how. The tingling sensation grew into something more painful than vexing.

"Sir, your face is changing colors. Your belly is glowing," Og exclaimed.

"We should get out of here, brother," Sihon looked at Og and said.

Elymas grabbed both of them by the legs and tried to speak, but no words came out. Suddenly, a blinding light shined forth from his mouth, then in a flash, Elymas and the two demons vanished into thin air.

NOTE FROM THE SCRIBE...

Gabriel had come closer than he knew to certain doom. There were some events, in particular that contributed to his rescue. Gabriel's prayer for help was one important factor and another was Elijah's appearance at just the right moment. Yet what truly saved the angel was the power of the Holy Spirit. For it was he who had set Gabriel free from the bonds of death and it was the Holy Spirit that spoke through Elymas. The enemy had been foolish to believe that their secret weapon called the Ruah was the only force capable of influencing someone, not only to lose control of their inhibitions, but to yield their body to another force. Moreover, the Ruah are no match for the awesome power of the Holy Spirit.

Gabriel hadn't realized it at the time, but the LORD had placed a covering of protection over him. A holy presence that was invisible to the naked eye, even to supernatural beings such as angels and demons. It was because of God's invisible covering, that he had not been detected by the Ruah. The angel's extensive training in warfare had not covered the advanced tactics of spiritual warfare needed to combat these dark, malicious spirits of Hell.

You have also previously read that Gabriel, eventually, met up with Michael. What's more, you've read of their battle against the monster called Babylon. What you have not read about is what else occurred during their battle against the dragon. The enemy exploited the situation, not necessarily on purpose, but more by chance.

The Warrior Within…

Judas and his minions heard the roars of a monster accompanied by excruciating screams of terror. They were in the midst of searching for the archangel. Truthfully, they too fled when they heard the dragon as it came towards Michael. As they stopped and listened to the terrifying noises, Goliath identified the cries for help as belonging to the demon, Saul. Judas ordered them to stay low and close together.

Goliath pleaded with him to save his friend.

"We shall see what we can do," Judas said.

Judas agreed to help Saul only because he saw it as a good opportunity to see to Haman's death. He thought that might redeem the situation they were in, because things were not going as planned. Judas had given Elymas the sorcerer this specific location and they were to meet him here. However, Elymas and the sergeants Og and Sihon were nowhere to be found. This greatly troubled Judas, but he knew he must remain with his strategy, even if he is without help from the sorcerer.

The monster might just eat Haman and it would be an accident. *Of course, that would work perfectly and to my benefit. No more Haman to worry about,* thought Judas. Haman, on the other hand, thought, *here is another opportunity to prove myself worthy; I shall rescue Saul from the monster and then I kill the foul beast. If all goes as planned, I am certain to be praised for my actions. Judas' governorship will be mine for the taking. Or even better, the dragon eats Judas and I will practically be handed the promotion of major. I can see it now: thousands of soldiers under my authority and bidding.*

He started running names through his head of possible candidates for Judas' successor, but he kept coming back to himself as the best soldier for the job. *Me, me, me. There's no one better for major than me,* he boasted to himself. *I can't let him know that I want his position, or I'll surely be done for. Judas would see to that,* Haman continued to think.

The demons hid behind a large shrub watching the monster toss the helpless demon in the air like a cat and mouse game. Suddenly, Goliath pointed to someone else who, he saw, was standing in the opening. He had a sword drawn and was taunting the dragon.

"Gabriel," Judas scornfully cried.

"This is going to be a challenge. If we go after Saul we risk breaking our cover," Judas thought out loud.

Finally they had found the Archangel's companion, which meant Michael was probably nearby. Judas ducked back beneath the bushes and ordered Goliath and Haman to do the same.

"Well, brothers, there is nothing we can do for Saul," Judas whispered in a sulking manner.

"The dragon is busy with the seraph. I can see Saul laying about two dozen paces from here. We can drag his body to the cover of these shrubs. If we hurry, we can save him," Goliath boldly said to Judas. Goliath had been peering through the bushes when he witnessed the dragon pursuing the angel of Heaven.

"As I was saying—" Judas repugnantly looked at him and said,

"—there is nothing we can do for Saul, unless you, Haman, are daring enough to rescue him. After all, you are quick on your feet."

"I agree Major, it is too great a risk. Saul would be proud to sacrifice his life for the kingdom," Haman replied cunningly. In his mind his courage was shrinking away, and what he actually was thinking was, *not me. I'll find plenty of opportunities elsewhere to promote myself or I could suggest—*

"Oh, he would be proud, you say," Goliath interrupted angrily. "That's ridiculous. I am smarter than you think, Haman. Saul would not agree to this. You're a coward, not a ruffian. You dare call yourself a soldier of Hell?"

Haman loved attention, but not this kind. He quickly diverted the focus of attention, from himself, to Judas by using his quick wits.

"Actually, something should be done for Saul," Haman recommended. "You are wise leader, so you should make the decision. However, if you will allow me, I would like to offer an alternative suggestion. It pertains to another matter, but not entirely—"

Another *roar* sounded and he was momentarily speechless from the horror of the dreadful noise.

"The king of monsters is Babylon," he whispered. "Major Judas, we are forgetting the companion to the dragon, Jezebel, the queen of monsters. This must be Babylon's territory for it's obvious that Saul encroached on the monster's home. Therefore, the dragon's nest or lair should be close by."

Judas' face appeared keen on this new idea. He thought, *why didn't I think of this first. Well, it's just another reason to rid myself of Haman.*

"Brilliant notion, Haman. You have made yourself worthy of sergeant," Judas declared.

Goliath was turning red with anger.

"Goliath. You are truly the best tracker on Luminarous," Judas looked him in the face and said. "Please use your skills and lead us to the dragon's lair."

Goliath relaxed his clenched fists.

"Major, I will do as you ask, but what about Saul," Goliath wanted to know.

"He's not moving," Judas stared at Saul's body lying on the

ground, and whispered. "I fear death has taken him. Unfortunately, there is nothing left for us to do here. Now you must take us to the dragon's lair."

Goliath was reluctant at first, but led them through the thick undergrowth. He caught eye of prints left by the dragon. They had to pass through a clearing and feared that the dragon might catch sight of them. Goliath, Judas, and Haman moved as swiftly as a pack of wolves on the hunt. The dragon and Gabriel were in the heat of battle, needless to say, the demons went undetected. The tracks led them down a large path that seemed to be clearly made by the dragon for ease of passage to his lair.

It was still night and the moon was under the cover of clouds. A hint of light appeared dimly on the horizon, but it gave no more light than the moon was already providing. Goliath came to a sudden stop. His eyes could distinguish something stirring in the darkness. A large scaly beast had turned and settled down on top of something that resembled a nest.

"Behold, the she-dragon, Jezebel," Goliath whispered. "She might have young with her."

"Or better, she might just have an egg or two under her. Be as quiet as you can. Goliath and I will move around the nest and launch an attack on her. Haman, you must approach her front side as closely as possible and create the distraction," Judas replied in a hushed voice.

Haman didn't like the idea of standing in front of a beast nearly ten times his size. He could be eaten. He'd never thought he would go like that. Well, no demon imagines dying from the slow digestive process in a dragon's belly or having their flesh and bones ground to powder by a dragon's fierce jaws. He did think, *if I can only kill the she-dragon, then I would be known as the dragon slayer. Then, taking the governorship of Luminarous will be easier still. Be strong and fearless, Haman.*

"You understand what to do. You are with us, aren't you," Judas grabbed Haman on the shoulder and whispered.

"Yes, I will create the diversion," Haman nodded and said.

When Haman came upon the dragon, she appeared to be asleep. She even sounded as if she was snoring. A strong breeze had picked up. Goliath told them to stay still, since the veil of darkness had been lifted. The moon had moved from behind the clouds and was shining brightly. Fortunately for the demons, the wind was blowing away from the dragon; therefore the dragon wouldn't be able to pick up their scent. Haman lay low, in a crouching position. He moved forward very slowly and quietly. He kept his eyes focused on Jezebel's closed eyelids. Under the moonlight the wrinkled leathery face of the she-dragon was revealed, and that's not all that was made known. One of her eyes wasn't completely shut. Then the other opened slightly and, in an instant, both of her eyes were wide open and she glared directly at the demon.

Haman froze in fear; he thought, *be fearless. Fearless. Fearless. I can't.* Then Haman turned to run and the dragon uncoiled its long neck like a snake and snatched the fleeing demon up in its teeth. Jezebel flung Haman through the air and into a tree with a violent thud. A hiss then a cry of pain sounded; Goliath had stabbed the beast in the foot and Judas had struck at its tail. The dragon whipped its tail through the air and smacked Judas in the chest. He fell to the ground as lifeless as a scarecrow. Goliath struck again, this time breaking her leg with a heavy blow from his sword. In a flash, Jezebel turned to bite her foe. Goliath ducked and assailed her blind side, catching her off-guard. He struck her in the side of her neck and this wound proved to be fatal. The dragon dropped to the forest floor and let out her last breath. Then, *poof*, and she had turned into ash and was no more.

Judas regained his breath and stood to his feet. Haman was still unconscious as he rested against the foot of a tree.

"Good work Goliath," Judas said. "I wish I had been more help, but the monster's ploy flung me helplessly to the ground. I must have gone unconscious for a moment and the next thing I knew you had slain the she-dragon. You're well-deserving of a promotion. I'll see to it."

Judas was relieved that the dragon was dead and that Haman was dead, or so he thought. Goliath leapt onto the nest and he dug through the brush and found two eggs.

"I found something. Major, you might want to take a look at this," Goliath remarked.

Judas climbed up, but he wasn't as agile or as strong as Goliath, so it took him a moment to mount the heap of brush that made up the dragon's nest. Judas stood on the rim of the nest and peered into the center.

"Ahh, a treasure, indeed. My good boy, what are you waiting for? Make a sack for the eggs," Judas said.

Goliath looked puzzled.

"Tear a piece of your robe. Use that," Judas ordered.

Goliath nodded and did as he was asked. He placed one egg into the makeshift sack and then he reached for the other. However, the egg rolled away from him. He chased after it and reached down to grab it; it rolled from him yet another time. He was becoming frustrated.

"Will you hurry," Judas scorned him. "We are wasting precious time. Morning will be here soon, and that means it will be light. The archangel isn't far behind and he can't see us. Not yet, not until everything is ready. Hurry Goliath. I don't have time for your games."

The major's comments weren't helping him any. Goliath's foot was caught between two thorn branches and he was struggling to free himself. However, it seemed that it was too late and the egg cracked open. A head covered with leathery spikes popped out of the shell and two seemingly curious eyes looked upon its world for the first time. Goliath's foot was still stuck in the nest. Judas curiously watched as the baby dragon wiggled to free himself from its shell. Then the shell crumbled and the dragon uncoiled its tail, which surprisingly enough, was about four feet in length. The dragon was instantly cautious of its surroundings, but its animal instincts soon took over. The first decision it made was to walk, ever so carefully, toward Goliath, who was still caught in the nest. The demon drew his sword and the dragon jumped back, but came close again its curiosity was too great for it to resist.

"Catch it Goliath. You'll be rewarded greatly in Hell. Now catch it," Judas ordered when Goliath finally freed himself.

Goliath ignored the major and crept slowly toward the dragon like a prowling tiger. He timed his jump perfectly and caught the dragon by the tail as it turned to get away from him. The dragon turned like the wind and in a split second it had landed a nasty bite on the demon's hand. Goliath yelled from the pain and lunged forward, sword in hand, but just missed it. The dragon swung its tail and struck Goliath, landing a spike in the demon's arm, which caused the demon to sway backwards and the egg dropped from the sack. The egg rolled right into the baby dragon and it sniffed the egg like it might be some sort of food. It gave the egg a swat with its tail and sent it flying out of the nest.

"No, you fool—you buffoon. The egg's no use now. You'd better redeem yourself right now and either catch the blasted dragon or kill it. Whichever you choose make it quick," Judas screamed.

Both of Goliath's arms had been badly wounded by the dragon and Judas' words ignited him with rage. He decided right then and there that he wouldn't stop until that dragon was smitten from the face of the earth.

"You're a dead dragon," he growled like a lion claiming its territory.

The dragon hissed back like a deadly cobra, it was more than determined and Goliath knew it wasn't going to back down. For having just been born, this creature truly lived up to its family name as the spawn of the king and queen of dragons. After all, he was twice its size and an experienced warrior. He was a soldier who had claimed the lives of many angels at the great battle in Heaven. He had achieved countless merits for his feats in battle and moreover, he possessed immense strength and power. Among all the demons in Hell, he was among the strongest and biggest. That alone is confounding enough.

As Goliath stared the dragon down, he thought, *what would my brothers think of me if they could see me now, battling a creature half my size, and still I can't manage to strike a significant blow. If I fail, I will never hear the last of it. I'll be seen as the demon that can't even defeat a baby.* Goliath sliced his sword through the air to intimidate the dragon. He received another nasty strike from the razor sharp point of the dragon's tail. This time, Goliath wasn't going to lose. He lunged forward with all of his might. The dragon leapt backwards onto the rim of the nest and off the edge. Goliath pursued the dragon to the edge of the jungle. The dragon made an unexpected move, instead of running for the cover of the dense forest, it turned and started running straight toward Goliath.

"Bring it down," Judas yelled, he was watching from the nest.

Goliath had his sword cocked behind his head, ready to strike. The dragon towards him with its thin, leathery wings stretched out. Goliath timed his swing and he let the dragon have it, but his sword only grazed the dragon's side and did it no harm. The dragon had taken to the air just before it had reached Goliath and its claws scraped flesh from Goliath's face as it flew above him. The demon turned around, took aim, and threw his dagger. He hit the dragon in the foot, but it wasn't enough to take it out of the sky. The dragon climbed higher above the treetops and was soon out of sight.

"Why don't you just let it go, Goliath," Judas yelled. "Let's get a move on it."

"You're pathetic," he added with a sneer.

Goliath's mind wasn't even thinking about what Judas thought of him. At the moment, he couldn't help but think what his brothers would say about him, since now he'd be known as the warrior that couldn't defeat a baby dragon.

"Warrior, you call yourself," Judas struck him in the face and said. "I think not. You're nothing more than a coward. All of Hell will jeer at you. You'll be disowned and you can be sure, I'll see to that."

Goliath wanted so badly to hit him back. He felt like a demon that had outlived his usefulness. But there was yet a chance to redeem myself, he thought. Goliath sulked for a moment, but his pride soon came back and in full force. His eyes peered at Judas with scorn in them, but he held his head high.

"Go ahead. Hit me again," Goliath dared, his fists were trembling with fierce resolve. Judas raised his arm and swung at him, but Goliath grabbed his bare hand, wrapping his fist around it.

"You're on your own now," Goliath said with a sly grin. Goliath pushed him down then turned and walked away.

"You can run if you like, Goliath, but I'll send a hunting party after you. One dozen of my most ruthless soldiers. You'll see. They will make you wish you were never created."

Goliath stopped in his tracks and looked Judas in the eyes. He stared right through the major and saw Judas for what he truly was: a mere coward.

"Tell your soldiers that I am hunting a dragon," Goliath said unflinchingly. "And Judas, I'll come back, just to find you and kill you."

His voice was cold and sober and Judas knew he wasn't playing around. He was serious. Judas couldn't help but be a little intimidated, so he said nothing in response. Goliath left and journeyed into the unknown regions of the jungle. He disappeared and was never seen again.

"The time is near to make our move," spoke an unknown demon. "By the looks of it, we have over one dozen gathered already."

"More are on the way, master," Baal said, slyly. "I recruited about two dozen strong demons as you requested."

"Have you seen Elymas the sorcerer," asked the mysterious demon.

"No, master," Baal replied.

"What about the sergeants Sihon or Og?"

"No, master," Baal said.

"This is troubling. They should be here. Captain Zoar informed me that they had been sent in secret to spy on Gabriel. Baal searched up and down the forest for them and keep an eye out for Major Judas. He should have been here by now."

"As you wish, master," Baal said.

"There's no need for that Baal. They aren't here," spoke the voice of Judas, from behind the wolf.

"Master Judas, please forgive me for acting rashly," said the unknown demon.

"Major Judas, I will do your bidding now," Baal bowed his front legs and said.

"I have come with two dozen of your strongest soldiers, Master Judas," spoke yet another voice.

"Captain Zoar, thank you for your service. Did you by chance see the sorcerer or the sergeants Og and Sihon," Judas said.

"No sir I have not," Zoar replied.

"Master Judas, maybe they have stationed themselves across the pasture," said the unknown demon.

"That could be, although highly doubtful. We must move in within the moment. Captain Zoar, make absolutely sure that your men know not to harm Archangel Michael. He must be brought back unspoiled."

"Master Judas, what about the other seraph," Captain Zoar asked.

"You may have some fun with him, but don't mess him up too badly. And killing him, by no means, is out of the question."

Captain Zoar left to address his soldiers.

"As for you, you know what to do. If things get out of hand, you must put our plan into action," Judas turned and said.

"Yes, Master Judas. You can trust me," the mysterious demon answered. He saluted and turned to walk away, but Judas stopped him.

"If you fail, if you stumble, if you wane even a little, there will be Hell to pay. You'll pay with an eternity in the dark pit with scorpions that make these earthly scorpions look like tiny ants. Do you understand me," Judas demanded.

The mysterious demon nodded, saluted once more, and was on his way. He walked down the line of warriors and met up with Baal.

There were far more recruits than Judas expected. He was well pleased.

"Captain Zoar, you who will be responsible for the ambush," Judas gathered the captains together and said. "I will signal you when your time to attack is at hand. Everyone else will remain with me. We will attack on my signal."

They assumed their positions at the edge of the forest and waited to make their move on the ambassadors of Heaven.

Michael turned his face towards Heaven and the LORD spoke to his heart.

"I created all of this in my splendor and majesty; but all of what you see will soon be sacrificed to remove the evil that resides here. Its cleansing will come soon and no angel or demon knows when that hour will be. Be strong and courageous, my child. Your trials and tribulations will be far from comfortable and the cup from which you will drink will be bitter. Michael, remember this though, I will never leave you nor forsake you. I am true to my word for I am the great I Am."

Michael soaked in the word he had just received.

"The woods are stirring," Gabriel moved close to him and whispered. "The animals have cleared the meadow; they know a storm is coming. Don't look in the forest, but I have counted at least three-dozen demons. Prepare for a fight, brother." Gabriel took hold of Logos.

"I can feel the strength of the LORD flowing through me," Michael gripped the hilt of the Sword of the Spirit and whispered. "Over a million seraphim are praying for us now. Their prayers come forth straight from the throne room of the Most High. It is time to show our valor. Our strength comes from the one true God. The LORD of Heaven and earth is on our side, and none can stand in his path. This will not be our defeat Gabriel, instead let them taste the fire of Heaven's wrath."

A smile stretched across Gabriel's face.

"Today, the foul retches of Hell will know that we are warriors of the LORD Almighty," Gabriel declared zealously.

They gazed towards the heavens and prayed. The jungle around them was in dead silence, the birds had disappeared and no animal could be seen or heard. Gabriel could feel his heart thumping; getting increasingly stronger with each passing moment. These were not heartbeats of fear, but of excitement. He took great joy in defending the kingdom of Heaven and the fact that they were greatly outnumbered made it even more exciting for him. They rose from the water's edge and sat on the rock. Michael prayed again and Gabriel was in agreement. Out of the corner of his eye, Gabriel noticed a company of demons approaching. They were crouching low like a pride of lions moving in to make their kill. Their swords were in hand and didn't notice that the angel had spotted them; Gabriel made a small grin. Michael was still praying out loud. Gabriel saw that Michael had a smile on his face, as pure and innocent as he had ever seen from his best friend.

At this point, Judas recognized the signs that they had been discovered.

"So you see them too," Gabriel whispered.

"Of course. Fear not, brother. Take courage, for today the enemy will fall by the power of God," the archangel replied.

Gabriel grinned from ear to ear. Then they both heard Judas' call to battle and the demons charged forward. The angels unsheathed their swords and unleashed the power of God flowing through their bodies. At this moment, the first battle occurred between the servants of the Most High God and the minions of Hell. This was history in the making.

The demons initial swarm was furious. Over two dozen demons attacked. Gabriel was fending off two, three, and even four at a time. The archangel's strength wasn't what it usually was. That is until he called out to the LORD to give him the strength he needed to defeat the enemy. That is when Michael felt a surge of supernatural power enter his body and the Sword of the Spirit pulsated with blinding light. Demons scattered in all directions. Then Judas jumped on the rock that Michael and Gabriel once sat on and gave the signal.

"Attack, you cowards, attack," Judas screamed at his soldiers.

Captain Zoar and his soldiers moved in from all sides. The plan was to close in on the angels and create a cage of demons and blades of steel to entrap them.

The light from Michael's sword faded and a demon with huge shoulders and a grotesquely ugly face charged the archangel. He was coming straight at him toward Michael's blind side so Michael hadn't noticed his attacker.

"Michael, watch out," Gabriel cried.

Every muscle in Gabriel's face cringed with fear; he was too far from his best friend to get there in enough time. Michael turned to face his attacker, but it was too late. The demon had leapt off the side of a hill and his sword was pointed straight at Michael's chest. The demon was in the perfect position to strike the fatal blow to the archangel's heart. Gabriel believed he had failed the LORD and most of all Michael. Now he would pay for Gabriel's shortcomings with his life. In a flash, even more fleeting than a single heartbeat, something grabbed the demon by the neck and pulled him into the air. Gabriel looked and saw a giant bird, an eagle to be precise, gliding with ease over the tree tops. The eagle had the demon firmly grasped in its powerful talons. The eagle turned upwards and soared a thousand feet into the sky in a matter of mere seconds it seemed, then let go of the demon. The demon dropped like a heavy stone and hit the ground and was no more.

"Our Salvation is here," Michael yelled and before Gabriel could respond, he struck down one demon and then another with a fierce swing from Logos.

There is fear in their eyes, thought Gabriel. *They know their doom when they see it.*

Suddenly, something incredible happened. A mighty peal of thunder shook the air and without a single cloud in sight, rain began to pour down so hard that the angels couldn't even see three paces in front of them.

This is a supernatural shower, thought Michael.

"It is time to be free from the enemy," he cried out.

Gabriel shouted for Michael, but he couldn't hear his own voice over the tumultuous shower. The sound of rain hitting steel reverberated directly in behind Michael. He turned just in time to see a blade lunging towards him. He knocked the sword to the side and struck his attacker; a large brutal looking demon fell in front of him.

The rain didn't let up, not even for a moment. Gabriel moved forward blindly reaching out for his best friend. It was hopeless he thought, *Lord, why send this shower if I lose sight of Michael. I am blinded. Help me, guide me.* As he finished his silent plea, a hand grabbed him by the arm.

"Speak now or lose your hand," Gabriel shouted, he had Logos securely in his free hand, ready to strike.

The rain was so loud he could barely hear his own voice. The hand squeezed even tighter and with every ounce of restraint, Gabriel refused to strike the hand.

"Who are you," Gabriel demanded. There was no response, but the hand pulled on his arm urging him to follow.

This could be a trap. I should strike while I have the chance, thought Gabriel.

"Follow me. You must trust me," said a voice suddenly and clearly over the peal of thunder that echoed overhead.

Gabriel knew he recognized the voice. *Who is this,* he thought. *Surely–this is no demon's voice.*

Everything was confusing. The rain was still coming down as hard as before and the arm pulled him faster. Then he bumped into a huge figure and his impulse was to attack so he did. A mighty blow blocked his sword and he lost his balance, but the hand that grasped to his arm pulled him up. His attacker, though, knocked him free of the grasp and was now standing over him. Gabriel knew this was the end. The fatal blow would soon strike him through and he would soon be home in Heaven, but he could never wield a weapon for the LORD again. His mind was racing so fast.

I will have eternal rest, but it can't be my time. Not yet, not now. My duty to the LORD has not been fulfilled. I have to fight for the Kingdom of Heaven and for the LORD Almighty, he thought.

A sword brilliant and shining came crashing down on him. Gabriel rolled and his attacker struck only mud. Gabriel retaliated and brought down his attacker. The rain grew thicker and Gabriel couldn't see but a single pace in front of him. The rain wasn't going to stop him from assailing his enemy. He took Logos and held it firmly under the attacker's chin. He was about to end the enemy's existence when a hand grabbed him and thrust him off. The attacker moved swifter than Gabriel had ever seen a demon move before and now he was helplessly on the receiving end. His chin felt the burning steel of the attacker's sword.

Gabriel grabbed a handful of the attacker's hair and pulled him closer. He wanted to see who the demon was that was about to defeat the Lieutenant General of the Host of Heaven.

"Michael," Gabriel gasped.

"Gabriel," Michael shouted over the rain.

They were both relieved, but before they could say anything a hand grabbed each of them and pulled them briskly to their feet.

"There's no time. Hurry and follow me. Stay close and do not fall behind," ordered the voice.

That's the same voice. Who is this, thought Gabriel to himself.

The rain was relentless, but fortunately it provided a dense covering from the prowling eyes of the enemy. Michael and Gabriel were pulled swiftly and steadily through the nearly impenetrable underbrush of the jungle. They didn't slow for even a moment. It seemed like maybe thirty or forty earth-minutes had passed and the rain still poured; thunder boomed and lightning illuminated the raindrops, but not enough to see clearly. Branches struck Gabriel in the chest and Michael was incessantly bombarded with palm leaves hitting against his face.

Where are we going, Michael wondered. The hike was making him weary.

Then suddenly, without warning or even a subtle decrease in raindrops, the thundershower ceased. With the rain now gone, the voice gave way to a body and a face that both Michael and Gabriel recognized. What they saw truly astonished their eyes.

"I thought you were imprisoned or even dead," Michael exclaimed.

"Yes, I was captured and put in a cage," replied the voice. "I nearly died, but I escaped. I fled as far as I could away from that dreadful place."

"Is it really you, Ahab," Gabriel said in astonishment, as if he was seeing him for the first time in ages.

The angel nodded yes.

"It's a true blessing from God to have found a fellow angel," Michael said.

"It is indeed," Gabriel added excitedly.

Ahab appeared different than when Michael and Gabriel had last seen him, of course that was in Heaven, which felt like long ages ago. And then again, he had been through the most brutal treatment—torture.

We Meet Again

Ahab wasn't a particularly large angel either, which is what originally made him perfect for spying on the enemy. Being smaller made him inconspicuous to watchful eyes. The enemy might expect something larger than just six feet in height. Ahab's physique was weak with narrow shoulders and a thin body. His once shimmering blond hair had become dirty and ragged from the fierce elements of the enemy's prison. His face was filled with tiny cuts and bruises, which he probably received from countless earth-hours of torture. His clothes were tattered and his once beautiful blue eyes were now swollen and puffy. To the two angels, he appeared as if the enemy had tried every attempt to make him talk.

Maybe the enemy failed in their questioning, thought Michael to himself.

Gabriel's thoughts were on the enemy's ambush. Hopefully they didn't get any information out of him. Then again, thought Gabriel, how did they know exactly where to find us.

"As I speak now, the enemy could be watching. We know now that they have many eyes alert to our movements," Michael whispered and then suggested they find refuge before they further discuss anything else. He pointed to an opening in a wall of rock about forty paces east of where they stood. Michael didn't recognize where they were. The trees were different than anywhere else on the island. The undergrowth was meanly dense and inhabited by vines of a thorny kind.

The cave was overgrown with vines. The entrance was barely detectable, so it was perfect for a hiding place. A temporary one, at least. The cave had a very detestable aroma to it: musty and stale.

As if something once inhabited it, thought Michael, *or might still be living here.*

The walls were cold and gray and covered with a thick moss dripping with moisture, although the floor was neatly swept. The ceiling was low, but not low enough to strike the top of their heads on except the archangel if he fully stood up. The depth of the cave was given not more than a dozen paces deep, give or take a few. The ceiling of the cave descended lower and lower with each few paces that it extended further back into the cave. The floor sloped steadily downwards, until the ceiling and floor met at a sharp angle at the deepest point in the cave.

Once the three angels were settled in, Michael spoke a few words of the ancient tongue and a small fire ignited in front of them.

"What was that? How did you—," Ahab said, taken back by what he witnessed.

"I know, I know. I thought the same thing the first time I heard those words and saw the fire they produced," Gabriel put a hand on his shoulder and said.

Ahab was thinking otherwise though.

"But Michael, is not sorcery forbidden by God," Ahab remarked. "Surely you were wrong to make fire."

"Ahab, there is no sorcery in Hell or on earth that is greater than the ancient tongue of creation," Michael looked straight at him and declared with great authority.

"It is the language spoken by the LORD of Hosts. The language was spoken long ago. In fact, it was at the dawn of creation, before you or I had come to life. Truly, with the tongue of creation, God spoke all the seraphim of Heaven into existence. That is something the prince of darkness, and his slaves fail to recognize or even remember for that matter. The Father generously chose to teach me the ancient tongue and I am deeply humbled by it being grateful beyond words."

"Are you the only one who speaks it, other than the Father," Ahab interrupted.

"There is one more who knows of it. I will not reveal his name; you will learn of it soon enough," Michael said, he was intrigued by his question.

"When we know you can be fully trusted, that is," Gabriel added, his eyes reflected the firelight with an intensity that represented the authority he was given by the LORD Almighty.

"Brothers, please, I assure you by our Father in Heaven that I am trustworthy. Have you already forgotten that it was I who rescued you from the enemy," Ahab pleaded; he was astounded at what Gabriel had said.

"Yes, you did come to our aid, but do not be mistaken by thinking you were our salvation. Do not take credit for what God has done, unless you enjoy treading on dangerous waters. For God alone sent the rain. And his ... " Michael said, almost revealing too much.

I can't reveal who the Eagle truly is, he thought to himself.

"I meant no disrespect," Ahab nodded agreeing with him, and said. "I'll give credit where it is due—to God. He is deserving of all honor."

"Now that we're clear where you stand, I need to ask you a few things," Michael lowered his brow and spoke with a gentle tone.

"What's become of our brothers: Caleb and Sethur," the archangel whispered. "Are they still alive? Does the enemy still have them?"

"When I managed to escape, Caleb was still in prison and Sethur—well, I fled before I they came back," Ahab replied solemnly.

"You left them behind like some coward," Gabriel interrupted. "A seraph of God never forsakes his brothers. If I find you to be a traitor I'll—"

Gabriel then rose to his feet and towered over Ahab like a mighty tree about to crash down on the axe bearer in vengeance. He was already on edge, and hearing Ahab's report is all it took to push the mighty seraph.

"Gabriel. Sit down. And you, Ahab, explain yourself now,"

Michael said, he stood up and grabbed Gabriel by the arm to prevent him from unsheathing Logos.

Ahab looked frightened, even though Gabriel had put Logos back in its sheath.

"It's alright Ahab. He won't hurt you," Michael said in a softer tone.

"You two don't think I have regrets for leaving a brother behind," Ahab uttered.

"Of course I do. In fact, I'm terribly grieved. I had to look him in the face, as he sat behind pillars of stone and steel that I could not break; even though I tried with all that was in me, and listen to Caleb's voice saying to me, 'Leave me Ahab. Go and may God save you.' It was the hardest decision I ever had to make."

Tears flowed profusely from Ahab's eyes. Michael felt compassion for him. Gabriel remained skeptical.

"How did you manage to escape when an angel, as strong and cunning as Caleb, could not," Gabriel stared intensely at him and asked sharply; he was skeptical.

"I'll tell you everything—if you must know." Ahab said the latter words under his breath and continued, "I was deep underground in some sort of cavern. I could not see the ceiling. It was far too dark, the cavern was too vast, and the torches were too dim for me to see clearly. I couldn't make out much around me, except for the demons that stood over me. The demons chained me to a stone wall. All sorts of creatures were summoned from the cracks of the walls. Giant centipedes crawled over my body. Hairy, prickly spiders ran across my face and through my hair. I think they bit me too, yes they did. They tore through my face with their fangs and filled my body with their poisons. Snakes were called to slither up my legs and bite me in my belly. They used everything they had to torture me. I was weakened to the point of breaking. It was horrible ... "

Ahab held back the tears.

"Judas, their commander, wanted to discover all that I knew and the demons were relentless in their efforts to please him. I suffered for a long time, and then, well, I'm ashamed to admit to this."

"But you must, Ahab," Michael asserted.

Ahab wiped more tears from his eyes and composed himself.

"I am ashamed to say, but I pleaded with them. I begged them to stop and let me go. I asked them to let Caleb and Sethur go, but then they told me that Sethur was already gone," he said with a sincere expression.

"That he was dead," Michael exclaimed with a dreadful look in his eyes.

"No—but death would have been better for him, I tell you the truth. He was delivered to Hell. The prince of darkness wanted to see him personally. I was told he was tortured until he denied God and submitted to Satan as his master and claimed allegiance to Hell. Still, it gets worse brothers. His spirit was perverted and removed from his physical form. He was transformed into something more horrible, far worse than death. They call these creatures the—"

"Ruah." Gabriel cried out.

"Yes, it is as you say," Ahab woefully admitted, with sore eyes.

"They must pay for what they've done. We must not delay, Michael," Gabriel demanded.

"This is sad news indeed," Michael said, his eyes were full of mercy as he searched his heart for the answer right, for this moment.

"There is hope yet, Gabriel. It is still possible that the enemy deceived Ahab in order to strike fear in his heart," he said in a serious tone and looked at Ahab. "Ahab did the enemy show you Sethur? Did you see him as a Ruah? Did you even see him in is original form as an angel?"

Ahab's face was buried in his hands. It was plain to see he was distressed by the whole ordeal. He was nervous, his heart was fluttering with anguish, and his mind was haunted with the horrific memories of his torture.

"Answer him, Ahab," Gabriel demanded impatiently.

Michael didn't pay attention to what Gabriel said, nor did Ahab. Michael put a hand on Ahab's shoulder. Ahab didn't look up at the archangel; he kept his face concealed behind his hands.

"Ahab, what you went through was dreadful I realize—" Michael said kindly, but persuasively. "—but if the enemy is to answer for what they've done, you must tell us everything you remember. I know it's hard to talk now, but if what you say about

Sethur is true, then Caleb doesn't have much time before the same fate befalls him."

Ahab finally took his hands away and slowly raised his head up

"Ahab, please forgive Gabriel's impatience. When you're ready," Michael spoke with compassion and searched for the right words.

"Ahab, I know your experience, what you went through, must have been horrifying and to escape is nothing short of a miracle from God. In spite of your struggles and for the sake of our mission, we need to discern all that you know. Now please tell us everything you've learned and don't hold back."

Ahab appeared troubled and upset. He paused for a moment or so.

"It grieves me to share this with you," Ahab said in a serious tone. "It is far more dreadful than we ever thought before. It greatly perturbs me to share this with you, though I must."

Ahab looked around the cave, as if there were ears listening in.

"The enemy has spies in every corner of the island," he whispered. "We have discovered that the enemy is in fact, using the island as training camp. It is indeed a breeding ground for evil and tyranny. Many have turned to him for protection from God. A demon named Judas, a major in Hell's forces is in charge of the legions stationed here and he's convinced many that Satan can offer them salvation from God's wrath and that angels of Heaven are not to be trusted."

He glanced past Michael and Gabriel, to survey the entrance to the cave.

"We angels have become the prey to the beasts of the forest. The enemy has perverted many beasts of the jungle to the point where they crave the flesh of angels. I was told there are hundreds of beasts across the jungles of Luminarous that wait in hiding to devour angels. I'm afraid to say their numbers are growing every day and more demons are arriving each earth-day that passes."

Ahab stopped speaking to signal them to come closer in.

"Truth be known, they are planning a war against Heaven. They plan on capturing Heaven and conquering all of the earth. If they continue to grow in strength and numbers, then nothing may stand in their way."

"There is nothing that our Father in Heaven doesn't already know, Ahab. He is all-seeing and all-knowing. The enemy will never prevail against the LORD of Hosts, the God of the universe," Michael cut in abruptly and sharply said.

Ahab scowled but managed to immediately hide it.

"I know Michael," Ahab said. "I know, but it does make me think why hasn't he done anything about it yet?"

"Blaspheme and treachery," Gabriel drew his sword and roared. "You heard it from his mouth, Michael. Logos will take pleasure in striking you, Ahab the traitor."

Michael jumped to his feet and restrained Gabriel.

"Enough of that Gabe. We've lost enough brothers already. We mustn't lose another," Michael pleaded.

Then the archangel turned around quickly and sternly pointed at Ahab.

"And as for you, Ahab, hold your tongue lest I personally cut it out," Michael said with a kingly poise. Michael settled down and took a seat.

"You have still failed to answer the question of your escape. Did you truly escape, or did they let you go freely," Michael questioned Ahan, looking him in the eye.

"I needn't warn you what would happen to you if you choose to lie to us. God has his own way of dealing with liars," the archangel added.

Ahab's expression changed from sad to bold.

"They let me go, but only after I told them why we were here on Luminarous; why Caleb, Sethur, and myself were spying. I told them that Caleb was the lead scout and that I knew nothing more than that—"

"You sold Caleb out," Gabriel interrupted, angrily. "Then it is true that you are a coward and a fiend. Where's your loyalty, Ahab? Do you retain any qualities of an angel of Heaven or have you given yourself to the enemy?"

Michael regained order once again.

"This time Ahab, I nearly did let Gabriel unleash his fury on you. You were horribly wrong to give your brother away. However it is not my place to judge, for only God is judge. Though, I will say this—justice will be done for Caleb's sake."

Ahab appeared relieved from what Michael said.

"Why look so comfortable, Ahab," Michael, noticing his appearance, said. "Only God can judge, so it is my duty to bring you back to Heaven where you will hear your sentence before the throne of the Most High."

Ahab's face froze in horror.

"Don't fret too son. We are going to need your help to complete our mission. You will lead us back to the place you escaped from, "Michael stared at him like a hawk and said.

"No, no. I won't go back, I won't," Ahab shrieked in protest.

"But you must and you will—friend," Gabriel, with a firm tone, said.

"When the time comes, may the LORD forgive you, Ahab, for your treachery. From this point on we have a clean slate between us, but you will hold your tongue," Michael said.

"Now please honor your duty and guide us to the enemy camp," Michael's tone was softer, but commanding all the same, as he spoke.

"I will do as you ask." Ahab hesitated for a second, and mumbled, "Come now, can I rest a bit before we leave? Then I'll lead you back."

"If I can remember the way that is, " he added under his breath.

NOTE FROM THE SCRIBE...

Michael and Gabriel stepped outside the cave for a moment to talk privately. However, they didn't know who or what could be listening, but they still thought Ahab's ears should be kept from their discussion. Their first day on Luminarous presented them with dangers of a different kind. At least they were able to put that danger to rest. That is, Babylon the dragon, whose strength could be measured. He was a monster they could see; a threat they could conquer. The third day on Luminarous presented them with a whole new threat that could not be fully measured or seen for that matter. The known fact that the enemy had found them meant that they had been spying on them before hand. Also, the fact that the enemy knew of their whereabouts, made the angels very uneasy. There was no telling now what monsters lurked in the jungle or what could be expected at each turn.

Michael and Gabriel fully understood that their power to defeat the enemy, in the midst of battle, came directly from the LORD. What about the power to see the enemy coming? That thought had become very real to Michael and to Gabriel. It was a fear that could surface in their consciences at any moment. However, the Holy Spirit reminded them that perfect love casts out all fear and doubt. In God, they had perfect love, and even though the LORD didn't always tell them what was to come, they knew to trust in him with all of their hearts, minds, and spirits. There was nothing he couldn't accomplish; nothing was impossible for the God who created all life. In him was the truth and with him was perfect love.

What they discussed outside the cave was the question of Ahab's story. Was it entirely true? More so, could he be trusted? They spoke as quietly as possible for them to hear each other. After all, they didn't know who or what could be listening. That was another matter they discussed in private: the fact that they must not allow themselves to be led into a trap. They prayed that the Holy Spirit would discern the matter for them. Michael felt the Holy Spirit telling him that there were seeds of evil in Ahab's heart, but they must follow him for God would turn what Ahab meant for wrong into good. They concluded their private meeting with the resolution that they will trust Ahab to at least lead.

The Warrior Within ...

"Michael." Gabriel grabbed Michael by the arm as he was about to enter the cave and whispered, "Your permission to strike him with Logos should he be found untrustworthy. If you know what I mean."

"You know that is not for me to grant, but for God. Pray, Gabriel, pray for discernment. If a sword is meant for his end, then God will make it happen," Michael replied in a sharp whisper.

Inside the cave they found Ahab asleep, or so he seemed. He jumped to his feet and a look of sheer terror was written on his face.

"It is only us, Ahab," Michael said.

"I'm sorry. I startle easily," Ahab calmed himself and said. "Since my capture, I can't close my eyes for a moment or else visions of horror haunt me."

"Then I have an answer to your problem. It's time to leave," Gabriel uttered, and without showing any sympathy.

"I won't close my eyes, but can I rest a little longer," Ahab requested, somberly.

"We leave now," Michael declared. He surprised Gabriel and Ahab when he grabbed Ahab by the arm and pulled him outside.

Ahab fell backwards on the ground, rose slowly from his feet and brushed off his tunic.

"There's no need to get rough Michael. We can leave," he said under his breath. "Now which way is it. I need a moment to catch my bearings."

Ahab licked his finger and took a measurement of the wind.

"Ah, yes. We go this way, due west I believe."

"You mean east, don't you," Gabriel pointed out.

"Yes, of course, east. That's it," Ahab quickly replied.

Michael was already beginning to doubt his story. On the other hand, Gabriel didn't believe Ahab from the beginning. *A heap of deceitful words* is what Gabriel determined from the moment he learned Ahab's story. Ahab led the angels slowly through a forest thick with hibiscus bushes and abundant in tall tropical trees. They spent the better part of the afternoon backtracking their steps and changing routes every few hundred paces or so. Gabriel was losing his patience. The truth was that Ahab was actually lost. The torture he had succumbed to had diminished his mind, especially his memory. They hiked until nightfall and made camp in a small clearing. The sky may have been above them, but they couldn't see it through the thick canopy. The quarters were tight and uncomfortable. Ahab insisted they light a fire, even though the night was warm.

"There will be no fire. Not now, nor from here on," spoke Michael.

I know why you want a fire, Ahab, Gabriel thought.

"Is that your signal for the enemy or perhaps you prefer to be a meal for all the beasts of the jungle," Gabriel said.

"I just like a nice fire, nothing more than that that Gabriel, I assure you," Ahab shrugged his shoulders and calmly said.

The night was not without its strange noises. An owl hoot was comfortable, but a low growl was definitely unwelcome. Michael took the first watch. Nothing eventful happened, except for a few howls in the distance and a terrible roar. Fortunately, the LORD comforted Michael and it didn't hurt that the roar seemed to come from many earth-miles away. When it was time to take his watch, Gabriel had to get past the feeling of sleepiness. It was still new to him and not entirely welcomed either. After Michael had fallen to sleep, Gabriel noticed something moving in the jungle. Initially, it was hard to make out, since the forest was covered in darkness. His eyes soon adjusted and he could see two giant yellow eyes glowing and staring at him. Gabriel didn't move an inch. He felt the creature staring through him, but he didn't feel threatened by the watchful eyes. *What are you, or should I ask who are you*, Gabriel thought.

The next morning, Gabriel didn't share his experience with Michael, even though he wanted to. What held him back was the thought if this was the same creature he had seen before he didn't want Ahab knowing about it. The day brought with it even more arduous hiking than the day before. The bushes were thicker, the vines were pricklier, the ground was mushy, and a certain stench, unrecognizable to either of the angels permeated the air around them. Gabriel walked in front of Ahab, cutting back the vines that hung from the trees and covered the bushes. The vines were as thick as ropes, yet they were, no match for Logos, thought Gabriel.

Suddenly, Gabriel stepped in something wet.

"There's muddled water everywhere. What *is* this murky place? Where are you leading us, Ahab," Gabriel demanded.

They were in fact in a marsh of some kind.

"I don't fully remember this place, but it does hold some similarities to my memories," Ahab answered.

"What is that supposed to mean," Gabriel asked.

Michael looked at Ahab too waiting for an answer.

"Just as I said. I recall parts of it, but not all of it. There are pieces missing," he, replied, in a forthright tone.

"That's comforting to know," Gabriel blurted.

"Ahab, what *do* you remember," Michael asked.

"I remember the wet muddy ground, but I don't remember how far from the enemy base we are."

"Just as long as we're moving in the right direction," Michael said.

"Oh, yes. We are definitely going in the right direction. I can say that with certainty," Ahab insisted.

"Now that you've confirmed that for us Ahab, point the way. And Gabriel let the vines taste the steel of Logos," Michael declared.

The vines grew thicker and the water deeper. Their feet were slowed to a sluggish pace now that the water was waste deep. After a thousand paces, according to Gabriel, they emerged from the water and the ground became more solid, but muddy nonetheless. The vegetation wasn't as thick either and the vines diminished to a few scraggily looking strings.

"This is much better. I also remember these parts, honestly," Ahab said, rather he did it to convince himself or Michael and Gabriel, is what's questionable.

"We'll rest here for now. Take a few moments to relieve your tired legs," Michael said, as they came to a large circular shaped clearing where the grass was tall and thin. In the middle was a huge tree that appeared almost as if it was deliberately planted, thought Michael. The tree was broad at the base and it climbed at least a few hundred paces into the sky. The hands of time had written countless lines in the bark.

"This tree must have been here when the LORD created the foundations of the earth," Gabriel said.

The branches of the tree were odd shaped; twisted and thick, they reached out in all directions from the tree trunk like giant outstretched arms. Although these characteristics were unique in themselves, this is not what set it apart from the other trees. The leaves were unlike anything Michael had seen before. Each leaf was red and circular in shape; in fact, a near perfect circle and in the center was a star-shaped hole.

"Nothing like this existed on Mount Horeb, nor have I seen a tree resembling this in all of Heaven," Michael said, as he admired the tree. His eyes were wide open, taking all of it in.

"I do recall this tree," Ahab said, studying the tree. "If I'm correct in my calculations, we are not but three, possibly two days journey from the enemy's lair."

"Good, then we should take a longer rest here," Gabriel said.

Ahab eagerly agreed with a nod of his head.

"We shall make our camp here until tomorrow, for dusk is upon us." Michael said, he turned to Ahab and added, "I have something for you to do, Ahab. See the very top of that tree? The branches appear sturdy at least for someone of your stature. I do believe a great distance could be seen from the top of the tree. Ahab, could you climb to the top and report back to us what you see?"

Ahab was terrified of heights. He was reluctant at first, but agreed after Gabriel told him he would get some delicious fruit for him to eat. There were many trees growing at the edge of the clearing that had mangos and bananas.

Ahab began his climb and before long he had nearly reached the top. Michael watched from below. Meanwhile, Gabriel walked to the forest's edge to gather fruit. Gabriel had an armful of fruit when he heard a noise stirring in the forest, not far from where he stood. He carefully stepped backwards, with the fruit in hand. He ran over to Michael and dropped the fruit.

"What do you see," Michael yelled up to Ahab,

Gabriel suddenly forced his hand over Michael's mouth and motioned for him to be absolutely still.

"There's something moving only a stone's throw from us. Wait, there's something else moving over there," Gabriel whispered and pointed ahead of them to a point at the forest's edge.

"Whatever it is, there is more than one. I believe we're surrounded, take guard Michael," he added.

"I see nothing but treetops; countless tree tops. Wait, there's something moving. The trees are shaking. Five, six, seven, no, eight trees are moving. Something is coming our way," Ahab shouted down to them.

Gabriel was trying his best to tell Ahab to quiet down without having to shout up at him but it was of no use. Whatever might be in the forest knew their exact location thanks to Ahab's shouting.

"He just gave us away, Michael," Gabriel uttered.

"This is not the time to place blame," Michael looked

Gabriel in the eyes and said. "Save your energy. I do believe we must prepare for a battle."

"May the LORD's protection go before us and his strength fill us," Michael drew the Sword of the Spirit and declared.

Gabriel pulled Logos from its sheath and he advanced slowly forward with the archangel by his side. Suddenly, the trees on the very edge shook violently and two reptilian creatures, slimy and gross, emerged from the jungle. They were about nine feet in height and covered in green scales. They stood on two agile-looking legs; the reptiles held two tiny arms at their chest with razor sharp claws. Their eyes were dark and piercing. Only a couple of dozen paces stood between the angels and the raptors. The monstrous creatures didn't move.

"Gabriel, the fear of the LORD is our strength. When the LORD is with us, who or what shall we fear," Michael declared.

"Mighty and steadfast are we—" Gabriel answered.

"—warriors of God," Michael, finishing his sentence, said.

The angels charged forward as the monsters ran right towards them. The distance between them was lessening quickly and the angels' hearts were pounding faster and faster. They were almost in striking distance of the monsters, when with perfect timing they leapt through the air and shoved their swords into each of the monster's chests. The beasts dropped to the ground and the angels stood unscathed and victorious.

"Glory to God in the highest," Michael yelled and just as he did, he heard the sound of steel flashing through the air. He turned and witnessed Gabriel take down another one of the slimy beasts.

"Thank the LORD. You have saved me brother. Down, quickly," Michael cried out.

Gabriel rolled to the ground and Michael lunged forward with his sword, stopping another beast in its tracks. Four monsters lay dead on the ground. The angels were fatigued from their fight.

"Watch out," Ahab yelled from the treetops.

Michael and Gabriel turned and beheld a gigantic grizzly standing on its hind legs. The angels stared at the beast and it stared back and for a moment everything seemed frozen in time. There were about three-dozen paces between the angels and the grizzly. Michael knew this grizzly was more than a mere bear or beast of the jungle. The bear stared intensely at them, but what made it unique was the fact it had only one eye. Michael knew this bear by name.

"Magnimus," Michael exclaimed. And like an animal that knew its name, the bear returned to its four feet with a huge vibrating boom and ran towards them. Only this was no pet, but a ferocious monster that served one master.

"Be still, Gabe. The LORD commands it of us," Michael said, holding Gabriel back by the arm.

Gabriel, in the face of danger, prayed to the LORD. There was no mistaking Magnimus now. His one eye glared viciously at Michael.

"You failed your mission once and you will not succeed this time," Michael uttered and raised the Sword of the Spirit to the heavens, threatening Magnimus.

Gabriel stood in a defensive stance with Logos drawn; he was ready for a battle. "You'd better give it your best, slave of Satan," Gabriel said.

Magnimus was closing in fast with each huge step. The grizzly was moving quicker than it appeared it was able to run. Everything was happening much faster than can possibly be described. The grizzly was twice the size of both Michael and Gabriel. What could they do against this monster that was bent on destroying them?

Michael brought his sword up from his side. He held the sword tightly with the blade in front of his face and braced himself for the impact. Michael stared death in its face and then it happened. The bear let out a fierce growl, there was an impact and crashing sound, and a boom shook the ground. Michael and Gabriel opened their eyes and witnessed a mighty tussle between the grizzly and what looked like a black blur.

"It's the panther," Gabriel exclaimed.

"The panther," Michael said, intrigued but grateful all the same.

"What's happening," Ahab shouted down. He was safe and sound still perched at the top of the tree. There was no answer so he shouted again. Michael and Gabriel ignored his shouting.

The panther surprisingly held his own against the grizzly.

The panther paced in a circle with its ears pointed back and with its front shoulders low to the ground. The grizzly stood on its back legs and let out a blood-curdling roar. The ground beneath the angels' feet vibrated, dozens of birds fled the trees, retreating to the safety of the air. The panther stood its ground, unmoving and undaunted by the grizzly's intimidation. The bear salivated and roared again, the ground shook again, and a shriek from a monkey echoed in the jungle. All of the jungle's inhabitants were apparently terrified, yet the panther steadied itself.

Magnimus was infuriated. The panther leaped through the air with the momentum and sheer power of a boulder released from a catapult. The panther latched on to the grizzly's face, imbedding its front claws deep into Magnimus' face. The bear roared and swatted the panther to the ground as if it was nothing more than an annoying fly. The panther regained its footing quickly and attacked from the rear, going for the bear's legs, then he swiftly returned to face the bear. The grizzly's stomach was now exposed and the panther, seeing this fortunate opportunity, pounced forward. The bear's stomach bore a serious wound from the panther and still it wasn't finished with the grizzly. Magnimus appeared unconscious as he lay frozen on his back and then Michael and Gabriel saw him open his eye. The panther was now completely on top of the bear's stomach clawing away.

"I will never leave you nor forsake you. Trust in me and behold I will deliver you," the Lord spoke to Michael's heart in that very moment.

The bear swung its arm back and with one mighty swing, the panther flew into the air and struck the tree in the center of the clearing. The panther fell dead to the earth.

"No! Lord of Hosts, wield my sword," Gabriel shouted and charged forward.

Before the bear could stand to its feet, Gabriel had jumped into the air and plunged his blade deep into the bear's stomach. The bear let out a final roar that faded quickly as Gabriel twisted the blade of Logos even deeper into its hideous flesh.

As the bear lay there struggling to breath, something strange indeed was happening; the bear's shape gradually started to change. The fur fell off and its color went from dark to light as its broad face narrowed and its naked flesh was exposed. What lay before them now was a fallen angel. Not just any fallen angel, but one of Satan's most favored demons. Michael and Gabriel stood over him. The demon choked and struggled to live.

"I am Magnimus, first lieutenant general of the elite royal army of Hell and most favored by Satan, may he live forever. I may perish, but our cause will prevail. Heaven will be vanquished and you Archangel Michael will perish in the flames of my master's wrath," he said and breathed his last. The demon then burst into a cloud of ash and dust.

"Now, that's something I've never seen," After the dust settled, Gabe said. "Thank you, brother." Michael said.

"You heard what I said," Gabe shrugged his shoulders and said. "My prayer was simply answered. Credit is due to the LORD, not me."

"The LORD has delivered us. Mighty is he and worthy of all praise," Michel said with his hand on Gabriel's shoulder. "Twice Satan tried to destroy me and both times the LORD had mercy on me."

Gabriel turned to see to the panther, but it was gone.

"He's vanished," Gabriel exclaimed.

"What or who he was, I don't know, but I do know he is a friend of God and he will be taken care of, Gabe. Fear not, the LORD is in control," Michael remarked.

Then, the seraphim were suddenly taken off-guard by a disturbing noise; the sound of snapping tree branches and a big crash against the ground. It was nothing more than Ahab. He had fallen from the tree as he was trying to climb down. Gabriel reached out his hand to a dusty and shaken Ahab.

"What happened," Ahab said.

"Nice timing Ahab," Gabriel said with a hint of sarcasm under his breath.

"What were all those beasts? I've never seen that kind before."

"Next time, I think I will climb the tree and maybe you can gather the fruit," Gabriel smiled at him and said.

"Gabe, don't let him get to you. Keep your focus. Ahab, those were no doubt slaves to Satan, servants of the prince of darkness," Michael remarked.

"Twice our position has been given away and twice Ahab has been present. Strange coincidence, don't you think Michael? That is, if I believed in coincidences," spoke Gabriel.

"Both times I was your help," Ahab said.

Gabriel clenched his fists together. He wanted so badly to strike that witless imbecile, Ahab, in the face.

"Just one punch, Michael—just one, that's all I want."

"There'll be no bloodshed today, Gabriel. I know he's been incorrigible, but do control yourself," Michael said, completely ignoring Ahab.

"Yes, of course brother. Well, do you feel it is safe to camp here tonight? Dusk is quickly setting in," mentioned Gabriel, completely worn out.

"I think it's a lovely place. The tree makes for a great perch," Ahab noted.

"We shall camp here tonight," Michael announced. "The lower tree branches are big enough to support Gabriel and me. As for Ahab, well, you can keep watch tonight. You better get going and climb to the top before all daylight is gone."

"Can I take some fruit with me? It would be a shame for all this sitting here to go to waste," Ahab said, speaking of the fruit Gabriel had gathered before the battle.

"Fine, take two pieces and get to the top and don't be choosy, just be hasty," answered Michael.

THE WRATH OF CARCHEMISH

NOTE FROM THE SCRIBE...

Ahab kept watch the entire night, staying alert for any disturbance in the jungle, so that Michael and Gabriel could rest. They
had slept peacefully under the stars, free from any interruptions.
Neither of them had a single vision throughout the night. The
LORD knew they needed a good rest and he provided one.

Morning came, and with it brought yet another day to be
thankful. The angels praised the LORD for his everlasting goodness and for his protection against the enemy. Ahab didn't
appear as if he wanted to join in with their worship and instead
he remained perched in the tree; insisting that he keep an eye
out so that they could praise the LORD freely. Michael and
Gabriel thought about it shortly and agreed that Ahab made a
good point; they still needed to be vigilant of the enemy. The
events to come in this chapter will prove to be helpful, so take
heed and read carefully.

The Warrior Within...

The morning was passing by quickly and the sun was now at its peak; the sweltering heat was suffocating, beneath the jungle canopy. What is more, the undergrowth consisted of mostly briar bushes that stuck to their clothing and tore at their skin.

"Curse these bushes for their thorns," Gabriel said.

Ahab noticed that the bush Gabriel had spoken to had shriveled up and died instantly. He was amazed at such powers and fearful of them as well. Even Gabriel, an archangel, does not possess supernatural power, he thought, who is he that he can command plants to die. Ahab had forgotten about the faith that Gabriel and Michael commanded in their spirits. That is why the LORD chose them, set apart from all seraphim, even before they took their first breath.

"How did you do that, Gabriel," Ahab raised his eyebrows and asked. "Faith," Michael said.

"Faith," Ahab uttered, with doubt in his voice.

"Yes, faith," Gabriel quickly asserted.

"The Father commands it of all his servants." Michael spoke up again, saying, "Faith is the foundation of my spirit. Without faith, my soul cannot be preserved; without faith what hope would there be? For faith is of the LORD and hope is born from faith."

"I see, I mean to say—ah—I know that," Ahab said,

"Then why ask," Gabriel was busy cutting away at the vines when he mentioned. "Do you not believe, in your heart, that faith can accomplish something as small as a drink of water or something as incredible as commanding a mountain to pick itself up and move its foundations into the sea? Perhaps, your mind has been polluted by the enemy and you thought my curse to the bush was nothing more than dark sorcery of Hell?"

The angels were hiking along even as they discussed the matter at hand.

"Well, of course not," Ahab answered. "That's preposterous. Keep your accusations to yourself, Gabriel. I am your only guide to the enemy's base and my memory might just fail me if you continue with such antics."

"We wouldn't want you to lose your memory and I don't think you would want me to lose my balance; I could possibly slip and my sword might come around and strike you," Gabriel laughed and said.

"Now, we wouldn't want that to happen, but of course it would be by accident. I would never intend to harm you, nor do I think you would intend to forget the way," Gabriel added.

Ahab was beside himself. "Archangel Michael, are you going to stand idly by while Gabriel blasts threats at me," Ahab said, turned and stared straight at Michael.

"I didn't pick up on any threat," the archangel simply replied. "Actually, I think he sounded more concerned for your safety than anything else; that is why you march between the two of us, for your safety, of course."

"I do believe, Ahab, you should put your false concerns behind you and march on," Michael added in a kind voice.

Ahab murmured a few comments under his breath.

Many earth-hours had now passed since they had left the tree in the clearing; how many, they couldn't tell because the jungle canopy covered most of the sunlight making it difficult to judge the position of the sun. The forest was becoming like an oven as the sun baked the treetops the heat became trapped under the canopy. The ground beneath their feet was firm for the most part, yet at times it became almost like quicksand. Traveling through this particular forest was much more arduous and strenuous than any of the other environments they had experienced on Luminarous.

Ahab babbled a few words to himself from time to time, but neither Michael nor Gabriel paid much attention to him. The humidity grew unbearable and the air was stifling; all three angels were drenched, head to toe, with sweat.

"Will you stop your complaining, Ahab," Gabriel snapped. "I said, stop your complaining Ahab."

Ahab's incessant murmuring had become completely annoying.

"I don't believe he's listening," Michael said as he grabbed Ahab's shoulder and gave him a shake.

"What—what is it," Ahab blurted out, a little annoyed.

"You've been chattering to yourself for the past hour or so. What's going on," Michael inquired as they hiked.

"I have? It must be this place. It's getting to me," Ahab said.

"Well, I don't like the situation either, but we'll just have to muster up the will if we're to make it through," Michael said with authority in his tone.

"Yes, of course. I'll straighten up," Ahab uttered in a bland almost emotionless voice.

At this point, it became apparent the landscape was changing and not for the better. Vines just as thick surrounded them, but now they were covered in sharp thorns. With every step they took, Michael felt like hundreds of small thorns were grabbing at his hands and feet.

"It's as if the jungle is closing in on us," Gabriel said. "It's as if an unseen force is bent on trapping us."

Strangely enough, traveling between the two angels, Ahab seemed to move along untouched. He evaded the long arms of the innumerable branches and he was just out of reach from the painful grasp of the thorny vines.

Dusk was soon upon them and that's when the jungle really began coming to life. The vines and branches became more aggressive and now even Ahab's thin body couldn't avoid the prickly sting from the undergrowth. Ahab cried out in pain with each step, his annoying mumbling had become more and more frequent. Michael and Gabriel endured the suffering without saying a word. The light was fading quickly and then Gabriel saw it.

"We're free. I can see the sky just ahead. Only a dozen paces or so and we'll be out of this dreadful, stinking forest," Gabriel said.

Though, the forest was bent on keeping them for itself. The vines grasped their ankles and the trees stabbed at them with their many branches. Michael found himself trapped. Hundreds of vines had wrapped completely around him, like a cocoon. Dozens of tree branches seized Gabriel, forming a crude cage around him. Enveloped by darkness, neither of them could see Ahab.

"Michael can you hear me," Gabriel cried out.

"Yes, I'm over here," Michael said. from about a half a dozen paces to the east of Gabriel.

"I can't move," Gabriel said.

"I can't either," Michael said and struggled to get free. "Is Ahab with you?"

"No–I thought he might be by you," Gabriel replied, trying to reach for his dagger. "What are we going to do, Michael?"

"Pray. Pray Gabriel," Michael said, determination was in his words.

A few moments went by and still they were trapped and there wasn't a single sign of Ahab anywhere. *Maybe he's trapped or maybe he's been knocked unconscious. Still he could be dead, or even worse, he could have run away, but why*—Gabriel thought—*he's treacherous, that's why.*

Gabriel stretched out his fingers with every ounce of strength he had left in him, trying his hardest to reach the dagger.

"Just a little further, a little more ought to do it," he said out loud as he touched the sheath, which was empty. "What. Where's my dagger? He took it! I knew he was a traitor from the moment I saw him."

"Enough is enough," Michael shouted with all the breath in him. "Satan you have no power here. In the name of the Lord of Hosts and the King of Kings I command you—stop in the name of God's Son."

Within a split second, the vines released their grip and recoiled into the ground, the tree branches that were determined on suffocating Gabriel came loose. Gabriel fell to the ground and Michael stood to his feet.

"Praise be to God," Gabriel regained his footing and shouted.

"Thanks be to God for he has delivered us and he is faithful," Michael remarked. "His words, 'I will never leave you nor forsake you,' now hold more meaning than they ever have before."

"Well, what are we waiting for," Gabriel laughed with joy and exclaimed. "God has freed us and yet we are still standing in this cursed forest; an open sky and crisp refreshing air await us. Follow me, let's go, Michael."

Earlier the same day and far away from the angels, the enemy camp was in an uproar. The demons stopped what they were doing to see what the commotion was all about. There was cheering and cursing. It was anarchy, but an orderly chaos all the same. More demons joined the crowd each second and more were on their way. It became apparent now, that this was a celebration. The demons quickly gathered in a tight group around three other demons that were dragging someone or something behind them in a net.

"We have returned. Nimrim summon the master Judas," Korah announced.

"Right away," Nimrim replied; he had come to see what all the noise was about.

Dathan and Abiram tied the net with its precious cargo to a large sturdy tree.

"That should hold him until we receive further orders," Korah said, a satisfied grin was on his face. "You did well brothers." He patted Dathan and Abiram on the back; they were exhausted from their struggle with Luminarous.

"It could, just as easily, have been any of us," Korah remarked. "Rehoboam was a brave fool. Brave, but a fool indeed. Well, his effort was not in vain and, in the end, his daring efforts did pay off. Look at Luminarous now, he's powerless."

Korah laughed at the fallen star. Though, he stopped right away, because he noticed that all the legions had gathered.

"Back off. Back away. Or Major Judas will have your head," Korah screamed; he was a fool to scold the legions. His pride, like usual, had blinded him.

"Watch out, Korah, or I'll have your head," a demon, much bigger than he, yelled.

"I'm asking for order. Order until Judas arrives," Korah demanded.

His brothers Dathan and Abiram jumped in front of him to protect him from the angry masses. It wouldn't matter much, though, for the masses could easily overpower the three brothers if they desired. All that it would take is for one demon in the legions to make a single move and the three brothers would be dead meat. Even if only one demon among the thousands decided to throw a stone at them, that is all it would take and the three brothers would be pummeled to death; trampled under the fury of a riotous crowd. Korah, on the other hand, was much too prideful or dense to realize what a foolish and possibly fatal, mistake it would be to taunt his fellow demons.

A demon, small and hideous, poked at Luminarous with a stick.

"He moved," the demon squealed.

Luminarous began to stir. He had been unconscious and was now awake.

"I said back off or I'll run you through," Korah screamed.

"Soldiers–I think we have a little trouble maker on our hands," the small hideous demon said in a shrill voice, glaring at Korah.

"Who does he think he is anyway? Judas," another demon added.

"I say we teach him a lesson, boys. What do you say," a brawny demon said.

Dathan and Abiram took a few steps back towards the tree where Luminarous was tied; Korah stood behind them.

"He's a coward, boys," the small hideous demon screeched.

"All three of them are," the brawny demon said. "Let's have some fun; a little scuffle might do 'em some good; teach 'em a lesson."

About fifty or so rough looking demons started moving in on the three brothers. They were drooling like a pack of wolves; feverishly anxious to bring down their prey.

"Korah, I told you if you touched me you would be dead. Fascinating how that worked out," Luminarous stirred and spitefully said.

"Stop, I say. What is the meaning of this," shouted a voice. It was Major Judas and his voice never sounded more menacing than it did now.

"My apologies Master Judas. We just wanted to have a closer look." the small hideous demon, who seemed to be the leader of the mob, said.

The legions parted instantly as Judas approached with his personal security by his side and a foreign or strange-looking demon following behind him.

"I believe you were about to kill without an assignment or at least first seeking my permission. That would be a fatal mistake. State your name," Judas ordered.

"Gee—gee—Geba, uh, Master Judas—" he replied, stuttering. "—We meant no harm. Please believe me."

"Major Judas, they were going to kill us and take Luminarous away from here," Korah blurted out.

"It's true, Major Judas–sir," Dathan added and Abiram nodded in agreement.

"Nonsense. Lies," Geba screeched.

"Lies, nothing but lies," shouted the brawny demon.

Judas signaled the strange demon, which had been standing behind him, to come forward. He whispered something to the demon, who was huge and he was of a different appearance than the rest of the demons. His clothes were foreign and strange looking; he had many badges adorned on his robe, and his hair was the color of fire.

"I'll show you how demons like Geba are dealt with," Judas turned and addressed the mob. "Geba meet Carchemish."

The foreign demon unsheathed his sword. Carchemish's sword was unlike any weapon the demons had ever seen. It glowed like hot embers; like steel that had been heated in fire. Geba's face instantly turned pale in terror. He tried to run, but Carchemish cut him off with a giant leap and he ran Geba through with his sword. Geba dropped to the ground and was dead.

"Now, is there any other demon who would like to lie to me," Carchemish said. "Speak up now. Well, round up the rest of this mob and take them below and shut them away." His menacing tone intimidated the crowds.

Carchemish, along with Judas' personal security, about one hundred tall and sturdy demons, took the demons down below. Only a few gave them trouble and they were given the exact same treatment as Geba.

After the mob had been taken to their imprisonment, Judas ordered the crowds to disperse. Only Carchemish remained by his side and a handful of personal guards and of course, the three brothers.

Korah approached Judas and saluted him. Judas inquired about Rehoboam.

"We captured Luminarous after three days of intense tracking and hunting. Rehoboam, sir, gave his life bravely. If not for his sacrifice, the fallen star would still be at large. That is the truth. All of it," Korah answered him.

Judas put forth his finest regrets possible but, honestly, he couldn't care less about Rehoboam or the rest of the search party. Instead, pleasing thoughts filled his head; he knew that with Luminarous in his custody he would be a sure candidate for promotion to lieutenant general. He knew that only Satan and Beltezar would command more authority than him and not to mention that the long desired title of demon prince would most certainly and deservingly be bestowed upon him. All that he must do now is deliver Luminarous personally to Satan's feet. To Judas, this was nothing but a technicality and needless to say, his ego was growing even larger. The sincere frown he had shown for the loss of Rehoboam soon turned to a devilish grin.

Korah thought this to be disrespectful to his comrade, so he confronted Judas in front of Carchemish and the major's personal guards.

"Sir, I should think this to be wrong, but your face reveals what the truth is," Korah boldly said. "You don't have a single nuance of respect or grief for our fallen comrade, Rehoboam."

"What disrespect you show for your commander. Carchemish, will you please deal with Korah," Judas stared him in the face and said.

"To Rehoboam's honor," Korah drew his sword in fury and shouted.

He raised his sword to strike a deadly blow to Judas, but the major quickly spoke an incantation and Korah's arm froze in its risen position; he couldn't move it no matter how hard he tried. His face was terror-stricken and his two brothers didn't have time to react; Carchemish suddenly swooped in and with one swift swing of his sword, Korah lay dead on the ground. Then Dathan and Abiram sprinted in to avenge their fallen brother.

Judas signaled his personal guard to stay put.

"Let Carchemish handle them," the major said, a sinister smile stretched across his face.

Dathan took no haste in delivering a blow to Carchemish, but it was quickly blocked. Sparks flew through the air as the noise of steel striking against steel pierced the air. Abiram, attempted to catch Carchemish off guard as he lunged towards him, but instead he immediately ducked and rolled to avoid Abiram's blow.

Meanwhile, many demons had started to gather. Sounds of

fighting would always bring a crowd, since demons would often have nasty rows among themselves. They thought it to be more of a sport rather than a division among their kind. The fighting continued as, both Dathan and Abiram strategically lunged at Carchemish, knocking the huge demon to the ground. Abiram moved in quickly to finish him off but, quicker than lightning, Carchemish dodged his sword, rolling right into Abiram. Carchemish stabbed him in the gut and dropped the demon to the ground. By now, nearly a thousand had gathered around the fight.

"No," Dathan shouted and ran at Carchemish with all of his force.

Dathan leapt fiercely into the air. He had jumped high above the huge demon; he had Carchemish sharply in his sights.

This is it. My chance to prove myself, thought Dathan.

He could avenge his brother and make a name for himself among the bravest in Hell and he would do it with one perfect strike to Carchemish's head. His sword was inches from Carchemish's head, but he dodged Dothan's swing and plunged his sword straight into Dathan as he was in midair.

"Blood and spit, you'll die for this," Dathan, with his last breath cursed. "Mark my words, you'll be run through the gut."

He closed his eyes and his spirit faded into oblivion.

"If anyone else desire's to defy Lucifer or his authorities, then you will have to come through me," Carchemish declared and pulled his sword from Dathan's chest and wiped it clean.

Carchemish's threat would surely remain unchallenged, for no demon present dare defy his words. Even among the legions on Luminarous, there was not a single demon that could match strength or power with Carchemish. Even a battle of wits would be hard to win against this high-ranking demon. Carchemish had arrived the day before; sent by Beltezar himself, to prepare for his arrival. Carchemish was larger than Goliath who was, until now, the biggest demon on the island. Even so, he outdid himself in the area of articulation. Truly he was as clever as a fox; having the ability to outwit the smartest of demons and, yes, even angels. Accordingly, his title Carchemish the Dreaded, suited him well. He was given his prestigious title for his feats at the great battle in Heaven where he supposedly had slain over ten thousand seraphim. Lucifer personally called him Carchemish the Dreaded from the day they established their dominion in Hell. There are few honors among the demons greater than being given a title by Lucifer. His title was quite befitting, since Carchemish's appearance was truly dreadful. His hair was red like the fiery pits of Hell. His face was rugged and handsome, yet terrible and hideous. However, it was his piercing jaded eyes that struck fear in his foes. Moreover, he possessed a stature that was solid as rock; he even intimidated the most powerful of demons with his sheer size and strength. Notably, when his anger flared he was known to deal brutally with those who crossed his path. The intelligence reports from Caleb have said that Carchemish wielded a sword too heavy for most any demon to bear. In fact, it possessed a supernatural power, since it was forged out of the fire from the deepest pits of Hell.

The few words that Carchemish had spoken captivated the demons' total attention. Thus, in complete silence, the thousands of demons had been held at bay. Judas thought that he'd better address the masses before there is an uprising.

"Brothers, comrades," Judas said. "I swear to you by our Lord Lucifer that what just happened will serve as an example. As you know brothers, total allegiance to the principalities of Hell is an essential part of our duty. Korah boasted such a sentiment to be futile. Neither he nor his brothers shared in our common faith. Therefore you must understand it was absolutely necessary to take extreme actions to assure the well being of the entire legion."

Half the legion looked dumbfounded at what Judas had said, yet others appeared ready to join together in a mob and make a riot of the situation. Judas took a brief moment to weigh his next words carefully, so he stood idly with the most sincere smile, which was cynical at best.

"Your needs and security are the foremost of my concerns," he said as the right words came to mind. "As your commander I promise to lead you to victory. Lucifer's will be done, may he live forever."

"Long live Judas, may Lucifer live forever," the legions chanted. The demons no longer seemed to care about Carchemish's executions. Judas breathed a sigh of relief for his dark magic had worked its spell over the small army.

They're contained for now. It's time to prepare for his arrival, thought Judas.

"Take the fallen star below," Judas commanded. "There's a special room prepared for him. Place four guards in front of his cell, four of my best personal security."

Carchemish saluted him and ordered a couple of huge brutes to drag Luminarous below to his holding cell. Meanwhile, Judas dismissed the crowds and slipped away, unnoticed, back to his quarters below the ground. He summoned a council with his most trusted demons. They met in secret room that could only be accessed through a hidden corridor in Judas' quarters. The room was dimly lit by thirteen candles that hung from an iron chandelier above a round table. The surface of the table had a symbol etched into it that ran from edge to edge. The symbol appeared as a five-pointed star called a pentagram.

Once everyone was assembled at the meeting and seated, the door slid shut.

"What's the latest word on the enemy, Nimrim," Judas commenced the deliberations with a question.

Nimrim had a medium to average build for a demon, but he was sharply confident, which earned him the position of command sergeant major of the secret intelligence.

"Sir," Nimrim saluted Judas and said. "Baal has reported they are on the move heading due west straight towards the forbidden zone. Ahab plans to divert them from the forbidden zone and lead them into the trap."

Judas nodded and told him to be seated. The major looked around at the demons in attendance. There were about thirteen total, including Carchemish.

"This council I have called together this evening concerns the seraphim of Heaven," Judas addressed them. "Thus far, my plans are working perfectly. Luminarous is in custody and there are none left from the hunting party that captured him. This is perfect, since none remain to play the witness or misconstrue the facts so to speak. The fact is I and Carchemish led a brave group of soldiers into the jungle to capture Luminarous. As far as we are concerned, Rehoboam, Korah, Dathan, and Abiram were never stationed on Luminarous. We have taken an oath on this matter, and as for the mob, they well be rightfully exterminated. They should have never stuck their noses into my business. They're deserving of death, do we all agree?"

The council nodded one by one around the table in agreement.

"Alright, I did act in accordance with the wishes of the council and as for the legions who personally witnessed the three brothers being slain, they are being taken care of right now. Carchemish delivered the initial threat, which was very menacing indeed."

Judas laughed haughtily and continued.

"Also, the spies have been planted among the legions to communicate any matters that require our attention. The spies have also been instructed to spread rumors throughout the legions, stating that Carchemish has executed at least three, four, five—maybe a dozen demons or more. The rumors may vary, but the message is consistent that whoever crosses Major Judas will be dealt with in a most serious manner."

Judas was interrupted by a sudden intrusion. The hidden door slid open and a small demon poked his head slightly in and started to speak.

"Carchemish, kill him for his intrusion immediately," Judas snapped.

"Please. Please don't kill me master," the demon begged for his life. "I bring news from Baal. The wolf only arrived moments ago."

"Well, tell us. Don't hold your tongue," Judas ordered.

The demon was still trembling with fear as he tried to speak. Carchemish's sword was touching the back of his neck.

"Carchemish, please relieve yourself from holding that dreadful sword. Go ahead and deliver the message."

"Ba—Ba—Baal tells us that—" the demon stuttered as he spoke.

Judas was impatient to say the least.

"Speak clearly or you'll be dead. I swear it," the major screamed.

"Baal tells us that Ahab awaits the rendezvous point. Baal is awaiting his orders above ground, as I speak," the demon cleared his throat and answered.

"We were about to discuss such matters, before your most

untimely interruption. Give Baal this message," Judas calmed himself and said. He wrote something down on a small parchment and passed it to Nimrim to hand to the demon.

"Please read the words before you leave. I just want to make sure they're written clearly," Judas said with a deceitfully sincere tone.

"I hereby deny my allegiance to Lucifer and swear an oath to serve the God of Heaven," the demon unrolled the parchment and read.

The council acted stunned at what they heard.

"You all heard it from his own mouth," Judas gravely said. "This is just awful. Such words, unfortunately for you, will be your death sentence. Carchemish, deliver justice as it is due."

"My pleasure, Major Judas," Carchemish raised his sword and concurred.

The demon shook in fear, but in a flash it was over. Those present looked a bit shocked, but they did not object, in any way, to the execution.

"It had to be done," Judas asserted. "No one outside this council can know of our proceedings, no one. Migron, drag him outside. Nimrim, deliver this message to Baal."

Judas handed the demon another piece of parchment that had been prepared before hand; written on them were coordinates for Ahab to follow. Nimrim saluted Judas and was out the door with the message before any of the council could speak.

Judas remained seated. He was sorting out his thoughts. No one at the table spoke a word. Carchemish took his seat again, and sat still. Around the table were many demons of important influence. There were thirteen demons in all; each of them either held prestigious ranks or they happened to be stationed on the island and were in Judas' good graces. One of the demons present was Migron who was a sergeant in command of many soldiers on Luminarous. Others in the secret council even hailed directly from Hell such as Carchemish, who had arrived just that morning accompanied by two demon princes who happened to be members of Lucifer's personal council.

The demon prince named Omri was an elder and ruler of the thirteenth province in Hell. He was a close friend and confidant of Lucifer. After all, one cannot rise to such a position of influence in Hell, without friends in high places. Omri was a strange looking demon. His beard was braided in thirteen locks to represent the province he ruled over.

The other demon prince, Baasha, was wicked indeed. It's a known fact that he killed the demon prince, Nadab, to seal his place among the demon princes of Hell. Furthermore, he was commanded by Lucifer himself to assassinate Nadab for being to forgiving of those under his command. Lucifer wanted someone cold of heart and ruthless and Baasha was pleasing in his eye. Since his fall from Heaven, Baasha had risen to become a demon prince by eliminating weak links like Nadab and other demons that he had been commissioned by Beltezar and Lucifer to assassinate.

"The plans are now set into motion—" after a moment of silence, Judas affirmed. "—but what I am looking for are a few ruthless soldiers to carry out the next phase in my plan. I have written down some names and I will pass them around now. Give me a *yea* or *nay* on each name."

The names of three individuals made their way through the council and only two received enough votes to be a part of the plan. The two who selected were Ammon, a captain in Judas' personal security, and Ishmael the proud and brutal warrior of the thirteenth province; he was with Omri as his personal bodyguard for the journey to Luminarous. The demon not selected was Nimrim, who was still above ground at the time the voting took place. Everyone was in agreement that he was not suited for the journey. He was too small a demon to fight against two of the mightiest warriors of God.

"I feel I am most capable and best suited to lead a mission, such as this one, of great importance," Judas said and stood up and paced around the table.

"But I must humbly decline, brothers. For my presence, at the moment is needed here to prepare for Beltezar's arrival, may he be feared. Now I am open to suggestions. Speak freely my distinguished council."

Migron was the first to speak. Migron was a brutally strong

demon, tall with broad shoulders and a rugged face. He was dark and menacing.

"Sir, I salute you most wise and prudent Major Judas," Migron boldly said. "Now, if you may allow me, I will proudly lead this quest. Furthermore, I swear that no hair on the seraphim's head will be harmed, as you have commanded. I will bring them personally to you at three days end."

Judas thought it over for a brief moment while he studied Migron's physique.

"Migron, if you do as you say, I swear I will put in a word for your promotion with Beltezar himself; but remember this, if you fail, you will rue the day that you volunteered your services. Moreover, I would be more than proud to deliver your head to Lucifer's feet."

"And on a silver platter, all the better," he added with a snicker.

"Now are there any objections to my appointment of Migron," Judas, after the matter, asked the council.

"Judas, most honorable and prudent commander under Lucifer, may he live forever," Carchemish daringly interjected. "I adjure you that in your infinite wisdom you will allow me to lead the mission. You know the powers I possess and I will assure a swift and clean capture."

As Judas considered the notion, Migron had to bite his tongue to keep from cursing Carchemish. He knew that if he opened his mouth against Carchemish the Dreaded he would most likely remove his tongue.

Judas lifted his hand and broke the foreboding silence.

"So, as you have spoken, Carchemish, so it shall be. Migron, you are second in command. Ammon, Ishmael, and Migron, obey Carchemish as you would Beltezar or Lucifer. Carchemish, you must leave within the hour. Go in secret and be swift."

HERESY

"**Baal** what news do you bring from camp," Ahab inquired.

"Master Ahab, I ran through the night a great distance to bring important news to you," Baal said. "A company of demons has been selected by Judas to capture the servants of Heaven. A powerful demon was selected as their leader. His name is Carchemish and his anger burns against heaven. He was ordered to bring them each back to camp in one piece and unharmed. They were to set out shortly after I left. Your orders are to lead them away from the forbidden territory and into the trap. Judas' commands your total cooperation and if you fail there will be Hell to pay."

"I understand fully," Ahab said. "He has my total—ouch— what was that for," Ahab screeched. The wolf had given him a nasty bite on the arm.

"Judas told me to give you a reminder. 'Just a taste of what will become of you if you fail,' his words exactly, Master Ahab."

"Alright then, no need to be overzealous. Return to camp and alert Judas that I will do as he commands," Ahab requested.

"As you wish, Master Ahab—grrrr—why'd you do that," Baal growled. Ahab had kicked him in the side and hard, too.

"Just to remind you who's master. Now go and be quick about it. There isn't much time," Ahab snapped.

"Morning certainly came fast," Gabriel remarked. "It feels good to get some rest. Especially after that dreadful forest nearly swallowed us both. Did anything interesting happen last night?"

Gabriel had just woken up, since Michael had taken the last watch of the night.

"I thank God that we're free of the enemy's trap," Michael drank a handful of water and said. "Nothing in particular really happened last night, but I will say the stars have never looked so good."

"I know exactly what you mean. Where'd you get that water? That wasn't there last night," Gabriel exclaimed.

"The water just appeared. I should have mentioned it right away, please forgive me," Michael uttered.

"It's already forgotten. I'm awfully thirsty," Gabriel said and dipped his hands into the water and drank of the refreshing spring.

"I wasn't asking for your apology, but I guess I should as well," said Michael and he laughed. Gabriel chuckled.

"It feels good to laugh," Michael said.

"And even better to drink," Gabriel added with a witty smile.

The spring of water was exceptional. It was about a half a dozen paces across and its origin seemed to come out of the forest. The water was blue, as clear as a crystal, crisp and clean. There was no debris in the water, which in itself was amazing to behold. The spring had a special quality to it that made it appear as if the water was much deeper than it actually was; in reality the water was even less than half a pace in depth. The spring was possibly the clearest water they had seen on earth, but then they recalled the waters at the meadow—the Pool of Bethesda.

"He is full of mercy and grace," Gabriel spoke softly.

"He is mercy and grace," Michael spoke with great zeal. "The very words have no meaning without his Being. As long as the LORD sits on his throne, mercy and grace will abound."

"That's as true of a word as I've ever heard from you brother. What shall we do now? Ahab has vanished, or fled is more like it. I honestly believe he is a traitor, even from the time I laid eyes on him."

"We will discuss the matters at hand soon, but for the moment my heart is longing to praise our Father. We shall worship here and give thanks to the LORD, and then we will know what to do next. When I worship, the LORD has a way of presenting all the answers I need."

The angels worshiped the LORD and thanked him for who he is and what he's done. They weren't alone, for the presence of the LORD met them there. The Holy Spirit came into their midst. Gabriel was enthralled in worship; his hands were raised high and his eyes gleamed with the joy of the LORD. He sang a new song onto the LORD.

Oh LORD, You are worthy of all praise
Your ways are perfect in every way
Worthy are you
Oh LORD, to you I give thanks
Your might and power delivers me from the enemy
Worthy are you
Oh LORD, in you alone doest salvation dwell
Your mercy and grace surrounds me
Worthy are you
Oh LORD, You are the King of Kings and LORD of LORDS
Your strength and might are my hiding place
Worthy are you … Forevermore

Under the influence of the Holy Spirit, Michael ceased praying and listened intently for the voice of the LORD. The LORD spoke a revelation to Michael's heart; something of great importance, but something that is not meant to be revealed for now.

From a safe distance in the forest he watched and waited for the right moment. He fully understood that he must not fail or else. He also thought about the punishment he would receive for his total allegiance to Hell, but he concentrated hard on blocking out any thought that even hinted towards punishment. *The LORD of Heaven cannot touch you. Under the LORD Lucifer's protection, you are safe from his wrath. There is nothing to worry about.* Those were the exact words he recalled the Major Judas saying to him. The words became impressed in his mind from the moment he had heard them, for all defenses in his conscious had been torn down. He was tortured until his spirit was broken. Now his spirit knew no consequences for his actions, only punishment for disobedience.

"You have my total allegiance LORD Lucifer. I will not disappoint you," Ahab whispered.

Worship brought a newfound strength to Gabriel. A renewed sense of hope had swept over him during worship, and he was more than ready to conquer the unconquerable. He felt fully prepared to take the enemy camp by storm. Even if they were on the threshold of the enemy's base, it mattered not to him, for the spirit of the LORD had come upon him.

"Michael I am ready for battle," Gabe declared. "The enemy won't know what struck them. Let's not waste another moment, I feel I know the way."

"Yes, I have seen the way in a vision, but there is still someone who must lead us there," Michael nodded and said.

Gabriel's expression turned to one of confusion for a mere moment.

"You mean the Holy Spirit," Gabriel collected his thoughts and asked.

Michael's eyes wandered away from Gabriel; they were searching the forest. Gabriel thought at first he had ignored him until he noticed something moving in the forest. He placed his hand on Logos, ready to draw at any moment. A hedge on the edge of the jungle shook restlessly. Then suddenly, someone appeared and fell to the ground sending a cloud of dust and dirt into the air. Gabriel unsheathed Logos. Michael remained surprisingly calm for the situation at hand. Whoever it was had become unrecognizable from the thick layer of dirt on their body.

"State your name," Gabriel demanded and stood between the archangel and the stranger.

"Please don't hurt me," a voice shrieked from under the mask of dirt.

"It is I, Ahab," he said and jumped to his feet and dusted himself off.

Michael signaled Gabriel to put his sword away.

"Not before you tell him to throw down his weapon," Gabriel insisted.

"He can hear you as well as he can hear me," Michael answered plainly.

"Please, don't hurt me, Gabriel," Ahab threw down his sword and stuttered a little as he spoke.

"I am here to help. I am your ally. Hear me out," he calmly said.

He still sounds frightened, thought Gabriel.

"Gabe, he sounds convincing enough. We should at least allow him the dignity to explain himself," Michael suggested.

"Dignity—" Gabriel, irritated with Ahab, blurted out. "—there is no dignity in fleeing from your allies. You heard it yourself. He says he's an ally, so why didn't he aid us."

"Let him speak and I'm sure he can explain himself," Michael said and turned to stare Ahab in the face. "You'd better be true to your word Ahab. Now tell us what happened."

Ahab was still dusting himself off.

"I am trustworthy, Archangel Michael," Ahab pleaded. "It was truly awful. I was trapped just as you were. It was terrible I tell you. I could hear your cries for help, yet I could not move. I can't recall every excruciating detail, but I'll tell you long did my suffering endure. Last thing I remember, I think, is the sound of tree branches snapping and the noise of leaves rustling and there were vines all around me. Yes, countless vines grabbing at my legs and arms and pulling me deeper into the jungle. Faster and faster they pulled me. I tried to scream, but my mouth was stuffed with a fistful of leaves and I can't even remember how those got there, but I'll tell you, I was petrified. I found myself covered with dirt and with the feeling that my insides were bruised up pretty bad. I heard Gabriel singing and I stumbled through the forest until I crashed through those bushes only minutes ago. That's everything I can remember. Oh, water. I'm terribly thirsty. May I drink? Oh, thank you, Archangel."

While Ahab quenched his thirst in the spring, Gabriel took advantage of the moment and spoke with Michael alone.

"Do you believe him," Gabriel whispered.

"He is convincing, but to answer your question, no, not in the least," Michael answered.

"Then something should be done about him now, and by now I mean *now*," Gabriel insisted. "What do you suggest?"

"I know Gabe, but we mustn't do anything irrational. Please trust me Gabe."

"I'm not asking you to do anything foolish. I suggest we tie him to a tree and let the wild animals deal with him," Gabriel recommended, a sly grin was on his face.

"I'm asking you to trust me. I'm your closest friend. Doesn't that count for something," Michael beseeched him.

"I do trust you. It's just that his story is as believable as Satan is good. He'll lead us into a trap and you know that," Gabriel whispered.

"I'm not saying he won't," Michael replied.

"Then why not just strap him to a tree," Gabriel insisted, yet again. "I'll find a hardy, sturdy tree and some vine as thick as ropes. It won't take long, and then we can be on our way. There are plenty of wild creatures out there, in the jungle, that he can make friends with."

Either he didn't fully understand Michael, or he was simply refusing him. "Use your ears, Gabe, and I mean that as a friend; he is meant to be our guide. Trust me, it is part of the call," Michael said with a sincere look in his face. His eyes alone spoke the truth, even without words.

"I will trust you. I may not comprehend why we should make him our guide, since he's a bold-faced liar—" Gabriel said before he stopped himself. "Please forgive me Michael. I meant to say that I may not understand, but I do trust you. As true as the LORD is to his word, I know you speak truthfully."

"Thank you brother; come, let us speak to Ahab before he suspects anything."

Although words were many, only a brief moment had transpired during the angel's private meeting.

"Ahab, we both agree you are the only one that can guide us. Do you recall the way now? Is it still fresh on your mind," Michael inquired of him.

"Why yes it is, Archangel Michael," Ahab replied. "I will lead the way. While I'm thinking about it—where did this water come from? It is quite possibly the most delicious and refreshing drink I've ever had."

"Please allow me to answer, brother," Gabriel chuckled and said. "From the LORD. Where else does creation come from? Did you think it was sorcery that brought it about?"

"Why of course not. Thanks to God for such delicious water," Ahab said.

"Ahab, is this the way," Michael said; he pointed down a beaten path that appeared well-traveled. The archangel, by the means of the Holy Spirit, knew the way to go. However, he thought it would be wise to demonstrate otherwise.

"I do believe you're correct. I won't ask how you knew," Ahab answered.

"Because you already know the answer, don't you," Michael smiled out of the corner of his mouth and said. "Now let's get going. My time is soon approaching."

Gabriel didn't say anything, but he couldn't help but wonder what Michael meant by such a statement. After all, Michael has said mysterious things before, thought Gabriel. Ahab seemed as if he hadn't heard the last thing that came out of Michael's mouth; he simply began hiking down the path.

The hours passed quickly as they hiked. The path was clearly unobstructed. Compared to what the angels had been through, this was an easy march. The air was still sweltering hot, but it was no longer stuffy or stale. The trees were spread apart which allowed for a cool breeze to pass through from time to time. They were roughly four earth hours into the hike when Gabriel noticed something out of the corner of his eye.

A pair of lions was on his left and out of his peripheral vision to his right he noticed a pair of large striped cats. They came upon a small clearing, only about a dozen paces in width with a dense forest of trees on the right and the left. There was a pathway straight ahead through a grove of what appeared to be fig trees.

Ahab suddenly stopped. He was out of breath.

"I'm having trouble remembering the way," Ahab said. "Please, give me a moment to find my bearings."

"Ahab, I know I'm not the one here who's been where we need to go, but it seems quite obvious where we need to go. Look ahead of you. There's a path clearly marked among those fig trees," Michael said and pointed straight ahead.

"I don't recall that being there before. Give me a moment," Ahab scratched his head and said.

"We'll go that way, but before we travel any further, we'll rest here to regain our strength," Michael put his hand on the guide's shoulder and frankly said.

Gabriel approached Michael, signaling him with a forefinger to come speak with him. The clearing wasn't particularly large enough to find room for a private meeting, so Gabriel pulled him aside.

"Michael, did you notice the creatures following us," he whispered.

"Yes, they've been following us for the past few earth-miles," Michael whispered, his back was turned to Ahab.

"Really," Gabriel pondered.

"There's a lion and a lioness and—"Michael stated before Gabriel abruptly cut in.

"Two tigers. I know this."

"There is also the eagle overhead. He is not the *one*, but he is guiding us," Michael said, a vibrant joy was in his eyes.

"I did not notice the eagle. Do you believe the lions and tigers are following the eagle," Gabriel queried.

"They are our guardians assigned to us I believe, and the eagle is their guide. The LORD does not intend harm for you or me. Not until—" Michael stopped himself short of saying too much.

"Not until what," Gabriel asked.

"Gabriel, not until our destiny calls for it, but only the LORD knows what the future holds for us. For now we must make sure that we travel in the same direction as the eagle. Ahab desires badly to lead us astray, but the sad truth is I don't think he clearly remembers the way. His confusion at times is deliberate I can tell, but at other times he is truly baffled by his calculations."

"What do you think his loss of memory at this moment is," Gabriel inquired. "I know that he knows where the path before us leads, but he was ordered not to take us that way. Actually, I believe he's led us too far in that direction already to make it look like an accident. The path before us was obviously placed there for a reason and it leads somewhere Ahab knows not to take us. Right now, as we speak, he has bought some extra time. Either that will work in his benefit or ours, is yet to be seen."

"What does your spirit tell you," Gabriel implored him; he looked as if he already knew how the archangel would answer.

"The Holy Spirit is urging us to go down the path, so to answer your question, I feel in my spirit that what lies at the end of that path will be hope for us."

"And despair for Ahab," Gabriel added, inquisitively.

"Quite possibly," Michael remarked. "We will see soon enough. It is time for us to depart. The Holy Spirit has spoken to my heart."

"I feel him speaking, too. We must get Ahab moving. Look the animals have started to move forward," Gabriel said.

"So has the eagle," Michael said, he turned and walked towards Ahab.

"Time to go, Ahab," Michael said with a smile on his face.

"Is it time already," Ahab whined. "I've barely gotten enough rest for my weary legs."

"The path isn't wide enough to walk side by side, so we must travel in a single file," Gabriel helped him to his feet and said. "I will go first, followed by you, and Michael will take the rear guard."

It was a gorgeous scene to behold. The fig trees were in bloom and the path was covered with a soft thick grass. The animals soon departed, Michael and Gabriel both noticed. Ahab acted as if he hadn't seen the animals, but Gabriel found it hard to believe. Michael, on the other hand, had a mysterious feeling deep down that Ahab's eyes were blinded from seeing the creatures, which Michael was sure were friends of God. That notion only confirmed in his spirit that God was leading them in the right direction, and not Ahab. As they walked, they noticed that the fig trees grew tighter and tighter together forming a tunnel that was barely high enough for Michael's head to clear.

The fig trees appeared older and more mature, as they walked further down the path. The fig trees on the outskirts had fresh buds and weren't old enough yet to produce fruit, but the fig trees they now came upon were heavy with lush delicious fruit. Gabriel was the first to pluck a ripe one from the tree.

"You must try one, they are simply delicious," he bit in and exclaimed.

Michael grabbed one and so did Ahab. After all, he wasn't going to deny his hungry stomach some food.

The path was long, but easily traveled. It wound from side to side and occasionally it sloped uphill. For the most part, though, it was level, straight, and narrow. There were no thorns, surprisingly enough, which took the angels many earth-miles to figure out. The path was also so tightly surrounded by the fig trees (no other tree grew here) that, even if they wanted to leave the path, there was no hasty way of doing it. They would have no other choice but to backtrack their steps or continue to the end.

Well, needless to say, the hike was absolutely the most wonderful part of the angels' journey thus far. It was unique in itself that it did, and yet it didn't, remind them of Heaven's landscape.

Dusk was closing in, so Gabriel decided to pick up the pace.

"We must move quickly," he yelled back. "Nighttime will soon be upon us."

"Must we go this fast," Ahab screeched as he stumbled along. "My legs feel like they're about to fall off." He tried in vain to catch his breath as they ran down the path.

"I'll be happy to take them off for you, if you like," Gabriel, under his breath, said, and Michael heard him for his hearing was quite exceptional.

"We must keep up this pace a little while longer," Michael said to Ahab. "We'll rest soon enough. Keep up the hard work and I promise you'll keep your legs."

The path grew even narrower and the trees grew closer together. The countless fig trees appeared to fly by as the three of them moved on faster and faster, until they came to a sudden halt. Gabriel noticed the path opened up and there was new landscape, or to say, there were more plants to speak of than just fig trees.

"We may be lost. I don't remember seeing these kinds of trees," Ahab said, referring to some cedar trees. He also knew deep down in his heart that he had disobeyed his orders and led the seraphim right into the forbidden zone.

Above, the sky opened up to them. There was still a faint amount of light from the setting sun, but the stars were out, and the moon. The horizon was in that dreamlike state between day and night where all elements of the universe seem to merge upon one another to form a majestic sky blanketed with stars and a moon and the last rays of the sun shining across them all. It's a beautiful sight to witness, the merging of such impressive figures in the sky. As the sunlight faded completely into its blissful state of rest, the stars twinkled and sparkled and the moon illumined like a giant lantern. Then something incredible happened. Suddenly, the most beautiful sound filled the air.

"We must turn sharply here and head in this direction," Ahab pointed in a direction heading away from the sound and said. "I think the moon will provide enough light to travel through the night."

"Quiet, Ahab. Do you hear that," Michael said.

"Why of course, my ears can't perceive what it is, but it is more beautiful than anything I've heard on earth before," Gabriel remarked.

"Yes, it's pure. It's heavenly," Michael exclaimed.

"Yes, it sure is, but we shouldn't waste anymore time staying here," Ahab quickly raised his voice. "I remember the way through these parts. We should leave now."

"This is the way, we can't squander any more time," he pointed in the opposite direction and added.

"Listen closer, do you hear that," Michael said.

"It's singing," Gabriel answered. "It sounds almost as beautiful as the cherubim in Heaven. Surely, whoever is singing is neither foe nor enemy, but an ally of the LORD."

"Ahab, you are right," Michael pointed right in the direction of the singing and said "There is enough moonlight to see the ground before us. I say we see what the source of the singing is. We will travel further into the woods. What do you say Gabriel?"

"I've known you to make wise choices, and this one is nothing short of wise. Let's go," Gabriel answered, his face beamed with joy beneath the moonlight.

"Move along. Our path has been decided," Michael nudged Ahab in the shoulder and declared; he pointed ahead to a path through the cedar trees and the angels moved through the holy enchanted forest

"We we'll find protection here this night. This forest is filled with the Holy Spirit. Don't you feel him Gabriel," Michael said as he walked slowly down the path.

"I feel him. It's like a vision of Heaven. What is this place—it's completely different from the rest of Luminarous," Gabriel observed.

"Do not mistake sorcery for the Holy Spirit," Ahab spoke up. "It could be a trap Michael. We could be walking to our dooms."

Ahab's face was wrinkled with fear. He knew he was fabricating a story in spite of the actual truth, but his fear was genuine. He feared a horrible torturous death in Hell. With every step they took deeper into the holy enchanted wood, Ahab's spirit grew more disturbed. A great conflict was taking place in his mind and his conscience. One voice in him was the conviction of the Holy Spirit and it told him to abandon his heresy and come back to the Lord.

"There is yet a chance for redemption," the Holy Spirit spoke to his conscience.

"You're too deep now, Ahab," a menacing voice, louder than the last, said. "Your soul and your spirit belongs to me. I own you. I can drag your spirit to Hell at any moment. If you disobey, a pit of hungry vipers awaits you. The snakes will pick the flesh off of your bones and they will take their time, prolonging your suffering. After the vipers have had their way with you, I may enslave you and make you like one of the Ruah forced to do my bidding, or I may destroy you completely. Your life is in my hands now, Ahab, not his. Forget your past and forget what you once were. That will never again be. Have you forgotten you can never again be like you once were for you have sworn the oath."

Ahab's soul shuddered with each verbal blow and with each word spoken, his conscience slipped deeper into a pit of despair.

"There is still hope, Ahab," the Holy Spirit declared. "You can make a choice. Repent of your actions. Salvation only awaits you in Heaven if you choose to follow the path of righteousness. There is yet time to turn back now, Ahab."

"You are and always will be mine, Ahab," the wicked voice countered, speaking in an ugly and tormenting tone. "By the power of Hell you belong to me. It's over, Ahab, over. Take the angels to their deaths and you will live."

While the battle within Ahab was taking place, the atmosphere in the forest underwent a sudden change. The air grew heavier. Not denser or stale, but heavy with the presence of the LORD. The music grew louder and voices, singing clearly, were added to the ambiance.

"This is amazing Gabriel. Do you hear the words," Michael exclaimed, his face beamed under the moonlight.

They had come to a clearing where the sky opened up again. What lay before them was a large smooth rock in the center of the small meadow and three paths clearly set between the trees in the forest. What was truly unique about their surroundings was the clear distinction between the landscapes. There were three completely different kinds of trees and the paths between them undoubtedly separated them. One path, which was to their left, went between groves of what appeared to be olive trees. The path to their right went directly through an orchard of fig trees. The center path was the narrowest of the three, and it ran through a forest of brilliant palm trees. The palm trees were greener than any other palms the angels had ever seen before. They moved as if they were swaying in the wind, yet the breeze blowing wasn't strong enough to move the palms as much as they were swaying. The music surrounded them on all sides and the words permeated the air. The words were:

> "Holy is the LORD God the Almighty
> Who was, who is, and who is to come"

"Listen. It's the rocks and the trees," Michael shouted. "They're praising the name of the LORD. This is incredible; hallelujah and Glory to God in the Highest."

Right then and there, he fell to his knees under the power of the Holy Spirit. He bowed his face to the ground and worshiped. Gabriel praised the LORD with dancing, although he was in worship he couldn't help but notice out of the corner of his eye that Ahab's face was in anguish.

"How can you stand this," the wicked voice snapped inside of Ahab's head. "Where is your sanity, Ahab? Curse it, curse it."

"I can't take it anymore," Ahab covered his ears and cried out.

"Why do you cover your ears," Gabriel grabbed Ahab's arm and demanded.

"Ah—" Ahab was reluctant to reply, but the voice inside his head fed him the words to speak. "—the noise is much too loud for my ears. My ears have grown sensitive since I've been on earth. Please understand."

Ahab's eyes then changed from clear to dark

"Cursed be the music. Damn it, curse it," an awful voice, different from Ahab, spat forth and screamed out of him.

"By the power of the Most High the LORD Almighty I forbid you to speak. Return to your dark realm, let go and return to Hell in the name of the God of Heaven," Gabriel became filled with the spirit of the LORD and rebuked the dark spirit that was in Ahab.

A dark shapeless form came out of Ahab.

"I'll return. And I'll bring reinforcements," it screamed.

In spite of the racket Michael was still bowed low in worship.

"Speak no more filthy spirit. Be gone and never return," Gabriel commanded the Ruah; it fled through the trees screaming, but the power of the LORD prevailed over its wretched and shrill cries.

The music grew louder and more beautiful.

"You are full of lies and deceit, Ahab the traitor, heretic from Hell. Tell me how long the Ruah has been your companion," Gabriel looked at Ahab and scrutinized him.

Gabriel then pulled Logos from its sheath and the music and singing ceased abruptly; the instant he held the sword to Ahab's throat. The music had stopped and Michael noticed immediately something was amiss. Gabriel had Ahab pinned against a tree and his sword was held at Ahab's throat. He jumped to his feet and seized Gabriel by the arm and pulled him away from Ahab.

"What's going on Gabriel? I need some answers now," Michael said.

"It is as we suspected brother," Gabriel replied. "Ahab is no angel. He's a traitor and nothing more than a demon. I tell you the truth. He brought a Ruah into our midst and only by the power of God, was it banished from our presence. Ahab is nothing more than a tool of Lucifer, wielded by the enemy to lead us into a trap. Ahab, tell Michael why you covered your ears. Tell him about your friend."

Michael looked to Ahab; he already knew in his spirit of Ahab's alliance with the enemy, but he also believed there may still be hope for his redemption. Michael stared at Ahab as he waited for him to speak.

"I'm begging you Michael, please spare my life," Ahab groveled at Michael's feet and pleaded. "I had no choice but to give into the enemy. I swear I am no demon. The enemy used me for their test. They made the Ruah to possess me; it was once an angel—he was Sethur. He took over my spirit and my soul was held at bay in the most inner recesses of my conscience. I've been trying my hardest to fight back, but I was powerless against the enemy. I had no choice but to give in. They were going to torture me until I was dead and gone. I am still an angel, a brother of Heaven like your and Gabriel. As a servant of the Most High God I'm begging you to have pity on my life."

"Pity, I do. Ahab, you must realize you did have a choice," Michael, looking at him with sheer disappointment, sternly said, "You always have a choice, and I'm afraid you chose wrongly. For there is no life in being in the service of the enemy; the only way to true life is through the LORD your God. There is only one God and Lucifer isn't him. The choice you made separated you from the grace of God. He will be your judge, but we will bring you in."

Ahab's face was stricken with grief.

"Ahab your spirit has become rotten from the poison of sin and evil," Michael sincerely, yet clearly displeased, said. "You have allowed your spirit to become one of the living dead that despises all adoration to God. For on the outside you may look like an angel, but on the inside your soul and spirit are black with the evil demands of Hell."

Michael then looked at Gabriel and noticed he still had Logos drawn from the sheath. He signaled Gabriel with his hand for him to put his sword away.

"Trust me on this one, Gabe," Michael asserted.

With the sound of metal against metal the sword was back in its sheath, and the music and singing resumed as it was before. Ahab covered his ears as quickly as his hands could get there.

"Ahab won't be able to resist the LORD's music if he can't use his arms," Michael grinned and said. "Gabe, if you will be so kind to tie his hands behind his back. We camp here tonight."

"With pleasure," Gabriel answered, he smiled from ear to ear. Gabriel took a handful of vines he had found, conveniently, hanging off the branch of a nearby tree.

"This is by far the best place we've had to rest since we've been here," he restrained Ahab's hands and said.

"I couldn't agree more, Gabe. I know we're safe from the enemy since the LORD's music is, most certainly, poison to their ears." Michael remarked.

The music made Ahab blue with grief. On the other hand, Michael and Gabriel joined the choir of rocks and trees and worshiped the LORD. Ahab dwelled on the words Michael had told him. He thought, *he is right, I did have a choice. I can't lead them to the trap. Maybe then the LORD will spare me.*

While Michael and Gabriel worshiped they were unaware that the enemy was on the move. Just after midnight Carchemish, along with Migron, Ammon, and Ishmael headed to the rendezvous point. The demons were making great headway.

"Follow me and do not slow down. We take no rest tonight," Carchemish commanded.

He had spoken an incantation before they left, so the group felt no need to rest; instead, they were driven with an evil energy fueled by sin. One thing about demons and their incantations is that it comes with a price. Their endurance to run without rest brings with it pain and anger. In fact, the demons couldn't stop if they wanted to. Their legs wouldn't allow them the pleasure of restful peace.

That night the angels rested peacefully. The music played like a soothing lullaby. They were completely at peace. Ahab even found rest that night. As Gabriel slept visions of Heaven played through his mind over and over again. He saw the Fields of Gladness and the Garden of Tranquility, just as he remembered. He walked through the golden streets of the Holy City and, to him it was as if he was there. It was merely a dream or a vision, but it felt more real than the air he breathed on earth. He felt the warmth of Heaven's breeze in the Fields of Gladness. He smelled the aroma of the flowers in the Garden of Tranquility and felt the refreshing mist on his face from the Fountain of Life. He saw his friends standing on the front stoops of their mansions; just as if he was standing in the streets, he could here their voices calling to him and inviting him to come in and visit. Oh how he wanted to, but he felt his heart longing to see the LORD on Mount Zion.

Before the sun had neared its time to rise, Michael suddenly awoke from his sleep; he lay still and flat on his back, while everything around him seemed as surreal as a dream. It was a vision and in it Michael could hear the audible voice of God calling to him. The cool, commanding voice carried through the wind. He sat up and found a smile was on his face. He was glowing with joy. For in his vision he had heard the LORD and seen his majesty. The music was playing beautifully and a calm cool breeze was blowing through his hair. He felt completely at peace as he took in his surroundings. Then the strangest sensation came over him. The cool breeze suddenly warmed and he peered towards the forest of palm trees, swaying gently in the wind. Michael noticed a mysterious glowing light traveling down the path, illuminating all that was around it as it traveled slowly towards him.

"Michael–I have come," out of nowhere, a voice spoke from within the gentle breeze. The archangel instantly recognized that the voice belonged to the LORD of Hosts.

"Yes LORD," he answered.

"Michael," the LORD said.

The mysterious light was growing brighter as it traveled towards him.

"Yes LORD, I'm listening," Michael answered once more.

"Michael, rise and follow me," the LORD said with a commanding tone.

All of sudden, the mysterious light transformed before Michael's eyes and he beheld the Author and Creator of life standing before him in all of his glory and majesty, and shining like the sun.

Gabriel and Ahab slept still. They didn't stir, not even a little.

"Should I wake Gabriel, LORD," Michael asked.

"No, let him rest. You must follow me," God answered, his voice sounded like the resounding of many waters.

Michael rose to his feet. His legs felt as if they were weightless and his shoulders were heavy in the Holy anointed presence, of the Almighty. Michael followed the LORD down the path between the olive trees. The music grew richer and deeper in sound. Everything around Michael was purely enchanting. The trees swayed to and fro in the wind. The dust beneath his feet stirred and twirled. The path, at first, was narrow; all that Michael could see in front of him was God's long flowing purple robe. His hair moved with the wind as if it was one with the element of nature. Everything around Michael was like a vision of Heaven. Hundreds of white doves, beautiful and graceful, danced above the trees in perfect harmony with the music. Michael noticed that each dove had an olive branch in its beak. He had no inclination why that was, but he trusted there was a reason; *for there are no such things as simple coincidences*, he thought.

The farther they traveled in, the wider the path grew. The fine dirt on the ground turned to a silky grass, which felt wonderfully soft on Michael's weary feet. He hadn't noticed his aches or the soreness up until the moment he felt the sensation of grass massaging the soles of his feet. He thought, *In the presence of the LORD, all worries, all pains, all things pass away except for his mighty will.*

Soon the path was wide enough for two to pass through.

"Come and walk by my side," the LORD called to Michael.

The archangel obeyed at once. Those were the first words he had heard God speak since he called to him, but the silence had mattered not to Michael. He was content to be in the presence of the LORD. He could spend a thousand ages not hearing a single word from God's mouth, just as long as he could be in his Holy presence would be enough for Michael.

He was utterly amazed, in awe, at how the olive trees began to literally bow as the LORD passed by them. To Michael, his walk with the LORD seemed to pass like ages of time yet it felt like it was passing more quickly than the clouds above. As he walked by his side, God spoke not a word; yet his face silently spoke a thousand words. It was clear to Michael that sadness had plagued God's solemn and wise face. And not just sorrow but concern, as well, reflected from his brow. Michael felt, in his spirit, that he shouldn't speak. Instead, he should wait on the LORD for the first word. Finally, they came to a halt at a small opening, surrounded by a grove of olive trees. The LORD raised his hand and the music stopped. The trees bowed one more time and returned to their natural state of swaying in the breeze.

"Sit with me a while," the LORD broke the grave silence and said. There appeared, from out of thin air it seemed, a large smooth stone big enough for two to sit upon.

Michael happily did as the LORD requested.

"Michael, I am about to reveal a vision to you. I will show you a world I created. A place where time stands still; where the aging processes of the earth has no hold. It is, indeed, hallowed ground where I love to walk. A realm where Heaven meets earth; a world that exists for my glory."

"Show me Lord. I am ready, " Michael said, his eyes overflowed with joy; he was captivated by each and every word the LORD spoke.

The LORD raised his right hand and suddenly, the trees before them obeyed his command and swayed forwards, bowing low to the ground. Then God revealed a vision to Michael. The most beautiful scene lay in front of him.

"How could such magnificent beauty have been hiding just behind those trees," Michael thought aloud. What he saw was a garden beyond beauty and measure, of grace and majesty. It was truly a reflection of God's glory.

Michael was in awe of seeing a flock of lambs grazing amongst a pride of lions. He couldn't believe his eyes. It was more amazing than anything he's seen on earth, he thought. And to have ascended the Mountain of God and still be able to lay hold to such a thought was incredible in itself. Countless creatures of every species were roaming freely, with no worry of harm. A panther walked among a herd of deer. Cheetahs ran alongside the antelope. A tiger frolicked in the meadow with a pack of wolves. The landscape was lush with bright flowers and exotic plants of every variety and species imaginable. The grass was greener and the water was bluer. The stars shone brighter above.

A peaceful sensation came over Michael's entire spirit and flowed through his body. Michael had been gazing at this wonderful place for many moments, it seemed to him. Finally he turned and looked upon the LORD sitting in brilliance, and remembered he was basking in the majesty of the Almighty Himself. Michael knew it was a privilege.

What a feeling to be sitting next to the LORD of Hosts, the Alpha and Omega, the Beginning and the End, the Ancient of Days. Who I am I to share a rock with the Rock of Ages, he thought. *What have I done to deserve a place of honor next to the King of Kings and the Creator of the Universe? To think he was here before this ever existed. He stood on the brink of Creation and like a beam of light his voice shot forth into nothingness and overwhelmed the darkness with the splendor of his glorious majesty. I am not worthy and yet he has called me. For as long as I exist this moment will never escape my mind.*

God's face was pure light, yet his face was filled with expression, with feeling, as he looked upon his beautiful creation. Michael's mind was dancing with visions of Heaven. It was as if he walked the streets of Gold and beheld the Father as he would appear sitting on his throne, ruling the universe with his mighty right hand. The smells, the sounds, and the way the golden streets felt on his bare feet was all coming back to him now. It was as if he had never left. This place he was in and the time that had passed, vanished from his mind momentarily as he gazed upon the Father of lights, the Holy of Holies, the Splendor of the Ages, the one who never sleeps, the Creator of all things. What was time, for it had no authority, in his presence. Time and the ages of the earth obeyed the LORD of LORDS.

Michael not only felt that time was standing still, but he knew it in his spirit that God had commanded the time to stop. Nothing could age as long as the Ageless One held it still. *In one finger alone, the Father has all the power he needs to rule the universe*, Michael thought. The LORD's face showed no age, yet it appeared as old as time itself. At times Michael would see a wise and aged face under the light and the next moment he would behold a young man. Although, one thing was for certain, Michael could only glance, momentarily, upon his face for it was shining, brilliant and intense, like the noon sun.

This all occurred quite fast, but words are slow. Suddenly, God raised his right hand and the trees returned to their position. The vision of Heaven's gardens was once more hidden behind a forest of palms. Then Michael looked upon the Father and saw that the light had faded from his face and he appeared as a man would. Michael was in awe of the handsome beauty of the LORD's wise and solemn face. One could only imagine how the LORD appeared at that very moment, but to Michael, he looked like a Father. A teardrop fell from God's eye. The single drop was purer than gold and it sparkled like a perfect diamond. The drop hit the ground and life sprung forth at once. Flowers, more gorgeous than any Michael had seen before, came to life. An intoxicating aroma instantly permeated the air. The LORD wept and Michael couldn't find the words to speak. He had never seen the Father so vulnerable before and he lacked the words to speak. Michael's heart ached as he searched for the right words, yet his spirit was telling him not to say anything at all.

"Be still," the Holy Spirit spoke to Michael's heart.

Before long, a garden of flowers flourished at Michael's feet. He wanted to sit at the LORD's feet and comfort Him.

"Be still Michael and wait upon the LORD," the Holy Spirit insisted.

A short moment went by, and then the LORD looked to Heaven. His large and loving eyes were saturated with tears.

"Michael, my heart is heavy," spoke the LORD.

"LORD my God, how can I help," Michael said, finding it hard to choose the right words. "Let me remove some of your burden from you."

God turned and looked compassionately into Michael's eyes.

"Michael, your heart is true and sincere," as another tear fell to the earth, God said. "Yet truly I say it is I who will remove the burden from you. The time is coming soon when you will be tried and tested. My heart is burdened from the pain you will endure on my behalf."

"My LORD, what is to become of me," Michael cried out, his heart was overwhelmed. Tears started to flow from his eyes and the harder he tried to hold them back the more they poured.

"I cannot reveal your destiny," the LORD uttered. "You are my child Michael and I love you dearly. You must remember my words. I will never leave you nor will I ever forsake you."

He embraced Michael with a fatherly embrace and held him tightly. The Father's tears rolled down his back and he wept on the Father's shoulders. He didn't want to let go of the LORD. His fatherly embrace was what Michael lived for. The Father's love is what held him together. When the enemy was against him, he knew that it was the love of his God that was his strength. The enemy had rejected God's love, but Michael wanted to hold onto the LORD forever. A thousand ages could come and go and Heaven and earth could pass away, but as long as the love of the Father remained that was enough. To know he loved him is what held his spirit together; it is what bonded his heart and soul together, his mind and conscience. What was life if the love of the Father was denied him? Where would he be without the love of God? His spirit would be rotting away in the pits of Hell with the enemy. *The enemy, I have still to face them*, Michael thought and wept more. The LORD held him tightly like a son. Michael was broken in the Father's arms. He didn't want the fatherly embrace to ever end. He wanted to stay in God's caring arms for an eternity; he held on to him even tighter. Then as mysteriously as God appeared, he vanished in the blink of an eye.

Michael sat alone on the rock and wept.

"LORD, I love you. I will follow you to death. For death can't overcome the love of God," he cried out to the dawn sky.

"Wake up, wake up, Michael," he was startled at the voice of Gabriel.

Michael opened his eyes and blinked hard, and sat up slowly.

"Are you okay? Did you rest well," inquired Gabriel as he stared curiously at him.

"Yes—yes I did," Michael rubbed his eyes and responded precariously.

Gabriel scratched his head. *He sounds like he's losing his mind,* he thought. It was only the break of dawn and even the birds were still waking.

"Did you see anything strange last night," Gabriel queried. "Ahab's still asleep. You can tell me. Did you have a vision, perhaps a dream?"

"No, not that I can recall," Michael replied.

Michael knew that his dream was no dream; moreover, it was no vision either, but he knew in his spirit that he had walked with the Rock of Ages, his Father. He felt the Holy Spirit telling him to keep his experience to himself, at least, for now.

"Can you please remove these ropes," Ahab, out of nowhere, begged. "They're cutting into my flesh."

"Yes, but I need not warn you of what Gabriel is fully capable of," he replied sternly. Michael then noticed that the music had ceased and he thought it odd.

Michael nodded at Gabriel and he removed the ropes from Ahab. As soon as he had finished doing so, the music started again. Ahab reached with both hands for his ears, but Gabriel gave him one look and he quickly placed his hands by his side.

"The time has come. Lead us through," Michael declared.

"I'll miss this place. I shall remember it," Gabriel said.

"Soon enough, you'll be telling Raphael and Uriel of this place," Michael smiled and said. "And you mustn't forget Remiel or Raguel, for they'll be eager to hear all about your adventures."

"Don't you mean we'll tell them," Gabriel raised an inquisitive eyebrow and said.

"Of course," said Michael, lightheartedly. "Like usual, nothing gets past you Gabe."

"Sleep was good for my memory," Ahab mentioned. "We'll journey through the forest of palms and that should bring us near the outskirts of the enemy's camp. Are you ready to depart?"

They hadn't hiked far when, out of nowhere, it started to rain. The showers soaked them, but the rain felt refreshing to

Michael's body and it felt cleansing on his skin. Gabriel reached out his hands as they walked and grabbed a palm leaf and he gathered the sweet rain and drank. Ahab, on the other hand, shivered from the rain. It felt cold and dreary to him. In fact, it was close to unbearable for him. Michael thanked the LORD for the shower. The rain lasted for about three earth-miles of their hike. Just as the rain stopped and the sun shined down on them, they stepped out of the palm forest and onto a hill. They were on the outskirts of the enchanted and holy forest.

"We are getting closer," Ahab observed. "Before the end of the day, you will be at the enemy's camp."

Michael placed a hand on Ahab's shoulder and startled him.

"Then we will waste not another moment," Michael said to him. "For if you say by the day's end, I say we should travel faster. The time has come to face my enemies."

The path was wide enough for the three to walk side by side. Michael was on the right and Ahab was on the left. Gabriel was in the middle and noticed, almost immediately that Michael had a solemn and sad expression on his face.

"You've looked like this since you awoke this morning. What's the matter, brother," Gabriel with concern, asked.

"I'm quite alright," Michael smiled and replied. "There's no need to worry, brother. I want as much as you to complete the quest. Then we can be home again."

"Remember, I have your back. The Father placed me here with you for just that reason," Gabriel asserted and just as those words slipped from his mouth, he realized he had said what Elijah had told him not to.

"I know you do, Gabe. The Father couldn't have appointed a better angel for the position," Michael patted him on the back and said.

Gabriel felt instantly relieved and better than ever. He found a new confidence rise up inside of him. He felt the spirit of God empowering him to do great things for the Kingdom of Heaven.

The hike was less challenging, that is, until they came upon a hill sloping upwards. Here, the landscape changed from predominately palms to a grove of olive trees. The aroma was enticing.

Gabriel picked an olive or two as they passed through the trees. Ahab even picked one and held it out for Michael, but Michael turned it down. His face was burdened with anguish. Ahab seemed to ignore his expression, but the truth was he knew that Michael knew. It didn't matter now though, since he was determined on changing the course. He would prove himself soon enough. They stopped for a brief rest at the highest point on the hill.

"What is wrong with you, brother," Gabriel pulled Michael aside and rebuked his behavior, he whispered. "Whatever it is that's troubling you, Michael, let me take care of it for you. I can help if you will just tell me."

"I must pray alone for a moment. I realize the time is at hand," Michael looked at him with a sober face and said.

Gabriel hesitated and let go of Michael's arm. Ahab was watching from a distance. He was nervous, but he was doing well at hiding it. Michael walked into a circle of olive trees to be alone.

A pair of crimson eyes hidden from natural sight lay in wait.

"You'll see what I can do now. Let us devour him," the Ruah, once know as Sethur, said as his eyes glared at Ahab with utter contempt.

Sethur was accompanied by eight Ruah: Resentment[1], Envy[2], Spite[3], Hatred[4], Wicked[5], Rage[6], Lust[7], and Pride[8]. The Ruah descended upon their nervous and unsuspecting victim. They entered him one by one. They securely clung to his spirit and infiltrated his conscience. All eight of the Ruah spoke at once. Confusion entered Ahab's mind. Pride overpowered the rest and took command of Ahab's spirit.

"I will make him do it. The rest of you must aid me," Pride said to the other Ruah.

Ahab thought, Oh no, what have I let in. They're taking over.

"Silence until after I speak," Pride told the other Ruah.

"You are better than this," Pride scorned Ahab. "Take control of the situation and complete your mission. It is you who should've been archangel. You are the greatest among all demons and all the seraphim will bow to you. You must do one thing."

"I can't betray my brothers," Ahab tried to fight back and spoke to his conscience. "I can still change. I can turn everything around.."

"Michael took everything from you. You should be God's favored angel, not him," Resentment contended.

"Don't you want to be archangel," Envy asserted. "And why can't you? After all, the title should be yours."

"Michael deserves what he has coming. Do it Ahab and don't think twice about it," Spite held his tongue no longer and said.

"You've despised him since he became Archangel," Hatred remarked.

"You've suffered long enough because of him. Hell will honor you. Just do it and be done with it," Wicked contributed.

"How long have you desired to be honored and loved by all," Lust, next in line, said. "How long have you yearned to be archangel? Take it, Ahab."

Pride was about to speak when Rage petitioned him. Pride allowed it to speak.

"Let the rage inside of you rise up Ahab," Rage demanded. " Let it take over. Let it drive you. It is the force behind your being. You couldn't have made it this far without rage."

"Well done Ruah, Lord Lucifer will be proud," Pride addressed the Ruah.

Michael felt a peace come over him as he knelt to pray.

"Have mercy on me oh Lord," he stretched his hands towards the heavens and prayed. "Let this test pass without pain and misery from the enemy. They desire to destroy me, Father."

Michael wept, for sadness had suddenly overtaken his spirit.

"How I long to be in your presence," he cried out. "How I long to be on Mount Zion and dance in your courts. Even if I must lie at your feet and never again behold the beauty of your majesty, my spirit would be filled. Just to be at your feet, oh Lord. Please make it go away; may it pass, my Father. Not my will, Lord, but yours be done. For you, my God, are King of my heart."

The sound of a branch snapping woke Michael from his prayers.

"Michael, I'm sorry to disturb you—" it was Gabriel and he sounded anxious.

"—but I think you must come. I spotted a host of demons approaching the hilltop. There are four I think, including one particularly huge demon about my size. What must we do?"

"It is time," Michael rose to his feet and said.

"What do you mean," Gabriel urged him, his hand was held tightly to Logos; he was already prepared for a fight.

"Never mind for now—let's vanquish the demons," Michael uttered and ventured out into the clearing with him, where Ahab was.

Gabriel looked and couldn't find Ahab.

"He's run away," Gabriel said, angrily.

"Michael the Archangel," a voice said, that sounded oddly like Ahab's. They turned and saw Ahab standing with four demons.

"Behold, the Archangel Michael," Ahab pointed to Michael and said.

The demon Migron went forth with his sword drawn. Baasha and Omri followed him and Carchemish stayed back with Ahab.

"I am servant of the LORD Most High," Gabriel pulled Logos from its sheath and cried. "Come no further unless I smite you by the power of God Almighty."

Gabriel's eyes lit up with the zeal of the LORD.

"Put your sword away, Gabe," Michael put his hand firmly on Gabriel's arm and said. "I must go with them."

"You are, here by, sentenced to death under the LORD Lucifer's orders. You must come with us," Migron came forth and declared.

"No Michael—we must fight," Gabriel uttered.

Michael stepped forward with his hands open in front of him. Omri took hold of his wrists and began to wrap a thick vine around them. Gabriel forcefully grabbed hold of Omri and threw him on the ground.

"Don't come any further. Go back to Hell or die by my hand," Gabe took Logos and pointed it at the demons and boldly said.

Baasha kicked Logos out of Gabriel's hand and knocked him to the ground. Omri jumped on Gabriel and held him down. Baasha kicked him repeatedly in the side. Gabriel tried to break free, but the demons struck him again and again. Gabriel wasn't about to give up. He broke free, but Carchemish was right there to strike him in the gut with his fist. Gabriel fell on his face.

"Enough," Michael shouted.

Gabriel stopped struggling and Carchemish stood still, as

did the rest of the demons. Sheer astonishment was on their faces, as Michael raised his hands into the air. His lips were moving like he was speaking, but no sound came forth for he was addressing the LORD.

"Here I am. I go freely," Michael said and then surprised Gabriel and even the demons when he held out his hands, submitting himself. Michael signaled Gabriel to put away his sword. Gabriel did so, and he thought he must have a plan.

Omri grasped Gabriel's wrist and began to tie his hands together.

"Take only me. I am who Lucifer wants aren't I," Michael said.

Carchemish looked quite intrigued at what Michael had just said.

"Only you," Carchemish mocked with a sly grin. "We need both of you, those were the orders, so we can take you both in alive or we can take you in dead. Archangel, you choose."

Carchemish ordered Migron and the others to bind Gabriel's hands. As Gabriel was being bound, he looked at Michael waiting for some kind of signal to retaliate. Although, to his utter dismay there came no signal from Michael; instead the archangel's head was bowed low.

"LORD, come now and deliver us from the evil one," Gabriel prayed aloud.

"Your God doesn't care about you," Carchemish broke out in cynical laughter and sneered. "My master has more use for you."

"What do you know," Gabriel snapped back. "You're a traitor. Your heart is as black as the dirt beneath my feet. You're a demon—filth of Hell—" but before he could get out another word, Carchemish struck him in the side and knocked the wind right out of him.

When Gabriel looked up, Michael had the most despairing expression on his face; Gabriel couldn't help but lose heart. All hope appeared to fade from Michael's face.

"You're the traitor you fool," Carchemish spit on Gabriel's face and whispered in his ear. "Dare to defy me now, infidel."

Carchemish brought his hand back to strike him again.

"What does your master compare to the Most High, the LORD

Almighty," Gabriel brought his head up and stared straight into his eyes and said.

Carchemish then struck him down and as he was about to kick him in the side.

"Your fight is not with my brother," Michael spoke up. "It's me your master wants. Isn't it?"

"To be honest, I don't know what he would want with a weak sap like you," Carchemish replied. "This one's got more fight in him."

He then kicked Gabriel in the side.

"Strike my brother once more and I promise you this—" Michael straightened up and asserted himself. "—when my time comes, I'll make an example out of you. Now do as you're told and take us to your master."

Carchemish, to Gabriel's surprise, ordered two demons to help him to his feet. Then he looked up into Michael's face and could see why. Michael's eyes had an intense, almost terrible, look to them. The power of the Holy Spirit was truly radiating from his face. Then it faded and once again he bowed his head.

Carchemish walked over to Michael and looked up and down at him.

"He's harmless, soldiers," Carchemish said. "Just look at him—he can't do a thing."

The other demons broke out in laughter and Carchemish laughed with them.

"Judas strictly commanded that we take possession of their swords," Carchemish said and ordered a demon to grab Gabriel's sword. "He desires Logos, the supernatural blade of Gabriel, for his collection and the LORD Lucifer, may he live forever, has need of the archangel's supernatural sword. I will carry it myself and I shall deliver it, personally to the LORD Lucifer."

Then, he reached out and plucked the sword from Michael's belt and, the moment his hand came in contact with its handle, an electrifying shock traveled through his body. The jolt was terribly painful for him.

"Let it remain in his sheath, for now," he said. "He isn't going to use it. The LORD Lucifer will know what to do with the Sword of the Spirit."

The enemy's camp was a day's run from the Mount of Olives. Carchemish wanted to get back to camp as quickly as possible. He wanted to please Judas, but there was someone he desired to please even more; not Lucifer, but the one closest to Lucifer— Beltezar the Terrible. Carchemish ordered the demons to pull the angels to their feet, for they had pinned them to the ground to secure the vines around their arms. Prince Baasha didn't especially like being bossed around and neither did Prince Omri. Migron pulled Gabriel to his feet and pushed him towards the two demon princes. Then he grabbed Michael by the hair and pulled him to his feet.

"Watch it, Migron. Judas wants them unscathed," Carchemish ordered.

Ahab stood idly by as the Ruah was busy tormenting his soul and spirit. He then knelt to the ground and in a fetal position, was rocking to and fro.

"It's time to go, Ahab. Move it," Carchemish yelled.

Ahab looked up at him as if he was listening, yet he hadn't heard a single word of what was said. Inside his head, the voices were growing louder and louder and Carchemish's voice sounded as if it was far away. Prince Baasha came over to offer his assistance. He yanked Ahab to his feet like a frail puppet, but Ahab fell back down and was rolling violently on the ground; he began foaming at the mouth.

"He's gone mad, leave him; besides, he's served his part, he's of no use to us now," Carchemish spoke with a haughty tongue.

The demons shoved the angels along as the caravan started to move on. Just after they had made their descent from the Mount of Olives, a scream pierced their ears. A shrill cry of death rang out and Ahab was never seen again. The demons pushed the seraphim along at an intensely quick pace. Carchemish wanted to be back to base before nightfall, and even before dusk was near. The demons ran with a supernatural power that made them tireless. Their endurance is baffling.

What strange power possesses them? thought Gabriel. He began to lose feeling in his legs as they ran. Even Michael was astounded at how the demons ran without tiring. The reason, the demons ran swiftly and were able to fend off fatigue with ease, was the power of the evil one. It was strongly at work in their spirits, driving them to run harder and faster. Dusk was now nearing and Gabriel couldn't go any further. His legs completely failed him. He fell and rolled on the ground. He tried to stand, by his own strength but he failed.

"Look at him brothers, he's pathetic. He can't even stand. And they call him a warrior," Carchemish sneered.

He ordered Migron to bring Gabriel over to where Michael stood. Michael was terribly out of breath and was struggling to stay on his feet.

"Your legs are still working. Pick up your brother," Carchemish ordered Michael. "You're going to carry him the rest of the distance."

Michael spoke not a word and, wrapping his arms around Gabriel, he heaved him up into the air. The archangel's legs quivered as he raised Gabriel over his shoulders. He stumbled for a few feet then fell over. The demons spit on Michael and ridiculed him.

"He's just as pathetic," Prince Baasha scoffed.

"I wouldn't even have him as a soldier," Prince Omri uttered.

"Enough," Carchemish commanded. "Help them to their feet Migron and make it quick. We haven't much daylight left."

Migron saluted and did as he was told. He hated taking orders from Carchemish, but he despised the seraphim of Heaven even more. After Migron had pulled Michael roughly to his feet, he reached down and scooped Gabriel from the ground putting him on Michael's shoulder. And once again, he bore the weight of his brother's body. Michael's legs were nearly buckling from fatigue but by the grace of God, he found enough strength to carry his friend. During the entire time of the journey Carchemish, along with the other demons, mocked Michael. They cursed him and spit on him. They laughed at him and ridiculed him.

THE GAUNTLET

The secret council had adjourned and withdrawn from the meeting chamber by way of the hidden passageway, only Judas and Nimrim remained behind. Judas had to resume the tedious task of making his preparations for Beltezar's visit and since the time for his arrival was fast approaching, there was still much to do before the base would offer him a respectable greeting.

Judas had written particular instructions to give to Nimrim.

"I've chosen you to supervise on the matter of Beltezar's visit," before he handed over the instructions, Judas said. "I want you to personally oversee the preparations. This is a milestone for you, Nimrim, and I am fully confident in your abilities to see that it is done, efficiently and precisely, according to my specifications. I'll begin with the weapons in storage. They must be inventoried; secondly, the soldier's quarters must be made spotless. I know it will be a formidable task but you will have my personal staff, two hundred count, at your disposal. See to it that it's done right the first time; I don't want to have to inspect every little detail or, for that matter, I don't want to have to do your job for you. I have no time for any mistakes, nor do I have the energy; there is simply no room for error. Now the legions must be in order, as well, absolutely no mischief and I don't want to hear of any disputes or petty quarrels over who's the biggest or who's the strongest. I've had it up to my ears with these soldiers' foolish behavior and, in all honesty, I am in charge of a legion of dimwits. Ever since I came to Luminarous, I've been asking myself what I did to deserve such a foolish appointment."

"Nothing sir," Nimrim spoke up. "I mean to ask, if I may speak freely master."

Judas gave a consenting gesture with his hand.

"Well if I may be so bold, I must say that you don't deserve to have such idiots under your command; you deserve far much better, sir," Nimrim swore.

Judas smiled. He loved what he heard, but he thought to himself, what a smug little weasel, thinking that he can use flattery to gain my favor. I wish I had more soldiers like him.

"Why thank you Nimrim," he responded in a sincere tone. "I'm glad that at least one soldier under my authority has some common sense. Your attributes are appreciated much more than you may realize. As I was saying before, my authority and dare I say my unique faculties are being wasted here on Luminarous. Regardless of the past, there is still a pleasant future to look forward to—a future where the archangel has been defeated and Gabriel has been destroyed. Yes, the future is looking promising, very promising indeed. You agree, don't you?"

"Oh yes, yes, Major Judas," Nimrim nodded and concurred.

Judas smiled and took a seat in his chair.

"I may be major at the moment, but soon enough that will change," he reclined comfortably and let out a sigh and alleged. "The LORD Lucifer will invite me into the inner circle. Yes, Nimrim, I will become what I've always longed to be: a demon prince of Hell. That is where you come in. If all goes well and as planned, your supervision being diligent enough, then I will appoint you as major in my place and you will inherit the command of many legions."

Nimrim was appreciative and Judas could see it written all over his face. Judas thought, I have him right where I want him. And, considering my choices, he's not really all that bad. He does have some redeeming qualities about him. After all, he does hang on to my every word and heeds every one of my commands, if I could only create more just like him. And I will. When I am made demon prince, I'll have the authority to experiment and enforce certain changes, coercing the soldiers to be more like Nimrim, and then I can exploit them for my own purposes.

"You have until the thirteenth hour to complete the job," Judas said.

Nimrim saluted Judas and vanished through the door.

Now to pay Luminarous a little visit, thought Judas. He had prepared an incantation that he thought just might work on the fallen star. He wasn't particularly an expert in the art of sorcery, but he did know a few helpful incantations.

Judas stepped outside his private quarters and walked down the dimly lit corridor. As he walked, he practiced the incantation in his head over and over again saying, *Allah-bessah Samih Dahij*. This spell was said to place one, of great power, under your control. However, it had yet to be tested on someone as powerful as Luminarous. In his greed he thought, you will find out his great purpose. You will wield his power against the enemy and destroy their kingdom forever. You *will* be demon prince.

The passageway seemed to be lengthier than Judas had remembered and the temperature seemed to be rising, as well. He hadn't recalled it being so warm or stuffy before. Then again, he thought, this is a strange place and unimaginable things do occur down here. He came to a fork in the passage and he veered to the left, finding what he was looking for—the cage that held the fallen star, Luminarous. Judas noticed, as he was rounding the corner, that the torches were put out and yet a strangely mysterious light cast shadows on the walls.

"Ah, is it time already," a voice called from around the corner. "Has Judas come to call on me? What spells or devious incantations do you have prepared for my entertainment—and will I be as fond of them as I am of this prison you had constructed for me?"

Judas gathered his pride, so it might swell inside of him, and he walked around the corner. The fallen star was standing in a small prison cell made of precious metals and stones and Judas was taken back at how much different his appearance was from when he had seen him above the ground. He was tall and slender, yet his shoulders were broad and masculine. Luminarous' eyes peered at him from behind the metal bars and stone slabs.

"Do you like your accommodations Luminarous," Judas asked with an arrogant tone.

"I can think of other places I'd rather be right now," he replied flippantly.

"I can also think of worse places for you to be," Judas was quick to say. "Perhaps I should remind you why you're on earth and not soaring through the universe or—why you're no longer a part of your *order* of stars and planets."

Luminarous, who was standing in the back of his prison quarters, came closer.

"Judas, maybe I should remind you why you're here speaking to me instead being a part of your original order, the seraphim, in Heaven," he remarked snidely.

"Blood and spit," Judas snapped. "Curse you Luminarous!"

"What do you know about curses," Luminarous crossed his arms and, after a good laugh, said. "Who are you to render judgment on me—are you not just a simple demon? Were you not once a seraph in Heaven and now you're a wretched spirit of Hell?"

"Enough of your babbling. It is time," Judas yelled, he quivered with anger.

"Look at you—you're just a demon trying to put on a show of intimidation; but can you really prove yourself," Luminarous taunted.

"*Allah-bessah Samih Dahij,*" Judas recited his incantation, raising his voice to a shout. "*Allah-bessah Samih Dahij.*"

"Am I supposed to be impressed," Luminarous uttered. "You're wasting your time speaking the forbidden tongue. Judas, did you actually believe your vain spell would work on a star that once walked in the heavens."

Judas became even angrier. *Why didn't it work*, he asked himself.

"What strange power do you possess," Judas questioned. "The reason that you're here is because the God of Heaven has abandoned you. What strange power could there possibly be that could remain in you? What is the source of your power?"

"Is that why I'm here," Luminarous asked. "Do you think you can take my powers and use them for your purpose—is that it?

You believe that just because I was banished to this godforsaken island that I have been totally relieved of all my power."

"To Hell with you," Luminarous yelled, and glared at Judas with contempt.

"Why else would we have gone to all this trouble to capture you," Judas coolly maintained. "We wouldn't have suffered ourselves in building these quarters for you unless we were certain that you possessed a great power. Luminarous, the question still remains. Where do you get your power?"

Luminarous stared at him, unflinching.

"Answer me or pay the penalty of death," Judas cried, totally losing his control.

"Judas, there is no need to get yourself so riled. Save your temper tantrums for your slaves, because I am someone you most assuredly do not want to anger. Before I request that you leave my presence, I will say I thought you wanted me here for the sole purpose of preventing the seraphim from finding me."

"How did you know," Judas eagerly demanded. "Have you seen them?"

"Yes," Luminarous replied. "I know of the archangel and his friend, Gabriel. Honestly, Judas, what do you take me for—a fool?"

"I am Luminarous—" Luminarous boldly declared. "—the seventh star of the heavens and I hold more power in my right hand than all of your legions combined."

"I know what the future holds for you, *Major* Judas," Luminarous said disdainfully and laughed at him.

"I've had enough of your mental trickery," Judas asserted. "You're nothing but a fallen star, banished from the heavens, forsaken, left to dwell on this retched dismal island. Truly I've squandered my resources and efforts on you; this whole venture has apparently been a complete waste of my time—valuable time, might I add. Time that I could have spent preparing for the battle to come." Judas stood back and waited to see if his conniving manner of speech would work to his advantage.

"Judas, must I remind you that you are merely nothing more than a fallen angel. You're lowlier than vermin. And, contrary to your opinion, it appears to me that I am the one who has had his time put to waste. Did you truly, actually, think that your soldiers captured me with their meager abilities?" Luminarous glared proudly at Judas.

"Beyond a doubt, it was the power of Hell that captured you. The master himself spoke the incantation over the trap that snared you," Judas spoke with fulsome arrogance.

"Your own, conceited, wicked spirit has deceived you, Judas. Satan has no authority over me," Luminarous stated, in a matter of fact way.

Judas didn't respond to him, but let his last words fall into silence, and he waited.

"Only the God of Heaven holds the key to my future," Luminarous slumped down, bowing his head, and uttered. "Once upon a time, I, Luminarous, was destined for greatness."

Luminarous looked up and a tear fell from his eye.

"In fact, I was meant to usher in the end of days," he said pitifully. "The Book of the Seven Seals was to be opened upon my arrival. I was to stand in the earth's path and—" he couldn't continue. He swelled with tears and was in anguish.

Judas stood silently by, listening to every word; he was intrigued by what he was hearing and, besides that, he took pleasure in reveling in the despair of others.

"Go on, Luminarous," Judas spoke softly. "You can tell me *anything*. I'm here to help you. I know I haven't communicated that clearly to you, but believe me it's true. You can trust me."

Luminarous wiped his tears away.

"I have left behind all that was promised for me," gritting his teeth, he cried out. "I turned from his promise for the sake of my own selfish glory. Who am I that I should disobey the Lord of Heaven? I have fallen and now there is no returning back to the heavens."

Luminarous' face took on a somewhat softer expression.

"I can see the heavens shining in their splendor and the parade of stars worshiping the Lord of Heaven. There is no longer any hope for me, now, of ever returning to the heavens. I am doomed to spend the rest of my days awaiting his judgment. I beg you, keep me locked in here for my heart has abandoned all hope. I have no desire to live."

He's playing right into my hands, thought Judas.

"If you have no desire to live, Luminarous, then why not join us? You no longer have anything to lose. Help us defeat the enemy," Judas cried with unbridled zeal.

"I cannot and will not be joined with Hell and its demons," Luminarous' brow was wrinkled with resentment as he gravely responded. "Never. For all I care, you can keep me trapped behind these bars for all eternity, never to see the light of day again and still, that's not severe enough punishment for what I have done. What I truly deserve is death."

Luminarous had let down his defenses and was now revealing what was truly in his thoughts. He was angry and bitter and troubled beyond words; moreover, he *knew* that he was deserving of punishment. Since his fall from the heavens, his mind had been dwelling, solely, on the consequence his actions had brought about. Now he was feeling woefully downhearted and in a moment of weakness, he left himself completely vulnerable; now, he was open to any proposals that the enemy might offer him.

Judas saw his opportunity and avidly jumped at it.

"Look what the LORD of Heaven has done to you," Judas suggested cunningly. "Look at how he has abandoned you to this forsaken island to await your judgment. Is this a pleasant way to spend your life—no, it's far from it. Don't you know that you exist for a mighty purpose?"

Luminarous seemed to be staring idly into nowhere. Judas wondered if he had listened to any of his words at all. Then it dawned on him exactly what he would say.

"What if I told you there was another way to fulfill your destiny," Judas uttered.

Luminarous, letting out a low moan, turned and looked at him with grieving eyes.

"There *is* something that you could do," Judas grinned and continued. "Something great that you could accomplish."

"What are you purposing," Luminarous asked, his face brightened with hope, for a moment, and then faded once again. "That I would join with you and Hell?"

"Not at all," Judas looked shocked and claimed.

"I am suggesting—" he calmly continued. "—there is still a

chance that your destiny can be fulfilled, thus redeeming your spirit from its bleak future and the despairing and dire straits of judgment. So, what would you say if that were possible?"

"Judas—" Luminarous looked away from Judas and bleakly responded. "You speak of the impossible and only the LORD of Heaven is capable of the impossible. I have grown weary of talking. Leave me be."

"Fine," Judas nodded and said. "However, I will return and when I come back, I will bring Beltezar the Terrible along with me. Then, you will have no choice but to listen. Take heed of this, I tried to speak to you with kindness and patience, but Beltezar will not be as pleasant to deal with."

Luminarous didn't respond or even acknowledge that Judas was there; he was far too depressed to think about anything other than his own demise. Judas stationed four of his heftiest soldiers at the entrance to the passage and then left to attend to other business. Beltezar was to arrive soon and he wanted everything to be perfect. His talk with Luminarous had gone well, but not quite as well as he had hoped. He wished that Luminarous had cooperatively negotiated with him, fully committing to his plan. However, that had not been the case. Judas now redirected his attention to assuring Beltezar that everything is going as planned. Needless to say, Judas' walk back to his private quarters seemed very long, for when Beltezar arrives there were going to be some things that would need to be explained or smoothed over, and anticipating the task was simply unnerving for Judas.

Above ground and about six earth hours later, Nimrim was busy overseeing the preparations for Beltezar's arrival. Below the earth he had many soldiers at work, laboring hard to bring every detail up to code. The weapons had been counted, sharpened, and polished. Now there were a few minor details to supervise and then his job would be nearly complete. He was standing on the mound that Judas usually used as he addressed the legions. He was carefully monitoring the captains as they took roll call to make certain that each demon would be in attendance for inspections. It was then, that he spotted Carchemish emerging from the forest, preceded by the demon princes Baasha and Omri and sergeant Migron. But what particularly caught his eye was a tall figure walking in the midst of the demons. He appeared to be carrying someone on his shoulders.

"Go summon the commander. Judas will want to be here to see this," Nimrim ordered a demon nearby.

Nimrim was feeling so proud that he could hardly contain himself. He had successfully supervised the preparations for Beltezar and, to add to his great accomplishment, he was the first to witness Carchemish and the others coming home victorious.

"Blow the trumpet three times. Let everyone come and see what Carchemish has brought back," Nimrim ordered a demon in the watchtower.

The horn bellowed out with a loud, resounding pitch and it didn't take long for the soldiers to respond to the call. Demons came by the droves and soon the camp was swarming with a few thousand curious demons. Nimrim climbed the watchtower to have a better look. Carchemish was only a hundred paces away now. He was in awe of the angel who was carrying his comrade on his shoulders.

"That has to be the Archangel Michael and is that Gabriel he's carrying," Nimrim said to the guard in the watchtower.

"This is so thrilling," the guard exclaimed. "Wait till the others, down in Hell, hear of this. We'll be famous indeed."

"My dear boy, Major Judas will be famous, *not* us. For we are but common soldiers," Nimrim remarked.

"I'm still proud to be a part of this, sir," the guard said.

"Me as well—me as well," Nimrim added with a grin.

Nimrim looked down and saw the crowds rushing towards the hilltop. Carchemish and the caravan began their ascension up the sloping hill. The legions cheered when they saw them coming with their prize. The ocean of demons parted as Carchemish led the way through camp.

Michael struggled with each step he took and Gabriel was still unconscious, which was much unlike him. He was usually as tough as steel and his endurance never wavered. Because of the mission God had given Gabriel, he had to remain unconscious throughout these happenings, so that what the LORD had spoken would come to pass.

Migron walked behind Michael, cussing at him all the while. Carchemish was leading the way, followed by the demon princes. As he walked, he raised his fist in the air and gave out a resounding cry of victory and the legions unanimously joined in. The crowd roared with excitement.

Michael's strength, by now, was almost completely gone; he felt as if he were balancing on the edge of defeat and yet, was holding on tightly to any hope that might remain for him and Gabriel. *Stay on your feet*, he thought, but he was helplessly weak; even his determination wasn't enough to keep him going. And suddenly, he collapsed to the ground, but not by his own accord. He felt a swift, ruthless jab behind his right knee. Enjoying it all the while, Migron had kicked him and hard; he knew it would bring him cheers of approval from the anxious crowd. The demons shouted curses and profanities at Michael, taking immense pleasure in mocking the archangel.

Gabriel fell limply from Michael's shoulders and met the ground with a jolt. Michael sat on his knees and swayed back and forth, as he was fighting to stay conscious. He strained his eyes in attempt to see, but his vision was blurring and fading in and out. He was losing his mental clarity, but the arduous journey had also reaped its havoc on his once magnificent frame. He was covered in dirt and sweat, he was filthy like a swine that had wallowed in the mud, he was dehydrated to the point that his lips had cracked and were bleeding, and he had been stricken with a fever.

Yet, with his impaired vision, Michael could still see Carchemish standing in front of him. He felt crippled as he listened to the jeers from the crowd. He wanted to be anywhere but there.

Oh Father, what will happen to me, he wanted to say, but he couldn't speak.

The demons continued to shout and yell curses at God.

Father, they persecute you. Give me strength so I may defend your holy name, Michael tried to speak the words, but his lips wouldn't move. He felt helpless and hung his head in his desperation.

Carchemish was eager to demonstrate his superiority; he beat his chest with his fist and raised his sword in the air.

"The great angel has fallen," Carchemish shouted. "Michael the Archangel has been captured."

Then Carchemish let forth a boisterous and sinister laugh; Michael's spirit shivered in its quake. Carchemish looked at him mockingly and scuffed dirt into his face. He then paced over to where Gabriel lay, unconscious and defenseless, and stood musing over him.

"And this pathetic weakling is Gabriel, a *true* warrior? I think not. He trembled with fear like a coward," Carchemish announced, with a self-satisfied, cynical sneer on his face and the entire legion broke out in laughter.

Suddenly an ominous silence overtook the demons and even Carchemish.

Judas had ascended from the cave and took position on the mound. He was adorned with a vibrant royal-purple robe, and he was looking down intently at Michael. Judas was ecstatic at just the mere sight of the archangel, helpless and kneeling on the ground. The demon princes looked upon him and noticed he is dressed like a member of the royal court of Lucifer. Actually, Judas now saw himself as one of them—a demon prince of Hell. He had good reason for his new appearance. He was responsible for the capture of the infamous archangel and the treacherous warrior Gabriel.

Judas, with regal carriage, descended the mound and posed himself for victory, as he arrogantly paraded himself through the multitude. He approached the archangel and turned to the crowd and bowed three times, so all may see him victorious. The legions had been completely silent as Judas bowed, but when they saw him raise his fisted arm high in the air, they erupted with cheering.

"Victory is Lucifer's," the legions raised their fists up and chanted.

As the horde loudly cheered, Judas summoned Migron to his side.

"Take Gabriel below," Judas shouted into his ear. "His

quarters have been prepared and four of my best soldiers are in armor waiting to lead you. Go and be quick about it."

Judas turned to quiet the unruly host of demons, which was nearly five thousand.

Michael sat motionless on his knees. His thoughts were on the LORD. *Oh God, my heart is broken. My God, my God, why have you forsaken me? I call to you, come and rescue me.*

The crowds settled down and Judas raised his voice so all could hear.

"Behold comrades, God's greatest angel. This is his masterpiece, the great Archangel Michael," Judas shouted and laughed, sneeringly.

Sinister laughter swept through the throng until Judas raised his hand and silence instantly emanated throughout the crowd.

"It's over Michael," Judas knelt down and whispered into Michael's ear. "Victory belongs to Lucifer—your soul is his to possess. In the pits of Hell you will make your home. Your only escape from torture will be to deny the LORD of Heaven and vow loyalty to the LORD Lucifer. What say you now?"

Michael remained silent while Judas stood to his feet and reveled in his own selfish glory. As the crowd shouted curses at God, a tear rolled down Michael's cheek. His soul was tormented and his spirit was despaired beyond description.

"Jehovahjireh yaw-rah,'" Michael cried out. "Yeh'-shah. Elishama." *My God sees your evil. I cry for salvation. My God will hear my cry.*

He had regained his voice and was able to shout out with strength and even Judas, over the noise of the crowd, had heard Michael's cry. He walked over to him and forcefully grabbed Michael by the hair on the back of his head.

"Comrades, the archangel has gone mad," Judas shouted. "Did you hear his words? He speaks gibberish. Maybe the Ruah have already claimed him for themselves."

Judas signaled to the demon princes to drag Michael forward. They reluctantly obeyed, for demon princes despise being ordered around. However, they feared the wrath of the crowd, since it seemed that Judas had them all under his spell. They carelessly heaved the archangel forward and laid him at Judas' feet. Judas took his royal purple robe and wrapped it around Michael's shoulders.

What proceeded next was extremely disturbing.

"Behold the archangel, mighty is he," Judas hailed, mocking him.

He struck Michael in the face and a wave of silence overtook the crowd. They were shocked and perplexed; for the demons didn't know how the archangel would react. Blood dripped from Michael's lips and his cheek had begun to swell and only a moment passed before Judas struck him again. Michael shuddered in pain with the impact of Judas' hard fist. He refused to give resistance or defend himself against the sinister demon; instead he turned the other cheek and Judas struck him even harder this time. The crowd, like a multitude of rocks, was silent. They remained speechless like trees in a forest.

"Archangel Michael, call on your God," Judas sneered. "Call on the ruler of Heaven to come and rescue you."

Judas struck him in the stomach. Michael doubled over in pain and Carchemish brutally hit him in the back of the head using the handle of his sword. Blood and spit poured out of Michael's mouth; yet he did nothing to defend himself. He was powerless and helplessly at the hands of the tyrants of Hell.

"Call on the Host of Heaven. Summon a million seraphim to come to your aid," Judas shouted; relentlessly taunting him, he spit on the archangel and kicked him in the face.

Tears of misery and heartache rolled down the archangel's face.

"The archangel is a coward and weakling. Death to Michael. Kill him, kill him," a demon, out of the crowd, demanded.

"Death to the archangel. Kill him," the legions chanted; their cheers were like a mighty tidal wave crashing on a shoreline.

Judas, from the corner of his eye, noticed a demon standing idly and the demon had something that Judas wanted: a whip made of sharks teeth, jagged rocks, and sharp steel shards. Judas seized the whip from him.

"Remember brothers, when Michael and the angels drove us from our rightful place in Heaven," Major Judas proclaimed.

The demons roared with anger and Judas loved it.

"That was their time, but now our time has come, brothers. Vengeance is ours and I say we take it," Judas declared.

The legions raised their fists and cheered.

Judas commanded Michael to take the Sword of the Spirit and defend himself. Michael ignored the demon's orders, as he gazed intently into the heavens.

"What insolence," Carchemish yelled at him, and reached for Michael's sword, pulling it from its sheath.

As soon as his hand made contact with the sword's handle, a painful jolt shot through Carchemish's body and he dropped the sword at Michael's feet.

"Defend yourself, great warrior of God," Judas demanded. "Call upon the Host of Heaven to come and fight for you. You're the general—aren't you? Pick up your sword and defend yourself you infidel."

The crowd shouted and hissed. Judas mocked him with laughter.

"Come closer," Judas provoked the legions. "Take a good look at the archangel of Heaven."

The demons moved in and crowded closely around Michael.

"Jehovahnissi," *God is my banner*, the archangel cried out.

"Listen to his mumbling, he's gone mad," Judas shouted.

The major then handed Carchemish the whip

"Carchemish, punish him with all you have. Hold nothing back," Judas leaned towards him and demanded.

"With great pleasure," Carchemish grinned and answered.

Judas ordered two demons in the crowd to pick Michael up. They ruthlessly yanked him up to a standing position. Judas told them to use the ropes to extend his arms outwards, to the sides of his body. The demons eagerly obeyed and pulled on the ropes with such might that his arms popped from their joints. Michael cried in agony and his eyes welled with tears. Carchemish stepped behind him and cracked the whip. To Michael's ears, the sound was as piercing as blaring peals of thunder. His body tensed up at the sound of the whip coursing madly through the air.

Judas positioned himself in front of Michael.

"This doesn't have to happen," Judas whispered cunningly into his ear. "You can escape your punishment. All that you must do is deny your God and swear allegiance to Lord Lucifer."

Michael gathered the strength to lift his head.

"Never," he boldly cried, looking Judas in the eye.

Judas nodded to Carchemish to begin. He suspended the whip behind him and with his all his strength, he fiercely slung the whip forward. The first strike landed solidly on the archangel's back and slithered down. Michael shuddered in utter agony, a tear rolling down his cheek. This was the moment the LORD had spoken of: *the bitter cup*. The next strike was far more painful than the last had been. The whip clung viciously to Michael's skin like the sharp claws of a lion. The shards of steel pierced his skin and the shark's teeth tore the flesh from his bone. Michael cried out in excruciating agony. He was trembling, his toes curled and his hands shook as the pain vibrated throughout his entire body. The hairs on his neck stood on end and his spirit cried to his Father for mercy. His flesh was tormented beyond words and his soul was crying for salvation, as his entire being hung at the threshold of death's door.

"Deny the LORD of Heaven, and all of this will end," Judas leaned towards him and whispered. "You won't have to suffer anymore. Just deny *Him*."

Michael didn't reply and as his head was hanging. He kept his sight directed toward the ground. Michael's body had given out completely and after all that he had endured, he was beyond the point of tears.

"Forty strikes ought to do him good. Prepare his spirit for Hell," Judas turned to Carchemish and said.

Carchemish grinned devilishly and, rearing back, he cracked the whip again and again. With each brutal crack from Carchemish's whip, more flesh was torn from Michael's body. He became torn on the outside; on the inside, he was bruised and broken. His face was beyond recognition and his outward beauty and splendor had vanished. The enemy had taken away his hope and his will to fight, yet the love he had for his Father never dwindled. In spite having suffered forty cruel lashes, two dislocated arms, two helpless legs, and a bloody and swollen face he never denied his Father in Heaven.

After Carchemish had finished his merciless scourging, the demons mocked the archangel and spit on him. Even still,

Michael spoke not a word. He yearned, with all that was in him, to rest at the feet of God.

Only if I could lie at your feet, he thought. He was desperate to feel the presence of God and inwardly he cried out, *why have you forsaken me, my God, my Father. Why have you abandoned your servant?*

The demons not only spit on him, but they beat him to a bloody pulp. He convulsed from the pain as the demons pounded him, again and again, with their fists. Michael was truly on the brink of death and in that moment, he felt that if he could gaze no more on the face of God nor ever stand, on his own two feet again, his soul would still be content to just *feel* the presence of God. His only desire was to sit at the feet of God, for his spirit longed to be near the Father and feel his loving embrace.

The demons stopped beating Michael, but only after each felt they had contributed their full share to the tortuous and merciless hammering.

Where are you my God, my King, my Father, thought Michael, *I need you. I need you.* He was crying in his spirit and his soul was trembling in disbelief of what was happening. Nothing could have prepared him for what was truly his darkest moment.

Judas degraded Michael one more time, just for sport. He put a crown of thorns on his head and cursed him.

"Behold the Archangel Michael, the God of Heaven's most favored angel. Among all the seraphim, the ruler of Heaven chose this one to lead his armies. Behold, he has a crown. Now look at him—even with a crown he's still nothing more than vermin. He once dared to defy Lucifer and, look at him now— he's battered and bruised. Who can look upon him and say he is the Archangel Michael?"

Judas leaned into Michael's ear.

"You are no longer the archangel. Your God has disowned you, Michael; Beltezar will see to your demise," Judas' voice hissed like a snake as he whispered.

Judas then ordered Carchemish to take him away. Carchemish grabbed hold of Michael and carelessly heaved his frail figure up on his shoulder like a dead animal from a hunt.

"Take him to my quarters below and stand guard until I arrive," Judas stepped up to Carchemish and whispered.

Judas ascended the mound as he intended to make a speech. He stood erect, as proud as a lion on top of the hill. The multitude hushed and was prepared to listen.

"The seraphim's time has passed. The Host of Heaven will come to an end. Today marks the beginning of the end for our enemies. It's our time now. Our time to rule the earth, our time to conquer mankind, and our time for victory."

The legions erupted in cheering.

"Long live Lucifer, long live Lucifer, long live Lucifer," the soldiers chanted.

Judas summoned Nimrim to the hilltop and put him in charge of dispersing the crowds. Then he walked briskly down the hill and slipped away unnoticed to his quarters below, as the demons continued they're chanting.

Michael, although barely coherent, could feel the walls and floors vibrate from the clamor outside. He was lying deathly still in a corner of the room. He was in Judas' private quarters and Carchemish was the only other one in the room.

"Hear that," Carchemish said. "That's the noise of your defeat–the downfall of Heaven is at hand. I can feel it in my bones and in my soul. It's only a matter of time now before your God is overthrown. Then Lucifer will take his rightful place on the throne."

He spit on Michael in contempt. He raised his fist in the air and was about to strike Michael when he was abruptly interrupted.

"Enough Carchemish. He's endured his share of pain today," Judas walked in and quickly said.

"Haven't you Michael," Judas approached Michael and sarcastically added.

Michael didn't answer, but remained quiet with his head hanging to the floor.

"Where's your power gone," Judas taunted some more. "Vanished has it? I hate to be the bearer of bad news, but your God will be overthrown and soon he will be—dead."

Michael could tolerate the mocking he received and he

endured the beating he received, but he had had enough of their ridicule toward his Father God.

Michael summoned his courage and what little strength remained in him, and tried with all he had to open his swollen eyes. With half-open eyes, he turned and peered at Judas.

"Without God, Lucifer would fail to exist," Michael, in a commanding tone, said. "Don't be a fool Judas. If it had not been for the LORD I would be dead and gone by now. It is by the power of the Most High that I am still alive. Truly you serve a false god."

He then lowered his head again. Judas snickered and wasn't going to back down from a debate. He viciously grabbed Michael by the face and stared cruelly into his eyes.

"You won't be so bold when you stand before the LORD Lucifer," Judas rebuked him. "Truly, if you speak those very same words, you will suffer greatly for your insolence."

Michael looked into his eyes; he peered into Judas's dark, condemned soul.

"I promise you—" Michael declared with authority. "—your arrogance will fail you and your lips will tremble in terror before the awesome power of the LORD of Hosts. There will come a day when you will stand before the LORD Almighty and your knees will cease to hold you for you will tremble before the King of Majesty. He is Jehovah my God, my Savior, and Ruler of the universe. In that moment fear will overtake you. You will prefer death over standing in the Almighty's presence."

"I've had enough of his insolence. You know where to take him," Judas struck Michael in the face and ordered Carchemish.

"You'll never again see the light of day," Judas looked at Michael and swore. "I hope you have a pleasant memory of Heaven somewhere in your bloody mess of a head, because you will never again walk on the streets of gold or ascend the stairs of Mount Zion."

"To your feet, swine," Carchemish grabbed Michael by the hair and barked.

Carchemish closed the door behind them and the sound of rusty hinges distressed Michael's ears like the screeching of swarming bats; when the door shut with a thump, Michael's soul began to fade. He thought, *was this truly the end.*

Carchemish ordered two demons to drag the archangel by his arms and he led the way. They traveled down a narrow passage that led to a winding stairway, which was carved out of the cave walls and descended deep into the darkness. Dreadful sounds of moaning, muffled shouting, and sickly shrieks of pain echoed from the inner depths of the darkness. The stairway wound around and like a giant snake; it made its way deep into the earth. The stairway finally came to an end.

Before them was a long and narrow corridor that stretched into the darkness. An icy breeze whirled and blew out of the passage. The way was dimly lit by a row of eerie green lanterns lining the walls of the corridor. More screams and shrieks echoed and vibrated the ground beneath their feet. The sickening, violent noises met Michael's ears as soon as he entered the passageway. Carchemish ordered the demons to move along faster. They dragged Michael's limp body hastily along the coarse ground, more injury being added to the archangel's legs as he was drug along the rough and punishing floor.

The dim green lights illuminated the darkness with a strange light and a dark shadow hovered to the left of where they walked. From out of the dark shadow came a shrill cry. Michael felt an icy cold breeze pass over him, as the lights dimmed and then flickered. He could hear a voice whispering.

"Ruah. Leave this place. You can't touch him. The archangel belongs to the Lord Lucifer," Carchemish commanded, a hiss sounded in the darkness and the Ruah stormed off in anger. The lights grew brighter and the air warmed.

"This place is overrun with the stench of Ruah. They're despicable I tell you," Carchemish commented to no one specific.

They came upon a fork in the path. The path to the left said *Desmeeos'* and the path to the right had no name. Carchemish had come to a stop here; he appeared like he was pondering which way to go.

"Should we show him boys what kind of welcome he'll receive in Hell," Carchemish pointed down the path marked, Desmeeos,' and sneered.

Cries of pain bellowed like a horrible and earsplitting blast from a trumpet. The noises were coming from the direction of the Desmeeos' passageway.

"Ah, it sounds like your friend, Gabriel, is having a grand time," Carchemish said and laughed so the two demons would join in.

A single tear made its way from Michael's eye and rolled down his cheek; this took him by surprise since dehydration had overtaken his body. *He's alive. Father, give me strength so I may deliver Gabriel from the hands of the wicked,* Michael silently prayed.

Carchemish led them down the other path, which was unmarked. The pathway sloped downwards and like the steep bank of a river, it was wet and slippery; it wound back and forth like a slithering reptile. The corridor was dimly lit with the same eerie green lanterns. The walls were slimy and wet and gave out a putrid stench; they glowed with an odd iridescence. The passage soon leveled out and Michael noticed that prison cells had been hollowed out of the walls that lined the passageway. Rows of bars enclosed the cells and protruding inward, from the bars, were long sharp spikes meant to keep the prisoners from reaching out from between them. There were rows and rows of empty prison cells. It appeared that the enemy was prepared to hold many prisoners captive. Michael wondered if a prison cell was going to be his ultimate fate; if his life was going to be spent rotting in a dungeon. Michael desired, with all of his heart, to be home and in the throne room of God. However, the reality of his seemingly hopeless situation sunk deep into his heart and he grew more despondent each passing moment. He closed his eyes and found himself drifting away. He felt as if he were falling into a bottomless pit.

PREMONITION

Judas sat comfortably in his quarters, sipping on a potion he had concocted for its rejuvenating effects. He was weary from the events of the day, although what tired him the most was the burden of Beltezar's impending visit. In an effort to put him at ease, he reclined comfortably in his chair and admired the Sword of the Spirit that now hung from the wall of his quarters. Logos hung directly next to it.

I'd best admire these swords while I can, he sat pondering, *Lucifer will definitely have the Sword of the Spirit for himself and I'm quite positive Beltezar will take Logos for its power and abilities. They are, truly, the products of master craftsmanship. Beautiful works of art and such perfection cannot be taken lightly. What if I hid Logos? I could always say it was stolen from my quarters; better yet, I could testify against Carchemish and say that he took it. Where do I get this incredible ability for plotting clever strategy? Many say I'm a brilliant commander; I agree, but I think of myself as more of a genius. Yes, a gifted genius. Surely, Beltezar will see me for the great leader I am.*

Forthwith, the door to the hidden passage swung open and Judas was abruptly taken from his deep and enticing thoughts. A hunched-over demon burst through the opening and in the dimly lit room, his face was hard to perceive, then he stepped forward and revealed himself, eyes beaming with exhilaration. He appeared very anxious as he attempted to catch his breath.

"Nimrim," Judas said. "You'd better have something important to say. You know that I refuse to tolerate such behavior, bursting in without even something as simple as a knock. You must learn to behave; you will have to be courteous if I shall consider you for the position."

"Major Judas, he is here—" Nimrim caught his breathe, stood up straight, and uttered. "—Beltezar the Terrible has arrived. As I speak he is on his way here, to see you. I thought it would be wise of me if I forewarned you."

"Did anyone see you come," Judas queried, his eyes ignited and not with anger or anxiety, but with fear.

"I swiftly made my way to the secret passage; no one could have seen me," Nimrim shook his head no and replied.

Judas stood to his feet and paced to and fro.

"Good. Have you seen Carchemish," Judas sternly asked.

"No," Nimrim answered. "Wait—I think I saw him. If that was him, he was with Beltezar and his party."

"Either you saw him or you didn't. Which is it, Nimrim," Judas slammed his hands on the table and snapped.

"Sir—" Nimrim stepped back, shocked, and said. "I am nearly positive it was Carchemish. Who else is as big and strong as he?"

Judas was growing more anxious by the minute and to add to it, he was becoming suspicious as well. Judas looked upon Nimrim's words as an offense.

"Carchemish maybe the biggest for now, but Nimrim, mark my words," he sharply retorted. "Once I am in power, I will create soldiers twice his size with strength ten times greater than his and with power that surpasses all sorcerers by at least twenty fold."

Nimrim discovered his back was to the wall and there was no room to move further away from his raving master. Judas continued to carry on, barking orders; while he ranted and raved, Nimrim was ignoring him and looking for a way to escape. He felt he had been too loyal of a servant to tolerate this madness. He slowly crept along the wall, acting as if he was listening.

Out of the corner of his eye, Judas noticed the demon's peculiar behavior.

"Nimrim, what do you think you are doing," Judas demanded.

Nimrim was too close to escape to turn back now, so he darted for the hidden passage. He pulled the lever on his way and the door came open, he had made it out. He could hear Judas cursing and yelling at the top of his lungs. He grabbed the torch he had left on the wall and ascended the steps as quickly as he could; he wanted to get away from Judas. More so, he wanted to escape from camp.

I'll make a run for it; I'll flee to the most remote jungle where no one can find me, he thought. Nimrim had made up his mind to flee. He came to the top of the passage and pulled the lever to escape. The hidden entrance slid open and he could see the millions of stars illuminating the night sky. *Freedom*, he thought. He stepped out onto the ground and there was absolutely no demon to be seen. He looked this way and that and still he could see no one. The ground felt good against his feet even though it was still muddy and wet from the recent rain shower. He breathed in the fresh air and it was a welcomed relief from the foul air in the cave below. He could hardly believe what he was doing, but a peace came over him as he thought, *I will finally be free to think for myself. Now, I can live for me.*

He crept slowly away and when he thought he was in the clear, he began running. Then it happened just as he was in full stride, he felt a sharp sting in his back and it crippled him. Nimrim buckled over, slipping and falling into the mud.

Earlier that evening, Carchemish had finished securing the archangel in his prison cell. That task having been attended to, he hastily returned to the surface and slipped away unnoticed. He traveled stealthily to the outskirts of the camp. He was in search of a certain waterfall, one that contained a portal to Hell. In fact, he had arrived by means of that exact same portal. Dusk had just set in when Carchemish came upon the waterfall. The light was dim, but the sound of the rushing water falling onto rocks had easily led him to it. At first, he had spent his time sitting patiently on a rock at the water's edge, but as time passed, his patience was waning.

He stood up and commenced to pace back and forth as he waited anxiously for Beltezar, the time planned for his arrival had already come and gone. Beltezar himself had told him that on this evening, when the moon was out and the stars were shining, that he and his party would meet him at this spot. Yet, the moon was out and the stars were spread like a blanket across the night sky, but there wasn't a single sign of Beltezar or his entourage. Carchemish was starting to believe he might have been lead into a trap.

Suddenly, something happened that caused him to abandon his suspicions. A mysterious glow lit up the waterfall. It began as a subtle light, but it soon magnified into an intense and blinding light. Carchemish covered his eyes, for it was worse than staring directly into the sun. A deep booming noise vibrated the ground and a flash illuminated the air around him, then he suddenly realized that water was spraying on him and all about him. The waterfall had parted and lifted into the air and a bridge was extending over the shimmering pool of water. A party of huge and daunting soldiers was marching across the bridge in a line, two by two. Carchemish, as intimidating as he was, trembled in fear at the sight of them; there were thirty soldiers in all and they encircled Carchemish until he was completely surrounded.

Then, just as suddenly as it had appeared, the intense aura was gone. Carchemish looked around and saw he was closed in on all sides; then the circle of soldiers opened, just enough to allow a giant and frightening demon to enter and shut tightly again. The soldiers drew their swords and a wall of muscle and steel now surrounded Carchemish. He found himself face to face with Beltezar the Terrible.

The General towered over Carchemish, dwarfing his large stature.

"Carchemish, my loyal captain, is everything prepared," Beltezar inquired in a deep intimidating tone. "Is Luminarous in custody?"

"Yes sir, General Beltezar, the fallen star has been captured," Carchemish replied.

"Is Judas alive and well," Beltezar asked, rubbing the end of his neatly trimmed beard. Carchemish nodded yes

"In your opinion, has he been a capable leader? Have you found him to be an efficient and competent governor of the island," Beltezar requested.

"General Beltezar, to be truthful, I was sent on this mission to specifically gather intelligence and from my observation Judas is a fool. Moreover, I've found that the soldiers complain, incessantly, about the major, if he is still worthy of the title. They have had enough of his foolish antics and outrageous speeches. I will be straightforward in telling you that if another day had passed, an uprising would be eminent. I believe that my presence here has been the only deterrent against an all-out rebellion."

Carchemish, honestly, didn't care for Judas, so he had eagerly grasped the opportunity to defame the arrogant demon. Beltezar appeared intrigued by Carchemish's report; his face was somber and, stroking the tip of his beard with his fingers, he was contemplating what he had just learned.

"According to your report, the situation is grave indeed and before we can go to war it looks as if some things will require my special attention. Take me to Judas this instant," Beltezar concisely said.

Carchemish complied, leading them directly to camp. Carchemish was anxious but nevertheless, he felt exhilarated. The chance to be rid of Judas was positively electrifying, but he most definitely did not want to take charge of his soldiers. He thought that the legions of soldiers stationed on this island are nothing but morons and idiots and complete fools. Having been lost in his thoughts, Carchemish recognized that they were now approaching the perimeter of the camp.

"We have arrived. Should I summon Judas or take you to him," Carchemish whispered to Beltezar's captain Zoan.

"You shall lead us to him. My soldiers will remain here and we shall escort Beltezar and his four personal guards," Zoan, whose brother Zoar was stationed on the island, replied.

The party was still crouched low, in the hedges, at the edge of camp when Carchemish noticed a demon moving rapidly from behind a tree.

"He looks suspicious," Zoan whispered. "Shall I send my men after him?"

"Wait, let's see where he's going," Carchemish suggested.

The demon scurried quickly towards a wall of rock outside the cave. He stopped and disappeared.

"What's that," Zoan queried. "Did you see that?"

"It's a hidden passage that leads to Judas' private quarters and the soldier is no other than Judas' personal servant, Nimrim," Carchemish answered.

"Then let us pursue him," Zoan drew his sword and uttered.

"It would be wiser for us to descend into the cave by way of the other entrance," Carchemish remarked. "Judas might be expecting us to come through the hidden passage. Now, situate your men and have them keep watch over the secret door. Station a few of your sharpest soldiers in the tree near the secret entrance; then, when Nimrim comes out he'll be met by an unexpected greeting."

"Perfect suggestion. I have the notion of just who to use for this assignment," Zoan grinned and said, he signaled a couple of his ablest guards and placed them, covertly, in the tree next to the hidden passage.

Carchemish guided them into the belly of the dark cave.

It's time. You're finished Judas; let's see what Beltezar thinks of your so called progress, thought Carchemish as they approached the corridor to the major's private quarters.

NOTE FROM THE SCRIBE...

With the highly privileged calling to be archangel, comes great responsibility and accountability. With a blessing of this magnitude comes a holy mandate, drawn out before the foundations of the heavens. With the honor that surpasses all others among the seraphim, comes a hallowed duty to serve the King of Kings with all of your heart, mind, and soul.

Michael had sought out the calling on his life, and by doing so; he had accepted the full requirements. There existed the devastating and very real possibility that he may, one day, have to give his life away... to the Glory of his Father God and for the sake of the Kingdom. The day Michael entered the enemy's camp was the day he faced his destiny. He was despised and rejected; brutally treated for the pleasure of a ghastly audience. No being should suffer as he did, yet there is still another who will endure a more severe punishment. For the sake of all mankind, he will suffer his fate having been determined before the foundation of time—a fate that would save the world.

The Archangel Michael endured the enemy's punishment for the sake of the Kingdom he bore the penalty from Hell. With all of their hate and malice, the demons savagely tortured the archangel; they mercilessly beat him. Michael was relentlessly degraded and made a public spectacle for the pleasure of Hell and its demons. The enemy rabidly despised him and everything he stood, they ridiculed him for his innocence and mocked him for his purity. They could not tolerate the fact that he was arch-angel; they hated the name and the office it stood for. Michael was the prince of Heaven and he stood by the Father and the Son. Among all the Host of Heaven, there was none like Michael.

Satan loathed him for finding favor with God and he detested him for his prestige among the Host of Heaven. For it had been Michael who was chosen by the LORD to command his armies as their general, it was Michael who had defeated Satan, and it had been Michael who vanquished all evil from Heaven, liberating the Kingdom of God. Out of millions upon millions of seraphim, Michael had been handpicked, predestined, preordained, chosen, and sanctified by the Eternal LORD of Heaven to stand on Mount Zion and dwell in the Holy of Holies with the Almighty and the four cherubim. He was groomed by the LORD, taught the knowl-edge of the Creator and the wisdom of the Everlasting God. This gave Satan, more than enough, reason to want Michael dead.

The day Michael looked death in the face was the day the Host of Heaven wept an ocean of tears. The million seraphim that had been assigned to intercede for him, felt his anguish and despair in their spirits; they continually prayed for Michael to have the will to survive. In the midst of Michael's darkest moment, the LORD was alone atop Mount Zion bent over on his throne. He wept for Michael as Michael was on the verge of death.

Then, the seraphim were instructed to pray for Gabriel; to focus all of their intercession on saving his life, for the mission depended on him.

The Warrior Within...

When Gabriel awoke, he perceived immediately that the situation had not improved; finding himself with no strength to move. He felt a firm grip on both of his wrists and his arms felt as someone were trying to pull them loose from his shoulders; then, he realized that he was being dragged along the ground. The last he recalled, Michael had helped him to his feet and the enemy had just taken them as prisoners. *Where am I,* he thought.

He opened his eyes and above him was a canopy of foliage with patches of blue sky showing through here and there. Immediately he noticed the uncomfortable pinch of rocks between his toes and the abrasive surface of rough rocky soil had cut into the soles of his feet. To Gabriel, it was like feeling his pain for the first time, as if his mind had blocked it out until now. He glanced down at his feet and looked upon his battered limbs with dismay; his toes were throbbing with pain and covered with his own blood. The feeling was insufferable to his wearied body and it was the reason he was now fully conscious. Despite the weakened condition he was in, Gabriel still felt compelled to make an effort to free himself from his captors. He wrestled to free himself, but it was to no avail. Satan's goons were simply too strong for him; even worse, he was subjected to a severe beating from the two demons.

"I thought he was already dead," the larger of the demons said. "What a tussle—too bad Sodom and Gomorrah had to abandon us for other duties and miss out on this."

"Yep, this one's still got some fight left in him," the smaller demon replied. "And, what about poor Migron, he's missing out too. If he weren't busy scouting ahead, he'd be busting a gut with laughter. Oh well, we'll just have to tell 'em about it."

They both had a good laugh at Gabriel's expense.

"The boys at Desmeeos' are going to have their hands full; he will be quite the challenge for 'em," the small demon added.

"Challenge," the large demon snickered and insisted. "They'll break him before the day's end." With those last words, Gabriel's hope had begun to fade.

He began thinking about what was in store for him; what ill fate had Satan planned for him. A dark gloom had overtaken him with despair. He had tragically failed his mission and it was too great a burden to accept. Deep inside his being, he felt his heart shatter, breaking into a million pieces. The sober truth was that he couldn't protect Michael from the enemy. That he hadn't done enough to prevent the archangel's capture, weighed heavily on his mind and soul. He began to wonder if he was doomed to death or even worse, he let his mind dwell on the horrible thought of being made into a Ruah. *Anything but that,* he anguished. *I would rather face a thousand deaths than wind up a wicked Ruah; becoming a wretched, hopeless, slave to Satan. I'd better escape, before I allow them to mutilate my spirit.*

Gabriel put all that he had into his heroic effort to be free; he had succeeded, but not without consequence. He had twisted his wrist to loose it from its fetter, but as he did, a sharp pain shot through his arm. In his valiant efforts to free himself, he had dislocated his wrist. Then he loosened the fetter from his other hand and it was free. Gabriel had but one useful hand now; yet he managed to heave himself backwards into the demons, knocking his enemy roughly to the ground. He too fell backwards but he was determined that his freedom was far too valuable a thing to lose without protest. The demons pounced on him and Gabriel responded quickly, kicking his feet and batting his arms, violently in every direction. A cloud of dust rose and filled the air, adding even more to the confusion. It was pure chaos, but Gabriel didn't cease in his pains to escape; needless to say, it would have to be the last man standing before he would let up. By now, the demons had their weapons drawn and were stabbing blindly at the seraph.

"Stop your madness, Gabriel," ordered the small demon, as he tried to land a strike on him with the end of his sword; either his aim was horribly off or Gabriel was just too fast for him.

Having avoided the demon's strike, Gabriel slugged him squarely in the mouth and freed himself from the demon's clutches. He kicked the other demon in the stomach, leaving him rolling on the ground wheezing in agony, and overcome with shock that such a powerful blow had come from the pitifully wounded seraph.

Gabriel tried to stand and flee from his captors, but his efforts were in vain. With all that he had been through, his legs were too feeble to stand. He looked around and saw that they were on a hilltop and it struck him that he could use this to his advantage. He moved across the ground using the strength of his arms and one good hand, to pull himself hurriedly along. The demons were now close behind, chasing him down. Gabriel scurried even faster, in his desperate attempt to escape. The fiends of Satan made a mad dash to seize their prisoner, fearing retribution from the Major Judas.

"Catch the vermin," the small demon yelled. "Judas will have our arms cut off if we let this one get away."

"Don't fret, I'll grab him," the large demon shouted back to him.

Gabriel saw the forest drawing closer to him; for some reason, that made him think of getting to the jungle. That would be a safe haven for him; a place where the enemy and he would be on equal ground.

If I can just get to the jungle, I can hide somewhere that they can't find me, thought Gabriel, frantically crawling down the hill. The hill had become steeper and Gabriel could hear his pursuer close behind. In his panic, he went rolling down the hill in a mad frenzy. He felt the sting of what seemed a hundred thorns piercing his skin, as he collided with the hedges. Finally, Gabriel had come to a stop. He raised his battered body to a sitting position. Recovering his senses from the nasty spill, he shook his head and wiped the dirt from his eyes, but he looked up just in time to see a demon standing directly over him.

"Where do you think you're going, swine," the demon said and knocked him out.

Gabriel awoke to find himself mounted on a majestic white steed, as it galloped through a barren desert plane. The sky above was a crystal clear blue, not a single cloud was in sight. The sand was soft and still, yet a violent gust of wind was blowing against his face. The sun was high overhead, but he didn't feel overheated. The atmosphere had an unnatural temperature; actually, it was pleasant, but still strange for the normal conditions of a hot desert plane. His horse was galloping at a fast pace toward a large dune that was far away on the edge of the horizon.

The wind was rushing through his hair, but he discovered

that he needn't close his eyes to protect them from the harsh force. Everything was peaceful; there was no noise except for the rhythmic pounding sound of the horse's hoofs beating against the sand. Gabriel was in awe with the serene feeling he had. It totally overshadowed each ache and pain in his body. Then he started to remember Luminarous and the agony he had felt; the excruciating injuries that his body had succumbed to and, not to mention, the anguish his spirit had bore since he had journeyed far from home.

Gabriel then remembered Heaven and all of its wonders and majesty. He envisioned the throne room on Mount Zion, he pictured the LORD shining in glory, sitting on his throne; his outstretched arms of compassion reaching out for him brought Gabriel to tears of joy.

"The Love of the one true God is all I need. I want to feel the embrace of my God and Father," he cried out. If anyone was listening, his voice truly would've carried for miles.

That was just the nature of his passion; his fervor for the LORD of Hosts. He desired more than anything now to return to his place in Heaven. The horse galloped still and the wind blew fiercely against his face.

"Onward faithful steed," Gabriel, courageous and lively, yelled. As his horse raced forth he contemplated if he actually died. *Why am I not in Heaven*, he thought, *or maybe this is Heaven? I don't recall this place, but maybe the Father, in his infinite wisdom, decided to expand the realms of his holy kingdom.*

The sun beat down on the desert plain, but Gabriel didn't feel its heat; it wasn't cold but it wasn't warm either. The atmosphere he was experiencing was simply too difficult to explain in words alone.

Suddenly, a horse and its rider drew near to Gabriel.

"Gabriel, I have come," a voice boldly proclaimed. That next second, Gabriel found himself riding, side by side, with the archangel of Heaven. Michael's eyes were gleaming with the power of the Holy Spirit.

"Victory is ours, Gabriel. Fear not, for the LORD is our strength. He is our glory and the lifter of our heads," Michael cried out with a great zeal.

Gabriel couldn't explain why he did it, but his instinct was to reach for the hilt of Logos. The last that he recalled, Logos had been seized and was in the hands of the enemy, and to his astonishment and delight, the sword was firmly in its sheath. His fingers felt the warmth of the handle and his hand fit perfectly. His heart skipped a beat and his mouth widened into an enormously happy grin. He grasped the handle tightly and drew the sword from its sheath; the blade radiated with supernatural power and shined intensely like an evening star.

"Logos, my friend," Gabriel looked proudly at his sword and exclaimed.

Gabriel still couldn't fathom what was happening, but his heart took great joy in knowing that his best friend was riding alongside him, strong and confident, like the extraordinary leader he was destined to be. If this were the life he was to know now, then he was prepared for it. Of course, Gabriel wanted to look upon the LORD again and feel his holy omniscient presence; he truly believed in his heart that he would see him again. In his newly found optimism he thought to himself that the end is not near. *I believe in the LORD all-powerful. Wherever I may be heading, I have faith that it will lead me to the Father.*

Out of thin air, a resounding trumpet blared; he and Michael were met by a multitude of angels on horseback.

"The Heavenly Host—my brothers," Gabriel remarked, overcome with what he was seeing. Even more so, he was thrilled at the wondrous sight of countless seraphim, riding in unison, armed with their weapons of war.

The horses and their riders came to an abrupt stand still. The archangel was seated tall on his stallion; he was richly adorned in shining armor. Gabriel looked upon the archangel in awe; Michael's face was full of vigor.

"Prepare your hearts, seraphim," the archangel addressed the army, shouting at the top of his lungs. "Today—we ride for the glory of the Lamb who sits on the throne."

The seraphim raised their weapons to heaven and cried, in one accord, "To the glory of the Lamb."

Gabriel's eyes grew wide and his heart pounded. Michael's eyes had changed and now blazed with the anointing of the LORD. A holy passion was impressed on Gabriel's heart as he scanned over the army of seraphim. The angels were beyond number and it was astounding. They were as numerous as the grains of sand in the desert. And then, in utter amazement, his spirit shouted for joy as he beheld Caleb and Joshua among the Host and his soul swelled with hope upon spotting Raphael, Uriel, and Saraqael, in the front line, seated on mammoth white steeds. Then, upon seeing the twin brothers, Remiel and Raguel as well, he shed tears of jubilation.

Suddenly, an ominous hush swept over the forces of light. The ground was trembling and began shaking violently; this was more than just a formidable noise or disturbance. It was an earthquake of such a frightening magnitude that it split the sea of sand before the army of Heaven. A great crevice in the earth, more than a thousand paces across, had spread itself open no less than ten thousand paces from where the Host of Heaven sat on their horses. Michael, Gabriel, and the Host silently looked on as hordes upon hordes of vile and wretched creatures spilled from the canyon and onto the sand.

A swarm of fire-breathing dragons, covered in a thick armor of slimy scales, took to the air in pursuit of their holy prey. Repulsive worms the length of many horses crept across the sand, seeping and oozing with poison, their horrid and filthy souls desiring the taste of angels. A brood of vipers, each the size of a seraph, slithered and hissed as their venom dripped from two scimitar-like fangs. Millions upon millions of bloodthirsty spiders crawled out and scampered about, as their eyes hunted for seraphim to destroy. And last, but certainly not the least, the legions of Hell emerged with a horrifying, resonating roar. There were millions upon millions of demons, malicious, evil, foul, and reeking and fully clad in armor and armed to their teeth with scimitars, pikes, maces, swords, and spears.

Without wasting a moment, the legions of dark spirits assembled quickly and tactically for one common purpose. Utterly devastating the Host of Heaven. Then in a display of fire and brimstone, a single being rose from the pits of Hell and took his place as commander of the legions of Hell. His name is Satan and upon his head was written blasphemous words against the Lamb. With the prince of darkness to lead them, the enemy was fully prepared to totally destroy the seraphim of Heaven. The horses reared, in fright and began to scatter. The angels still mounted upon their backs. Then Michael reached for the ivory horn, inlaid with precious gold, and removed it from his belt. He held the horn in his left hand and taking in a deep breath, he put it to his mouth sounding out a resonating call to battle. The earth trembled and Michael's eyes were glowing with a holy fire. The seraphim came together in ranks as they steadied their horses.

"Not by might, nor by power, but by my spirit, says the LORD of Hosts," Michael valiantly cried out. Upon those words the earth opened a hundred paces or so, in front of the hordes from hell, and just as they were charging towards the Host of Heaven.

Gabriel sat on his horse, thoroughly, dumbfounded by what he was witnessing. A swarm of hornets and locusts, too infinite in number to calculate, had erupted from the earth and the vibration of their wings resounded like thunder, frightful and menacing. The hornets struck first; fast and furious they sank their stingers deep into the hides of the dragons, worms, and snakes, and felled them to the earth. The locusts swarmed onto the spiders like a tidal wave, completely covering them; they suffocated the hairy creatures.

The ground swallowed the manifestations of evil erasing them from the face of the earth. The locusts and hornets restored themselves into the ground and with rumbling and a resolute bang, both of the gaping fissures closed; the desert floor appeared as if had never been opened. After the cloud of dust cleared, it was evident that only the cursed legions of Hell yet remained to face the righteous Host of Heaven. Gabriel was astounded.

THE DARKNESS

Judas, even now, was in his private quarters pacing back and forth, mulling over what he should say to Beltezar. His nerves were disquieted to say the least. Truthfully, he was at his wit's end. He knew that the situation with Luminarous was unsettled; for this reason, Beltezar would not be pleased.

"What am I to do," he pondered into thin air. "What am I to say to Beltezar?"

Ah-ha, there is still time to persuade the fallen star, he thought, *I can win him over before Beltezar comes to see me.* Judas rushed toward the door assuring himself if he leaves now and takes great haste, he can get to him before Beltezar arrives. As he opened the door into the hallway, he could hear the sound of footsteps approaching his quarters. Someone was coming toward him.

Judas panicked and quickly retreated back into the safety of his quarters. *Ah, the hidden passage, I can escape,* he thought and hurriedly with tenacious resolve, he scuttled towards the passage. Escaping would be simple now; all he had to do was pull the small handle hidden behind the torch that hung on the wall opposite his desk and he would be gone.

Beads of sweat dripped from his forehead and his hand trembled with alarm, as he grasped the lever and tugged at it forcefully. The lever budged not an inch, for unbeknownst to him one of Zoan's soldiers was on the outside of the door bracing it firmly in place. Judas' heart was racing now, throbbing louder and harder against his chest with each beat.

A trap, he thought. *Nimrim deceived me, he betrayed me.*

"How could he? And after all I've done for his worthless hide," Judas clenched his fist and cried out loud. Every fear and doubt that had ever loomed in Judas' mind surfaced, but worse than ever he was totally unnerved.

All of sudden, the door to his quarters swung wide open and the handle struck against the wall. A few small rocks and pebbles fell from the ceiling and skipped lightly across the floor. Truthfully, the sound was no louder than a few pins dropping, but to Judas it seemed as loud as an avalanche. He cowered in the corner, afraid to move or turn his face towards the door. He whimpered like the spawn of a wild boar, terrified to acknowledge that the door had opened. Madness had prevailed over his spirit and stolen his sanity. His soul became gutless and pathetic, his spirit turned into spineless mush and his clever facade vanished. He hid his face in futile hope that whoever had entered his quarters would be unable to see him, thus exemplifying the extent of the insanity that had possessed him. He whispered to himself with incantations or so he thought. The words may have begun as spells in his mind, but they escaped his lips humming like the ramblings of a raving lunatic.

For a few moments Zoan stood silently in Judas' quarters simply observing; he was astonished and appalled at the demon's condition. Then he loudly cleared his throat to get Judas' attention and with a strident and assertive tone to his voice, he announced.

"Beltezar the supreme general of Hell, second only to Lucifer, and commander of the armies of Hell seeks a private audience with your Lordship Judas, major and counsellorship of Luminarous. Will you please rise to your feet, sir?"

Judas slowly stood up. His appearance was like one in mourning. His eyes were swollen and puffy from crying, his hair was tousled and looking unkempt, his body was bent over, plagued from stress and his spirit and soul were besieged with panic and anxiety. Judas gave an effort to stand up straight and at best, he looked like a fictional warlock with his long, narrow, pointed nose dominating his profile. His back was hunched over from the burden of his sins; his face was sour from loathing this moment.

"Please enter my humble abode—oh most revered of demons—Beltezar the Terrible." Judas replied, stuttering.

Zoan moved himself from the doorway and made way for the general of Hell. A giant and intimidating figure dressed from head to toe in black and wearing a blood red cloak, made his way in. The massive demon lowered his head to clear the doorway. He was truly a terror to behold. The torches suddenly flickered and dimmed. The walls trembled and creaked as he entered.

Then the foreboding figure unveiled his face beneath his hood and there stood, before Judas, the most menacing of all the demons. The most feared next to Satan. Wrought with doom and the challenger of peace, the bringer of pestilence, and the warden of death, Beltezar himself. Like a pillar of wrath, the general towered menacingly over Judas, with his dark brows and looming gray eyes, he peered through Judas' soulless body.

"Sit and listen closely," Beltezar uttered, breaking the silence with a deep, harsh, and petrifying voice. "The LORD Lucifer, has given you, Judas, control over the realm of Luminarous. What have you accomplished with this generous appointment?"

Judas stood behind his desk, speechless. He doubted he was going to make it out of his private quarters alive. While he stood stricken with fear, Carchemish walked into the room and Beltezar ordered Zoan to shut the door.

"Choose your words carefully for I am not a forgiving general," Beltezar spoke, using an especially severe tone.

"My lord and general, Beltezar, welcome. Welcome," Judas collected himself and said; he was now alone, left behind by trusty Nimrim, to confront three horrific demons: Zoan, Carchemish, and Beltezar the Terrible.

"Only Lucifer is lord," Beltezar retorted spitefully. "Now tell me Judas, what have you accomplished? Is Luminarous inline with our plans?"

Judas cowered and stepped back against the wall, nearly knocking Logos from its place. Beltezar snapped his fingers and Zoan walked over to Logos and removed it from its mount on the wall. He swiftly and gingerly laid the sword on the table, since its touch had sent painful waves of shock through his arm. Beltezar stood looking at Judas with a penetrating glare, waiting for the now feeble-minded demon to answer him.

Judas wanted to concoct a lie—bend the truth as he did best, but he found his lips refused to utter a word. Unbeknownst to him, Beltezar had prepared for the distinct possibility that Judas might lie and beforehand had cast a truth spell over him. Judas, unfortunate for him, was utterly and vulnerably at Beltezar's will. He had no choice but to succumb to the power of the spell and speak only the truth.

Judas opened his mouth and the words came out, "General Beltezar, I have spent some time with the fallen star talking with him. I have gained, or earned—well—I have not yet won his trust, nor have I been successful in making him believe in our war."

Beltezar moved, suddenly, towards Judas with one great stride. He slammed his giant fists down on the table; it cracked and shattered right in front of Judas, sending Logos to the ground and Judas, as well. He had startled with fright at Beltezar's sudden violence, stumbled, and fell to the ground.

"We had an agreement," Beltezar roared, his voice was loud and shrill and echoed and through the room. More rocks and pebbles crumbled off the ceiling and bounced across the floor.

This time the noise did not reverberate like an avalanche, it sounded, to Judas, like the rumble of a giant guillotine chopping off the head of a poor condemned soul. Judas melted away as waves of agonizing fear ran through his spineless body. Judas retreated to the corner of the room like a dying dog or a prisoner awaiting his punishment.

"Judas, you are hereby relieved of your duty as major and governor of Luminarous," Beltezar towered over him and grimly proclaimed. "Moreover, as general of the royal legions of Hell, I charge you with multiple acts of treason and you will stand trial for heresy. You will be tried before the high council of the LORD Lucifer's supreme court of demon princes." The words had barely sunken into Judas' demented mind, when Carchemish yanked his inert body up from the floor.

"I am supposed to be a demon prince," Judas cried out.

"Demon prince," Beltezar sneered and said. "Hah. Judas, be

sure to testify of this before the court," and he added under his breath, "I'm sure they'll find it amusing."

"General Beltezar, what would you like me to do with him," Carchemish asked, the general had his attention focused on Logos and was bent to the floor feeling the sword.

"What would you suggest Major Carchemish," He responded, curtly. Judas shuddered in disgust at the general's words, but Carchemish swelled with pride at just the sound of them.

"Maybe, if it pleases the General, I shall send him to Desmeeos' and give him a taste of his own punishment," Carchemish suggested.

"Not bad for your first order as major," Beltezar nodded agreeably and said. "Do as you say, only order four of Zoan's soldiers to escort Judas to his new and improved private quarters."

Carchemish bowed and said, "As you wish, master." He proceeded to bind Judas' hands behind his back and, having just been promoted and highly pleased to be the new commander of the island, Carchemish proudly marched out the door taking Judas along with him.

Judas was now defeated and broken; he contemplated that the tortures awaiting him couldn't be worse than the blows his pride had already taken. He was miserably mistaken, for what awaited him in Desmeeos' was Hell on earth. Carchemish returned within mere moments, but enough time had passed to give Beltezar his awaited opportunity to hold Logos in his hands. Carchemish was amazed to find the general wielding the majestic blade with ease and style. A true show of talent and incredible swordsmanship, Beltezar swung the sword with a fierceness that could cut straight through stone and he did just that, slicing a chunk of rock out of the stonewall. Logos came through unblemished and glowing with heat.

Carchemish was speechless. He recounted to himself the shock he had received the instant his hand came in contact with the sword. *What great and mysterious power does the general possess*, thought Carchemish, *that it does not hurt him.*

Carchemish was startled from his thoughts as he heard Beltezar say, "What marvelous craftsmanship. The blade appears to be constructed of the same unique steel as the LORD Lucifer's sword, Prioust Ohly. This precious metal is most certainly the strongest in all of Heaven and earth. There are only three swords in the entire universe that have been crafted from Prioust Ohly: Gabriel's sword, Logos, the archangel's weapon, Sword of the Spirit, and our LORD Lucifer's blade of darkness, Awven, slayer of angels. Fate has given all three into our hands. What a momentous day this is to possess the power of the three blades of supernatural power."

NOTE FROM THE SCRIBE…

To appease your curiosity, I must inform you that Lucifer crafted the sword, Awven, in secret before the great battle. Awven was a weapon he had fashioned out of the precious metal, Prioust Ohly. The sword was beautiful in every aspect and perfectly flawless. Nevertheless, Satan's heart had become black with evil and malice, so his fingers couldn't grasp the handle to wield its power, for its touch scorched his hand and radiated pain throughout his entire body. Thus, he was forced to create a second sword of different metal and this sword was the one he used in the great battle.

At the great battle, Satan had girded Awven to his belt; when the ground opened the powerful sword, along with Satan, plunged in to the dark abyss, Hell. It is not known yet what unique powers Awven may possess. However, it is rumored that Satan has wielded Awven against his demons and turned them to ash from a single stroke of the supernatural weapon.

The Warrior Within …

Beltezar took Logos and placed it in the sheath, which was now firmly attached to his belt. The general then approached the archangel's sword, hanging on the wall.

"This is the infamous Sword of the Spirit, the weapon that disintegrated the blade of our LORD Lucifer," Beltezar remarked as his hand gripped its handle.

As soon as he removed the sword from its sheath, the blade radiated with an intense heat. The aura traveled into the handle and through the general's body like a small bolt of lightening. He jolted from the sudden electrical shock and felt as if hot lava was coursing through his veins. Beltezar dropped the sword to the ground and screamed in pain, examining his wound.

"My liege," Carchemish blurted out. "I should have warned you not to touch the Archangel's weapon. It's cursed, I believe."

"Yes, you should've, boy," Beltezar said, irately. "Look at me now. My perfect hand has been welted. It's an abomination, I tell you." He held his hand up to the light and was aghast over the lesion the sword produced.

"My general, please forgive your servant; my humblest apologies, Beltezar the Terrible," Carchemish said, bowing submissively on the ground. He was terribly frightened by Beltezar's hostile words.

Carchemish was sufficiently informed of the general's reputation, so he knew perfectly well how to influence the situation. Even one as prestigious as Beltezar can be manipulated and persuaded; in any case, it's common knowledge that the general swells with pride and self-esteem at just the sound of his title, Beltezar the Terrible, thought Carchemish as he awaited the general's response.

"I will not forget this Carchemish," Beltezar asserted. "Know that I spared you from your insolence this time, only because you're of more use to me alive than dead. Remember, though, that with the snap of my fingers I can turn you into something detestable to look upon, or make you a Ruah if I so desire. I can even make you vanish out of existence. Not even the records in Heaven will show that you have ever lived."

Carchemish knelt and thanked Beltezar for his munificent pity, finishing by addressing him with the same three patronizing words, Beltezar the Terrible. When he saw the conceited smile upon Beltezar's face he thought Beltezar's pride made him like a lamb being lead to the slaughter.

"Stand to your feet, Major Carchemish," Beltezar ordered. "It is time that I see Luminarous, for I have much desire to speak with the fallen star. Now take haste, before I change my mind and do something you'll regret."

While Beltezar interrogated Luminarous, Gabriel was awakening from his vision. To a large extent, his memory of the vision was vague; the truth of the matter was that he recalled only bits and pieces of what he had seen. For instance, he pictured a horse, but didn't remember galloping across the desert plain on its back. A voice had called out to him, but he couldn't picture the face.

He found himself wondering, was it truly a dream or was it something else. Many visions and images passed through his mind, but not a single one of them could be clearly seen. He felt as if he was traveling at an incredible rate of speed, while all that surrounded him stood still or, for all he knew, it may be it was just the opposite. His eyelids were still tightly closed.

Although Gabriel was outright perplexed, he knew one thing was for certain; the horrible throbbing pain he was feeling in his head. *Now where did that come from*, he thought to himself. Gabriel looked to the Holy Spirit for strength, *empower me with your presence, oh Holy One*, he prayed silently. He sensed the confidence of the Holy Spirit from within. At last, he opened his eyes and the first thing he noticed was an eerie green light glowing on the wall.

Actually, he found he was peering at several strange, glowing flames. Then it dawned on him, he was having trouble focusing his eyes; for there was only a single mysterious green illumination, and it was glowing about a dozen paces away from him. What was most odd about the torch was that it did not spark or hiss like an ordinary flame would; it simply pulsated with mysterious waves the color of jade and within each flicker and wave of its unnatural illumination, were bizarre yellow hues. He noticed that shadows were moving and waving across the ceiling, as if they were wicked dancing demons. *Where am I*, thought Gabriel.

Gabriel tried to move his hands and found he had no freedom. Instead, he heard the clanging of chains and the clattering of metal against stone. His hands were bound with shackles and his feet were clasped with iron fetters; he discovered he was anchored to the wall and unable to move but a solitary inch. *LORD of Hosts, what has become of your lieutenant general, your servant, and your child*, he thought. His eyes grew weary, as he searched the vicinity for any inhabitants; his eyes failed to focus in the darkness, but as far as he knew there was no one there.

Upon discovering he was alone, Gabriel became desperate for God. He prayed silently to himself, but his prayers seemed to be of no use; his intentions were pure, but his effort had been futile. It was as if his prayers were hitting a wall that solidly blocked each one of his thoughts from reaching the LORD, both figuratively and literally speaking. *What is this hideous strength*, he thought. *I am wearied continually, my words ascend but to the outskirts of my mind, only to return empty and vain.*

Gabriel wasn't about to give up that easily. He prayed continually from his heart, yet the words rolled off his tongue, merely to come back void and lifeless. To the seraph, the prayers felt systematic and dead, instead of spontaneous and life-giving. There was something lacking. *Perhaps passion*, thought Gabriel, *No, that mustn't be it. I desire with all that is in me, to be in the presence of the Most High God. What is it that's absent from my prayers, or what is missing from my heart? With all that is in me, with my entire being and with everything I have I want, I need, I long for the presence of the King of Kings and LORD of Hosts.* Gabriel found himself in a crisis and he couldn't hear his God; he didn't know where he was and he was in a total state of confusion.

Eventually, he gave in to the prospect that this must be his new life and with immense reluctance, he commenced to accept the constraints that came with the new way of life. His mind soon wondered into dark territories where his thoughts dwelt on the notion that he had been kidnapped and was actually in Hell; and perchance, he was being held captive for the inevitable, the imminent threat of succumbing to the will of the dark one; being tortured until he was disfigured, tainted, perverted, and transformed into a Ruah.

"Have mercy on me, oh LORD," Gabriel cried out with a loud voice, frantically and desperately. The instant his voice rang out, a terrible shriek echoed; it sounded as if he was imprisoned in a cavern.

Then, a chill swept over his entire body and his eyes grew with horror as he realized that the shadows, which had been dancing on the ceiling, were not really shadows at all. They were not illusions of sorcery, but all along they were the Ruah. All of a sudden, each of the Ruah unveiled a set of menacing red eyes. All six pairs stared, with wicked cruelty, upon Gabriel. Gliding in unison the six Ruah descended upon the angel of Heaven.

"Holy Spirit come now and deliver me from these wretched spirits of Hell," Gabriel prayed aloud. "Ruah be gone in the name of the LORD of Hosts." They hissed at him and they cursed him as they continued moving in closer, he could feel the Ruah's icy cold breath upon his face as they mocked him with evil, ferocious laughter.

"Gabriel you have no power over me," a Ruah announced itself. "I am Sin, the prince of the Ruah. The LORD Lucifer has given me the authority to rule over all Ruah and the power to resist the enemy's attack. Your words are foolishness, seraph of Heaven. Your prayers are powerless. Do you have any more prayers to beseech your master with? I should think not, because your hope has faded and your spirit, I sense, is waning even as I speak to you now. Deny it if you like, but I can clearly perceive that your time is running out."

Gabriel gathered his strength and held his head up.

"Who do you think you are, Sin, that you threaten an angel of God," looking Sin directly in the eyes, he said. "You're helplessly at the whim and authority of the Holy Spirit and if I call upon him—before a moment has passed, you will flee before his power."

Sin hovered closer to Gabriel. His presence emitted pure evil.

"Holy Spirit? I think not," uttered Sin. "Beyond this cave I have over a thousand Ruah at my bidding. Their combined strength has created a shield, ten times thicker than a stone wall and impenetrable by any supernatural forces, which includes the Holy Spirit whom you, so willingly and foolishly, serve and obey. Now that I have settled that matter, I'll explain all that you ought to know. My captains and I have been assigned to watch over you until our order comes from Beltezar the Terrible to destroy you. Although, if the mood strikes him right, he may permit me to take possession of your body and he might even authorize many other Ruah to invade your body; if that comes to happen, then we will utilize your body to its fullest potential. And by fullest, I mean to say your body will be exploited to fight against the Host of Heaven, your brothers. The lieutenant general of Heaven waging war against the seraphim of Heaven—it's quite the paradox. And who would be at the front of his mind, commanding every move and each word spoken? I, of course, Sin prince of the Ruah."

The other Ruah heckled and mocked Gabriel while the angel peered contemptuously into Sin's wicked eyes. Anger was welling up inside of the angel and was about to surface with an eruption of fury, one that would set him free from the chains that bound him.

"Let him alone Ruah, vile and wretched spirits of Hell," without warning, from out of the darkness, a voice boldly shouted.

Gabriel could hardly believe his ears, a familiar voice that seemed to have come from across the dungeon. His spirit soared with renewed hope.

"Caleb, mind your tongue you feeble and worthless seraph," the vile spirit swept its formless body across the dungeon and roared. "Why the Lord Lucifer has kept you alive thus far, I'll never know."

Gabriel was utterly amazed to hear Caleb's voice. He so wanted to look upon Caleb with his own eyes, but the Ruah had formed a dark cloud blocking the seraph's vision. Even though he couldn't see Caleb, hope and courage rose from within his spirit and pervaded his heart.

"Ha. Sin, you think you can frighten me with your idle threats," Caleb declared. "You and your band of Ruah are nothing but a mistake; a perversion of Hell stumbled upon by chance. All Ruah are naught, rejects of Hell. You were not only banished from Heaven, but as well, you've been thrown from the favor of Hell. So I ask: who are you Sin that you think you can prevail against a servant of the living God?" Caleb's voice was music to Gabriel's ears.

"Your words are trivial, Caleb," Sin hissed and scorned him. "You speak boldly for one who is bound in shackles. When the time comes, I'll enjoy eating your spirit while you suffer to death." The Ruah's hideous, shrill voice was unsettling and repulsive to the angels' ears.

"Sin, why do you waste your time with Caleb—after all, it is I you want, the lieutenant general of God's armies," Gabriel cried out, his spirit was flooded with the power of the Holy Spirit. The threats of the Ruah served only to boost his zeal.

Sin focused a hateful stare upon Gabriel and rushed at the angel in a mad frenzy.

"You can gawk all you want Sin, but if you want to strike fear in my heart, you'll have to attempt a bolder effort than that," Gabriel declared.

Sin deafeningly screeched but its wishes to strike trepidation into the heart of the seraph proved to be futile. Gabriel was holding on to the hope that the Holy Spirit would deliver him. Sin sensed what the angel's spirit was feeling, so he commanded all the Ruah to screech and parade around the angel like lions moving in for the kill, the spectacle appeared frightening but it was to no avail.

"Speak the words of truth Gabriel and the enemy will flee," the Holy Spirit spoke to Gabriel's heart. Despite the enemy's plethoric ruckus, their attack was not strong enough to silence the voice of the Holy Spirit.

The Ruah abruptly stopped their frightening display, when a foreign Ruah pervaded the room and presented itself with a hiss.

"Sin, my prince, I come bearing a dreadful report," the Ruah announced in a grave voice. "There are rumors that a foreboding presence has made itself known. On the outskirts of camp, it has been alleged that several Ruah have vanished; they have not responded to any calls from their captains. The Ruah who are missing are: Resentment, Envy, Spite, Hatred, Wicked, Rage, and Lust."

"Sethur, these rumors are very interesting. They're nowhere to be seen, vanished you say," Sin was intrigued and perplexed,

"Yes, your lordship," Sethur responded.

"Do you find this interesting or in the least bit alarming, Sethur," Sin asked.

"I am a member of their legion, so, yes, my prince," Sethur replied.

"Yes you are," Sin stated. "But the fact remains that you led each of those Ruah in invading Ahab's consciousness, thus possessing his spirit; therefore, aiding in the capture of the archangel and the retched angel you see, over there, chained to the wall."

"My prince, then you must protect me from the enemy's wrath," Sethur pleaded.

"I would offer my protection Sethur if I could," Sin uttered. "However, seeing that you are one of the newer additions to my squadron of elite Ruah, I cannot spare any resources on you. The truth, Sethur, is that the LORD Lucifer fully realized what would become of the Ruah who possessed the one who betrayed the seraphim of God; the Prince of Darkness knew what demise my soldiers would meet, what fate would befall them. Therefore, I was given a list of Ruah to commission for the job and your name was at the top, as well as the names of the Ruah who have evidently met their fateful demise."

"So be it then. I'll flee from here and leave this forsaken place," Sethur retorted.

"Your complacency was admired at one time, Sethur," Sin brought up. "Must I remind you though, that your spirit is under my authority, and without my permission you cannot forsake this island; no matter how greatly you desire to do so. You're my possession, Sethur, to do with whatever I like."

Gabriel had paid little attention to the Ruahs' heated altercation until he heard the mention of Michael and himself. Since Sethur had entered the room distracting Sin, Gabriel had seized the opportunity to meditate on the LORD and seek the Holy Spirit. The more he prayed silently, the further he delved into his spirit and the closer he came to the presence of God. Once again, he could feel the touch of the Holy Spirit on his heart and his soul came alive with the rejuvenating effect of the love of God. More astonishing yet, physical manifestations of the Holy Spirit's presence started to become evident throughout his body. The feeling began in the tip of his fingers; the trembling sensation passed from his hands into his chest, to his head and down to his feet. It was the eternal power of the Holy Spirit. He prayed even harder as the Ruah continued to exchange words in a fierce bout.

Surprisingly, Sethur was holding his own against the prince of the Ruah. Just as Sethur was challenging the prince to a contest another Ruah broke through the wall.

"Prince Sin, more have fallen," yelled the foreign Ruah. "Dozens and dozens, maybe hundreds have been utterly destroyed. We're diminishing in numbers and quickly, master."

"Sin, I believe your claim to huge numbers have been a falsehood all along," Gabriel boldly uttered. "What happened to the thousand Ruah you have under your command. Vanishing are they? What say you now, prince of the Ruah?" The angel's words emanated the impending threat to Sin and his rule; the prince's arrogance was quickly waning.

"Gabriel, join me in praying brother," Caleb shouted forth.

Gabriel was suddenly reminded of what the LORD had once said to him, *if two or more are gathered, in my name, agreeing in spirit and in truth; then nothing is impossible for them. Speak to this mountain to move and it will move.*

"Caleb, agree with me; let us demolish the principalities of Hell and breakdown the strongholds of Satan," Gabriel cried out. He thought, *it is time to command the mountain to move.*

"Agony and Defeat make attack on his spirit with pain," Sin, furious with the seraphim's words, drew his commands. "Sethur redeem yourself and make Caleb wish he had never been created. Be swift, Attack now!"

Gabriel sensed the spirit of God come upon him that moment and he cried out in a mighty voice, "Ruah, I banish you to the dark abyss. Return to the fiery pits of Hell."

Sin flew over to Gabriel and focused every ounce of its hatred upon Gabriel.

Just then, Agony cried in dismay, "I can't take his spirit. There's an invisible force protecting him and it's too strong for me."

"Let me through Agony, I am able," Sethur haughtily declared, and soon discovered that the same impenetrable barrier was blocking his path as well. Nevertheless, he wouldn't give up, but continued trying to press in toward Gabriel; he believed he could overcome the powerful shield as he forced himself against it.

"No," Sethur screamed. "No—it's the Holy Spirit. Flee—save yourselves, brothers!" Then Sethur burst into a flame and sizzled into oblivion.

"Sin, I have you right where I want you," Gabriel declared, his eyes lit up with the mighty power of Jehovah. Sin, mystified at the authority in his voice, stared at the angel with fear; the Ruah's piercing-red slanting eyes opened wide in horror.

"Sin—through the power of the Most High you have been defeated," Gabriel declared, mightily. "By the precious name of the Son of the one and only living God—you have been overcome."

"By the power of the living God, Jehovahnissi, my banner of victory, Sin we command you to leave this place and never return," Caleb added, with much passion and zeal.

Sin fumed violently. He grew desperate for his power was fading. Sin made a fierce attempt to possess Gabriel and like running into a stone wall, so was the impact against the angel's chest. Sin ordered the other Ruah to attack, but it was too late.

Out of nowhere, a mighty swirling wind stirred up in the cavern. The eerie green torch that had illuminated the walls with its mysterious and evil glow suddenly blew out and an intense and pure white light shone from the ceiling of the immense cave. All around, wind was flooding the room; it blew with fury and then formed into a whirlwind in the center of the cave. The light from the supernatural windstorm pulsated and glowed like the light of day. The Ruah screeched and cursed, and were sucked straight into the whirlwind; their screams echoed, fading until all that could be heard was the sound of the fierce and holy storm. Then as mysteriously as the windstorm materialized, it completely vanished. Gabriel and Caleb were then enveloped in total obscurity.

The lieutenant general hung his head from exhaustion; he was thankful for the LORD's deliverance, but at the same time he was left in the dark wondering what would become of him.

"Caleb, are you still there," he asked, but no answer came. Soon enough, the darkness prevailed in silencing Gabriel's new found hope.

A PROPHECY FULFILLED

An uncanny glow illuminated the corridor to the fallen star's prison cell. Luminarous' quarters were composed of three walls of tightly packed rock, each a hundred feet thick, and one barrier crafted of mysterious steel, fixed securely together by bizarre looking gemstones. The space inside the enclosure was compact and outright suffocating. In addition to these already extremely staggering living conditions, there was something putrid in the air. A disgusting odor that was foul and unbearable at best.

When the company of demons appeared outside his cell, Luminarous was slouched on a bench in the corner, sitting still. The star's appearance had dramatically changed and the glow that had once radiated throughout the universe was no longer with him. His figure now appeared thin and his skin was darkened from the sun; his face was gaunt and bore a downtrodden expression.

"Ah, Beltezar the Terrible—is that not what they call you," Luminarous looked him in the eyes and said. "I see you've brought some of your companions; to whom or to what do I owe the satisfaction of such an impressive visit?"

Even in his apparently meager condition Luminarous sat himself up straight and broadened his shoulders.

"Allow me to formally introduce myself. I am Beltezar the Terrible, general of the legions of Hell, second only to LORD

Lucifer," he proudly said; ignoring the star's haughty remark, he acted the role of a proper host.

"Splendid. I've wanted to meet you ever since I came here. I've heard much about you," said Luminarous, clapping his hands together with mocking enthusiasm.

"How are your accommodations? Do you find them suitable to your liking," Beltezar said. He had picked up on the obvious sarcasm, but he remained calm and composed.

Luminarous briefly studied his environment before he responded.

"It's not much, but I think it could grow on me. Do I have a choice of more spacious quarters," Luminarous uttered, his voice sounded facetiously pleasant.

"This cell was created specially for you, Luminarous, traitor of Heaven," Beltezar appeared offended and he verbalized his contempt. "Enough of this nonsense—I'll get down to business, let's discuss the real matters at hand."

"What about Judas? Where is the governor," Luminarous interrupted.

"He is indisposed at the time. Now, I will begin," Beltezar said.

"You got rid of him," Luminarous interrupted. "He is the kind of leadership that was disposable and easily replaced, if you understand my meaning."

"You will hold your tongue," Beltezar yelled. "Or I shall cut it from your mouth and I wouldn't hesitate to gouge your eyes out as well."

"By what authority and by what power," Luminarous demanded and arose from the bench. He walked to the front of the prison chamber; posing a challenge to the general, whose eyes were now glaring with indignation.

"Zoan, open the cell. Carchemish, go in and demonstrate for this disrespectful and ungrateful reject, how we deal with treachery and insolence," Beltezar ordered, he had clenched his fists so tightly that his nails had drawn blood.

"Yes, master Beltezar," Zoan answered.

Luminarous stood up straight; his shoulders were broader than Carchemish's, who was huge and powerful, and the star was also taller; but as soon as Zoan opened the door to the cell,

Carchemish stepped in and struck Luminarous in the side bringing him to his knees.

"How dare you defy Beltezar the Terrible," Carchemish barked.

Carchemish brought his hand back to strike him once more and his punch was blocked. Luminarous grabbed him by the arm and overpowered him, taking him to the ground. Zoan quickly placed the key in the lock, attempting to intervene, but Beltezar ordered him to stop. The fallen star and the demon rolled around on the floor striking against the three walls again and again as they brawled, the advantage went back and forth. A few moments elapsed, and suddenly Luminarous had the upper hand, literally.

"Feel the burn from beneath my fingers," Luminarous said, loathingly, and placed his right hand squarely on Carchemish's face. "Even in my palm, a power flows that is far beyond yours scoundrel of Hell."

Carchemish screamed with pain and Luminarous removed his hand. Carchemish's face was now permanently scarred with the mark of the star. Luminarous pulled Carchemish to his feet and gripped the demon's throat.

"See this mark," Luminarous stared at the general and said scornfully. "Take a good look at the welts on his face; let this serve as a reminder to you, Beltezar. You're playing with fire."

"Release Carchemish; let us discuss your future in a more sensible manner," Beltezar requested.

"You chose to provoke my anger, Beltezar," Luminarous uttered and threw Carchemish into the cell door; Zoan promptly opened the door and freed the wounded demon.

Then Luminarous stepped forward unpredictably and eyed Beltezar haughtily.

"Luminarous answers to none. My powers may have decreased, but they are still more powerful than the dark sorcery of Hell. Hence, only once, will I warn you and the rest of your rebel host I can still destroy all of you if I wish," Luminarous declared.

Beltezar paused for a dramatic effect and then burst into sinister laughter and Zoan followed suit, as did Carchemish, even though it hurt him to laugh.

"You think you can destroy me," Beltezar looked him in the eyes and questioned. "You dare defy the forces of Lucifer? You have the gall to challenge the dominion of Hell? Your words are vain–foolish is more appropriate. Moreover, I have yet to demonstrate my powers. And you have the guts to confront my authority? You can't bring Beltezar the Terrible down that easily, you insolent fool."

Luminarous turned visibly red from anger.

"Now, if you will but control yourself for a moment, I will make you a proposal," Beltezar spoke in a calm and menacing voice. "I offer you Lucifer's protection for your unwavering loyalty."

"You think you can protect me from the God of Heaven," Luminarous lost his temper and responded, heatedly. "When he finds me I will surely pay for my transgressions. I knowingly disobeyed his orders; one simple commandment and I broke it."

Beltezar then spoke an incantation over the fallen star and before Luminarous realized it he was on his knees bent over in agonizing pain; his hands firmly placed over his ears. The General had conjured an earsplitting spell to prove his superiority.

"Silence fool," Beltezar demanded. "You have carried on long enough. You displayed your power and might; therefore, I have demonstrated my skills. Now you know what I am capable of—just a taste of the sorcery I can wield. Dare defy my authority again and I will display all my power to the glory of LORD Lucifer."

Beltezar then softened his voice a bit and said, "Luminarous, this situation we've gotten ourselves into isn't exactly what I was anticipating when I desired to speak with you." Beltezar noticed Luminarous was listening intently.

"Initially, I wanted to discuss the issue of your future in a peaceful manner, cordially that is, but I lost my bearings in the middle of my heated words. Please accept my apologies. I want to offer you something more than protection."

"I accept your apology. Beltezar, continue if you will," Luminarous narrowed his eyes and answered.

Beltezar took note of two things he disliked: the fact that Luminarous didn't offer forgiveness for his actions nor did he address him by either of his proper titles, General or Terrible. He pushed these distasteful actions to the back of his mind, so that he wouldn't be distracted. Beltezar ordered Zoan to unbolt the prison gate; he ducked his head and entered the cell.

Luminarous may have been large and brooding, but he wasn't as big or menacing as Beltezar the Terrible. The fallen star's confidence seemed to wane in the shadow of the general's enormous stature; the audacity he once felt compelled to speak with had vanished. *Where's your impudence now; have you no more courage,* Beltezar thought, and closely examined Luminarous, like a warden inspecting a prisoner.

"Please take a seat, Luminarous. Listen closely to all I have to say," Beltezar spoke. His words formed on his lips like an intoxicating potion and like a pet dog, Luminarous obeyed. *Like clay in my hands,* the general thought to himself.

Once the star was seated, Beltezar commenced to pace in front of him.

"Luminarous, your power is great and the purpose you once served, even greater," Beltezar said calmly and persuasively. "I understand the dilemma you're in. After all, I once lived in the one and only Heaven. I fell many ages ago and fortunately, my mind has ceased to dwell on any visions of Heaven. I tell you the LORD of Heaven would have you believe that you fell from his grace, but the real truth is: he can't accept anyone who won't mindlessly obey each and every one of his commands. Certainly, I followed many of the guidelines and statutes of Heaven, as did many so-called demons; but I won't lie to you, we didn't obey all of the rules. I'll also admit that I'm not perfect and, there in, lies the problem."

"You must understand, Luminarous," the general continued. "The LORD of Heaven sees himself as perfect and absolutely flawless in every aspect of his being. He expects the same. My LORD Lucifer sought to capture God's throne and for good reason too; his cause was simply to rule with fairness, a quality that the God of Heaven refuses to acknowledge. Truly, the God of Heaven became jealous of my LORD Lucifer when he heard the rumors that millions of angels were joining my master's cause for equal rights of all seraphim of Heaven. Lucifer despised Michael, because the LORD of Heaven favored him above all others. Lucifer gathered all the angels to his side that agreed with his principles and values: equality for all seraphim. And for his passion and for his cause, he was banished along with all angels that swore their allegiance to him. As you know, we became demons but we truly are angels who recognize that ranks and positions, rights and privileges must be earned to be exact, deserved and awarded."

"Luminarous, the time is now at hand," Beltezar declared, he noticed the fallen star was listening intently. "The Archangel Michael has been defeated and his lieutenant general, Gabriel, is imprisoned and awaiting his sentence. We are planning our offense, strategically implementing our devices and soon the God of Heaven will be overthrown. With such a grand victory will come equal rights for all demons and not only will Heaven and earth be ruled fairly and equally, but you will be acquitted and exonerated. Free to live for an eternity in the heavens or wherever you choose."

Beltezar ceased his continual pacing and awaited an answer; he acknowledged the advantageous position he now held with the fallen star. Luminarous appeared interested and fascinated with what he had just heard; his attention was captivated.

"My friend, may I address you as such," Beltezar commenced, before Luminarous could answer. "Good, because I sincerely think of you as one. We may have started off going in opposite directions, but I believe we have come together as kindred spirits. Therefore, I have no hesitation in sharing the following information with you. LORD Lucifer has given the decree to go to war. We are amassing a great force of demons and Ruah alike and with numbers of such immense magnitudes the Host of Heaven won't stand a chance. The reality of the situation Luminarous, we are at the threshold of victory and we want you to join our cause. The best part is you will not be in the forefront of the battle. That is to say, we have far bigger plans for you so important I fear uttering them for the sake of keeping them secret."

"Please tell me more," Luminarous whispered.

"Even now, there is a band of elite sorcerers," Beltezar continued. "Which I'll add, is the first time an assemblage of sorcery with such impressive and superb talent, has ever been gathered. As we speak, they are working diligently and tirelessly to formulate a very unique and extraordinary incantation, one that has never before been uttered. One so powerful and impressive, that it has been saved for a momentous occasion. Moreover, the incantation can be completed now; for the missing ingredients have been found and seized. The Sword of the Spirit and Logos, the two supernatural swords of power are in our possession. And the final ingredient, you shouldn't be surprised to discover, is the most powerful. You, Luminarous, star of light, are that ingredient."

Luminarous' eyes lit up and he was beginning to hunger for power, a return to self-glory. Beltezar incisively read the greed on the fallen star's face, so he spoke up.

"This spell, when properly employed with precise measurements will allow us to combine the power of the three swords with your special powers, thus creating a weapon so powerful that all of earth will be shattered to a million pieces and like dust in the wind, it will float through the heavens. Then, at that moment, we will be transported to Heaven where we will strike the final blow. Not only will we annihilate all seraphim, but we will imprison the God of Heaven. We will punish the LORD of Heaven with the exact fate he allotted to my LORD Lucifer: a millennium in the dark abyss, after which he will be destroyed."

Luminarous' face now possessed a much different façade than before, a few moments ago he was obtrusive and audacious and unwilling to negotiate. However, the fallen star now appeared agreeable and well disposed to the general's ideas.

Before he would confer to the plans presented by Beltezar, he raised his eyebrow conspicuously, and curtly asked, "Sounds almost perfect, almost being the choicest of words. Although, I must know, how do you expect to enter Heaven without first being granted entry by the Creator?" Luminarous sat back with his arms crossed awaiting a response.

"Luminarous, my friend," Beltezar promptly said. "I believe you should know better than to ask such a foolish question. Have you failed to hear any of the words I've spoken to you? And do you not realize how dominant the realm of Hell has become? Or how great and powerful LORD Lucifer actually is?"

Beltezar toned down his voice and continued in a more agreeable tone.

"My friend, can you not grasp the notion I've presented? Have you yet to comprehend the reality that you are the key to our victory? Or is it just that you fail to see your full potential? You,

Luminarous, have traveled the heavens and seen the universe; it is this gift, you possess, that will permit us to journey across the universe. As for invading Heaven; leave that to the sorcerers and the master sorcerer, the LORD Lucifer, may he live forever. Luminarous, up until this point, I thought I had made myself perfectly clear. I am offering you freedom from your bondage, your captivity. Once in power, the merciful LORD Lucifer will award your deepest desires. If you wish to explore the heavens, even to the farthest edges of the universe, then he will grant your wish. Still, if you aspire to dwell in Heaven or have a planet all to yourself, it will be given you. Whatever your yearning may be, consider it fulfilled. Ultimately, with your extraordinary abilities combined with the three supernatural swords, and joined with the fearless legions of Hell, not even God himself will be able to match our power and strength. We'll be unstoppable. Will you join in our cause and deliver the throne to my master, the rightful king? What say you, Luminarous, star of light?"

The fallen star stood up and came close to Beltezar.

"I join my life force with Hell," he answered assertively. "Let us go to war and to the glory of the LORD Lucifer, victory will be ours." Luminarous' eyes ignited like flames and Beltezar's glowed a deep red as they grasped arms with one another, thereby sealing the pact.

NOTE FROM THE SCRIBE...

It was finished. Luminarous willingly sold his soul to Satan, unwittingly fulfilling words found in ancient prophecy. A prophecy not disclosed until this point in the story. Granted, I have had the prophecy in my possession the entire time. I have not felt compelled to share the words with you, save this moment the words of the prophecy are contained in an ancient scroll written by the Father himself and dated older than time itself. The scroll is entitled, The Beginning.

The parchment it was written on is fragile; hence bits and pieces are missing. Nevertheless, the following words have now been fulfilled: *The captive and the wicked conspired against me. An agreement was made in secret ... between a luminary and an adversary. Terms were spoken in the darkness ... the fall of mankind was quick-*

ened by their words. The time draws near when the Son will rise ... and cometh in the name of the LORD.

Unbeknownst to Beltezar, he played an essential part in a timeless prophecy foreseen by the Ancient One. Eternally omniscient in all his ways and omnipresent throughout the universe, his age-old wisdom foresaw the creation of the world and his peerless vision has foreseen its ultimate doom; even beyond the end of humanity, when mankind will cease to breathe the air of their earthly realm. The LORD of Heaven knows all and sees all. Therefore, his capacity for caring is unmatched; his compassion is unparalleled; the depth of his love is unfathomable. Without a nuance of doubt, his forgiveness is unequaled and his mercy is from everlasting to everlasting; as far as the east is from the west, so far hath he removed man's transgressions from them.

Even though you have just now learned of this prophecy, do not be alarmed or allow it to distract you from the pertinent details of this saga. Presently, I will turn back the clock, a few earthly hours earlier, and take you to the place where Michael is being held captive. He had been in a deep sleep and when he awoke, he was horrified to find that he couldn't move his hands or his feet and he could barely turn his neck, so he couldn't see what strange devices were encumbering his freedom. Worse still, he was enveloped in darkness and a heavy haze clouded his mind. Could it be the Ruah? He began to panic, but there was no adrenaline left in his body to give him the strength to even wrinkle his brow in his anxiety.

Out of the surrounding darkness came a glow. Michael couldn't comprehend its distance; he was having extreme difficulty in focusing his eyes on the light. For all he knew, the light could be far away, or it might only be a mere dozen paces in proximity from him. Strange as it may seem, although the light shined in the darkness, its glow failed to illuminate or define its perimeters. Michael still could not see anything else, save the light, and all was deadly silent except for the intermittent sound of water dripping from the ceiling.

The following description is entirely and accurately portrayed as the archangel dictated to me for the House of Scrolls.

The Warrior Within ...

I awakened in a cold sweat. My heart was throbbing like a drum, within my chest; my soul felt grief-stricken and my spirit was filled with despair. Woe was me, for I found myself cloaked in an eerie darkness—a darkness that enveloped everything except for a single mysterious light glowing in the distance. Where was I? *What strange light is that, which fails to pierce the darkness,* I thought. I vaguely began to recall having been led deep beneath the ground, through a maze of corridors illuminated by green torches mounted along the wall and the unnatural light oddly cast no shadows. I also remember passing by many prison cells, of which all were empty. I pondered the thought that these cages were empty, because they were waiting to be filled with seraphim. And that's when it happened. I felt my body drifting off into oblivion.

My mind faded into a dark and dire state of unconsciousness. My head was filled abruptly with horrible visions; daunting thoughts teeming with demons bent on destroying me. I was in Hell and on a red throne sat Satan, the dark prince, taunting me with malice and spite and before my eyes he mercilessly executed hundreds upon hundreds of my brothers and friends, the seraphim of Heaven. It was most dreadful and it got worse still; for the prince of evil claimed that Heaven had been utterly destroyed and that I was now the last of the seraphim. He even dared to boast that I was, in fact, the only one remaining out of all the Host of Heaven; that even the LORD had been destroyed and was gone forever. Satan didn't stop there, but he continued his ranting and raving; nearly all of his rage-filled words have slipped my memory, but one thing in particular he said has not evaded my mind.

"You will now be bound and thrown in the lake of fire; where your thirst can not be quenched and your spirit will dwell without comfort or peace. There you will suffer for an eternity," Satan uttered, he reveled and laughed in his own arrogant glory, even as a pig would wallow in the mire. Satan's wretched cackling echoed through my brain and tormented my spirit like the clamor of a million bats' wings flapping through a dark cavern, so was the hideous noise of his cynical laughter.

Satan ordered the demons to drag my body to the lake of fire, but before they could take hold of me with their beastly hands, I cried out in a loud voice for the LORD to save me. That is when I must have awakened, because I can't remember anything beyond my plea for salvation. The odd green light was the first thing that was noticeable and, within a matter of moments, the light grew brighter. However, it wasn't the single green glow that intensified, but it was the coming together of several torches. How many torches I couldn't ascertain, but there were at least three more, all shining with a strange emerald glow.

Then I heard voices whispering; I failed to perceive clearly all that they were saying, but I did gather that instructions were being given. Actually, they seemed more like commands than instructions, since one voice in particular was very stern and direct; whoever was dictating the orders was concise and to the point and he spoke like one with great authority. The murmuring carried on for a few moments and when it finally ceased, I saw two lights ascending from a dark passage.

Then suddenly I heard the clattering and creaking of iron bars being bent and moved. Two demons, each holding a torch, stood on opposite sides of their makeshift entryway. A towering figure, enormous and menacing, now stood before me. On his right and left stood two demons: one huge and one slightly smaller.

The huge demon stepped forward and his fist struck my face.

"Rise to your feet infidel," he demanded, in a low growling voice. In what seemed an instant, the torches magnified and the entire chamber was illuminated with an intense radiance, a green eerie glow.

"I said, rise to your feet infidel," the huge demon barked, threatening me. "Pay your respects to the general of the legions of Hell, Beltezar the Terrible, second only to Lucifer." He struck me again in the side and I groaned in extreme pain.

"Carchemish, please control your self," shouted the tall and menacing demon.

He lowered his tone and continued, "Allow me to properly introduce myself—"

Before he could get any further I spoke out, "I know who you are. Your heart is as black and void as the darkness of night; your spirit is wicked and depraved and twisted horrendously beyond the pure and innocent being you once were. You're no longer a creation of the Almighty, you're a perversion of Satan tainted with malevolence and spawned from evil. You disgust me Beltezar."

"Why thank you Michael. I appreciate the compliment, but there's no need for flattery," Beltezar quaintly replied.

The general stepped closer, though he maintained a safe distance from me his red hair appeared to ignite with the glow of the torches, his jade eyes gleamed intensely in the light of the emerald flames and with each dreadful stare he cast upon me, another ounce of hope diminished from within my soul. His entire being radiated sin in its most wicked form; his spirit emanated with the stench of Hell. Encompassed with evil and the dark powers of Hell, his presence was atrociously daunting and terrible to behold.

His face was bursting with pride as he uttered, "Archangel Michael, how I've anticipated this moment; for a long time I have relished the thought of standing here before you and I have envisioned you, Michael, countless times imprisoned in shackles; bound by supernatural chains and rendered helpless and defeated, disowned, and forgotten. Although, those thoughts I had were truly grand, I must say they failed miserably to measure up to the actual moment. In fact, I've practiced exactly what I would say to you; I've run the words through my head time and time again. This is what I've been waiting for. Truly what my life has been leading up to. Since the time I rose to general of LORD Lucifer's legions and was banished from Heaven, to this very hour I've sought to destroy you. In fact, even as I existed in Heaven, my thoughts were conspiring against you. Even as I worked diligently to establish the LORD Lucifer's kingdom in Hell, I was determined that I would not find any rest until you were wiped completely and utterly from existence. Finally through hard work, relentless determination, and ruthless efforts I hold your life in my very hands; now that the long-awaited moment has arrived I am overwhelmed with an immense gratification. I want to savor this moment in time forever. I want to indulge in this vision for an eternity and never forget what the archangel looks like held captive in manacles and fetters. You were once the archangel, but today by the authority of the kingdom of LORD Lucifer, I hereby strip you of your God-given title. The power you once commanded no longer holds any worth here or any-where else. Furthermore, the prestige you once held claim to is hereby denied to you. Revel in any memories you have left that pertain to Heaven and your God. I'll give you the chance now to recollect whatever thoughts or visions you have of your broth-erhood of seraphim, because what you once held dear is being taken from you. What you pertained as joy and happiness will be destroyed in the blink of an eye. I am Beltezar the Terrible, fear my name and tremble in my presence, infidel."

I feared him not. I stared upon the general of Hell and with a fiercely defiant look in my eyes I dared him to come closer and speak those words to my face. Beltezar had made his charges against me while pacing to and fro, hiding between the dark shadows and the green glow of the torches; from time to time he would cast a glance in my direction, but never did he look me straight in the eye.

Finally, Beltezar stopped his pacing and with heavy deliberate steps, he approached me. He appeared as a prowling monster that had its prey finally within its grasp. Although, I was help-lessly bound with chains and fetters, I held on to hope. My spirit was balancing on the edge of doom, but I wasn't about to give in to my vile enemy. I had already settled in my spirit that the LORD was going to come to my rescue. I knew beyond a shadow of doubt, that the Holy Spirit in me was greater than the powers of this world, the powers Beltezar trusted completely. Ultimately, in my spirit, my soul, and in my heart, I made a vow that I was not going to surrender my spirit to the principalities of Hell.

I held on dearly to the image of my God sitting on his throne on top of Mount Zion, ruling with justice and mercy; shining in all his splendor and majesty. He promised he would never leave me nor forsake me. Those were the last words he spoke to me and he is true to his word. Even if Heaven and earth should pass away, his word will stand always and forever.

Beltezar, feeling less threatened, moved in toward me even closer now; he was examining me with an incredulous expression on his face. His glare was intimidating; he wrinkled his brow with displeasure and then turned and stared at Carchemish.

"He's hideous. What happened to him? Be forthright and tell me now," Beltezar addressed him.

"General Beltezar, it was Judas. He ordered that he be beaten and put through the gauntlet," Carchemish kneeled straight away and humbly replied. He cringed in fear, anticipating a strike from the general's fist for this treacherous act. *The torture of Michael was a deliberate and rebellious act, contrary to the general's orders.*

"The gauntlet, eh," Beltezar shouted angrily, his voice boomed like thunder. "And did you have any part in this disobedience, this deviation, this treachery? Answer me now." He did not strike a blow with his fist, but his voice was just as effective.

"No, my master I assure you that I had nothing to do with this," Carchemish prostrated himself and replied. "It was Judas, I tell you he had gone mad and was on a rampage. The legions stationed here obeyed his commands as you had ordered; and in the heat of Judas' anger, the soldiers mindlessly heeded each and every one of his commands. I swear to you by the LORD Lucifer, I removed myself from the gauntlet and I played not a single part in it."

Beltezar appeared skeptical. Carchemish remained bowing on the floor.

"Can you confirm his testimony," the general turned to Zoan and sternly inquired.

"He has no reason to be untruthful," Zoan answered. Beltezar nodded, appearing to concur, while Carchemish held his face meekly on the ground and appeared sincere in his reverence.

"Call this a test, if you will, Zoan," Beltezar uttered. "I am putting his life in your hands. Should he live or should he die?"

"Sir," Zoan looked nervous but clearly answered. "He is one of our best and strongest. He will be sorely needed in battle."

Beltezar grinned and he appeared pleased with Zoan's answer.

"Well, you can stop your groveling now Carchemish," Beltezar commanded. "Get up, you coward, and behave like a major of Hell. I can't have you parading around like an incompetent buffoon. I'll let you live, but remember I can have you destroyed at any moment, with only a snap of my fingers."

For being such a large demon, when Carchemish was in Beltezar's presence, he actually conducted himself like one who was faint of heart and easily manipulated.

I did not confess that Carchemish was not only among the perpetrators, but he was the one who cracked the whip across my back for forty grueling lashes; in all reality, it was his hand that stripped my flesh of its strength. Nonetheless, Beltezar continued to be oblivious to this notion and instead, he assumed he had settled any discrepancies there may have been and focused his attention, once again, on me.

"Have you anything to add archangel," Beltezar said.

I said nothing. He walked slowly and as he moved even closer to me, his steps echoed like booming thunder. I waited until he drew near enough and then I spit on him.

"Is that your answer," he asked with a smirk strung across his face.

I still did not answer. I waited for the Holy Spirit to come and give me the words to speak. Then I remembered specific instructions I had received from the Father. He spoke them shortly before my journey had begun; he held that, *when and if you find yourself surrounded by the enemy, wait on my spirit to penetrate the veil of evil. He will speak for you when you need it most.*

Beltezar kneeled, since my body had drooped from the weight of my burden; the sharp edges of the iron clasps, by now, had cruelly cut through my bleeding wrists. He reached out his finger and plucked a drop of my blood from midair, as it was falling from my wrist. He looked me directly in the eyes and his face was etched with lines, caused from years of bitterness. He examined me with a conceited, judgmental expression. I could tell he was trying to enter my mind, but a mystical barrier hindered his efforts. It was the spirit of the LORD. I knew in my darkest hour Jehovah was with me, he is my strong tower. Beltezar stared intently into my face from merely inches away and with his cold and sinister eyes he sought a way into my sub-conscious. Even with all his concentrated wizardry he was failing; the Holy Spirit had kept my thoughts safe. Beltezar's expression became frustrated, it was quite apparent his sorcery had failed to work on me. He stood up straight and his appearance was like a statue carved from granite: chiseled, strapping, and unbreakable.

A sly grin came across Beltezar's face. His voice was bitter and shrewd as he spoke to me, asserting, "Your stature was once strong and mighty. Now look at you. You're a frail creature, beaten, bloody, and beyond recognition. Even as I speak, I sense your power slowly draining from your useless body, which soon enough will be totally lifeless and forever dead. You sense it too, don't you?"

I cared not what he said against me, but my heart was concerned for my friend and brother, Gabriel; so I ignored his words and gathered courage from within my spirit.

"Free Gabriel and I promise I won't destroy you," I boldly said. The words formed like thunderbolts on my tongue, but they escaped my lips sounding like nothing more than meek utterances.

Beltezar laughed and straight away Carchemish and Zoan joined in his amusement. They all were in an uproar with cackling, solely for my benefit; then the general lifted his hand to command silence.

He knelt down, looked me straight in the eyes, and said, "We don't know if Gabriel is even alive. There was a cave-in, but my soldiers are clearing the rubble as we speak. If he breathes still, my soldiers will finish him off. As for you Michael, I'm suddenly stricken with sympathy and mercy. Yes, I said I want to see you destroyed, but now as I look upon your frail emaciated body, I am having second thoughts about your demise. Thus, I will offer you this once and only once, you understand me? I can restore to you, your power and glory. I can even make you greater than you were before. You can be freed from your bondage and captivity. All that you must do is renounce God, swear allegiance to my master the LORD Lucifer and then you can reign side by side with the princes of Hell. I possess the authority and power to grant you freedom. What will it be?"

I lifted my head, gazed into his hateful demonic eyes, and peered into his heartless soul; a resounding valor began to rise from the inner recesses of my heart. I discerned that this was the time to speak for the Holy Spirit had arrived, bringing with him the strength and boldness to speak the words of truth.

"I would rather die a servant of the Most High, than live and serve the evil Lucifer," I cried out, my words echoed like thunder and they shot forth from my mouth like arrows blazing through the air. For my words, Beltezar had spit on me.

"Your punishment will come," I spoke out with utmost confidence. "The day is approaching when you will stand before the throne of the Most High, and on that day my God will show you no mercy. I pray he will torment you with pain and suffering a thousand fold greater than what Hell has dealt to me. Heed my words Beltezar, 'vengeance is mine,' says the LORD."

The general of Hell's legions grinned with evil malice as he said, "Even in his final hour, he speaks out of arrogance. You fool—your spite has doomed you." He spit on me and with his fist he struck me hard in the face. I could taste the blood running from my lips.

I defied him, declaring, "When my God comes to save me, mark my words Beltezar, I will come for you." I belted the words out with all that remained within me.

"End his existence and make it quick," Beltezar turned his back to me and ordered Carchemish and Zoan. "I'll summon the Ruah to harvest his soul."

The demons answered with a zealous nod.

"Allow me the privilege, my master," Carchemish requested.

Beltezar, with his back turned to them, signaled his approval with the raising of his right fist. Beltezar exited the room briskly. Zoan stood idly by, pleasurably observing as Carchemish prepared himself for the job. Carchemish pulled his sword from its sheath. He did not hesitate when he approached; in a fleeting moment he had plunged the sword into my flesh; the blade pierced my stomach, and when he removed the sword, blood and water flowed from my stomach.

"It is finished. Let the Ruah have him, for victory is now at hand," Carchemish cried out, and he and Zoan quickly left the room.

A single torch and that is all that withheld complete darkness from consuming me. I was suspended upright by only chains and my arms had been dislocated; my legs were twisted but not broken. My hair was ripped from my scalp and lay before me on the prison floor. My eyes were nearly swollen shut and all but a few of my teeth had been knocked from my mouth. Tears poured freely from my eyes, the salty drops stung my wounds as they trickled down off of my face. I was completely alone now, left to die in seclusion like some abandoned animal, until the torch burns out and then the Ruah will move in to harvest my spirit and devour my soul. Was this to be my fate, I thought, was this to be my calling? The end is near, death is approaching and I can feel it.

"My God, my God, why have you forsaken me," I cried out and closed my eyes.

MANY PREPARATIONS

"Gabriel, is that you," cried the voice in the darkness.

"Yes—are you alright," Gabriel answered, coughing from the dust in the air.

"I think so," Caleb answered. "I'm still in chains, wait, I can move my right leg; but that is all." Gloom was in his voice.

"Don't worry Caleb. Fear not, for the LORD will come to our rescue. The power of the Holy Spirit has defeated the Ruah," Gabriel declared.

"I thank the LORD for his goodness and mercy," Caleb uttered. "If it wasn't for his saving grace, I wouldn't have been able to keep the Ruah at bay. They would have devoured me for sure." Hope had returned to his voice.

"What has happened," Caleb continued, asking. "Why is the air filled with dust?"

"There was a cave-in, I'm certain," Gabriel answered. "I heard the sound of rumbling, like huge rocks tumbling, crashing against one another, and slamming to the ground. Didn't you feel the earth trembling beneath you, Caleb?"

"Surely, I would remember that happening," Caleb remarked. "The last that I can remember the Holy Spirit was coming in the form of a whirlwind and then I recall something, most likely a rock, struck my head and then I must have lost consciousness. Ah, now it's all coming back to me. I remember seeing an angel and he appeared to be a distinguished seraph. He was dressed in a long green robe and a brilliant circle of light, an orb or glowing ring of some sorts hovered just above his head. He was noble, very noble indeed."

"Are you positive that this is what you saw," Gabriel asked eagerly, his eyes although enveloped in darkness, were sparkling with joy. "Did he say anything to you—did he tell you his name?"

"I'm trying hard to remember more. It happened so fast and my head, it's throbbing with pain. No, no, I can't recollect," Caleb answered, his voice was lively when he began speaking, but it soon sounded despondent.

Gabriel hung his head in despair with the solemn thought that Caleb couldn't remember. He needed disparately to hear a message from his God.

"Wait—it's coming back. Slowly but surely, yes, I remember," Caleb cried out with pure delight. Instantly, Gabriel lifted his head in anticipation, eager to hear every word, he listened closely.

"He introduced himself as the chief of the messenger seraphim," Caleb recalled. His name was—Elijah. It wasn't the first time I had seen him; he had visited me previously—in a dream."

"Did he tell you anything; did he say anything, anything at all," Gabriel queried.

"Yes, as a matter of fact, he did tell me something," Caleb replied. "He gave me a message. The vision is forming again in my mind and I can see him reading from a scroll. Give me a moment to gather myself. Thanks be to the Almighty, I have it now. Elijah said. 'Caleb, brave and loyal seraph of Heaven, I have a message from God. The LORD of Hosts says this, 'My servant, you have been courageous and true of heart in all your deeds; in the face of danger, you have trusted in me and now I tell you that the enemy will be overcome.' Elijah then dictated a message from God that was specifically for you. The message read: The LORD says, 'Gabriel, lieutenant general of the Host of Heaven, you have answered your calling. You have pursued me with your whole heart, not turning to the right or the left, but following me with all of your heart, soul, and spirit; you have overcome the attacks of the enemy. You have fulfilled your duty to the Kingdom, yet there is still more for you to accomplish in my name and to my glory.' That's all that I'm able to remember."

"That is exactly what I needed to hear; I am at a loss for words," Gabriel said. He was overwhelmed with much needed encouragement; his eyes were saturated with tears.

Before Gabriel could speak any further, they heard a disrupting clamor and it sounded as if it was coming from the other side of the stone walls, enclosing their dungeon.

"What was that," Caleb blurted.

"I'm not sure," Gabriel answered. "It sounds almost like digging."

"Do you hear those voices," Caleb whispered loudly.

"I hear them, but I can't make out what they're saying," Gabriel answered quietly.

"Gabriel, what are we to do," Caleb said, his tone was anxious. "We're bound in chains and soon the demons will break through the rocks."

"Pray, pray now. Do not whisper, but pray. Pray like this is the end," Gabriel said.

"Is it the end," Caleb asked in a dreadful tone.

"No, no it's not, Caleb," Gabriel answered with vigor in his voice.

At this precise moment, the enemy's plans were unfolding.

"Is it done," the general asked.

"Yes master—he is done for," Carchemish nodded and answered.

"Well then, I'll summon the Ruah. They'll go rabid, slobbering in greed over his spirit," Beltezar said with an evil, satisfied grin.

"Master Beltezar, we need to know what to do about Gabriel and Caleb? The soldiers are unable to break in," Migron uttered, who had just approached, in a terrible hurry, as he emerged from up the passage.

"Leave them. Let the Ruah devour them," Beltezar answered, curtly.

"That's just it," Migron stuttered as he caught his breath. "There's been a breach. According to Pride, the enemy has broken through our perimeter defenses. As many as a hundred Ruah have been massacred."

The company of demons had been walking along the corridor as they talked, up until now that is. As soon as Beltezar heard the report, he stopped and slammed his fist against the wall. He was outraged and his eyes blazed with fury in the eerie light of the passageway.

"Tell me, has Prince Sin been destroyed," Beltezar demanded to know. Migron gulped and using no words, he nodded yes. Beltezar shook his head in disbelief.

Migron swallowed his pride and somewhat fearfully muttered, "Sir there is still another matter that requires your attention." Beltezar's face ignited with rage like a blazing inferno.

"Speak up," Beltezar shouted.

Inwardly, Migron was shuddering in fear; it took all he had to compose himself.

"It is the matter of Judas," Migron gathered his senses and said. "We were escorting him to Desmeeos' when an evil spirit seized him and threw him to the ground. I can't say for sure if it was a Ruah, but what I do know is when the spirit took hold of him he went into a terrible fit; his body convulsed and his mouth was foaming. His eyes rolled back into his head and he began to bleed from the mouth. It all happened so fast that neither my soldiers nor I had any time to react. Before we could restrain him, he clawed his way across the ground and viciously bit one of my soldier's legs. The sudden turmoil had put us all in a state of confusion and I'm sorry to say, Judas escaped down the passage. The soldiers, though, are rapidly pursuing him as we now speak."

Migron braced himself for the general's reaction. He knew beyond all doubt that he would receive a harsh reprimand or even death, if Beltezar truly was mad enough. The general grabbed him by the throat and lifted the demon up off of the ground; Migron's feet dangled limply in the air and he was now at the mercy of Beltezar the Terrible.

"Did you actually believe that I would allow your incompetence to go unpunished," Beltezar demanded. "You should think twice before you reveal the disturbing truth to me. However, there will be no second chance; for I find that you are of no further use to me Sergeant Migron."

Beltezar then spoke an incantation in the forbidden tongue and Migron ignited into flames. Carchemish and Zoan protected their faces from the blistering fire and in a fleeting moment, Migron had incinerated and vanished before their eyes; not even a speck of dust remained as proof of his demise.

"From light he was created and into the darkness he goes to dwell for an eternity, never to return. A just reward for a bungling idiot," Beltezar, with no emotion or remorse in his voice, plainly said.

Zoan had witnessed this deviant spell once before, but as for Carchemish, this was his first time. From that point on, Carchemish greatly dreaded Beltezar and he no longer sought to challenge the general for supreme power. He knew now to tread carefully when in the general's presence and choose his words carefully; after all, they could be his last words should he choose wrongly. Carchemish thought about what he should say to the General now, considering the circumstances, he sought to gain favor from the general.

"General Beltezar, give me but two soldiers and I will clear the entrance to Desmeeos' or if it pleases the general further, permit me but an hour's time and I will hunt down Judas and vanquish the measly traitor from our midst," Carchemish asserted.

"Do not bother with the seraphim of Heaven; it would be best to forget they ever existed," Beltezar replied, stoutly. "A matter of fact, order the soldiers assigned to Desmeeos' to retreat to the upper ground. There is no need to waste our resources by digging Caleb and Gabriel out. On the contrary, I believe we should allow time itself to strip the flesh from their bones; we can revel in the thought that the infidels will spend the rest of their existence withering away, trapped in shackles that are resistant to any supernatural force of the enemy. However, if the LORD Lucifer does find a use for the seraphim, his power is more than ample enough to capture their spirits. He'll see to that."

"And as for Judas," Beltezar made a fist, clenching his hand until his palm bled; then he composed himself and maintained a calmer façade. "If the soldiers don't catch him, his madness will eventually destroy him; we need not waste our time worrying about that fool. More importantly, we will now move ahead with our plans."

The general's eyes ignited with a hellish passion.

"Zoan, Carchemish, gather the legions to the mound; order them to prepare for war. I will address them within the hour. Now go and waste no time," the general ordered in a commanding tone.

Now that Beltezar was alone, he thought to himself, *Now, I must see to Luminarous. The sorcerers should arrive shortly and I have still to summon him to the surface.* He traveled down the dimly lit passage using his long strides to his advantage; with each huge step, the general thought, *I am closer now than ever. Vengeance will soon be mine. Yes, Heaven's throne will belong to the LORD Lucifer, but the earth will be my footstool.*

"Caleb, Caleb," Gabriel called.

"Yes, yes, I'm listening," Caleb answered with a somewhat weary voice.

"Do you hear that," Gabriel asked, curiously

"What do you mean, Gabriel," Caleb uttered. "I hear nothing at all."

"I think they're gone," Gabriel noted. "It's dead quiet outside and I believe they've left, because only a few moments ago I overheard what sounded like a dispute. Before long, there was the sound of footsteps leaving in a hurry. I'm positive now that there's not a single demon posted outside."

"If that is so, then why do you suppose they've gone away," Caleb queried and stirred his feet trying to regain the feeling in them, making a clatter with the chains that echoed loudly throughout the cavern.

"Caleb, save your energy," Gabriel uttered. "I'm not quite sure why they've left. Actually I just might. I can discern that something foreboding is coming; one thing is clearly evident and that is the enemy camp is stirring above ground. I can feel this entire place shaking and vibrating; there's quite a commotion going on above us."

Gabriel continued with a revelation, "I know this might come as a shock to you, though, I must still tell you the reality of the situation; there are more than just a few thousand demons stationed here. There are over eight thousand at least. The enemy is preparing for something big and Satan has been planning and scheming; whatever he is up to involves the fallen star Luminarous. And if they have captured Luminarous, then they are ready to move forward with their plans."

"Do you mean *war*?" The intensity in Caleb's voice escalated.

"Yes, and it is what I have been expecting; actually, the moment I discovered there were thousands of demons stationed here, my spirit discerned the severity of the situation, "Gabriel said.

"How did you come to find this out," Caleb asked; his eyes although hidden in the darkness, gleamed and widened inquisitively.

"It was he, who you saw in your vision; Elijah, the chief of the messenger seraphim," Gabriel uttered. "At the risk of sacrificing his life, he revealed to me and Michael—I'm sorry Caleb, it's just I am anguished to the point of death over my brother. I fear the worst has befallen him." Gabriel's voice quivered from grief while he struggled to speak of his dearest friend and tears rolled silently down his face.

"Gabriel, I know you've probably heard this before, but still, hear me out," Caleb said. "The Lord is not predisposed to abandon his most favored seraphim. Although, we are inherently imperfect, he who created us is perfect; therefore, he will not abandon Michael nor will he forsake him. What does your spirit tell you?"

Caleb, while he may be a much younger angel, spoke these words with a Godly wisdom and his zeal for the Lord shone through with each and every word he uttered.

"Caleb, I sense the Holy Spirit telling me to have no fear," Gabriel said. "I believe the Lord will not leave us here to suffer until contempt for ourselves and bitterness for our enemy's rule over us making us rot away like the undead, the Ruah. Wait, can you feel him?" Gabriel's voice suddenly changed as he spoke those last words; they filled the air with excitement in anticipation of the presence of God.

"He is coming," Gabriel cried. Caleb shouted for joy.

Out of nowhere, a light grew out of the darkness in the cave. The light danced on the ceiling and traveled across the walls and the colors changed from one shade to the next, bringing the opaque rocks instantly to life with their vibrant beams. The illumination covered the dreary and cold walls with numerous remarkable colors. It was spectacular to behold. What was once used by grimy and wicked demons for detestable and unspeakable acts of torture had now been transformed in the blink of an eye into a beautiful work of art; scenery created by supernatural power overtook the seraphim with awe and wonder.

Suddenly, the cave's floor and walls shook. Stones tumbled down from the ceiling; rocks bulged out from the walls and small cracks traveled across the floor. Needless to say, Desmeeos' could not withstand the awesome power of the LORD and the presence of evil had to flee before the Holy Spirit. All of this took place in a matter of mere moments and Caleb and Gabriel were in fear before the LORD for his display of strength and might. The earthquake ceased and a still and peaceful presence permeated the dungeon. A silent rumble could be felt for the preparations were taking place. Gabriel knew in his spirit that something or someone great was being ushered in. Caleb's hearing was crackling with static from the vibrations in the air. Before it was over, a whirling ring of fire appeared; its flames burned brightly and a being of light, appearing more like a pillar of fire, hovered between Caleb and Gabriel. The fire dwindled away in a second's time; then a brilliant light shone and in it's midst stood Elijah. He was clothed in an emerald robe and suspended in mid-air was the crown of light bestowed upon him by the Father of lights for the angel's mighty valor and deeds as the chief of messengers.

Above ground Carchemish and Zoan were hurriedly going about giving orders; abusing their authority, being true to their tainted characters. They sentenced quite a few demons to death for disorderly conduct. In other words, these were the demons that did not recognize their authority or show them respect; it mattered not to Zoan or Carchemish, since they both could care less for their comrades, but cared solely for themselves.

Nevertheless, no demon had courage enough to challenge their authority and having seen their brothers being brutally slain, they formed ranks quicker than ever before. The legions were ready for the general Beltezar's inspection.

"Captain Zoan, have you seen the general," Carchemish said.

He and Zoan were standing outside the cave.

"No Major, not since he gave us our orders. I took care of my part. My soldiers are neatly in ranks and ready for inspection," Zoan answered.

"As have I, Captain," Carchemish proudly added, speaking with authority. "Send two soldiers below to see if the general is in Judas,' I mean to say, my quarters; or perhaps he is elsewhere. Beltezar does as he pleases, takes what he wants, and does whatever he wishes. If he does not arrive within an hour's time, I will address the soldiers myself." Zoan was dumbfounded at what he just heard, and his face expressed it as well.

Carchemish resumed his arrogant posture and commenced to travel to the mound; he had already thought about what he would say, should he need to speak. What was baffling, even to him, was the fact that he still greatly feared Beltezar, but of course he hadn't stopped desiring the title of General Carchemish. He truly knew deep down inside that it could never be, but his infatuation won over his senses and so his entire being followed along with it. *What is this madness*, he thought to himself as he traveled through the forest. *Why do I insist on being disobedient? I am, after all, faithful to Hell and the advancement of the kingdom. Maybe, the LORD Lucifer will see my passion for his cause and I will prevail over Beltezar's wrath.*

I must not speak to the legions for if I address them, I put at risk all that I have worked so hard to accomplish. That's it. I'll maintain my position and respect the general's authority and the position will fall into my lap. Well, on the other hand, if I address the legions, I might just win them over to my side. Maybe I can establish my own kingdom on earth. What is wrong with me? I am stouthearted and mighty in power, so I can withstand his incantations. I'm almost to the mound. I can hear the soldiers—there must be ten thousand. That could be enough to challenge Beltezar.

Little did Carchemish know but Beltezar was a few earth-miles away. He wasn't alone either; Luminarous walked along side of him. The fallen star was as intimidating in stature and from a distance the two appeared as equals. However, Beltezar didn't think of Luminarous as his peer, nor did the fallen star see the general as his equal or even as a friend for that matter. He saw him merely as a demon of Hell that had handed him an opportunity to escape his sentence of doom handed down to him from God the Father. Beltezar felt almost the same about Luminarous, but he wasn't about to reveal his contempt for the fallen star; at least not until Luminarous had helped him achieve his ultimate revenge. The general didn't intend on offering all that he had promised Luminarous once his oath was fulfilled; instead he planned on having the fallen star imprisoned and if that couldn't be done then destroyed. If that proved to be impossible didn't want to think about that. Beltezar, for now, was inclined to dwell mostly on thoughts of vengeance.

"We are nearly there," Beltezar said, as they passed by an unusual looking palm tree. "The sorcerers should be awaiting our arrival."

The threshold was one of the entrances to Hell, but the only one that was located on the island. The LORD Lucifer and his sorcerers had conjured it up after the Ruah had located the island. The portal, as you know, is behind a waterfall; but what wasn't revealed before hand was the fact that the portal is positioned exactly in the middle of the island. The shape of a star with five points encircled in a ring was measured out precisely using the Ruah and their speed of travel. The five-pointed pentagram, Satan believed, was a source of power. As a matter of fact, he ascertains that the stars in the heavens command much authority and by honoring them in his incantations he can utilize the stars' supernatural powers for his own devices. This power he conjures up is no creation of God, but it is an evil abomination.

It was nearly noon now and the sun was high overhead, glaring down on their backs from above. Beltezar found the extreme heat to be intolerable; he was sweating profusely and he hated the feeling of being hot. The surrounding jungle felt like a stuffy inferno to him. The palms, the bushes, and the various vibrant colors of blooms were all disgustingly horrid, as far as he was concerned. *If I was in charge,* he mused, *I would obliterate all life on earth. Plants especially, after all, what usefulness do they serve other than to clutter my pathway.*

The closer we get to the portal, Beltezar thought, *the nearer I am to having my long-deserved vengeance. This is just one step of many, but it all seems surreal to me much like a pleasant and satisfying dream. The archangel is dead. Gabriel, the warrior will soon be dead and it isn't a bad thought that Caleb will soon be dead and gone too. With the archangel and his lieutenant general out of the way,* he pondered, *who is there left to lead Heaven to war.* He continued quietly in his thoughts, while he kept the fallen star in his peripheral vision.

Shortly after passing the palm tree, where the way had been marked, Beltezar spotted the path to the portal; the path consisted of brownish-yellow dead grass.

"I can see why the Creator made this island your prison," Beltezar remarked. "It's a dreadfully stale place. I can't tolerate its existence. I declare this day that the island's doom is near. When the LORD Lucifer is in power, I will have this place destroyed; flattened to the ground, along with the rest of this dreadful existence." He was visibly disgusted with everything about the island. Nothing pleased him about this place.

"It's tolerable," Luminarous answered him subtly.

This response angered Beltezar greatly because he assumed it to be disrespect; in fact, he knew that Luminarous had made his reply just to spite him. And to compound his frustration, he knew that he couldn't reprimand the fallen star for his words, since the general absolutely needed him for his war against Heaven. So Beltezar bit his tongue and clenched his fists; he held his hands close by his side, so he wouldn't be tempted to strike Luminarous.

Luminarous was perceptive enough to tell that the general was exasperated by the response he gave and not just by what he said, but how he said it. *Meditate on that for a while you pompous demon,* thought Luminarous. He pondered how something as simple as two words could agitate the general and make him lose his composure. Therefore, the fallen star took great delight in soaking up the hot rays from the sun; he clearly showed his pleasure by reaching out his hands to feel the warmth of the sun and sighing with pleasure. Nevertheless, to Luminarous, the heat was wonderful compared to the disagreeable conditions of the confining underground prison that he had inhabited only hours earlier. Beltezar continued to bite his tongue in contempt for Luminarous. The fallen star was pleased with the response he was getting; though, he hid his feelings from view and he was quite satisfied.

"We're here," Beltezar declared, smugly.

Where are the sorcerers, thought Luminarous.

"The sorcerers are waiting for me," Beltezar said, as if he was answering the question. The fallen star peered at him skeptically, searching for an answer to the general's ability to see into his mind.

"Did you actually believe I lacked the power to read your thoughts," the general revealed in a cool steady voice. "I am Beltezar the Terrible, but some call me Beltezar the Seer."

Luminarous only nodded in response and steadied his mind; concealing his thoughts from Beltezar's probing psyche. There were powers, after all, that the fallen star possessed but would not speak of; for these times alone, he was grateful for his strength that he had kept hidden from the demons. Beltezar approached the edge of the water and spoke a few words, an incantation; with demonstrative powerful effects. The wind blew fiercely and the water seemed to pull together; gathering in the center of the pool, the water rose fiercely and hardened quickly into a solid mass. A bridge lay before them now, clear as crystal, yet strong as granite.

Who is this, Luminarous thought, *that commands even the elements and they obey him.* He started to have serious doubts about the pact he had made with Beltezar. Luminarous contemplated to himself, *I made a deal with a prince of Hell. What have I done?*

"Cross over, Luminarous. The time has come to meet the brotherhood, the circle of strength, the conjurers of unholy spells more powerful than the heavens, the all-mighty and omnipotent sorcerers of Hell," Beltezar declared, arrogantly.

Luminarous had never seen Beltezar appear so intimidating than at this moment. It was as if the horrendous power of Hades was flowing directly into the prince of Hell. Gathering more strength, Beltezar seemed to be growing even larger and more menacing with each passing second. Quite frankly, Luminarous felt disparaged in his presence, so he instantly obeyed; without hesitating he took a single step onto the solid bridge of water; then another and another until he was half-way across. Beltezar followed with long heavy strides. The general spoke a few words in the forbidden tongue and the waterfall before them parted like a curtain and turned from brilliant turquoise to blood red; at the same time transforming the beautiful crystal pool into a cesspool of evil.

Luminarous shivered as an icy chill swept across his body; his spine tingled and his spirit trembled in the wake of the dreadful breeze blowing up from Hell. He stood at the threshold of the dark foreboding cave and he felt now that he was helplessly at the mercy of Beltezar, general of Hell and conjurer of evil.

"Enter," Beltezar said, calmly, yet with an underlying malign tone.

As the fallen star took a step, he heard a multitude of voices; all speaking with a foreign tongue, or the forbidden tongue more like it. Beltezar stayed closely behind Luminarous, so the fallen star was urged to take steps further in without hesitating. He felt his legs take on a will aside from his and even when he desired to stop walking they would not cease to move forward. The cave, like a starless night, was pitch black; for the waters that had so easily parted for their ingression had transformed back into a waterfall and were now, once again, flowing from above and into the pool.

Luminarous still could hear the voices speaking in the forbidden tongue.

"*Rah Soonegiro Gehenna*," their voices grew steadily louder as they chanted over and over again. Then the chanting suddenly ceased and a red iridescence illuminated the cave, which opened up into a spacious cavern that seemed to have no end to its depth.

Luminarous found himself surrounded by several tall black and red stalagmites protruding from the cave floor. The pillars stood straight and smooth and encircled the fallen star on all sides; he seemed to be at the center of a circle of great stalagmites. Then he gazed above him and looked in horror upon sharp stalagmites, suspended from the ceiling of the cavern like hundreds of swords laying ready to plunge from their heights and thrust their sharp tips into his flesh. He turned and there was

Beltezar gazing intently into his eyes; his mouth was opened in a huge ghoulish vile grin, his eyes were crimson red and piercing into the depths of the star's soul.

The general then stepped forward and stood in front of Luminarous.

Beltezar spread his arms outward and, spinning his body around in circles, he cried out, "Zawrak *Kashawf*." At those very words, the red iridescence grew more intense and violent gusts of wind stirred in the cavern.

The winds seemed to have no particular direction, but they blew from all directions; crisscrossing and intertwining with one another they swept the floor clean of any dirt or rocks. The wind became a storm and its fury had no match except that of the most violent tornado. Surprisingly Beltezar appeared to be unaffected by the force of the wind, but Luminarous no longer able to stand upright in the force, lost his footing and fell to the ground. He searched for something solid to grab hold of; some secure holding that would keep him from blowing away. He crept along the floor towards one of the pillars of rock, though before he could come within its reach his body rose off the floor and he found himself suspended in mid-air.

"Beltezar, stop this. Stop it now," Luminarous demanded, shouting vehemently.

Beltezar's lips slanted into a sly grin, and he shouted above the storm, "*Zawrak Kashawf.*"

Luminarous' mouth gaped in complete shock and horror as he witnessed the pillars of stalagmites shift their shapes into demons. They threw back their cloaks to reveal twelve sorcerers; tall and menacing, they maliciously glared at him; they looked wickedly pleased with their prize catch.

"I will smite all of you. Stop this now and I will let you live," Luminarous yelled at them.

The demons only grinned devilishly and chanted, "*Rah Soonegiro Gehenna.*"

Beltezar joined their circle and the demons locked hands and walked in a circle chanting the words while Luminarous remained elevated in mid-air, mercilessly at their total control. The air grew warmer and the red glow became brighter and denser. Red waves of light streamed out from the sorcerers. Their silhouettes were edged in the red glow; their faces were radiating with hellish light. A putrid stench had permeated the cave; the air now reeked of decaying flesh. Then another odor began wafting through the room, even worse than the last. It was the foul smell of sulfur and, one whiff from the ghastly gagging stench, was enough to overpower Luminarous.

Succeeding the unspeakably repulsive odors, the fallen star found himself surrounded with a cloud of flames and reddish smoke. He was suspended in mid-air and trapped. He was powerless and completely at the mercy of the conjurers of Hell; he could do nothing to combat their supernatural sorcery. Luminarous could feel that his strength was depleting rapidly and that his power was being drained from him; it was as if the flames were the fingertips of Hell grabbing at him and dragging him straight into Hades. Finally, the battering wind and the wicked stench overtook the fallen star and he lost all consciousness.

"Rah Soonegiro Gehenna," the sorcerers of Hell continued to chant louder and louder yet with their voices shrill, almost screeching, as they methodically repeated the words.

Their sinister spell was coming to fruition and Luminarous' body was changing and shifting back to its original form as a star of heaven. The fallen star's skin turned into pure light, his body now shined with a bright yellow light. His luminosity started to slowly and steadily merge with the iridescent red glow and they fused together to create a terrible and shapeless blinding light. The wind whirled faster and faster until a tornado of rushing wind rotated steadily in the center of the sorcerers' circle. A crack emerged in the ground and the wind and light were sucked into the funnel and vanished just like that, gone in the blink of an eye. The wind ceased and Luminarous had disappeared.

"It is done," Beltezar, poised and confident, uttered. "At the present, the LORD Lucifer will prepare him for the ritual. First, as Elymas had instructed us, the power of *Awven* must transform the star's entire being: his spirit, soul, and mind. Then and only then, can the power of Luminarous meld with Logos and at last become one with the Sword of the Spirit."

"We will begin our preparations for the portal incantation and the spell for teleportation," one of the sorcerers, Magos, said.

"You are positive the spell is ready," Beltezar nodded and inquired.

"Once the hour approached for Elymas to leave for this island, he entrusted me with his sacred scrolls and all of his incantations are written here," Magos, speaking assuredly, answered. "He had been working on a spell for teleportation and an incantation that could invoke enough time needed to transport legions upon legions of soldiers at one time. I have taken it upon myself to finish it."

Beltezar nodded as one peer to another and said, "I am pleased with your work Magos. The Lord Lucifer will hear of your great sorcery, as will all of Hell. For the time being, I must excuse myself from your presence and return to muster the soldiers for war. When I send word, I expect the portal to be fully operational."

The sorcerers again formed in a circle and began their tedious work on what would be the largest portal ever conjured. Beltezar, moreover, left in the same manner he entered, by speaking the exact incantation he had before, he walked across the crystal bridge and made his way back to base. *Victory is nearly at hand*, he deliberated, *and vengeance is mine for the taking*.

MARCH TO WAR

"**Major** Carchemish," Zoan nervously said. "The General is not in your quarters and Luminarous is gone from his prison cell. In fact neither of them are anywhere to be found. I have sent a dozen of the royal guard to the portal to search for him there. It is a possibility he is gone there. To add to the chaos, the legions are getting rowdy, you could say. I don't think the soldiers can stand the heat any longer; the sunlight is weakening them."

"What do you mean he's gone to the portal," Carchemish inquired, ignorantly, staring at Zoan like he was transparent.

"General Beltezar mentioned it prior to coming here," Captain Zoan spoke up clearly this time. "He stated that the brotherhood of sorcerers was coming here to prepare the portal for the regime stationed on Luminarous. The General means to transport the soldiers in mass numbers—to send them to war, that is."

"Huh, then it's decided. Chaos is abounding among the legions and I am left no choice; my only option is to address them myself and prepare them for battle. Beltezar has obviously busied himself with other matters, of which he finds more important. Even so, it would it avail him more if I addressed the soldiers. As the portal is made ready, so will the troops," Carchemish said.

Zoan and Carchemish were carrying on their discussion at the threshold of the cave. Beltezar had been missing for more than five earth-hours. The legions had been fully assembled for a while now and the sun had been blazing overhead the entire time; to the soldiers, the heat was intolerably scorching.

"Major Carchemish, I would think twice—" Zoan uttered. "—before giving orders that supersede the General's commands; his authority cannot be challenged. You know that as well as I, sir. I am the captain of his guard and I know him nearly as well as the LORD Lucifer himself. His wrath is merciless. He is unforgiving of actions such as you are contemplating."

"Respect my position," Carchemish became angered and yelled. "I am your senior and you must not defy me. Beltezar is the general, but on this island the Major is second in command in the General's absence and I give the orders. Do you understand?"

Carchemish ceased speaking suddenly; someone was coming. On the edge of base a figure emerged from the dense foliage. It was the general. He walked tall with broad shoulders, a muscular torso, and an arrogant smirk on his face. Before he was within a dozen paces of Zoan and Carchemish, they had already stood erect and were saluting.

"Major Carchemish, I trust you have prepared the legions for inspection," Beltezar queried. "Captain Zoan, I hope you have kept the soldiers at bay until my return. They are assembled and awaiting my speech, are they not?"

"Yes sir, General Beltezar, sir," Carchemish and Zoan, still saluting, said.

"Captain Zoan, good work; major, I hereby assert my authority and will resume the chain of command. I must address the legions; the time to depart is nearly at hand. Major, lead me to the mound where I shall speak to the masses. Before I ascend the mound, major, you will give me a proper introduction," Beltezar declared.

Carchemish saluted and nodded. He was envious still, but he knew better than to concede his thoughts bare before Beltezar the Terrible, who could read his mind if he desired. The walk was a long one for Carchemish, who knew now that he would have to start over on his plans to overthrow Beltezar. Zoan had summoned the rest of the general's private guard. They had been awaiting orders and sitting in the shade only a stone's throw from the cave entrance. The captain walked along side general

Beltezar. Zoan's allegiance was strongly tied to the general, and Carchemish was foolish to speak his mind to Zoan and now he was paranoid and without a solid strategy.

Major Carchemish had no choice but to merely follow orders, needlessly obey, and hope the general won't expect anything. The major caught himself in the process of developing a thought time and time again; it was hard for him to keep himself from pondering the questions that were in his head, but he fully knew of Beltezar's ability to read one's mind and if the general delved deep enough he would discover Carchemish's treachery and execute him right away.

"Major Carchemish, climb to the top and prepare the way for my presence. Now, major," Beltezar ordered. Carchemish had been so busy with preventing his mind from sparking any thoughts that he had completely ignored his surroundings; it dawned on him that he was standing at the bottom of the great hill and the legions were unruly and noisy, to say the least. He obeyed at once and scaled the mound.

The ground was soft from a recent shower and his sandals sank into the terrain. From the top, he became instantly enamored by the view; out of nowhere a cluster of dark clouds rolled in and blocked the sunlight. A dreary and rainless sky moved in and thunder rumbled and lightning boomed overhead. Carchemish was in awe and gazing out upon the thousands of demons, all assembled in ranks and placed in their specific legions, he was rendered speechless. In that moment, he realized how badly he wanted to take command of the legions of Hell. Adoration took him by surprise. He was overwhelmed with a deep respect for the soldiers and he desired more than ever now to be their leader. His wish would have to wait, since the powers to be were too strong. General Beltezar was feared and admired by nearly all of Hell. Lord Lucifer had chosen him and by doing so, he raised him up to the status of general; the prince of darkness had built him up and promoted him as a fearsome leader, even to the degree that Beltezar was considered by many to be Lucifer's peer.

This worked to Beltezar's benefit more so than the Lord Lucifer's, but that isn't what mattered to Carchemish at the moment. The better good took precedence and in Carchemish's eyes. It was worth fighting for. The advancement of the kingdom was his priority; that is for now. He repressed his rebellious notions and tucked them away in a safe place in his conscious, where Beltezar hopefully could not penetrate. Nevertheless, he thought, *I will have my day, Beltezar; you wait and see. I will prove my merit in battle; that, I am sure of.* Only a few moments had taken place, in fact, between the time Carchemish ascended the mound and the moment he addressed the legions. Despite all of his bitter resentment for Beltezar, the major gave a fine introduction. The speech was incredibly drawn out and lengthy. Carchemish would rather overindulge in the flattery of his rival than relinquish his position from on top of the world.

"I give you, your General, commander of the legions of Hell, Beltezar the Terrible," Carchemish announced, ending his speech with a bang.

"Long live LORD Lucifer and long live the General," the demons chanted, fanatically.

Beltezar was pleased with his introduction and he displayed his approval by patting Carchemish on the back as the two passed one another on the side of the steep hill. There was actually a time when Beltezar was quite fond of Carchemish and he respected him as well; but now he had come to perceive the demon's spite and seen through his petty façade, all the way to the core of his being where treachery and deceit have been found hiding. The general, however, was far too arrogant to worry himself with the meager threats of a lower-ranking demon; nor did he intend to disband him for his heretics, which even if unproved, could still be punishable by death according to the code that Beltezar lived by. Instead, the general was over-confident in believing that Carchemish would somehow be done away with during the war. Beltezar thought that Carchemish's pride would be his downfall and the enemy would see to that in battle.

The instant Beltezar assumed his place on the hilltop and was within sight of the soldiers' view, the legions roared louder. Beltezar reveled in the praise from the soldiers. He raised his arms and the crowds cheered even louder. Beltezar lowered his hands and commanded silence, and just like that, the soldiers ceased making any noise.

"Soldiers, warriors, you are gathered today for one purpose," Beltezar declared. "Our planning and our preparations and our efforts have come to fruition. The fate of Hell has come to rest in your hands. Our destiny has arrived. The prophecies have been fulfilled."

The demons cheered, but quieted as they witnessed two demons hoisting two objects up the hill. Zoan dragged something across the ground, covered in sheets of silk and attached to a chain, and as did another demon. Zoan and the other demon raised one of the masked objects off the ground and brought it to Beltezar. The general stood in between them with the mystery item wrapped in silk before him, he reached out and yanked the silk away and unveiled the object.

The object was no mystery now for Beltezar raised a sword above his head and shouted, "Logos. This weapon once belonged to Gabriel, lieutenant general of Heaven's forces. The power it possesses is purely mystifying and its potential is inconceivable, it belongs to Hell now."

The legions burst forth in chanting, "Long live Lucifer. Let Hell prevail."

Beltezar took it all in and was pleased with their response although he silenced them, because he had something even more incredible to show them. He grasped hold of Logos with both hands and stuck the sword straight into the ground. The ground around the sword was not engulfed in flames; the general was expecting some supernatural power to radiate from the blade. He thought, at least, the sword might send sparks flying and that maybe the grass and earth might be singed by the blade of Logos. However, nothing happened and Beltezar was displeased, moreover he was compelled to suppress the rage and frustration that had come to crush his spirit. Then thunder boomed and shook the heavens and a bolt of lightning stuck the lofty palm growing at the side of the mound, instantly splitting the tree in two.

"Legions of Hell, I give you Logos," Beltezar intuitively cried out; his proud wit took charge of the situation.

The soldiers, at once, were moved to shouting. Their cheers were louder than ever, but soon enough their silences were stilled as a tree in a windless day. Beltezar raised his arms to command silence.

"Even the power of the heavens must obey me," Beltezar said with an arrogance that could only be equaled by one—Satan. "What I am about to show you next will truly tantalize you; the strength of Heaven flows through the veins of this supernatural blade. The vastness of the universe and the wonders of the heavens have been intertwined in its steel." The masses were hushed in awe of his words.

"Bring me the sword of the archangel," Beltezar ordered.

The legions anticipated what was coming next. Two demons brought an object wrapped in chain mail. He ordered them to unwrap the outer-covering. They carefully removed the chain mail and it dropped to the grass like a heavy rock. Beneath this covering was the finest red silk, weaved by the most skilled craftsmen in all of Hell. The demons methodically unraveled the silk in midair and after many tedious and careful revolutions, the demons had created an altar of firmly pulled silk and on it rested the Sword of the Spirit. Beltezar gazed upon the sword with a lust for supreme power. He had tried once already and failed to wield the sword of the archangel. Its cruel touch was terribly penetrating, even beyond merely scorching the hand; on the contrary, its burn reached the depths of the soul and singed the core of the spirit, roasting alive whoever was forbidden from wielding this holy sword in their hands. Four demons, alone, had died while preparing the sword for the ceremony.

Beltezar reached out with hands that nearly trembled.

"*Behtakh Gehenna,*" he spoke an incantation, with his hands hovering above the handle. The words resonated out of his mouth with self-assurance; a sinister grin creased his face and his eyes glowed red. Beltezar touched the handle's edge with his fingertip and, to his utter relief, nothing happened. No burning sensation, no pain, not even a hair on his arm was raised.

"Heaven hath no power like the sorcery of Hell," Beltezar said, daringly.

Then he wrapped every finger around the handle and a pure satisfaction came over his whole spirit. Power-hungry thoughts masqueraded pleasurably in his mind; sinister ambitions were brought to light, and for the first time he felt what it would be like to be the supreme ruler of Hell. Although, he promptly recanted and quietly thought to himself, *forgive me my* LORD *Lucifer. You alone are the ruler of Hell.*

General Beltezar picked up the sword with both hands. The two demons standing idly by gripping the silk sheet with sweaty palms were completely amazed at what they were witnessing. Carchemish watched from below in shock. He had thought that surely the Archangel's sword would have destroyed Beltezar; he was sadly mistaken. *I have sorely underestimated the general's sorcery*, pondered Carchemish and once again, he greatly feared Beltezar the Terrible. Moreover, out of dread for Hell's admonishment, he further suppressed any rebellious feelings. He blocked his deepest thoughts to keep them secret from the merciless general. Carchemish made sure that he joined in all the cheers and clapping and the chants; this way, he could escape notice and carry on as a major of legions.

"The sword has no power over Beltezar the Terrible," a demon from the crowd shouted and the legions cheered. Beltezar raised the weapon mightily above his head. What a display of showmanship it made and the legions roared and the ground vibrated from their stomping feet.

"Behold the Sword of the Spirit," Beltezar shouted at the top of his lungs. The instant he finished speaking a terrifying clap of thunder echoed and then another rang through the sky. There were four total and with each outburst from the dark clouds and with every blast came an explosion of lighting; four huge and ominous bolts of lighting came crashing down to earth. Before the air settled and calmed, the lightning had blasted four palm trees, splintering each tree and shattering their wood into a thousand pieces. The effects were devastating. Long, sharp stakes of wood flew through the air, stabbing and wounding hundreds of soldiers, impaling and killing many, and instigating chaos at once.

"Soldiers of Hell listen to me. Brothers, servants of our LORD Lucifer, heed my words," Beltezar, instead of resorting to panic, yelled in fury.

The crowds were in an uproar. Hundreds were on the ground, slain, dead, and gone. Beltezar shouted a spell and struck the earth with the tip of the sword's blade. He drove the sword into the earth until it was halfway into the ground. Suddenly, a commanding silence pervaded the air. *My spell has worked its magic*, thought Beltezar conceitedly. Now that he had a captive audience, he was determined to take advantage of the prevailing situation.

"Brothers, do not fear for your life any longer," Beltezar declared with the utmost authority. "There is no reason to. I must tell you, regrettably, that the Sword of the Spirit demanded a sacrifice. Our fellow brothers will be remembered as victims that gave their lives for the cause of Hell—" Beltezar stopped his speech short, since rain had begun to pour down.

Nevertheless, as their general and ruthless leader, Beltezar had easily managed to grab their full attention, thus persuading them with no difficulty whatsoever. Seeing as there wasn't a single skeptic among the demons, no one protested the general's reasoning. Even Carchemish bought into Beltezar's explanation.

Beltezar signaled captain Zoan to draw near.

"Summon two of your swiftest runners," Beltezar shouted into his ear. "Send them to the portal to alert Magos that the legions are coming. Have them tell Magos that if the portal is not ready that my anger will burn against him and all the sorcerers. Now go and tell them to run their fastest."

Zoan descended the mound in a hurry. Beltezar turned to address the legions.

"Brothers, warriors of Hell, servants of the LORD Lucifer," Beltezar's voice was emphatically earsplitting, as he yelled. "The time has come. The moment has arrived for us to gather ourselves together for one purpose. This hour we make war against Heaven and the Host. The God of Heaven will rue the day he ever threw us from his kingdom. Today we take back what rightfully belongs to the servants of Lucifer. Legions of Luminarous, you have been set-aside for this hour. Your part in the war will be nothing short of spectacular; for I have deemed each and every one of you worthy warriors deserving the right to fight in the front lines and to lead in the battlefront. You will head the charge against the Host of Heaven. Take up your weapons and follow me Let us march to victory!"

"Victory belongs to Hell. Victory is the LORD Lucifer's," the

Legions chanted and rallied behind Beltezar and his company of sergeants, captains, princes, and personal guard. The earth shook beneath their plodding feet; the rain teemed down upon the demons' backs.

On the outskirts of the forest, a black panther watched and waited as the last troop of demons disappeared into the far jungle across the enemy camp. The panther was hidden under the covering of some dense foliage and he was not alone; just behind him and out of sight an immense multitude of creatures, both great and small, crouched low in the midst of the underbrush.

Moments ago while Beltezar was proudly addressing the legions of Hell, something monumental took place below the earth, secluded in the depth of the dungeon called Desmeeos.'

"Hail Lieutenant General Gabriel. Hail Caleb, captain of the guard," Elijah addressed the seraphim. "In the name of the LORD of Hosts, your salvation is here. I have been commissioned by God Almighty to come and deliver his word. I have been sent to free you from captivity. You will see Heaven again."

A tear fell from Gabriel's eyes from the words that poured out of Elijah's mouth; he was overjoyed at just the thought of his bare feet touching the golden streets of the city of Zion, the Holy City of the Most High, Jerusalem, where God's dwelling place stands, Mount Zion. Just to look upon the face of God and to sit once again in his presence made Gabriel to tremble from sheer delight.

Elijah's staff ignited in a pure red flame; it flickered and took the shape of a tongue, suspended above the staff, neither touching the staff nor abandoning its place. Elijah's crown of light glowed deeper than before; he appeared even wiser than Gabriel had last seen him. The seraph's face had aged with creases, yet his face looked smooth and soft. Elijah's eyes were different; they had a keener sense about them, and they gleamed in the light of the holy flame from his staff. His serene quality was the same as before, maybe even a little more profound than before. He looked upon Caleb with a gentle and compassionate smile, and Caleb nodded like a silent agreement had been made between the seraphim. Elijah turned and walked towards Gabriel. His steps made no echo. The angel seemed to hover above the ground as he moved.

Who is this chief of messengers? Who knows the power the LORD *has placed in him*, pondered Gabriel as he stared at Elijah with hopeful eyes. Elijah stared with sympathy at the shackles and chains; tears streamed from the angel's eyes.

Elijah reached out his staff and his eyes cleared up and shined with the authority of Heaven and cried out with a booming voice, "*Elyootheros*." The chains and shackles that imprisoned Gabriel disintegrated instantly at his commanding words.

Elijah turned and gazed at Caleb. He stretched out his staff and shouted again, "*Elyootheros*." The chains that kept Caleb burst into a cloud of dust and Caleb fell to the ground and gave thanks to God.

"Rise Gabriel and receive the word from Father God," Elijah turned to him and said; he noticed that Gabriel was humbly prostrate, praising the LORD.

Gabriel stood to his feet and looked Elijah in the eyes. The chief of messengers was smiling at him when Gabriel noticed his strength returning to him. At first his ankles gave way under his weight as he had stood up, but with each passing second he felt a surge of supernatural power enter his head and travel all the way down to his toes.

"Gabriel," Elijah placed his left hand on Gabriel's shoulder and declared. "The LORD says: 'you answered my call and you have fulfilled your duty to the Kingdom of Heaven. Your loyalty has been unwavering, even in the face of death. The enemy has tried in vain to destroy you, my faithful servant, for they have failed. My holy presence has been with you even from the beginning of time, and my protection has been by your side and kept the enemy at bay. Gabriel, your time is now at hand and your time to fulfill the destiny to which you have been called. Fear not, for I have redeemed you, I have summoned you by name, and you are mine. When you pass through the waters, I will be with you and when you pass through the rivers, they will not sweep over you. When you walk through the fire, you will not be burned. The flames will not set you ablaze. Not even the gates of

Hell will prevail over you.' Gabriel I have been sent here to take you to your destiny. There is more to be accomplished to the glory of the one who sits on the throne. Are you ready to go?"

"With all my heart, I will follow the LORD," Gabriel answered, zealously.

"The LORD says take up your sword and follow me," Elijah declared; he revealed a sword in a sheath, and Gabriel's eyes lit up immediately.

"Logos—but the enemy had taken it," Gabriel uttered in disbelief.

"The enemy will soon discover their folly," Elijah said with authority in his voice. "Nevertheless, I say expand your mind, have faith Gabriel, and remember this: not even the universe is vast enough to contain the Almighty's power and glory. The time is coming when you will see the LORD of Hosts display his splendor and majesty for all to see, but for now, you must believe with all of your heart, for nothing is too small or too great for the creator of all things, great and small."

Elijah then approached Caleb, who was still thanking the LORD.

"As for you Caleb, captain of the guard. The LORD is deeply pleased with you and you have been raised to new heights in the Kingdom of Heaven. The Father looks forward to greatly rewarding you for your service and valor. Jehovah does not look lightly on loyalty nor does he take courage and perseverance for granted. God the Father has prepared a place for you," Elijah said.

Elijah called the angels together and Caleb and Gabriel embraced as brothers. Although, they knew little of each other they had fought together in the great battle and together their prayers defeated the Ruah.

"The time is now at hand," Elijah said. "You must depart with me Caleb, and Gabriel the LORD has need of you here—" an immense rumble shook the cavern they stood in, so Elijah stopped speaking the instant the ground shook.

Rocks tumbled from the ceiling and Elijah raised his staff above his head.

"Makaseh' *Jehovahnissi*," Elijah shouted and a dome of light appeared, enveloping the angels, of which no rock could penetrate.

"The enemy is departing and leaving this island to go make war against the Kingdom of Heaven," Elijah kept the staff over his head and said. "Gabriel, the LORD has summoned you to battle; but before you must go, you must rescue his servants from danger. The friends of God have been called by the LORD and are on their way. By the time you leave this cursed place and ascend the passage, there will be hundreds upon hundreds gathered above and awaiting your help. The spirit of the LORD has filled you with supernatural speed to run at speeds unheard of before now and you will not grow weary. You must lead them to the outer recesses of the island to the white sands of the beach. There the LORD has made ready their passage into Eden, a realm where no harm can befall them. This is their reward."

Rocks and giant stones fell from the ceiling. The entire place was collapsing.

"I must first save Michael. I will not abandon him," Gabriel cried out.

"Fear not Gabriel—" Elijah smiled, and even under the pressure of a great earthquake, he remained calm and said. "—for lest you forget the Almighty is all-knowing and all-powerful. The LORD will not leave the archangel here to die nor will he forsake him to the enemy. The LORD has provided a covering of protection for you. Time is of the essence, so you must not delay in rescuing the friends of God. You will travel due south; you should face no resistance, since the enemy has traveled in another direction. The beach is but a dozen earth-miles south of here. The LORD has given you the power and the protection you need. Now go and make speed Gabriel."

Elijah's voice had echoed and boomed like thunder above the destruction of Desmeeos.' As soon as the last word rolled off his tongue, he and Caleb vanished into thin air. Gabriel was alone, but he was thankful that the dome of light yet surrounded him and protected him. The rocks continued to tumble and fall and the floor jutted and separated, forming huge crevices and gaps in the floor. Gabriel got a move on it and if he hadn't, the floor would have swallowed him up. The walls cracked and split open from another earthquake, the biggest thus far. Molten hot lava gushed from the seams and crevices as Gabriel made his way to the exit. The boulders left from the cave-in had miraculously crumbled into pebbles and the angel ran with incredible speed jumping over holes and cracks in the cave floor.

Gabriel reached the passage and as if it was second nature, he knew exactly in which direction he must go to reach safety. Close behind him, the walls buckled and the floors split apart; tons of lava seeped from the walls and soon the rock gave way to the magma and the lava came gushing down the passage. Like a great tidal wave, ablaze with fire, it was gaining momentum as it nearly caught up to him. Even so, and not a moment too soon, Gabriel reached the stairway that climbed to freedom just as the lava was about to engulf him in fire.

With the blue sky high above his head, he ascended the stairs faster and faster to safety and his strength seemed to have no end as he ran at a supernatural pace. He sprinted like the wind, and with each step he took another wound on his body healed. The dashes and cuts and the bruises and the blood, were miraculously washed clean from his body by the healing power of Jehovah. The threshold of the cave was now in sight for Gabriel, but the hot magma was climbing fast and filling the cave from end to end. The light of day was peering just beyond the cave's entrance; the stairs above were shining brightly from sunlight. Each crack, each crevice, was revealed on the walls, but to Gabriel the dirty, blood stained walls signaled freedom from the dreary and horrid dungeon.

THE WITNESS

NOTE FROM THE SCRIBE...

The enemy's plans have been set in stone. And their strategies were seemingly strengthened by the downfall of the seraphim of Heaven and now they have only to flawlessly execute the campaign they've devised to overthrow the throne of God. The wheels of destiny are turning and although Michael is at the brink of death, staring it in the face, there is still a chance. Hope lingers yet, even though it is at the edge of defeat, it still remains within the archangel's grasp if only he can seize it.

Now, the enemy had just departed and Elijah was in the final moments of his deliberations with Caleb and Gabriel. During this time, in another part of the cavernous dungeon, Michael had been drifting into darkness and beginning to lose consciousness. At this stage, it is vital that I again return to Michael's personal epic.

THE EPICS OF MICHAEL...

My pain had grown excruciating, even to the point that my beaten, broken, and torn body began to convulse uncontrollably. I fought hard to resist the pain, but each time I lost I shook with unspeakable agony. Each bout was pure torture, intolerably cruel to my flesh. The spells of trembling came and went as they pleased, bringing gloom and heartache when they came and when they left they stole a little more hope from my already downtrodden spirit. I grew apprehensive and began to speculate rather or not these attacks might actually be coming from the Ruah; that they had come to harvest my soul like Beltezar had said. The fits of trembling continued to pummel me and with each spell of utter misery, I felt more of my life drain from my body. I could no longer sense the presence of the Holy Spirit and it sadly seemed that the spirit of the LORD was nowhere to be found.

Eventually, my body became numb and my eyes grew heavy. I discerned the end was near. Death was knocking at the door of my soul, ready to drag me away. I found I could no longer open my eyes and my body had gone numb; I was, in fact, completely paralyzed as one last faint breath escaped from my mouth. But, in what seemed to be only a fleeting moment, I had regained all feeling and was breathing easily once again. Then, I experienced the most invigorating sensation; I felt the touch of warmth, pleasing and wonderful, caressing my entire body. Next, I perceived a brilliant and concentrated light as its intensity shone through my closed eyelids. I, ever so gratefully, soaked in the soothing ambiance that was surrounding me.

I discovered that my hands were no longer restrained and I was free to raise them. I touched my face and it felt clean and smooth, then I gathered the courage to open my eyes and as I did, my ears also opened; I found myself able to hear and see clearly once again. In that moment, I beheld the most glorious sight and my ears were delighted by the most splendid sound I have ever heard. I directed my gaze downward and saw that there were no longer any shackles bound to my ankles either. Filled with marvel, I studied my entire body, it was miraculously smooth and untainted; I felt my hair to find that it was intact, clean, and untangled. Not even a single hair on my head was unaccounted for.

The ground around me had a radiant glow and the air was filled with enchanting music. I suddenly realized I was now situated on the utmost heights of the Crystal Mountains, tens of thousands of feet above the ground I stood admiring the magnificent jagged peaks adorned with countless precious gemstones. Each jewel was a uniquely beautiful creation, sparkling with vibrant color and brilliantly fashioned by the limitless creativity of the Father God; hence, each separate gem was radiant enough to shine marvelously on its own but being placed together in harmony, they shimmered more beautifully than a hundred majestic sunrises. I hastily stood to my feet and serenity washed over my senses, for I knew I was finally home in Heaven, but it was not quite as I had recalled; it appeared exceedingly more wonderful than ever before. The moment I had been anticipating had finally arrived. I was home where I belonged. I stood tall on the highest peek in Heaven gazing at the Holy City of Jerusalem and I was awestruck with the beauty of Zion.

I discovered that my eyesight was at least tenfold greater than what it once was; I took in every minute detail of the city. The golden streets came to life and it was as if I was seeing them for the first time; every golden brick was engraved with a seraph's name. Never before had I noticed the extraordinary detail nor did I pay much heed to the painstaking effort that had gone into the street's excellent workmanship. Not only were the streets amazing in craftsmanship, but the buildings and the gates; even the towering walls covered in gold were undeniably breathtaking. Suddenly, my eyes captured the sight of my mansion, my beloved home. I have longed to walk the hallways and linger in the passages and feel the coolness of the marble upon my feet. And lest I forget, relaxing in my favorite chair, and conversing with my closest friends, Gabriel, Uriel, and Saraqael; along with Remiel and Raguel. And I mustn't forget the mighty Raphael. Oh, how I have missed my dear friends.

I stood reminiscing while an intoxicating breeze swept over my entire body. As I did, I observed the grandeur of God's holy city with a reverent silence. I was rendered speechless by the LORD's wondrous works and brought to my knees in humble admiration for what he had done. All along, as I my eyes explored Heaven I listened to the four cherubim along with the angelic choir. They were singing the song of Zion and it was soothing, purely comforting to my ears to hear their beautiful enchanting voices. I had taken in the holy city and I was pleased beyond measure with what I had seen, but I felt ashamed for I had yet to seek the LORD.

Up until this moment, I had spent my time venerating his creation; it is folly to worship the Creator's designs, for all adoration and praise belongs to the LORD of Hosts. He alone is worthy. My heart only desired one thing and my mind served but one purpose; to dwell in the house of the LORD, bow at the Father's feet, and worship him for all eternity. I fixed my eyes on Mount Zion where I knew I could find the one true God sitting on his throne, clothed with beauty, adorned in majesty, and crowned with glory. He sits upon his throne where he rules with mercy in his right hand and in his left hand there is justice; he is constantly surrounded by the four cherubim, who continually offer him praises from their lips.

I found myself taken back with sudden alarm, as I looked upon the throne, even though the cherubim were around the throne, the LORD of Hosts was missing from his seat of power. Where had he gone? Then, I felt the Holy Spirit urging me to look in the Fields of Gladness, so I gazed out upon its expanse of rolling foothills covered with soft grass, which is so soothing to the feet, and its flowing valley blanketed with fragrant lavender and sweet-smelling cicely. The sky above was as smooth as a velvet canvas with soft strokes of magenta and turquoise painted across the horizon. The view was nothing less than spectacular.

What I witnessed next was unlike anything I had ever seen before; it was as if my eyes were suddenly opened and I beheld a multitude of beings; they covered the entire expanse of the Fields of Gladness. Among the millions of seraphim gathered, stood a sea of faces that were much different from the angels; they were also set apart by their shorter statures, these creations were most definitely not seraphim. The beings, moreover, were beyond number and yet there was room among the streets and the other fields and the meadows for many more. My fellow angels and the new creations, all together, were worshiping and facing in the same direction. Then I looked once more on Mount Zion and the LORD was still not on the throne.

"Where have you gone my God, my King," I said aloud.

"Do not be so narrow-sighted Michael, my servant; broaden your vision and open your mind to what I can do. Then and only then will you behold the beauty of the LORD," the Holy Spirit spoke to my heart.

Out of nowhere, a rushing gust of wind blew across my face.

"Look down Michael and believe," the Holy Spirit said.

Obeying the direction of the Holy Spirit, I looked down and saw that everyone who had been standing in the Fields of Gladness were now bowing in unison; as the beings prostrated themselves, their appearance was like the sudden surge of a tidal wave and then I knew that the mighty breeze I was experiencing had been stirred up by the movement of the multitude. Suddenly, without warning, the ground trembled violently and the foundations of Heaven shook fiercely. Even though I was frightened, the multitudes seemed to not heed the earthquake or at least they did not appear to be alarmed by any means.

"Fear not, Michael," the Holy Spirit said and then, just as suddenly as it had started, the earthquake ceased and once again peace filled the air.

"Look to Zion. Behold, I have come," spoke a voice, unlike any other I've heard.

I turned my gaze towards Mount Zion and there stood the LORD, shining in all his magnificence. I gasped at the sight of him and tears flowed freely from my eyes, his glory shined with a brilliance that was almost too great to bear. His presence had permeated the air and even on the highest peaks of Heaven where I stood, I could feel the all-encompassing, omnipresent spirit of the LORD; his face shone forth with the purest light I had ever witnessed. Power and majesty radiated like thunder and lightning; a whirlwind of light encircled the LORD of Hosts. The multitude, all at once, rose to one knee and sang a new song onto the LORD; their voices melted together flawlessly in beautiful harmony as they worshiped the LORD singing:

Worthy is the Lamb
Who sits on the throne
Worthy is his name

And forever may he be praised.
Worthy is the Lamb
Who rules the heavens and the earth
Worthy is his name
And may His kingdom last forever.

Trust me when I say that words fail to describe how intricately the myriad of voices came together in one accord. The melody was alluring as it beckoned me to join with the multitudes in their worship. I proceeded to the edge of the cliff, treading carefully, to search for a path down the mountain. My heart yearned to walk among my brothers and, not to mention, acquaint myself with these new and wonderful creations of God. I peered over the edge where the mountain steeped down many thousands of feet and only four, maybe five ledges, stood between the valley and me. If I were to falter or miss my step, I would plummet uncontrollably downward like a tumbling boulder, but reassuring myself, I remembered that I was in Heaven where anything is possible.

"Nothing can keep me from the presence of God. I am coming LORD," I cried out.

I gathered my courage and lowered myself carefully over the edge as I grasped onto the cliff, and that's when I heard a loud voice clearly calling my name. I steadied myself and looking up I witnessed a being, like the others below, approaching me.

"Michael the Archangel," the being reached for my hand and said; surprisingly, he was able to pull me up, even though he was much smaller than me.

He helped me to my feet and immediately I noticed his shorter stature; more peculiarly, he was dressed in clothing that was strikingly different from that of the Host of Heaven. He was clothed in a tunic made of coarse cloth and a leather belt was girded around his waist. I found his appearance to be quite unusual; what was most unique about him was that he had a dark beard and long scruffy locks of dark brown hair. This strange being carried himself like an esteemed warrior of God; not with pride, but as one with great confidence and trustworthiness. Truly, his eyes belonged to one who ought to be adorned with royal garments rather than the ragged clothing he was wearing.

As I gazed upon him, he seemed oddly familiar. I couldn't help but somehow feel that I had known him all my life. *Who is he and how did he climb to such heights*, I asked myself. His presence is commanding and he must possess extraordinary ability in order to have climbed to the summit of the Crystal Mountains. I was overwhelmed with curiosity and wondered why he was here on the summit.

"Michael, I have come to witness to you," he boldly said.

"Who are you," I asked him.

"My name is John," he answered in a noble voice. "I was fashioned, like you, before the creation of time. Before the heavens and the universe were shaped or the foundations of the earth were set, I was conceived by the Almighty. Albeit, I am only a man, yet the Father of Lights has ordained me for a great calling; however, my time is yet to come. I have come to bring you hope, Michael. I was sent to minister to you. For your life is not over. You are not dead on the contrary your spirit is hanging in the balance. The enemy wants to imprison you for an eternity; hundreds of Ruah have been summoned from the dark abyss to harvest your soul and spirit. Your spirit may be hanging in the balance but I am here to assure you that, you are covered with the shelter and power of Jehovah. Satan despises you still and he will stop at nothing to destroy you."

John's voice then grew solemn as he told me, "In as much as he hates you, there is another that he loathes even more. He is the King of Kings and the LORD of LORDS, the Messiah, the salvation of mankind, Emanuel, Jesus, the son of God."

"LORD Jesus," I was instantly enamored uttered in amazement.

John took me by the arm and walked me to the edge of the cliff.

"Behold the Son of God," he pointed straight towards Mount Zion and uttered.

As the very last word rolled off of his tongue, the brilliant aura that encircled the LORD veiling him from sight shot straight up into the sky like a beam of pure light. Flashes of lightning bolted across the horizon bringing with them ominous rolls of thunder that shook the heavens. I shrank back in fear and squinted from the intensity of the illumination but when it was over, I gazed back to Mount Zion and saw the LORD not as I had become accustomed to seeing him, but more glorious than ever before. His face had a gentle softness about it, yet it was entirely masculine at the same time; his long, dark hair rippled softly in the breeze and I was awestruck and breathless in the wake of his splendor and majesty.

At that moment, the two seraphim, Justice and Mercy, abandoned their posts at the threshold of the throne room and joined together at Emanuel's side. Justice, handsome and brawny, stood valiantly to his left and Mercy, true and humble, placed himself by the right hand of the Son. Mercy and Justice each held a great trumpet, made of pure gold, in their hands.

"Blessed is he that cometh in the name of the LORD. Hosanna in the highest," Mercy gave a great blast on his trumpet and announced.

Shouts of praise rang out and in one accord, the multitudes bowed to the floor showing their reverence for the Son of God. Out of thin air it must have been, lest my eyes were fooling me. I suddenly observed that not one single being was without a palm branch in his hand.

"Truly I say to you that every knee shall bow and every tongue will confess that he is LORD," Justice heralded in the forthcoming word with a loud and mighty blow from his trumpet, and proclaimed in a deep, resounding voice.

The assembly burst forth into worship and waving their palm branches high in the air they sang:

Hosanna, Hosanna
Blessed is he who comes in the name of the LORD
Hosanna in the highest.

I was overcome with rapture by the song they were singing; the music was immensely pleasing and I longed for it to continue forever, without ceasing. Then Jesus lifted his arms to the sky and the singing came to a sudden halt. My spirit trembled as I looked upon his majesty; my heart felt a longing to be only in his presence. Tears were flowing from my eyes; I yearned, like never before, to walk by his side and hear is voice speaking to me. It was as if I was seeing the LORD for the first time; yet, mysteriously, something deep inside of me seemed to sense that I had walked with him before long ago, before the foundations of the heavens were yet formed or there was yet to be any voice other than his.

Jesus' face was soft and serene and his eyes were kingly and kind; even though he spoke not a word, his face alone issued a thousand heralds. The Son of God stood gazing out upon his flock…his children.

"Michael, you are a witness of what is to come, what you are seeing, has yet to come to pass," John turned to me and proclaimed. "Many ages shall come and go before the Messiah's time will come, and when it does, he will create a new Heaven and a new earth, for the old will pass away. Look out upon the multitudes, Michael, and behold the beings; humans are greater in number than the seraphim; they are called the *redeemed*. They have been bought with a great price. Their lives will never end and in his presence they will spend all of eternity. The time has now come for them to receive their reward. Truly, the new Heaven and the new earth will soon be joined together and when that time comes, there will be no barrier separating the redeemed from his love or his grace from everlasting to everlasting. Their praises will ring. Listen to them worship, let the redeemed of the LORD say so."

I was speechless, as these events had never been revealed to me before this time.

"I have been created for a purpose, much like yours," John studied my face carefully and continued to say. "The LORD has commanded: Prepare the way of the LORD and make his path straight. That is your purpose Archangel Michael. You are the deliverer of justice and the guardian of the seed of Emanuel, the salvation of the world."

I was awestruck and avowed, "I am taken back, truly speechless in his presence. Who am I that I can look upon the face of God's only Son? Who am I that I can even begin to be considered for something of such great magnitude? For whatever I have gained thus far, I consider it all loss after beholding, with my own eyes, the Son of God in all his glory."

John looked tenderly and kindly into my eyes and as he did, I established that his capacity for love was like that of the Father's, deeper than the deepest ocean. He said nothing; instead, he peered into my eyes with compassion and zeal purer than gold.

"Read from the scroll, Michael," he finally said and then, without any warning, he vanished into thin air right before my eyes.

At that very instant, I was reminded of the scroll Elijah had given me. I searched my memory and found the words that had penetrated my heart as he had spoken them to me: *He will reveal to you the time and the place to open it.* I thought, *surely the enemy had searched my robes and found it. It couldn't be there, could it?* I reached into my robe with my right hand and I felt the dry smooth edges of the parchment.

"The scroll," I exclaimed with great delight.

My hands shook uncontrollably as I held the parchment and my heart was racing with anticipation; I steadied myself and welcomed the sound of the heavenly choir's music as it soothed and calmed my spirit and, with gentle steady hands, I carefully unrolled the parchment.

The words were a scarlet color, as if written in blood, and it read: *Your time has come Michael for your destiny to be fulfilled. Behold, you have been put through the refiner's fire and you have come forth pure as gold. I have redeemed you and by my grace you have been set free.*

I had read the words aloud and then, when the last word rolled off my tongue, the writing on the scroll ignited into thin blades of flame and to my astonishment, the words then turned to gold and vanished from the parchment.

"Under the shadow of my wings, you will find rest," a voice, sounding like it came from above me, said. Then an immense heaviness came over me and despite all my efforts to hold myself upright, my legs failed me.

"Hush and be still," spoke the voice, calmly to my heart. I fell on my knees and worshiped Jesus, the King of Kings. His presence was all around me, surrounding me with warmth and love.

I heard God's voice, like one crying in the wilderness, calling out to me, "The time is at hand Michael. Your salvation is here."

When I opened my eyes, I was aghast to find myself in the dark dreary cell, still captive in shackles. *Was I in a dream*, I thought, *was it merely a hallucination brought on by a fever?* Nevertheless, I felt the sting of death fast approaching and even as blood dripped from my lips.

"Father, Father, I need you," I cried out to God with all that was in me. "You promised you would never leave me nor forsake me. Father, come to my rescue."

In spite of being dehydrated and on the brink of death, tears poured from my eyes burning my wounds with salt as they ran down my face. I became overwhelmed with utter despair; for it seemed that all hope was gone. Desolation fed on the remnants of my soul, and I could feel the Ruah hiding, looming at the threshold of my spirit; rabidly waiting to devour my life force and they wouldn't be satisfied until they had completely drained every bit of life from me. Their wicked stench increasingly filled the room; countless pairs of cruel, red-glowing eyes emerged from out of the darkness. The air suddenly grew cold as ice and the walls echoed with the Ruah's bellows of hideous, shrieking, screams.

I was petrified with fear but the Holy Spirit rebuked me saying, "Ye of little faith. Fear not, for where the Light is darkness cannot prevail."

The Ruah had now taken on form and they manifested themselves as dragons, serpents, and other evil beasts too horrible to describe. Slowly and methodically they slithered and crawled across the ground, making their way closer to me by the moment. A thick mist-like substance was pouring from their mouths and I presumed that it was drool but at the moment, what it was held no importance to me. I was frantically praying for the LORD to come to my rescue.

"In the name of Jesus, I condemn you to the pits of Hell. Return to the darkness you slaves of Satan," I cried out. The Ruah quivered and shook nervously at the name of the Messiah.

"I am bought, I have been redeemed by the Christ Jesus. You cannot touch me," I boldly proclaimed. The spirits trembled and hissed; some scattered in all directions and others cursed the name above all names.

After speaking forth with boldness and proclaiming my redemption, an immense courage rose up from within my spirit; a reassurance and confidence filled my entire being, overshadowing all fear and doubt that had lingered in my soul.

"Flee now or suffer the Holy wrath of Jesus my deliverer," I proclaimed one last time. The Ruah jeered and cursed once again but this time, a light suddenly broke through the darkness destroying the spell of the Ruah. The sound of a thousand screams rang through the air.

I could feel the warmth of the intense illumination against my face and I peered through my eyelids and was blinded by the light.

"I am the great I Am. Flee before my might and power, spawn of Satan," from within the light, a voice boldly called out.

I squinted and beheld a dark, black mass gathered in front of the light.

"In my name, be uncreated Ruah, wrought of evil," a voice, mighty and bold, spoke forth from the light. Suddenly, the light flashed, shattering the mass into oblivion and a resounding boom shook the entire cell. Rocks crumbled and dust fell from the ceiling. When I dared to I look again, the blinding light had faded away but a bright glow lingered, illuminating the cell.

"Lord, my God," I called out towards the light.

"You called to me and I have answered," the voice of God said.

I heard his footsteps approaching me and then I felt the warmth of his breath caress my face as he stood before me. I began to weep uncontrollably.

"I have failed my mission. Please forgive me Lord for I have failed you," I pleaded.

"Michael, you have served me with all of your heart; you gave all you had for my kingdom," I Am replied softly but assertively. "You have made the ultimate sacrifice. Well done good and faithful servant."

He then placed his hand gently, but firmly, on my head and said, "Alas, you have died to this earth my child, but I come to bring you new life."

Then I felt his power enter through my head, stream through my body, and travel all the way down to my toes, reviving all my senses at once.

"By my might you have been set free," I Am shouted.

The chains that had bound me broke at his command and my body began to rise from the floor. The power of I Am continued to pass through my body; all pain and anguish vanished as I was being filled with a new and greater strength; a radiant light beamed forth from my mouth. My body then lowered gently to the ground; all my wounds were healed and I was wiped clean. My flesh had been restored and there, in the cell, I knelt before the most beautiful sight of all; the one from my vision.

"My child, the old has gone and you are now a new creation, more precious in my sight," Emmanuel said and took a hold of my hand and raising me to my feet he lovingly embraced me like a father embraces his child.

The walls of the cell gleamed with the radiance of his glory and my eyes could not hold back the tears of joy, for Jesus had come to my rescue.

"In your most desperate hour, salvation has come to you; for you were once lost and now you have been found," the Son of God placed his hands in mine and pronounced with a kingly tone.

I was at a complete loss for words and in total awe of the splendor of the Messiah. As we stood there together, a mighty tornado, filled with light, swirled all around us.

"Michael, your purpose is yet to be fulfilled," Jesus grasped tightly onto my hands and declared. "There are still many great and mighty deeds destined for you to accomplish to my glory. I have created in you a clean heart and in you I have set my power, which has been made complete in me. Be aware that your strength is not your own, but the power that resides within you is the Holy Spirit. Now and forever more, you will be able to do things that would have seemed unimaginable before; but through me, all things have been made possible. You now stand in my presence a new creature, reborn in my power and glory. You are forever changed, set apart from this world, for my plan and purpose. The road ahead will be difficult, but now all things are possible. Do you accept your purpose and my plan?"

The wind blew harder and the luminosity intensified, now throwing out intense heat, it felt as if my skin was being scorched by raging fire.

"I accept your purpose, with my whole heart and all that is within me. I accept your plan," I squeezed the Son's hands tighter and answered him with great zeal.

"It is time," Jesus then proclaimed.

The floor vibrated and the walls trembled in the quake of his awesome power. The immense and terrifying tornado wrapped itself around us. Sparks were flying outward in all directions; all the colors of the rainbow shimmered and glowed in the wind and light that enclosed us. All of a sudden, I felt my body leaving the floor. I was floating upwards. I closed my eyes and when I opened them I was surrounded by daylight.

I was, in fact, hovering in the sky and the island was far below me. I looked and saw that I was standing on a cloud, my hands still holding on tightly to Christ's hands. Suddenly, a great rumble sounded throughout the sky and a mighty blast of fire exploded from out of the volcano below. Flames were shooting high into the air, coming too near for comfort; then the blaze retreated back down into the earth. In its place, it left an immense black cloud that hung heavily in the atmosphere.

"I've never seen such devastation. What's happening," I said.

"It is not for you to know these things now, but my Father will reveal them to you in due time. Alas, do not trouble yourself with what you see. Concentrate on what is to come for this will prove to be your biggest challenge yet," Jesus said and in the twinkling of an eye he vanished into thin air.

I stood alone, floating upwards towards the heavens on a cloud.

THE WARRIOR WITHIN

"I'm almost there. I can see the threshold," Gabriel said to himself as he swiftly ascended the stairs. At last, he had reached the top safely, but he was by no means out of harms way. Danger was still looming and it wasn't far behind him; it would only be a matter of minutes before a burning flow of lava would engulf the enemy camp and then flood over the entire island, setting it ablaze and burying it beneath hot magma.

Gabriel quickly scanned over the area for any sign of the enemy and to his relief, there were no demons in sight. *Lord, I've trusted in you always, and I've never forsaken your ways*, Gabriel prayed silently, *now what do you want me to do.*

Gabriel sprinted across the abandoned base. Instinctively, he ran towards the mound, the highest place in the camp, and he knew in his spirit that he was to climb up to the top. *From here you'll be able to see your surroundings*, God spoke to his heart. Standing on the mound, he looked around the base searching for any signs of life and saw only a forsaken place. Then he looked outward to the perimeters of the camp, which bordered the jungle, and it was desolate as well.

"God, I need your help oh Lord, guide my path," Gabriel stretched his hands up towards the heavens and cried out.

A horrendous roar sounded out from somewhere deep within the jungle, startling Gabriel. His heart pounded relentlessly within his chest and then another beastly cry resounded, and then another getting nearer each time he heard it. Unseen, numerous creatures began roaring, shrieking, and howling. Gabriel's eyes opened wide with fear, but then he heard the LORD speaking to his heart saying, *Have faith, Gabriel.* The ground vibrated, tremors shook the mound and there was a steadily intensifying rumble that sounded through the air. *A stampede,* he thought. Whatever it was, it was getting closer by the second. Suddenly it stopped and a lone creature emerged from the edge of the forest lunging forward was a huge black panther.

The bold black beast came to halt; its broad chest was defined and muscular and it stared intently at the angel with its piercing yellow eyes. The panther remained standing a few hundred paces away.

"You made all that noise? You're big, but not that *big,*" Gabriel said.

As if Gabriel had been beckoning the animal to come nearer, the panther ran towards him with giant leaps and bounds. The noble creature mounted the hilltop in one effortlessly smooth long leap. Gabriel was taken back by the panther's immense size and noble carriage. It seemed to him that it was the same panther that had stealthily surveyed him and Michael throughout their quest and most likely the same panther that bravely came to their aid during the struggle with Magnimus. Gabriel pondered how it could be. *I witnessed Magnimus slay him.*

"Ah yes, I remember now," it suddenly dawned on him and he exclaimed. "You were nowhere to be found after Magnimus had died so you did not perish after all; quite the opposite, I'd say, for the LORD must have revived you."

Gabriel fondly patted the panther on top of its head; in response, the creature purred affectionately and looked up at Gabriel staring keenly into his eyes; then, without any hesitation, he turned and let out a thunderous roar, which reverberated out in the direction of the jungle. The panther's roar had taken Gabriel by surprise, but what followed left him totally dumbfounded. The earth trembled and the trees were shaking as hundred's upon hundreds of animals were on a stampede as they came pouring out of the jungle. As they entered the clearing they began to slow their pace; Gabriel beheld creatures of all sizes and varieties as they moved towards the mound. Approaching the mound they quickly gathered around its base and intently gazed up at Gabriel and the panther as if awaiting instruction from their leaders.

Amongst the multitude of creatures were majestic lions, ferocious tigers, enormous bears, sleek brawny panthers, vociferous monkeys, chirping birds all colors of the rainbow, and even mice and many more creatures that would take scrolls to describe. However, there was one creature that stood out from the rest: a baby dragon, which hovered above the myriad of animals, one of kind.

The panther placed its huge paw on Gabriel's side as if to get his attention and then, with the same paw, he motioned in a southerly direction. At that precise moment, a dazzling shaft of sunlight passed through the treetops and beamed down directly on Gabriel.

"Gabriel, my faithful servant, lead my precious creatures toward the light," God's audible voice said. After God had spoken, the beam receded back through the treetops.

Every animal vocalized their support and desire to follow Gabriel by roaring, howling, chirping, squawking, shrieking, and barking.

The panther briskly turned around and came out with a low, but urgent sounding, growl; Gabriel turned just in time to see lava spilling out of the cave. The blazing flood was surging right for him and the animals; it toppled trees in its path and disintegrated boulders in its flaming wake, wreaking total devastation. The panther jumped from the mound and the animals parted down the middle, creating a clear path for the angel to pass through. Gabriel was filled with undaunted courage as adrenaline pumped through his veins; his heart was racing not from fear, but from exhilaration. He swiftly scrambled down from the mound and he was soon surrounded by the multitude of animals.

"Friends of God, follow me. Let's fly," he shouted and off he sprinted, and right by his side, ran the panther. The brave creature's leadership was unswerving in the face of imminent danger; Gabriel was astonished at the speed the panther was running.

He was flanked on his right by the panther and on his left by a cheetah; all the other creatures followed right behind the three that were leading them to safety. What a spectacle it was indeed, as a mouse hitched a ride on the back of a lion, monkeys swung nimbly from tree to tree, quicker than lightning and the birds glided overhead, keeping pace with all the creatures. The baby dragon took its place at the head of the pack, hovering right above Gabriel's head, as the angel sprinted forward with supernatural speed.

The monkeys suddenly began shrieking with terror. Alas, the lava was gaining on them, and it wouldn't be long before the devastating river of fiery magma would catch up to Gabriel and his huge entourage of friends. Nevertheless, Gabriel was filled with an even greater strength to run even faster; at the same time, the LORD endowed the creatures with added strength enabling them to keep pace with him. With the help of God's hand, the gap was widened between the friends of God and the rushing stream of molten lava. Trees and shrubs flew by like specks on the landscape, as Gabriel and the vast horde of animals ran with incredible swiftness; suddenly, much to his relief, Gabriel felt his bare feet now treading through fine soft sand. He hadn't even noticed, up until now, that he had lost his sandals as he was running so rapidly toward the light and away from the threatening flow of lava.

He came to a halt as the animals poured out of the jungle and onto the white virgin sand. The pearly white shoreline and the endless turquoise waters were the refuge Gabriel was seeking. He had obeyed thus far, but what to do now? The bulging flow of magma was a mere hundred paces from them now, ferociously smothering and destroying everything in its path.

"LORD help us," Gabriel cried out, as he and the creatures stood anxiously by. Then, the light that led them there suddenly changed into a brilliant sphere. The sphere mysteriously transformed into a large being of pure light.

"Come my servants, come to me," spoke God; his voice was like the flowing of many waters.

And from out of his right hand, God revealed to them a small orb of light. He tossed it up into the air and as soon as it struck the sand, the small ball of light began to grow larger with every passing moment. Then, in the blink of an eye, the light became translucent. The only word worthy to describe such an event is the word *miracle*, yet no word that can do justice to the stunning panorama set before them.

Gabriel peered into the sphere and discovered that another place, another world, existed within its seemingly endless borders; moreover, it was daylight within this parallel universe. Truly, this other world was more beautiful than the earth. It was one that could even rival all of the gardens and valleys of Heaven. The brave animals, with a reckless abandon, ran towards the light and one by one they entered into the sphere.

Gabriel stared into the sphere and beheld alluring green valleys plush with soft silky grass. Beyond the valleys, lush trees grew abundantly and bore fruit as simply as a bird spreads its wings. Flowers bloomed everywhere and bowed low to the glory of the Creator. Truly, the LORD's creation transcended all imagination. *Only God himself could conceive a world so majestic and beautiful; its tranquility and alluring nature is beyond description*, thought Gabriel.

"A fine choice," Gabriel said with a bright smile.

Then, suddenly remembering where he was, his attention was averted to the river of magma that was still behind him. The entire jungle was submerged in lava now and it had almost silently crept onto the white sandy beach covering it with glowing hot dark magma. Gabriel looked to the LORD for help and in the blink of an eye the angel was lifted upwards and away from certain doom by the power of God. He was enclosed in a sphere of pure light. Gabriel wanted to look at this marvelous new surrounding; he attempted to open his eyes but found that he wasn't able to. He could sense that he was not alone.

"Open your eyes, Gabriel," the LORD said softly and assertively.

Gabriel opened his eyes and he saw no one there or at least, it appeared as if he was alone. But he wasn't by himself and the spirit of the LORD had been with him the entire time.

"I am here, Gabriel," God said. "I have never left you alone. I am with you always; even in your darkest hour, I was by your side."

"Forgive me Lord, for there were times when I felt that you had abandoned me. Please help my unbelief," tears welled in his eyes and he cried out.

"You have endured much on my behalf and have served me with your whole heart," the Lord, with a compassionate and solemn voice, said. "Truly, rescuing my servants was not a simple task, nor do I look lightly on such a great deed. Gabriel, I reveal the truth to you: my creatures are loyal and steadfast, set apart from the entire kingdom of Luminarous, to serve my plan and purpose and because of their allegiance and resolute courage, they fended off many of the enemies; protecting you from the harm the evil ones had intended for you. You were faithful Gabriel in answering the call, and you have proven your unwavering devotion; it is for that reason, and to your credit that the friends of God are now safe and basking in their reward."

The Lord then said, "Look below, Gabriel, and witness the tragedy that would have befallen my friends had you not intervened."

As he looked down, the island appeared as small as a footstone. Suddenly, a colossal eruption boomed forth from the volcano. Fire and brimstone smothered the horizon until the island was blocked entirely from view and the dark clouds were an ominous sign that the island had indeed been blasted out of existence.

"Several creatures have lost their lives this day; but as for my servants, because of your steadfast faithfulness and bravery, they survived to live for all of eternity in Eden."

God continued, speaking with a tender voice, saying, "Nonetheless, what I require of you now, will prove to be your most difficult trial yet. Every ounce of your strength will be required and each sharply honed skill that I have bestowed on you will be vital to your mission. Will you wield Logos with fierce justice? Will you fight?"

"Yes Lord," Gabriel answered, fervently.

"Will you go to battle, even if it were to mean your demise," the Lord asked.

"Yes Lord, I will go to battle for you, no matter the cost," Gabriel zealously replied.

"Will you go to war in my name to defend the kingdom of Heaven," the LORD asked once more.

"LORD, anything you ask of me, you can consider it done for your glory," Gabriel answered, passionately.

"From the moment Satan fell from my grace, he has been ruthless and cunning in establishing his kingdom," God said, solemnly. "He rules Hell from his throne making judgments and issuing forth decrees. In his wicked heart, he has foolishly conceived the notion that he is God calling himself Beelzebub the ruler of the universe. And his treacherous conceit doesn't stop there. He has set up for himself a royal court of demon princes and with their aid, he has been deviously plotting and scheming against my kingdom. Truly I say to you that, deep in the dark abyss of Hell, the principalities have hatched a sinister agenda aimed at destroying all that is holy and righteous.

"Even now, as I speak, the dominion of Satan dares to threaten the very sanctity of Heaven and earth; for at this moment, hideous strength has been summoned forth and soon the wickedly depraved legions of Hell will cover the earth with their malevolently evil presence. Satan wishes to completely annihilate all the Host of Heaven and as for those he doesn't kill, he plans to destroy their righteous spirits and make them like the Ruah. If he is successful in defeating my holy and righteous warriors, then nothing will prevent him from making the earth barren, destroying completely the friends of God."

"I have called you, Gabriel, to battle against the legions of Satan. In my name, you must drive the enemy back to the pits of Hell. Will you accept this mission whole heartily?"

"LORD I accept it, with all of my heart. I will follow you with all that I am, for I serve you and you alone," Gabriel replied with hands held high.

"The host of Heaven has been gathered and as I speak, Raphael has temporary command of the forces. He awaits you and Michael to lead them into battle," God said.

"He is alive?" Gabriel was overwhelmed with excitement and yet intrigued at the same time.

"He's alive and well and expecting you," the LORD declared.

All the while he was speaking to Gabriel, the spirit of the

LORD was taking him higher and higher into the sky. He ascended into the stratosphere, where the outermost recesses of the blue sky encounter the beginning of the heavens. The stars twinkled brightly; blazing comets streaked by them, their tails awakening the heavens with an aura of sparks and pulsating colors. Gabriel was rendered speechless taking in the beauty of it all; in fact, he was so intently and completely wrapped up with the breathtaking spectacle that he failed to notice that a being was descending upon him. As the being came near, he caught sight of him from the corner of his eye and as he turned his head to look, he was filled with immense delight as he beheld Michael the Archangel, commander of the Host of Heaven.

It was a glorious reunion between two long lost friends closer than brothers; and each of them had believed all along that the other had perished. They were both ecstatic and overwhelmed with joy; then, their emotional exuberance was taken to even greater heights when they beheld the sight of Jesus, rapidly approaching riding on a comet, of all things. Christ appeared as a mighty warrior riding like the wind, and he was richly adorned in a regal purple robe.

Michael and Gabriel suddenly became as silent as mist and they found themselves utterly awestricken with the sight of Jesus, that is, until Michael could no longer contain himself.

"The Messiah," Michael cried out, passionately.

"The King of Kings," Gabriel, with adoration, exclaimed.

Before the seraphim could blink twice, Jesus stood before them clothed majestically in holy light; his kingly poise was awe-inspiring. Jesus' eyes had been blazing with a supernatural light when he arrived but the flame in his eyes had now faded; and his eyes welled up with tears of compassion and joy.

"A great destiny awaits you," the Son of God said; his voice echoed the gravity of the situation. "The time has drawn nigh for you to go to war. Satan has delivered his challenge for the throne. The principalities of Hell have assembled for battle, and the prince of darkness has sworn that Hell will stop at nothing until the Host of Heaven is utterly annihilated and he has complete dominion over Heaven and earth. The battle will be fierce; as well, your enemy is cruel and merciless and their tactics are malicious and ruthless. Possessing a guile and corrupt nature, they will take any advantage they can possibly seize. Their count is innumerable; for deep in the pits of Hell they have been breeding wicked perversions of creation. Truly, Satan is so merciless that he tortures his own even to the point where their spirit breaks and alters into an even more horrific abomination; thus, Satan's deviant faculties are to blame for the existence of the Ruah whose numbers have grown profusely, so that they are now equal to half of the legions of Hell."

Jesus appeared deeply concerned as he continued, "I will tell of something of grave importance and dear to the Father and the Son. I can only give you a glimpse for now; at the appropriated time, the Father will tell you more. My Father has created a man and woman in his image and he loves them deeply beyond measure. The man he created first and then the woman; she has only just now begun to breathe, and Satan has already plotted evil against her and the man. This is truly why the enemy must not prevail this day."

Michael and Gabriel were in need of words, for the immensity of the situation was too much to bear. Only a short moment had passed when tears began to pour from Christ's tender and loving eyes.

"Truly, I say to you I bear the weight of your destinies on my shoulders; for my burden is light and my yoke is easy," Jesus boldly proclaimed.

Christ's eyes beamed with supernatural power as he stretched out his arms.

"Take hold of my hands, for the time has come," Christ declared.

The three held hands, forming a circle, and straight away their bodies transformed into a brilliant light. The intense glow, for both Michael and Gabriel, seemed to transcend space and time and when the radiance at last faded, they found themselves dressed in magnificent armor and not just any armor, but Pirist Olhy, the most precious metal in all of Heaven and earth. Its strength is unmatched in all of the universe and what is more, the flawless metal is as weightless as a feather and in the heat of battle it comes to life; adhering itself to the warrior's body and forming an impenetrable defense. This precious metal is supernatural indeed and since it is so rare, few things have ever been forged out of Pirist Olhy.

Michael and Gabriel were astonished by their impenetrable supernatural armor; they were speechless, overcome with awe having just beheld such a miracle. As they looked themselves up and down, each of them were marveling at their own unique shining armor of unblemished metal; they touched it feeling its smoothness and complexity.

"Do not be taken back by the Pirist Olhy. Is this not only an example, a mere shadow, of what I can do? Increase your faith and abounding courage will come forth; be steadfast and your valor shall pass the test. Open your eyes and see what has become of the wicked; the perverse generation who rejected my grace," Jesus said.

Michael and Gabriel were caught up in the moment and they hadn't taken notice of the scene below them. Situated in a deep valley between two great mounds were millions of beings. These beings were actually huge ugly demons but as Michael and Gabriel looked down on them from high above, they appeared to be as small as ants. It was blatantly obvious that nearly all of Hell had assembled for battle; the legions were well organized and arranged in straight, orderly lines. Hell's ranks were so large that their numbers were beyond count and even though the angels were high among the clouds and miles above the earth, the demons' chants echoed upward sending chills down Michael's and Gabriel's spines. Their chants, both wretched and vile, were in the forbidden tongue, which is spoken only by the fallen ones. Truly, in that hour, the earth shook with the rage of the dark prince's slaves. This was the hour that Hell had been anticipating and it had finally arrived; indeed, this was the time they had been long in preparing for since their revolt in Heaven and their fall from God's grace.

On the opposite end of the vast ravine, a safe distance from the forces of Hell stood another army. They were as still and as silent as statues, lined up in perfect formation. In comparison to the countless legions of Hell, their numbers were inordinately small. Michael and Gabriel were dumbfounded at the scenario that was unfolding right before their eyes.

"You are gazing upon the plane of Megiddo," Jesus, breaking the ominous silence, declared. "It is here that Satan's dark legions have come to make war against Heaven and the righteous."

Christ then looked at both of them with righteous zeal in his eyes.

"Destiny has arrived. It is knocking at the doors of your hearts, waiting for you to answer—" Jesus paused as tears began to swell in his eyes and he wept.

"Will you go," with loving compassion in his voice, he said. "Will you fight in my name? Will you believe on my name that you can overcome the enemy? With all of your heart will you trust in me?"

"Yes Lord, we will follow," in unison, Michael and Gabriel replied with an unbridled passion and zeal unsurpassed by any angel that ever was or ever will be.

"With all of my heart, I will follow you my King, my Savior, even to the ends of the earth," Gabriel said; he now appeared taller than ever and there was boldness in his eyes.

"I will follow you always, Jesus. I would give my life for you a thousand times over if I was able and, even then such a sacrifice would not be adequate enough for your glory and majesty," Michael uttered, sincerely; he appeared royal and magnificent in his shining armor.

The Son of God smiled upon them, in appreciation of their unwavering loyalty.

"My grace is sufficient for you. Truly, I have searched your hearts and behold your words speak the truth. For that, you are eternally rewarded. See now, my breath of life has filled you both," Jesus said.

In that precise moment a miracle occurred, for the Spirit of the Lord came upon them both and their faces beamed with the glory of the Lord.

"Lord, let not I or Gabriel lead the battle, but you. Surely, the enemy will flee before your mighty presence," the archangel boldly said.

"Fear not, for I am with you," Christ boldly declared. "Do

not be dismayed, but behold, I am your strong tower. I will strengthen you; I will be your help when the way is dark; I will come to your aid when evil is near. Truly, I will uphold you with my victorious right hand."

What Jesus spoke next would shape the pending ages to come.

"Remember this, when you see the Son of God riding on the clouds and descending upon the earth, truly then, the end is at hand. All evil will then be vanquished from the heavens and the earth and the enemy will be defeated once and for all."

Jesus lifted his hands towards Heaven.

"*Yawshah' Adonai*," Christ blessed the angels, in the age-old tongue. The words went forth like a mighty rushing wind; for Christ's tongue was like a mighty scepter; his voice transcended the natural realm, surpassing all powers of the universe and igniting a Holy fire in their hearts.

Suddenly, a cloud of brilliant light surrounded the Son of God and in the twinkling of an eye, he vanished into thin air. And just as suddenly as Jesus had left, so was the suddenness with which the cloud began to descend towards the earth with Michael and Gabriel still standing on it. The angels turned to prayer.

"Yea, though I walk through the valley of the shadow of death, I will fear no evil, for you are with me. Your Son and your Holy Spirit, they comfort me," they prayed.

The battlefield was a mere thousand paces below them now. The thought of encountering millions upon millions of vicious demons in battle would have intimidated even the most stout-hearted soldier, yet Michael and Gabriel remained steadfast and courageous, for the Spirit of the LORD was upon them. In one accord, the demons were chanting in the forbidden language. Demons of all shapes and sizes were gathered for war: some were giant and burly, others were twisted and distorted with malice, and others were angelic in appearance but still horribly wicked. The presence of evil was so heavy that it was suffocating and the morale of the righteous ones was beginning to wane in the shadow of the massive army of Satan's minions.

Michael and Gabriel watched in horror as a dark foreboding mist materialized on the horizon. The Host of Heaven was held at bay, helpless, as the darkness devoured the light of day with its foul vapor. The mist blew and churned, swelling into a massive black cloud of evil, as it rolled over the Plain of Megiddo, gaining momentum and strength as it moved along. This eerie storm did not flash with lightning nor did it rumble with thunder; this was not an ordinary storm that was produced by nature, but it was a hideous force of evil that had been prepared by the Prince of Darkness for this moment in time. He had concocted a silent weapon, with the most sinister of intention: to wield destruction on the earth and to annihilate all things righteous. Contained within this storm was the manifestation of iniquity in its vilest form; it was saturated with all things unholy, everything wicked and sinister dwelled in its rank mist. The demons fed off of its evil and sinful energy and, without it they were powerless; but with it they were invincible.

Michael and Gabriel grimaced as they descended lower into dark vapor; it reeked with the foul stench of decaying flesh. The angels gasped from the heaviness of the putrid air and coughed to clear their throats and then they prayed against the malevolent power of Hell. Even so, it didn't stop there; for they knew they were moving in closer to the enemy, as the demons' chanting grew increasingly louder. The angels could now hear nothing but the roaring mantra of the millions upon millions of demons, foaming at the mouth and raring for battle. Like drums beating in the dark, the seraphim's hearts pounded in anticipation of battle. This was the ultimate event that Michael and Gabriel had been preparing for, and the time had arrived for them to implement their sharply honed skills of warfare and to summon up every bit of knowledge and wisdom that they had acquired from the Ancient of Days for battle is at hand.

"The darkness may have blinded our eyes, Gabe, but never God's vision," Michael put his hand firmly on Gabe's shoulder and said. "Be strong and courageous and fear not, for this hour the power of the Almighty is upon us."

"Fear? What is fear in the midst of his presence; his perfect love banishes all fear. My hope is in the LORD and in him alone do I trust," Gabriel uttered.

"Gabe, your words have truly lifted my spirit," Michael smiled at him through the thick haze and said. "The enemy may vastly outnumber the Host of Heaven this hour, yet I will declare that I will not back down."

At that same moment, the Host of Heaven was far below them, trembling in absolute terror at the presence of an evil, darker than a moonless night. Raphael sat on a noble white steed at the head of the ranks. He peered across the battlefield to determine the position of the enemy, but the darkness had obscured all vision.

"Pray! Pray, you seraphim of Heaven," Raphael shouted orders to the seraphim.

The horses neighed and stirred restlessly; they were nervous and frightened by the chanting and the darkness. Sweat was running down the angels' faces and their eyes were stricken with fear. Chaos had not yet prevailed, but it was at the threshold; eagerly attempting to disrupt and stifle the seraph's praying.

"Shout to the LORD. Claim victory," Uriel stood by Raphael's side and cried out.

Across the plain, standing upon a mound, was Magos the acting chief sorcerer. Magos stood with the brotherhood of thirteen sorcerers forming a circle and with hands joined they spoke the dark incantations in the forbidden tongue. Magos' eyes were menacing, glowing like red-hot embers filled with the fire of Hell; being the chief sorcerer, he chanted the spell Elymas had suffered hard and long to create. As the brotherhood repeated his words after him, their eyes became filled with the fiery reflection of Hell. Suddenly, a great earthquake shook the battlefield and the earth trembled with fury; a crack ran across the center of the mound and it widened into a large gap. Fire and ash violently erupted from the gaping crevice and a large being rose up in the midst of it.

"Behold, Luminarous, the seventh star of the luminaries, ruler of the stars and principalities of the universe," Magos uttered; his voice was deep and menacing.

A revoltingly sinister laugh rang forth from the fallen star's mouth; followed by an immense earthquake that rumbled and shook violently throughout the valley.

"Time to finish what has begun. The inevitable annihilation of

Heaven's Host," Magos whispered to himself. The chief sorcerer summoned every bit of malicious wickedness that was within him and uttered the final part of Elymas' spell; the brotherhood boldly repeated each word and their chant grew increasingly louder until every demon present on the plain could hear the incantation. The spell flawlessly achieved the purpose for which it was formulated and to the demons' advantage, the Host of Heaven appeared to be even more daunted and confused now.

"Is that all you have," Uriel stared into the darkness and shouted. "Is that it? What is your power compared to the Most High."

"That's it brother. Let them know that the Host will not stand idly by," Raphael said. He then prayed silently. *Open my eyes oh LORD, so I may see the wicked devices of the enemy.* Immediately, the Holy Spirit revealed to him what Magos and the sorcerers were doing so he knew exactly how to counter the spells of the enemy.

Raphael's dark red hair blew wildly in the fierce wind, and his stunning green eyes were sparkling with the power of the Holy Spirit.

"LORD my God, part the evil that is before me so I might look upon my enemy and speak your words of deliverance," Raphael cried to the LORD.

The dark cloud parted and Raphael took sight of Magos; although Raphael's strength is mighty among angels, his keen eyesight is the greatest among all the Host of Heaven. He gazed clearly across Megiddo and fixed his eyes on a stunned Magos, who stared back at him.

"There you are," Raphael uttered.

"Where has your help gone, Raphael," Magos, as if he knew Raphael could hear him, said. "Where is your general, the archangel? What about your great warrior, Gabriel? Watch as I dismantle Heaven's pathetic army, Raphael." And then Magos put all of his focus upon conjuring up each and every Ruah of Hell.

"I've borne through this long enough, Uriel. It is time that I offer them an opportunity to surrender," Raphael uttered.

"Brother, allow me to ride by your side," Uriel eagerly requested.

"Stay here Uriel. You are to assume command of the Host should I not come back alive," Raphael answered, concisely, and reared his horse up to its hind legs.

"The LORD is with you, Raphael," Uriel shouted; as Raphael headed across the plain towards the enemy line, Uriel prayed, *God, go with your loyal servant and protect him with your power.*

The gap between Raphael and the enemy was rapidly closing, as his steed's hooves pounded furiously against the ground. Although the wind was whipping harshly against his face, he kept his sight aimed straight ahead; across the battlefield, he espied a large menacing figure moving towards him. It was Beltezar seated on a scaly gray monster, a ghastly intimidating beast with long burly legs and a set of sharp fangs dripping with the blood of a fresh kill. Raphael met up with Beltezar and his beastly mount in the center of the vast battlefield. His horse became uneasy, being frightened at the sight of the monster, but Raphael quickly gained control of the steed.

"It appears he thinks your horse would be quite delicious," Beltezar mocked.

"Keep your distance, lest I slay that foul beast you ride," Raphael snapped back.

"Please do forgive me for not properly addressing you," Beltezar said, derisively. "Now, that I have cleared myself of any discrepancies, I must say it is fancy meeting you here, Raphael. I thought you had more sense then to take sides with a company of fools."

"Spare me your poisoned tongue, lest I properly address you with the blade from my sword," Raphael boldly said.

"Fine, fine. There is no need to be boisterous," Beltezar, annoyed by Raphael's words, said, somberly. "Here's the offer, and I do advise you and your measly army of seraphim to take it. I will offer it once and only once."

Beltezar spurred his beast to move closer to the angel and the demon leaned in towards Raphael, facing him closely, eye-to-eye and glared at him with utter confidence.

"Your forces will be totally annihilated within the hour," Beltezar proclaimed, arrogantly. "Earth will be destroyed and Heaven will be conquered. Why do I say this? Because I know that Hell has the three supernatural swords. I have wielded Logos myself and Lucifer has held the Sword of the Spirit in his palms. Hell now holds the true power, the same power that your God possesses is now ours to wield against him and his kingdom. You know, as well as I, that all of Heaven is doomed unless you can agree to the LORD Lucifer's terms. That is to say my master has promised he will generously spare your life if you heed his request. He asks only that—"

"Beltezar the puppet," Raphael interrupted his rhetorical rambling, and declared, defiantly. "I think that title suites you quite well. You are nothing but a mere slave to your master Satan. Send him a message for me, will you? My God makes no compromises. He is who he says he is. He is the great I Am and before him there was no God and there is no other god besides him. I will give you less than an hour's time to gather your legions and go back to Hell, where you belong. Or else God's army will march on you and like a fierce tidal wave we will show you no mercy. By his spirit we will be triumphant." Raphael glared into Beltezar's eyes.

"Fool, you forget who you're dealing with," Beltezar exploded with anger and screamed. "You dare speak to the general of Hell's royal legions like that? Raphael, you're not a general and you're certainly not the archangel; you're nothing but a worthless infidel. Your archangel is dead and your great warrior, Gabriel, is rotting away as I speak. You and your meager army stand not even a chance. I'll spare my soldiers from battle and send the Ruah to devour your spirits. All of Heaven will now pay for your insolence. Before the hour has ended, either you will be dead, lying face down in the mire, or you will be my master's newest slave. Either way I say death to all of you infidels."

Beltezar presumed that his arrogant words had pierced Raphael's heart with total trepidation. Raphael turned his gaze to Heaven and prayed for strength from the God Almighty. As he was in the middle of praying, he beheld two beings shining brilliantly and descending from above on a white cloud. The darkness began to give way to light and the beings came closer, radiating with a blinding holy light.

"Your prayers are but empty words coming from an empty vessel," Beltezar reared his lizard in a display of intimidation, and said.

As they were descending, Michael and Gabriel were not aware of the glorious aura all about them that shined forth so brightly, yet the radiance that poured forth from them shattered the darkness scattering the hideous strength in all directions. Uriel and the Host watched in awe as they witnessed their brothers alive and riding on clouds.

"To God be the glory. It is, indeed, a miracle," Uriel shouted to the warriors.

Magos was taken by complete surprise; he ceased casting his spells, as did the brotherhood. The chief sorcerer peered into the sky and beheld the bright and righteous beings.

"No, it can't be. Call on the Ruah. Summon the principalities of Hell. We cannot be defeated and we must conquer," Magos put his hands to his head and screamed.

Magos quickly turned and ordered his servant, "Bring me Logos and the Sword of the Spirit. It is time to finish my ultimate incantation—Hell's Fury."

Magos then greedily mumbled to himself, "The culmination of all of my suffering and labor has finally come to fruition. The doom of Heaven has been made ready."

Across Megiddo, Michael and Gabriel had completely descended now and as they came to light at the frontline of the Host, the heavenly warriors shouted out loud praises to Heaven, shattering the arrogant confidence of the enemy and dismantling Hell's devious devices.

"Michael? Gabriel? Inconceivable! The archangel is dead. I saw to it myself. Gabriel, he's trapped beneath the earth," Beltezar muttered to himself in disbelief.

"You had better rethink your strategies, because it looks like Jehovah has a few surprises in store for you," Raphael looked Beltezar in the face and uttered.

Raphael pulled his horse around and swiftly rode off to meet his brothers. Beltezar knew this meant war; he turned his scaly beast and sped back to lead the legions of Hell.

"Praises and honor to Jehovah, for he has delivered his salvation to us all," Raphael rode like the wind and shouted, just as he was approaching the host.

"My brother Raphael, it is the Christ who is our salvation. He has sent us to you in your darkest hour," Michael boldly proclaimed. Then Uriel rode up on his horse, accompanied by two brave warriors on white steeds.

"Then the glory and honor belongs to Christ, for it is he who has revived our hope this hour," Uriel exclaimed; by his keen hearing, he had overheard their conversation. Uriel dismounted his horse and the two warriors with him climbed off their steeds. Raphael jumped off of his horse and then, he and Uriel heartily embraced Michael and Gabriel like long-lost brothers reunited.

After their joyous greetings had been exchanged, Uriel walked over to the horses that the two other warriors had ridden and he led them to the general and his lieutenant.

"These extraordinary white steeds are for you, Michael and Gabriel," Uriel said. "Their names are revered among the majestic breed of horses: Doonatos, meaning mighty and strong, and Tifawrah, denotes bravery, splendor, and glory. These noble steeds were sent down by the Almighty himself, reserved for the moment that you should arrive."

"Take your places and lead us into battle," Raphael said, fervently.

"What strength. What valor. Doonatos, together we will smite the enemy," Gabriel said, patting the horse on its side. And eager to fight the enemy, he immediately jumped on Doonatos.

"Tifawrah, your bravery shall carry us valiantly through battle," Michael whispered into the horse's ear. Then he climbed on Tifawrah's back; he was the larger of the two horses and had a long flowing mane. The archangel sat himself confidently erect upon Tifawrah and turned him to face the Host, who were one thousand in number.

These were the seraphim warriors who had been selected by Jesus, meticulously chosen from among the millions of angels in Heaven because of their dauntless courage and immense stature. Michael raised the Sword of the Spirit straight up, high into the air; the herald angels, who were interspersed throughout the army of host, took heed to his signal and sounded their golden trumpets, announcing that the battle was at hand.

"Victory belongs to our God," general Michael proclaimed, loudly.

"Victory is the LORD's," Gabriel, Uriel, Raphael, and the entire host of Heaven followed his lead with great enthusiasm, as they boldly shouted.

As their shouts rang out, a brilliant light with unequaled intensity, suddenly burst forth through the shadow, and the sinister army of darkness fled before the unbearable glory of the LORD. The warrior seraphim shouted out their praises to the Most High, their deliverer and their mighty shield.

The enemy forces trembled in terror at the sight of the pure light and they screamed out curses as they shook their fists in the air. Beltezar, sparing not a moment, turned his mount quickly. The legions parted to make way for him as he charged to the rear of the army, jumped off the beast and hurriedly ascended the mound where the sorcerers stood.

"Unleash the Ruah!" Beltezar sternly ordered Magos.

Magos, without question or hesitation, immediately opened the portal from Hell and hundreds upon thousands of dark spirits came pouring out onto the plain. The demons roared with enthusiasm for they believed that with the Ruah was their assurance of victory.

"Pay heed, demons," Carchemish shouted. "The Ruah will devour the enemies' spirit and feast on their souls."

The legion roared and cursed Heaven.

"Conquer the enemy, Ruah," Carchemish demanded; the evil spirits obeyed his command, passing swiftly overhead.

Meanwhile, Beltezar was inquiring of Magos, "Is the incantation complete?"

"Yes, my liege," Magos answered. "We have but to add the final weapon and the portal to Heaven will be open."

"Luminarous will be unbeatable and Hell will be unstoppable," Beltezar, grinning with arrogance, declared.

The fallen star was restrained in the middle of the brotherhood; he had been bound by the sorcerers' spells and was helplessly at their bidding. His mind had been perverted and his body was distorted. Who could recognize the fallen star? The beauty and splendor with which he once illuminated the heavens had vanished. His thought process, his mind and heart, had been cruelly stripped from him and were no longer there. He was now a soulless creature; an evil abomination that was created for the sole purpose of destroying all that is righteous and holy.

The archangel took command of the army and reared Tifawrah on his hind legs.

"Join with me, my brothers, and ride by my side," raising his sword high, he addressed his captains, Raphael and Uriel, and his lieutenant general Gabriel.

Michael rode along the front of the ranks of seraphim warriors.

"Raise the banners," he shouted as he passed before them. "Hoist the standard of Christ. Proclaim victory in Zion."

The herald angels lifted their banners high into the air, waving them to and fro. Some banners bore the image of a lamb and other banners had Zion written across them; still others were displayed with the image of a cross. The angels quickly organized their ranks. The foot soldiers bearing shields and swords moved to the front and the warriors mounted on steeds brought up the rear. The herald angels lined the perimeter of the army, but a few remained in the midst of the host, bearing the banner of the cross. Michael suddenly sensed the presence of immense evil approaching.

"My general, look," Gabriel pointed across Megiddo and shouted, urgently.

The Ruah were charging directly towards them and their numbers were so great that they cloaked the sky with a blanket of ominous darkness. As the menacing enemy charged toward them with the speed of rushing wind, the army of seraphim was becoming steadily more anxious and fearful. Their steeds became rowdy with uneasiness.

Michael immediately took command of the situation.

"Blow the trumpets for Zion. Raise the banners on high," Michael looked to the heralds and shouted. Then, the archangel looked out and surveyed the entire army.

"Do not fear them," Michael boldly proclaimed. "Do not tremble at the Ruah. The enemy has no power over you. The Ruah cannot claim your spirit, for you have been redeemed by the Christ Jesus, Son of God and by his power we will overcome the dark powers of Hell."

Michael then turned his horse around and faced, head on, the imminent threat of the Ruah. The Archangel raised the Sword of the Spirit and pointing it directly at the enemy.

"*Adonai Sotayreah–Yawshaw*," he shouted with all his might.

As he bravely faced the enemy, Michael's face glowed with the glory of Heaven and his eyes were ablaze with the power of the Holy Spirit. The force of the Ruah, as they neared him, felt like a mighty gust of wind blowing harshly against the archangel's face; Tifawrah stood firmly in his place like the noble, valiant steed he was created to be. Michael glared fiercely at the advancing Ruah and he swung his sword, slicing it through the air. In a single stroke, a flash of lightning emanated from Sword of the Spirit and like a swift wave of shocking illumination, it shot out towards the enemy. The vast hoard of Ruah screamed in horror and shrieked from pain and in the blink of an eye the Ruah burst into oblivion, vanishing into thin air.

The Heavenly Host cheered, offering loud praises to their Almighty God.

Beltezar was livid that his plan had been foiled.

"Ready the portal and prepare to unleash Luminarous upon Heaven's gates," Beltezar rode his scaly beast up the mound and ordered Magos. "It is time for me to initiate an all-out onslaught on Michael and his feeble army. Their total annihilation is now at hand, mark my words, Magos."

The general rode off in a fury to lead his legions into battle.

"Soldiers of Hell, servants of the LORD Lucifer, rise to your duty. The hour has come to destroy the heavenly host. We must kill them all. Spare not one," proceeding to the front of the ranks, the general shouted at the top of his lungs.

The demons refrained from their usual roars and chants; instead, they straightened their lines and formed into tighter ranks; nearly all of Hell was assembled on Megiddo and prepared to fight a fierce battle.

Beltezar summoned his sergeants and captains to his side.

"You will lead the surge," he ordered, speaking directly to Carchemish. "Your legion will spring on the enemy like a blood-thirsty dragon. You know what to do. Now deliver my orders and make it quick. We launch our assault within the hour." Beltezar rode off to address the legions again, to boost their moral. Carchemish assumed the role of lieutenant general and delivered the general Beltezar's strategies to the sergeants and captains. There were a total of ten thousand sergeants and one thousand captains gathered to hear the lieutenant general; Carchemish kept it brief and terse, so the demons could resume their command positions and prepare to march on the Host.

With Gabriel by his side, Michael prayed for renewed strength from the Almighty; he felt physically drained from the intensity of the spiritual battle with the Ruah. He pondered upon how, not long ago, he had been held prisoner in Desmeeos'; beaten and abused by the demons and tormented by the Ruah until he finally died. The LORD had resurrected him from death and Jesus had given him new life. He was thankful for the strength the LORD had given him to come against the multitude of Ruah, just moments ago. And now, even in his exhaustion, the archangel began to feel new strength rising from the inner depths of his spirit; it was a gift from the Father of Lights.

The heavenly host was filled with the fear of the LORD. This moment had marked the confirmation of their faith; for the fear of the LORD is the beginning of wisdom and the knowledge of the Holy One, is understanding, and without it the host would be unable to believe for the miracle that was needed to defeat the enemy this day. The enemy's numbers overshadowed them a thousand times over and more.

"Let your voices reach the gates of the Holy City," Raphael cried out, commanding the seraphim warriors to send up their prayers as an offering before the throne of God.

"The time for war is nigh. Pray, seraphim of God," Uriel shouted; he rode up and down the ranks calling out and as his horse galloped along the ranks, its hooves resounded loudly against the earth.

The enemy's confidence was impregnable like a wall of steel. Demons were foaming at the mouth as they anticipated this battle to be the ultimate opportunity for them to totally annihilate their disinherited brothers, the angels of God. As far as the demons were concerned, the echoes of the seraphim praying to God were nothing more than pitifully desperate cries for mercy.

In the meantime, Gabriel was interceding for Michael and ministering to him.

"May new strength soar within you, like the wings of an eagle taking it to new heights," Gabriel prayed with a holy passion.

Michael felt the power of the Holy Spirit swelling inside of him and coming forth. The archangel knew that his time had arrived and his destiny was about to be fulfilled.

"It is time Michael, for your new character to come forth. You are now the embodiment of my salvation; in your heart I dwell forevermore. Michael, your destiny has arrived and I call forth the warrior within," a voice of Jesus spoke to his heart, it was calm and soothing, yet commanding.

Chills raced up and down Michael's spine as a narrow stream of radiant light flashed down from Heaven and beamed on Michael, and he alone.

"Come Forth Warrior of God!" the voice of God thundered from above like the sound of many waterfalls. Suddenly, Michael's Sword of the Spirit illuminated with the power of the Holy Spirit and his armor shone vibrantly with the glory of God; a tongue of fire appeared over his head and he began speaking in the ancient tongue of creation.

Gabriel, taken up in awe with what the LORD was doing, happened to be standing in Michael's shadow and a tongue of fire materialized above his head. He began uttering words in the tongue of creation.

The entire army of Heaven beheld the miraculous scene unfolding before them and they were totally entranced by the marvelous things the LORD had done. Then, in the blink of an eye, tongues of fire were resting above Raphael and Uriel's heads. The two captains immediately took off on their steeds, going in opposite directions and riding along the ranks of heavenly warriors, they spread the tongues of fire throughout the entire army of Host.

Before the enemy had time to even realize what was happening, a tongue of fire now rested on each warrior; the entire army of Heaven began shouting at the top of their lungs in the holy and renowned language of God. It was a remarkable sight to behold: a thousand strong were praising the LORD in the ancient tongue, the herald angels were each waving their banners above their heads and raising high the standard of Christ. There was the general, Archangel Michael, riding on his magnificent white steed, Tifawrah, as he valiantly led the heavenly host. Michael's face was shining with the splendor of the LORD and all the angels took on a glow, in the light of God's holy presence. The anointing of the Holy Spirit had fallen on the one thousand seraphim warriors and the truth be told, they were now each empowered with the strength of a hundred mighty warriors.

THE END OF THE BEGINNING

The entire army of Satan had witnessed the miraculous transformation of the Heavenly Host, as they stood and watched from
their ranks across the battleground. Beltezar was nothing short
of perplexed and trying desperately to recover from the shock of
it all; the demons were growing anxious, the sergeants, captains,
and all the commanding officers in the army were losing control
of their legions. Beltezar was well aware that, if he didn't do something fast the confusion and chaos would surely run rampant.
The general reared up his giant ugly beast and charged towards
the mound where Magos was. The beast stormed through the
midst of the legions, parting demons like the wind against shafts
of wheat.

Beltezar sighted a glowing ring in the sky above the mound.

"The portal," Beltezar cried, in utter relief.

"Luminarous should be complete by now. Why is he stall-
ing," the general mumbled as he scurried up the mound get a
closer look.

On top of the mound, he spied two tall sorcerers, who happened to be widely renowned for their dark magic. They were
dressed completely in red and sported green cloaks that flowed
down their backs. The sorcerers were walking slowly towards the

fallen star; they each held a mysterious object in their hands and the objects were veiled in secrecy.

Beltezar, incredulously, took note that Luminarous had nearly doubled in size. He remarked to himself that this was not the same fallen star he had dragged to Hell from that murky and fusty cave; at this moment Luminarous was more menacing and terrifying to look upon than ever before. To be forthright, Beltezar was quite frightened by him. More daunting still, a hefty wound was in the side of the fallen star presumably where the LORD Lucifer had pierced him with the supernatural sword, Awven. This was part of the incantation that would allow Luminarous to breach Heaven in order for the forces of Hell to raid Mount Zion.

Now, all that was needed to complete the spell was for the last two supernatural blades to pierce Luminarous' hands. The two tall sorcerers removed the covering from the objects they had brought to the mound; one of them was securely holding Logos and the other had his grip on the Sword of the Spirit.

"What power does he possess that he can wield the archangel's sword," Beltezar remarked. It then dawned on him that it could not be the true Sword of the Spirit.

"It's a fake," Beltezar uttered, but it was too late; for just as he had spoken those words the sorcerers were already in position. Two more sorcerers, tall and brooding, were in position and they fearfully grabbed hold of the fallen star's hands to raise them precisely into position. With trembling hands, the sorcerer holding Logos and the sorcerer wielding the Sword of the Spirit plunged the tips of the swords through Luminarous' giant palms. The fallen star groaned in agony from the pain, clenching his jaws and gritting his teeth, he growled angrily at the demons around him.

"The spell is working," Beltezar cried out; relief came over him.

This would give Luminarous the ultimate power that only God possessed. But suddenly a violent wind blew out of the portal. The powerful wind encircled Luminarous, swirling around like a powerful tornado. The four sorcerers, who had performed the ritual, were lifted above the ground by the wind and sucked straight into the portal. Luminarous roared and growled. He fought madly to free himself, but his struggling was in vain; he was helplessly trapped within the storm that had engulfed him.

"Do something. Conjure a spell," Beltezar screamed at Magos.

Magos was frozen with fear; speechless and immobilized with horror by the unexpected events unfolding right before his eyes. Beltezar jumped off the leathery beast and drew his sword in a fit of rage. He kicked Magos to the ground. Magos was beginning to hallucinate; the dark magic and malicious conjuring that he so cunningly practiced, had come to haunt him, confusing his mind and tormenting spirit. As he cowered on the ground in front of Beltezar, he imagined the general to be a ferocious monster, hungry for demon flesh.

The tornado blew and twisted with such terrible force that it was shaking the foundation of the mound. As the ground shook and trembled, Luminarous was roaring like an angry ferocious lion.

"Must I do everything myself. You're pathetic. Utterly useless, I say," Beltezar scorned Magos, focusing all of his hatred and frustration on him. And in a mad frenzy, the general drove the blade of his sword straight through the belly of the sorcerer. Magos let out a piercing shriek and then his body shriveled into dust, the punishing effect of Beltezar's blade.

Beltezar turned and stared into the twisting funnel of wind; he knew that Luminarous was somewhere in the middle of the blinding whirlwind, but he couldn't see him. The general spoke every incantation he knew and conjured up whatever spell came to mind, in desperate effort to combat the supernatural power, but nothing was working. Instead, the wind was gaining even more strength and speed. The great general was forced to concede to its power, so he backed down, jumped onto his beast and scurried down the mound. Just as he reached the bottom, the sorcerers on the mound were suddenly sucked into the portal, vanishing from sight.

The velocity of the tornado had increased to twice the speed, raising its intensity and doubling its force; then, in the blink of an eye it expanded, totally engulfing the mound. Fortunately for Beltezar, he had ridden to a safe distance and all legions had fled for safety. Chaos ensued and spread like wildfire among the forces of Hell. Beltezar, out of anger and utter frustration, became like a bloodthirsty wolf barking orders out, here and there, in a frantic attempt to muster his troops.

Michael was filled with the Holy Spirit and mounted on the back of Tifawrah; he appeared like a mighty king leading his people into battle. The archangel rode like the wind down the battle line with the Sword of the Spirit gripped tightly in his right hand.

"Glory be to the Lamb of God," Michael raised his sword high into the air and shouted. "Give thanks to the King of Kings and LORD of LORDS. He has sent his spirit to confuse the enemy and dismantle their sinister device."

Michael slowed Tifawrah to a canter and steadied him at the center of the front flank. Michael gazed across the multitude of heavenly warriors; a tongue of flame flickered brightly above each angel's head. Yet, even as impressive as this display of warriors was, Michael's face lit up with pure delight when he caught sight of Caleb's face amongst them. Everywhere he turned, he beheld friends and brothers among the host of seraphim. A tear as sweet as honey rolled down his cheek and then another; for the first time he truly saw the angels as the LORD did. God had opened Michael's eyes and his heart was filled with a deep love and compassion for the seraphim

"Michael, you are truly mighty among the seraphim," a small still voice spoke to his heart. "You are the greatest in height and mightiest in strength, but that is not why I have chosen you. For I look not on the exterior, but my eyes peer into the heart; and in you I have found a heart of gold, a heart after my own. This is why you were chosen, from among the innumerable Host of Heaven, for a destiny unlike that of any other angel in the history of creation. Michael, now look before you and see my servants with whom I am well pleased; I have entrusted them into your hands, my archangel.

When you gaze upon the enemy, do not fear their size or their vast numbers. Instead, fix your eyes on me and trust wholly in me. Rely entirely on my holy name, the name above all other names. And remember this, my power is made perfect in weakness. The time is neigh. Take hold of your destiny, Archangel, and lead Heaven to victory."

Michael had been engrossed with listening attentively to the voice of Christ and then it came to his attention that his captains and lieutenant general surrounded him.

"The enemy is busy reforming their ranks," Gabriel stated.

"What of Luminarous? Can you see him," the archangel gripped to the Sword of the Spirit, and inquired.

"Raphael has gone to scout sir," Uriel replied, quickly, before Gabriel could.

At that exact moment, Raphael galloped up on his horse and skidded to a halt.

"The enemy has re-organized," Raphael said. "They have positioned three of their smaller legions to the eastern perimeter of their forces. Another three legions, larger than the others, have converged to the western border of their camp and Beltezar has taken his position in command of a vast legion at the rear of their army. Also, the giant mound has vanished. Truly a miracle has taken place, for the sorcerers and even the fallen star Luminarous, have vanished into the portal."

"The enemy can no longer use him. Luminarous is now in the hands of the Almighty, the only true judge," Michael expressed, solemnly.

"Gabriel, take up leadership of the rear guard," Michael said, ardently. "You shall lead the four hundred on horseback. Raphael, lead the right flank with one hundred of the tallest and strongest on foot. Uriel, take charge of the left flank and bring with you one hundred of our swiftest warriors on horseback. I shall command the front rank of the remaining four hundred seraphim on foot."

"Brothers, know this, the hand of God is upon us and by the discretion of the Holy Spirit, each angel has been chosen for your particular leadership; they will follow your command. Trust in the LORD always and his strength and power will go with you. Now go and take your positions and I will address the heavenly host," the archangel declared.

Gabriel mounted on Doonatos and rode swiftly around the ranks to the rear of the army. Raphael and Uriel rode their steeds away, fast as the wind, and took their places on the right and on the left. Michael positioned himself on top of Tifawrah at the center of the front flank and, with the presence of command in his eyes he gazed steadily upon the Host.

Seeking the voice of the Holy Spirit, the archangel found the words to speak.

"Seraphim, warriors, you have been chosen from among the countless Host of Heaven. Christ selected you, the Son of the Almighty, not for your sheer strength and power, but for what he has seen in each of your hearts. He sees you as warriors, defenders of his kingdom," Michael declared. Cheers erupted amongst the Host and the noise carried over into the enemy camp.

"Hell has come to earth to destroy all that our God and King has created," Michael continued. "They have assembled against us to annihilate the Host and all of Heaven. Their sole purpose is to kill and destroy. Satan is bent on conquering Mount Zion and claiming the throne from the God of Ages. Long has he prepared for this hour; he has summoned nearly all of Hell to Megiddo. He dispatched his Ruah against us and the mighty power of Christ banished the evil spirits to Hell. So I say to you this hour, do not tremble before them, even though the enemy is as great in number as the grains of sand on a desert. We will not fear them. For greater is he who is in us than all the legions and principalities of Hell."

The enemy began to chant blasphemes against Heaven. The demons were so numerous and their voices were so loud that the earth shook from the sheer magnitude of their noise.

"Host of Heaven, shout to the LORD. Let your voices reach God's throne," Michael, gathering all of the might within him, shouted; his voice blasted like a trumpet.

The demons roared and cheered even louder.

"That's it. Time to strike fear in their hearts," Beltezar shouted.

Suddenly a sound like the rushing of a mighty monsoon swept over the legions of Hell. It was the voices of a thousand seraphim joined together in unison and giving glory to the LORD.

"Worthy is the Lamb," the warriors of God shouted. Again and again, they boasted loudly in the LORD; raising their voices like peals of thunder, they sent forth their praises.

Beltezar commanded the demons to roar even louder, to overcome the shouting of the angelic army, but it was to no avail. The hand of God was upon the heavenly host and there wasn't anything

Beltezar could do to rival their noise. Millions upon millions of demons could not match the praises of a thousand angels.

The angels carried on with their praising for many moments until Michael motioned for them to be still, and peace commenced.

"Be still and wait upon the LORD, for he alone is our strength," Michael cried out with a commanding voice. As soon as the words rolled off Michael's tongue, a deafening rumble thundered throughout the air and at the same time an earthquake violently shook the ground beneath the seraphim's feet.

"Behold the enemy is on the march," Michael shouted, steering Tifawrah around.

An estimated five million demons were marching right down the center of Megiddo. Rocks and stones crumbled beneath their marching feet; the earth cracked beneath them and expanded into crevices from the sheer force of their momentum. The sky darkened, the atmosphere became oppressive and the ominous force was looming on the horizon. Lightning cracked and thunder rolled, as the power of sin and iniquity permeated the air, playing host to the legions of Hell.

The approaching legion of five million demons, malicious and bloodthirsty, appeared intimidating on a grand scale. Even so, the imminent threat of millions of demons awaiting their orders at the right and left ranks, held even more peril. There were still at least ten million of the strongest demons, all eager to fight, standing on the rear perimeter of the camp and waiting to join the battle.

"Lucifer reigns. Death to Jehovah," at general Beltezar's command, all the demons chanted, raising their voices in unison.

Michael grimaced with disdain at the enemy's words. Then the spirit of the LORD came upon him and the archangel was provoked to anger; he glared at enemy as they were preparing to attack and defying their ranks.

"Jehovahjireh. My God sees your sin," the archangel shouted, mightily.

Michael then surveyed the army of God and, looking upon

their faces, he could see that the Holy Spirit was resting upon them; all of the warriors' faces were glowing with a terrible light from the glory of God. Their eyes were gleaming like fire with the zeal of the LORD and even in the dismal light; the host's armor shimmered with a candescent light.

The four hundred warriors, under Michael's command, all carried swords with blades that shined magnificently and their shields bore the sign of the cherubim, the anointed worshipers of God.

The warriors joined to Gabriel were all on horseback; they were equipped with strong spears that were plated with silver, bearing sharp tips that were covered in gold. Their royal steeds neighed and scuffed their hooves against the ground in anticipation of a fight.

The seraphim led by Captain Raphael, were among the tallest and strongest; they had the broadest shoulders out of all who were in the army. Their long golden hair blew fiercely in the wind as they held their lances high.

The angels assigned to Uriel were probably the most eager to confront the enemy. They were keenly alert and kept their sights totally focused on the enemy line as it advanced toward them; and their confidence was unshakeable because their hearts remained steadfast in Jesus.

The herald angels were stationed throughout the ranks; their banners held high and proudly waved the standard of Christ for all to see. The warriors of God were, indeed, fully prepared for battle.

Little did Michael and the Host know, but there were more than one hundred million seraphim interceding for them in Heaven; only when the enemy was nearly upon them was Michael informed of this news.

"Do not be anxious," the LORD spoke to Michael's heart. "This is your destiny. Lead my angels to victory. For even now, hope is stirring in the hearts of my seraphim. Michael, all of Heaven stands behind you this hour; their hearts are with you. And in spirit and in truth, I am with you my loyal servant, my mighty archangel, and my beloved child. Ride to victory Michael, Archangel of Heaven."

The enemy line had advanced even closer; they were now just

about a thousand paces from where the archangel sat on Tifawrah. Michael's heart was so filled with courage that fear no longer had a place to reside. The hearts of the seraphim were fully turned to Christ; their strength was multiplied a hundredfold and they were ready for battle. Their eyes were shining with boldness and victory was written across their faces. This is the hour.

The time has come to be the warrior I was called to be and the leader I was destined to be, thought Michael, *the defender of God's throne, and the guardian of the crown of Christ.* He looked with love and admiration upon his brothers and friends, his cohorts in battle.

Then, suddenly but not unexpectedly, the enemy began their charge. The demons rushed towards the Host like a brutal sandstorm, menacing and ruthless.

Michael stretched out his arm and raised the Sword of the Spirit above his head. "Mighty and steadfast are we. Warriors of God," Michael shouted, fearlessly.

Raphael, Uriel, and Gabriel echoed their general's cry throughout the ranks.

"Mighty and steadfast are we, warriors of God," Michael's eyes shined with a fierce light, as he heard his words ringing out among the army.

"Charge on my command," the archangel shouted.

Adorned with their breastplates of righteousness; armed with swords and shields; spears and lances, the Host of Heaven stood firmly prepared and waited zealously for the battle cry to ring. The legions of hell were coming like an avalanche; the demons were armed with spears, swords, pikes, crossbows, and every deadly and torturous weapon that one could imagine. Beltezar raised his hands high and stretched them towards the plain. He chanted an incantation of fear and destruction over his enemy, but to his aggravation he found that his spells were utterly in vain. Nevertheless, the fallen angels stormed forward continually chanting war cries in the forbidden tongue; as they drew nearer to the Host, their war chants were sending tremors through the earth, shaking the ground beneath their enemy's feet. And riding in the head position was, none other than Carchemish, mounted on a large, ugly, scaly beast.

Michael looked out at the enemy and they were only a hundred yards away; he keenly directed his focus on Carchemish, staring fear directly in its face. Michael then turned and confidently looked over the army of God.

"Who is our shield and our high tower? In whom shall we trust," Michael cried.

"The LORD God Almighty," the host of Heaven loudly shouted.

Empowered with the might of the Holy Spirit, Michael raised the Sword of the Spirit and as it blazed with the light of God's power, he pointed it towards the enemy.

"Not by might. Nor by power. But by my spirit, says the LORD. Charge, you fearless warriors of Christ," Michael shouted, valiantly.

The fury of the LORD ignited Michael as he charged out onto the battlefield and riding on Tifawrah's back, he flew like the wind. Right behind him were the four hundred foot soldiers, running with the speed of a cheetah and charging full on towards the enemy.

The Battle had begun and the collision between the two enemies proved to be catastrophic for the demons. Tifawrah easily hurdled over the front line of demons and came crashing down, still on all four legs, trampling at least a dozen demons to death with his massive hooves. The Sword of the Spirit glowed with the power of God and its light blinded the enemy; when the four hundred foot soldiers arrived armed with swords and shields the enemy was already at a great disadvantage. Tongues of flames were glowing above the angels' heads and cast light into the darkness that was around them.

The fearless angelic warriors unleashed their might upon the demons; steel hit against steel and sparks flew. The enemy's shields literally shattered as seraphim's swords struck them; the demons were powerless in wake of the attacking angels. The four hundred easily maintained their line; the demons were being driven back by the sheer force of the angels' momentum. The seraphim's strength and speed were unwavering in the heat of battle. The screams and shrieks of countless demons rang through the air; fear ran rampant among the enemy, scattering their ranks in all directions. The blades of the angels' swords were dripping with the blood of demons. Michael fiercely cut down the enemy, toppling their forces as if they were merely seedlings in a forest.

Beltezar grew dramatically more furious. He clenched his hands into fists with such strength that he drew blood as his fingernails dug into his flesh. He screamed blasphemes at God, then he ordered the right and left legions to flank the host while he preserved the rear and largest rank; saving them until the moment they were needed.

"Now that should take care of your pathetic force, Michael," Beltezar grumbled, proudly. "Let's see how you'll deal with my swift and brutal surge."

Meanwhile, Carchemish barked at his soldiers, "Hold your ranks. Do not flee, but look, the reinforcements are on the way." Having heard that help was on the way, the demons regrouped and fought even harder.

The seraphim's endurance was barely stable. Their strength began to wane in the face of the enemy's persistent onslaught.

"*Yeshooaw,*" Michael raised the Sword of the Spirit and yelled in the ancient tongue. At his words, a beam of light pierced the darkness and shined on Raphael and Uriel.

"*Eloheem, Epeetaso,*" Raphael and Uriel cried out.

Raphael's one hundred mighty and strong seraphim charged like a stampede of elephants. Raphael flanked the enemy's right legion, colliding against them with the strength of a storm surge. The angels were taller and stronger than the demons, but they were hugely outnumbered and their momentum was beginning to fade.

Uriel and the mighty angels on white steeds moved in like a tidal wave crashing down on the enemy's left flank. The attack was brutal and effective; the two million demons had scattered in all directions. Uriel went after their captain, who had a lead on him of about one hundred paces, but throwing his spear with deadly aim, it shot through the air impaling the fleeing demon. The remaining left flank of the enemy saw that their leader was vanquished, so they ran away going off in all directions.

Michael and the four hundred held their line and had defeated a million demons already. The hand of God was surely on them; Beltezar was even trembling with dread at the sight of the seraphim warriors.

"The right flank is prospering, but we have lost our left flank and Carchemish's once huge force is now dwindling," Beltezar addressed the captains at his side. "I am through giving the archangel false hopes for victory. Prepare our strongest legion. We move out shortly...we'll finish what we have begun."

Raphael's forces were being driven back. The enemy had surrounded the lone seraphim on all four sides, thwarting any chance of retreating. It was only a matter of time before the warriors would fall to the demons.

"Joshua, I can't hold the line much longer," Raphael, fighting at his side, uttered.

Michael peered across the battlefield and saw his brothers, desperately in need.

"*Yeshooaw,*" the archangel cried; he raised his sword high above his head and shouted. "*Yeshooaw.*" Just as soon as he uttered the word, a beam of light shined down on Gabriel.

"*Eloheem, epeetaso,*" the lieutenant general yelled with a commanding voice.

Raphael turned and gazing up at the sky, he witnessed the light shining down.

"Joshua, God's help is on the way," Raphael proclaimed.

"Fear not seraphim. God's holy warrior is on the way," Joshua's flame burned brighter above his head as he boldly announced, for the other ninety-nine angels to hear.

Michael and the four hundred were shattering the enemy's defenses as they were hastening to Raphael's aid. Uriel and the ninety-nine joined up with the archangel's forces; Michael and his warriors were instantly empowered with strength and courage at the sight of their brothers.

Uriel rode up to Michael's side, fending off a dozen demons on the way.

"Raphael needs your aid. Take twelve of my strongest seraphim with you," Uriel said to the archangel.

"Mighty and steadfast are we—" Michael said and saluted him.

"—warriors of God," Uriel finished the sentence with a shout.

Meanwhile, Gabriel was coming up on the right flank. He and the four hundred on white steeds were rushing over Megiddo like a blinding force of wind and sand. Carchemish, joined by five hundred burly demons on scaly beasts, was leading an assault against Gabriel's forces.

"Charge seraphim," Gabriel pointed Logos at Carchemish and shouted.

"I have eagerly awaited this moment, Carchemish. Vengeance is the LORD's," Gabriel added, zealously, with a grin of pure satisfaction on his face.

Doonatos galloped faster and faster as Gabriel spurred him on towards the enemy. Carchemish's sword had seen no blood thus far; he had not defeated a single angel yet, and he was growing anxious to run his sword through an angel. Not just any angel, but the lieutenant general Gabriel. Oh how he hated the holy warrior of God.

"I will taste your blood, Gabriel," Carchemish uttered and kicked his beastly mount, forcing it to ride faster.

Just as Doonatos met head-on with Carchemish and his beast, Gabriel nudged the daring steed with his heal and Doonatos leapt into the air. Gabriel swung Logos with such force that when he struck Carchemish in the head, the demon's helmet shattered and he flew off the beast. The seraphim on horseback cut through Carchemish's ranks of beastly riders as if they were merely blades of grass. The demons, being left vulnerable, fell rapidly before the seraphim's holy fury. Gabriel had sent Carchemish scurrying for his life and the four hundred majestic riders emerged victorious over the enemy's attack.

Beltezar's forces were falling apart left and right.

Michael had come to Raphael's aid. He and the other twelve, on white steeds, were battling bravely against a million demons. Uriel and the mighty seraphim with him were winning the fierce fight against more than three million demons.

"Enough. Muster the legions. We move out, now," Beltezar shook his fist and yelled. The captains obeyed and signaled the legions to charge.

"Brother, we are winning. But, look over there," Gabriel said to Michael; his forces had crushed the enemy's right flank and they had just joined with Michael.

A massive force of demons was coming their way.

"Keep the hope alive, for the hand of God is with us," Michael proclaimed.

The archangel then pointed the Sword of the Spirit upwards towards the heavens.

"*Jehovahnissi,*" Michael cried out with a mighty voice, and suddenly, the sky opened up and Heaven's light shined down, piercing the veil of darkness and the portal to Heaven reappeared.

Beltezar stopped dead in his tracks and stared up at the portal.

"Soldiers, Luminarous is victorious. He has come for us. We will defeat Michael's forces and then, Heaven is ours for the taking," the general shouted, confidently. His arrogant bliss soon turned into complete horror.

The portal flashed with a terrible light and then blazing chariots of fire driven by seraphim came pouring out from the heavenly door.

"Christ's salvation has come," Michael cried with eyes full of joy and passion.

"Tell me Michael, did you already know of this," Gabriel asked, an inquisitive expression was on his face.

"Even I am taken by surprise," Michael uttered.

The seraphim cheered and shouted praises to the Lord. One thousand chariots of fire and their angelic riders streaked through the sky with a fearsome light; two larger chariots led the way and in them rode Remiel and Saraqael, carrying the banner of Christ.

Suddenly, fire rained down from the chariots as thousands of flaming arrows streamed down on Beltezar's forces. The legions were engulfed in flames and thousands upon hundreds of thousands were burned to ashes by the holy fire of heaven. Yet, there were massive numbers of Hell's legions that still remained alive and ready to fight.

Michael focused his energy on leading the charge straight towards Beltezar and all 999 seraphim followed behind. Michael had centered his sight on Hell's general.

"Beltezar, time to taste the wrath of my God, Jehovahnissi, the Almighty," the archangel boldly shouted for him to hear.

"Blood and spit. I'll destroy you Michael, even if I must die to do so," Beltezar shouted back; he stood heading up his remaining ranks of a million demons.

The chariots of fire rained more flaming arrows down on Beltezar's forces.

"No, no. Victory belongs to Hell," Beltezar screamed out of frustration and anger.

Suddenly, Michael was filled with a surge of supernatural strength, as was Tifawrah and they charged out ahead of the heavenly force. Beltezar kicked his beast to make him run faster so he could meet up with the archangel in battle and do away with him for good.

"Must I always finish what my soldiers fail miserably to do? You won't escape alive. Not this time, Michael," Beltezar uttered, as he stampeded towards the archangel.

Then, in a flash, it happened. Michael jumped off of Tifawrah and Beltezar leapt off of the scaly beast. Michael's sword glowed with the supernatural power of the Holy Spirit and the general's blade of Hell was ablaze with the sinister power of Hades. Gabriel couldn't believe his eyes; he was astonished as he looked on in total silence. All of the heavenly Host was speechless. Demons were still dashing madly in all directions, running for safety from the Hosts' flaming arrows.

Then, in what seemed like a timeless continuum, but in reality was only a fleeting moment, they lunged out towards each other and collided in mid-air, the general of Hell and God's only archangel. Sparks flew as an explosion of sheer power shot into the atmosphere and the earth shook violently as the two supernatural beings battled against one another. Their dual went on for what felt like countless ages.

Beltezar blurted out all of the incantations that he knew with his wealth of sinister knowledge; he conjured every ounce of sorcery he could wield, but to no avail. Michael, being the stalwart archangel, had fearlessly defended himself from each and every attack his enemy had launched against him. Now it was time for Michael to mount his offense. Valiantly, he bounded forward, going right at Beltezar. His sword was glowing with a blinding luminosity, and his eyes shimmered with the resurrection power of Christ. Beltezar was stricken with terror in the shadow of the archangel's wrath; Michael went after him with the mighty force of God, breaking his sword of Hell into shards.

The general cowered before the fury of the archangel and Michael stood over Beltezar like a towering pillar on Mount Zion.

As Michael stared Hell's proud and arrogant general keenly in the eyes, he caught a glimpse of the demon's true character: he had been truly weak against God's avenger and he was pathetic in the wake of God's wrath. He was repugnantly ugly and treacherous.

Michael pointed the Sword of the Spirit right at his throat.

"I told you before, Beltezar," Michael declared. "I would come for you and unlike your despicable precedence, I stand true to my word. By the power of Christ that lives in me; I hereby order you to return to Hell where you and your condemned army belongs."

Then, at that moment, the earth quaked and rumbled. A crack, small and straight, surfaced from the ground drawing a line between Michael and the Host, and Beltezar and Hell's legions. It was at that line in the ground that the Plane of Megiddo suddenly gaped open and fire and lava spewed into the air. Rocks splintered and shifted; the demons were falling and tumbling over each other as the ground swallowed them up, returning their wretched spirits to Hell. Then, just as fast as it had opened, the ground closed back up again, and not a single demon, dead or alive, remained in sight. Satan's rebellion to conquer Heaven and destroy the earth had been thwarted and his legions were utterly defeated before the fury of the LORD Almighty.

"Let freedom reign," Michael raised the Sword of the Spirit to Heaven and shouted. "To God be the glory, forever and ever; the Lamb of God be praised."

The army of Host raised their voices to Heaven and gave glory and praises to the King of Kings. The heavenly host rode back to Heaven, victorious, in chariots of fire.

NOTE FROM THE SCRIBE...

Only if you could have been there, then you would have felt the tremors for miles on end; you would have seen the supernatural display of God's infinite power. I remember the celebration in Heaven that day; I shall never forget, for as long as I exist. For this was the dawning of the time of Jesus and soon the countdown for his coming will begin. The prophecy of his reign is to be fulfilled on earth.

This chapter has come to an end, but I revel in the fact that this is not the end; instead, it is only the beginning. Soon I will inform you further on the history of Heaven and the epics of Michael.

Until then, children of God, remember this: nothing can rival the spontaneous praise and worship of the LORD of Heaven and earth and when the people of God lift their voices in unison, the Heavens and earth will shake with the splendor of his majesty.